Atlanta Rain

Eugene Goss

authorHOUSE®

AuthorHouse™
1663 Liberty Drive
Bloomington, IN 47403
www.authorhouse.com
Phone: 1-800-839-8640

Published by AuthorHouse 2/21/2013

ISBN: 978-1-4772-8895-5 (sc)
ISBN: 978-1-4772-8894-8 (hc)
ISBN: 978-1-4772-8893-1 (e)

Library of Congress Control Number: 2012921257

I would like to dedicate this book to my son, Mark David Goss, and daughter-in-law, Rebecca S. Goss, and to Brenda Kelly, my reader and Brenda Cassim, my secretary of forty-three years.

CHAPTER 1

BATON ROUGE, 1968

Emily Fortune. Homecoming queen, Louisiana State University; sparkling black eyes, little wispy curls around the temples which she got from her mother who came from southern Louisiana Cajun stock; given somewhat to tantrums; spoiled by her planter father; pampered and schooled in the way of "ladies"; sheltered; catered to; every muscle, every molecule of protoplasm, exactly where it ought to be; playful, giggly voice; nose slightly askew just enough to give it character; a smile that occupied the entire face; a princess of Lafayette-Baton Rouge beau monde.

Richard Boomer. Atlanta Central High School, Valedictorian; National High School Debate Champion; Undergraduate of LSU, pre-law; LSU Law School, Editor, *Law Journal*; Inducted in the Order of the Coif; quarterback, LSU; highly recruited by law firms; accepted employment by Getty & Jacobs in Atlanta; friendly, nice appearance, serious, hard worker.

"I first met Boomer when we both were seniors at one of my sorority parties," she would say. "You know, one of those 'come alone' parties between sororities and fraternities. He came into that room all dressed up in that blue blazer—you know, the kind with the gold buttons on the sleeves—and those gray pleated slacks, and black shoes. He was a great big tall, good-looking thing. He walked into that room and I said to myself, "Thatun there's mine. Better nobody else touch him. If they do I'll scratch their eyes out."

Walking briskly toward him, she had smiled and gave him her hand. "Yes, I do believe I want to dance."

He led her to the dance floor and held her hand aloft. They moved easily across the floor. As they danced he first held her away slightly as though he was afraid their bodies would touch. She, however, moved closer to him and felt his muscular body.

Laying her head in the crook of his arm she sighed to herself, "Yes, I believe you will do. You will do nicely."

When the music stopped, he thanked her and moved to leave the floor.

"Where are you going, Boomer? You stay right heah." For the rest of the evening, she was his. Rather, he was hers.

He remembered leaving the dance at one o'clock feeling dizzy from the drinks and dancing. He had just walked into his darkened dormitory room when the phone rang. Remembering his grandfather had been ill, he grabbed the phone afraid it might be bad news. He was relieved to hear a small voice on the other end.

"Boomer, it's Emily. At the party? I just couldn't sleep without calling to thank you for paying so much attention to me. Why, you just swept me off my feet. You did! Why I just didn't dance with anybody but you. I'm so happy! I had a real good time Boomer. You're just the funniest boy. Are all the boys from Atlanta like you? I hope so. Well, goodnight, Boomer."

Boomer went to sleep trying to figure out what was happening. He had never been called funny before. He thought he had always been too serious.

The next morning, Saturday, the phone rang. Looking at his watch, he saw it was only eight o'clock.

"Who could that be" he groaned? He picked up the receiver and shouted a rude "Hello!" into the phone thinking it was a wrong number or some prankster. "Hello, yeah. This is Boomer. Who? Emily?"

"It's early, I know," she replied, giggling. "Hope I didn't wake you up but I did. Papa's having a homebrew hoedown today at my house near Lafayette. We always have the best food you ever ate. Cajun. You ever eat any Cajun, Boomer? Crawfish, gumbo, pig, and lots and lots of home brewed beer. I thought to myself you just might not be doing anything today, it being Saturday and all, and you might like to go along. So pick me up at twelve noon and we'll just go right on over there. Is that alright?"

He paused for a moment, trying to get awake. As he was about to decline the invitation the voice, giggling again and before he could answer, said, "Well, its all set then. See you at twelve o'clock, front porch of the sorority house. Bye."

Boomer drove his 1950 MG back to the sorority house. "I sweah, you Georgia boys drive the sweetest little cars. There isn't much room though. We'd never be able to cut up much in this little thing, now, would we?" Boomer blushed. He knew exactly what she meant. He felt a rush of excitement.

"Why, Boomer! I do believe I see you blush!"

They arrived at Emily's house at one o'clock. Boomer hadn't expected what he saw. As they turned off the main road, they faced a large limestone entrance. On either side were giant oaks, festooned with Spanish moss. In the foreground were large planters landscaped with a profusion of sweet-smelling tropical flowers and plants, skillfully arranged, with fountains on either side. A bronze plaque said "Chaumiere." A state historical marker identified the place as an antebellum plantation, owned continuously since 1840 by the Fortunes. Boomer remembered. Emily was a Fortune.

"Hell, he said out loud. I've run into Scarlett O'Hara."

As they pulled into the drive, Emily reached across, touched the horn button and waved. The wrought iron gates creaked open. As they drove by the gate house, Scarlett, rather Emily, sang to the black attendant.

"Can't get it up. Can't get it up in the morning." The old man grinned and waved them through, shaking his head in feigned disgust.

After they were inside the compound Boomer felt a slight stirring in his stomach from the night before as he drove a mile up the oak-lined drive. An old stone fence, carefully placed, lined the drive on either side, built by hands long since dead. The cobblestone drive made the little sports coupe rattle and shake. Emily didn't seem to mind. She just laughed.

"Boomer, I just believe you need a bigger car. Can't have any fun in this little old thing."

On either side of the roadway, he saw row after row of crops gleaming while cattle stood under trees, swishing their tails and trying to avoid the flies and the hot summer sun. Old blacks raked and mowed the roadway, their white hair gleaming brightly.

"See that one. That's Jasper. I love that old man. He used to make me dolls out of corn shucks. Calls me Miss Priss. My great-granddaddy freed his granddaddy in the 1850's. Worked him, though. Gave him 10 acres, built him a little house and paid him a good wage. Jasper lives there in that same house. Can you imagine, Boomer, people owning people like horses. This was the only plantation in the whole state of Louisiana where all the tenants were free men. That's what my granddaddy used to say."

Granddaddy, as it turned out was a damn liar. When great-granddaddy died, sixty slaves were listed in the inventory of his estate.

As they neared the house, Boomer smelled hickory smoke and meat cooking. An oven in the side yard was smoking. A leather-faced black wearing a white chef's hat and cooking jacket turned meat and threw wood onto the hot embers, smoke boiling into his grinning face. He wiped the tears from his eyes, broke off a little piece of rib, dipped it in a sauce and ate it, grinning, licking his lips, and shaking his head in wonderment as he eyes danced gleefully. To the left of the house, a good distance from the smoker, was a large veranda with a swimming pool shaped like a seahorse. Around the pool were twenty or so round tables with places for six. Arranging the tables were young girls, all wearing cut-off denims, checkered shirts and ponytails.

"Pull over there, next to Daddy's pickup. That's about all he drives anymore unless he's going to New Orleans or somewhere like that."

As Boomer opened the door for Emily, he heard a gruff voice say, "Hey whatchadoing baby? Come on out heah. How's my baby girl? Hey, who is this scrapper? Damn big-un ain't he? I'm Marcus— Marcus Fortune."

"Hi, I'm Richard Boomer from Atlanta. Thanks for inviting me to your party."

Marcus' eyes turned toward Emily. He gave her a quick wink and nodded his head in approval.

"Damn big scrapper ain't you?"

"Emily," a voice shouted, "come here to your mamma girl." Florence gave Boomer a quick glance. "Bout time you come to see your mamma. I swear, I believe you put on some weight. Better watch it girl, fat runs in your stock." Emily reddened with embarrassment.

"This is Richard Boomer. Everybody calls him Boomer. I met him last night at the sorority party. Danced with him all night. Wouldn't take a no. He's going to be a lawyer, a big criminal lawyer," she said giggling. "He's from Atlanta."

Florence stepped forward, stumbled and caught hold of Boomer's arm. She put her face close to his.

"Hello Boomer. Welcome to Chaumiere du Prairie." Boomer sensed the smell of stale alcohol.

"Why, Mamma, I believe you've been in the punch bowl already." Emily blushed again with embarrassment. "Let's go inside, I want to tell you everything that's happened to me this week." She took her mother's arm and they strolled together toward the big Georgian house.

Marcus put his hand on Boomer's shoulder.

"Come on Boomer. I want you to meet Emmy's brother." The two walked over to the food table where Jeff was, with a slab of pork ribs in his hand, sauce all over his face.

"Jeff, meet Boomer. Emmy brought him out from school. Show him around will you, while I see about things. People will start coming in pretty soon and I want to check the new run of homebrew and make sure it's good and cold."

Jeff shrugged his shoulders as Marcus walked away.

"Not much to show you, you've not already seen. Here, I'll get you a drink. What do you like?"

"Just anything," Boomer said. "Had a little party last night and I'm still a little jumpy."

The silence was broken by car horns sounding as people began to arrive in everything from Cadillacs to pickup trucks. A van arrived. The "Louisiana Fiddlers" unpacked their faded fiddles, banjos and mandolins and began tuning up. Red-faced Louisianans emerged from their cars and pickups, chattering their hellos and heading straight for the liquor barn. Rooster Jack Napier stepped to the microphone to test the crude PA system.

"Testin one... two... three... four. Testin four... three... two... one. Everybody hear me? Work alright?"

"Turn up the volume, Rooster," yelled a listener. "A few dead ain't come awake yet."

Someone in the crowd made a sound like a rooster crowing. Rooster took out a red handkerchief and tied it around his forehead to catch the perspiration pouring off his shiny bald head and he cackled back into the microphone.

"Shore is hot today, ain't it. But we're here to have fun so gitcha some of Marcus's home brew—iced down real good over there by the old wash house. After two doses, ye may not notice the heat. Matter of fact, ye probably won't notice anything' for awhile. They say its going to git into the high nineties here in Baton Rouge so let's git ourselves iced down real good. They's plenty of it. This temperature reminds me of a Louisiana tune. Some of you old-timers get out there now and I'll call one. Okay, here we go."

Rooster laid his chin on top of the old fiddle, stomped his foot to establish the tempo, and attacked the poor fiddle so violently that Boomer thought both the fiddle and bow would splinter into a thousand pieces. Having established the cadence, Rooster began to call the dance:

Now, down in hell Swamp Water Dan
Had a conversation with the Booger Man
"Come on Devil, turn up the heat

Ya gotta do sumpin to warm my feet.
    It's cold down here!"

Come on now, swing it!

The dancers fell into their clogging steps as Rooster continued:

Now the Devil's face was 'drippin' wet
"You got all the heat you're gonna get"
"Well, you got to do sumpin", Swamp Water replied
"If I had known this situation I never woulda died-
    I'm freezing!"

Well, Dan called a meetin of the Looziana clan
They all attended to the very last man.
There was Soup Bean Boudreaux and Fat Daddy Mack,
Big Tom Crazy and Crawfish Jack.
    They all wuz a'shivering.

"Boys' we got to do sumpin," Crawfish began,
"Let's send a message to the Booger Man.
Stoke up the fires, kick some butts
We didn't come here to freeze our n__s.
    We're cold."

"He won't do that," Fat Daddy cried
"I know what we'll do," Crawfish replied
"Let's send a request to the doggone scrooge
To transfer us all to Baton Rouge.
    It's real hot there!"

Rooster put the fiddle under his chin and concluded the number with,

"Shave and a haircut. Six bits. Who's the barber? Tom Mix."

Boomer and Jeff found a spot and sat watching the sweating crowd mingle, slurp their drinks, and turn Chaumiere du Prairie into a Louisiana brawl.

"Here, you boys try some of this new batch." Marcus handed each of them a huge mug of homebrew beer. He blew the brown foam from his third mug and gulped it down, wiping his mouth with the sleeve of his denim shirt and giving a deep sigh of contentment. The brew was dark brown and smelled strongly of yeast. Boomer took a deep swig from his mug and felt the cold brew open his stomach. He took another drink and began to feel a warm glow. He downed the rest and asked for another. Marcus obliged.

Boomer looked around. The sweet smell of jasmine and honeysuckle enveloped him. He listened to the cadence of the fiddle, mandolin and banjo and sank slowly into the soft contentment of the waning day.

The next morning, Boomer was awakened by a quiet movement and a sigh. Emily raised up on an elbow and whispered,

"Good morning, lover. I've got to go now. Daddy will be getting up about now, and I don't want him to catch me in here. I promised to ride jumpers with him this morning. I'll be back soon. Reba will have the coffee on by now. She'll fix whatever you want for breakfast."

Breakfast? He wretched at the thought. "Got to get back to the campus. Finish that damn term paper. Sort this thing out. Figure out what's happened."

Emily went quietly and quickly, leaving her pink panties draped across the bed stand.

"My gosh," he said out loud. "I don't believe it." Then he remembered all of it.

From that day on, it was all Emily: Wake up call in the morning; meet at the grill for rolls and coffee; supper; goodnight call; weekends at Chaumiere; hot gasping nights at the White Lattice Motel; beer parties at the frat house; ballgames. Then the school year ended.

That summer, back in Atlanta, the phone rang. It was Emily, crying into the phone.

"Oh God, Boomer, Marcus is gone—heart attack. Last night. Oh, you will come, won't you Boomer—I need you so bad."

Boomer quickly packed his bag and headed for Baton Rouge and into the life that now was his. After Marcus' funeral, Boomer went with Florence, Jeff and Emily to Chaumiere.

"I need to talk to you Boomer, Emily said. "Come on, let's take a walk." They walked among the giant oaks, down to the bank of a pond of brackish water.

"I've been wanting to call you Boomer and tell you something. I hate to tell you because I don't know how you will take it. Boomer, I'm pregnant. I'm pregnant Boomer. What am I going to do?"

Stunned, Boomer thought, *"How can this be. How could this have happened. She must be mistaken."* Then, he said, "Are you sure? Have you been to a doctor?"

"Sure, silly," she replied giggling.

Boomer was stunned. He had been so careful.

"We'll get married," he murmured hardly able to say the words. After the ceremony, Boomer learned two things. Marcus had died broke and Chaumiere would be lost. Emily was not pregnant. It was all a mistake.

JACOBS' MANSION, ATLANTA 1969

Soon after they moved to Atlanta, Boomer handed Emily a cream-colored envelope which had the appearance of a formal invitation of some sort with free-hand calligraphy and wax seal. "It is Boomer. I just know it is." Emily put her long thumbnail under the flap easily fishing the contents of the envelope onto the refractory her mother had hidden in the barn when the Marshall came to take away her treasury of antiques. Emily squealed loudly, " It is Boomer. It is. It's some kind of invitation." Look Boomer, it's at some big mansion and its formal. That means tuxedos. I bet you have never been to a formal dinner party. We used to have them all the time at Chaumiere. It's to celebrate your passing the Bar and starting to work at Getty and Jacobs. Oh Boomer, I'm so happy, oh merveilleux.

Thus, it was then that Richard Boomer got his first glimpse of the stately Jacobs' home. Returning to Atlanta as a recent graduate of LSU Law School, he had been employed by the law firm of Getty and Jacobs in the criminal law division.

His new bride was an instant favorite of the partners. At the annual cocktail party and dinner, held at the home of Jacobs to welcome that year's crop of new associates, she cornered old Jacobs and, by flattery and flirtation, reluctantly accepted him into her court of admirers.

"Why, Mr. Malcomb Jacobs. I believe your big old law firm is just what my Boomer needs to exercise his considerable talents as a lawyer—or should I say attorney. We call them lawyers back in Baton Rouge—and he just admires you and all you have accomplished as an outstanding trial lawyer at the Atlanta bar. You're just an inspiration to him and he talks about you all the time. He does! And, I say, 'Boomer he can't be all that great,' but now that I met you, I know what he means."

Old Jacobs beamed, took Emily by the hand and kissed her gallantly on the cheek, a gesture not unnoticed by the other fledglings. By the time the evening was over, little Emily had skillfully made her way through the gathering, teasing and flirting with the staid old gray-hairs and establishing herself as an asset, to both Boomer and the law firm.

Before dinner, Jacob's wife, Miriam, moved cautiously toward Emily, a cane in her right hand.

"Hello, my dear. I'm Miriam Jacobs. I believe you're Emily Boomer, Richard's bride. Let's see, you are from Baton Rouge and you and Richard were only recently married. Am I correct? Well, welcome to Atlanta. Welcome to Getty and Jacobs, and congratulations to you and Richard. I hope you both will be very happy here. My husband just spoke of you and your husband. Said I should be sure to meet you. You will have to pardon me. I have this awful bone problem and I can't stand very long. It makes it difficult, and somewhat embarrassing at social gatherings, but I manage. One reason I wanted to speak to you is that I have a very good friend in Baton Rouge. Her name is Millie Asher. She and I were at Vassar 'way' back in the thirties. We've remained close through the years. We write and sometimes talk on the phone. Do you know her?"

"Why, of course I know Miss Millie. Her granddaughter, Sarah, and I once belonged to the same manage—horses—jumpers, you know. She sometimes stayed overnight at Chaumiere—that's the plantation where I grew up. We're just real good friends."

"Then, you'll have to come by sometime so we can talk. I'd love to hear all about Baton Rouge and Millie and spend an afternoon with you. Will you sit beside me dear so we can chat?"

Old Jacobs smiled across the room at Miriam. He crossed the room, took her carefully by the arm and drew her to the sofa.

"Better sit down, Mom. Don't overdo it."

"Oh Boomer, Mr. Jacobs was so nice to me," Emily beamed as they drove home. "And, Mrs. Jacobs, too. She invited me to come see her soon to spend the afternoon. What do you think of that, Boomer?" She smiled, mischievously. "Not a bad start," she whispered to herself. It was the first time they had been to Jacobs' mansion, but it was not the last. They soon became regulars at social functions and often went with them on vacations.

In spite of their ages, Boomer and Jacobs after their first meeting became instant friends and companions. On days when they played golf together, he picked Jacobs up in his old 1960 Chevy and drove to Atlanta's Plantation Club. Jacobs always cautioned him to drive carefully or get a better car. He encouraged Boomer to park the old Chevy next to somebody's new Mercedes.

"Give the place some class," he would say giggling.

After a round of golf, they would retire to the clubroom where Jacobs would have his usual two martinis—two olives. After his second martini, Jacobs, who had been a nationally known trial lawyer and past-president of the Georgia bar, would begin to lecture. Boomer called the session his weekly seminar—"Jacobs on Trial Practice."

"Remember, boy," he might say, "a law case is a story you have to tell. It's part truth, part fiction. No matter how complicated it is—you've got to make it simple, boy, so the dumbest sonofabitch in the courtroom can understand it. And you've got to believe your story—even the fiction part—or you'll never make the judge and jury believe it. A lawsuit, boy, is 50 percent preparation. The rest is penetration. You've got to put it in and put it in deep—screw the other guy, I mean. That's what makes the difference. You can give a dull-witted, tongue-tied jackass the best case in the world. Let him work and sweat a year over it. And he'll get the stuffing kicked out of him—blow it—that's what he'll do. Some slick-tongued, half-prepared shyster will shove it to him. In the final analysis, the best lawyers are the best actors. Remember it, boy. They don't teach any of that in law school now, do they?"

"By the way, boy," he said one day, "here's an application for membership. Usually takes twenty years and an act of Congress to get in this crappy place. I'm on the board and I've made the necessary arrangements. It's expensive, but good for your career. Good investment in your future—good contacts. Besides, I want you in the club tournament this year. You'll win it."

The next day Boomer and Emily borrowed fifteen thousand dollars from Third National Bank and, while living in a rented duplex, became an applicant for membership in the Plantation Club. That's how a nearly broke, young lawyer, got to be a member of Plantation Club, Atlanta's most prestigious country club and qualified for his first club tournament.

CHAPTER 2

ATLANTA NEWS WLAK, JULY 6, 2000

"Now today's weather for Fulton, Cobb and Dekalb Counties. Expect cloudy skies this morning with rain for Atlanta beginning in the early afternoon hours and continuing until late afternoon. It's a cool sixty-seven degrees at the airport which will rise to seventy degrees by noon.

Today, July 6, 2000. The time is eight o'clock, Central Standard Time. Stay tuned now for the latest news from WLAK:"

"Good morning, this is George Preston with breaking news. Beginning at one o'clock tomorrow, churches and synagogues all over the Atlanta area will gather in historic Piedmont Park in a vigil to pray for the safe return of nine year-old Tommy Perelli who was apparently a victim of an abduction. He disappeared three days ago shortly after he was dropped off near his home in northern Atlanta by a William Fentrell, driver of the Holy Trinity School bus. According to the latest weather report those attending the vigil face Atlanta rain but Father Boniface, rector of the Perelli's parish, has predicted an outpouring of loving concern for the child and his parents regardless of the weather. Stay tuned for updates as they become available."

In a somber and troubled voice Preston reported that the police had no explanation for the child's disappearance but that they were pursuing all leads in the case hoping that he might be found.

Boomer had learned from years of criminal practice that the longer such cases go unsolved the less likely it was that the victim would ever be recovered alive. Young Perelli had been missing for over three days and his case was the talk of Atlanta. It was on practically everyone's mind, putting great pressure on the police of Atlanta for a solution. Seeing that the probability of an abduction was growing more and more likely, the Department had already begun to assemble a task force consisting of the most experienced homicide officers and had already entered into a discussion with the Federal Bureau of Investigation with a view of determining who would have jurisdiction, who would be charged with the actual investigation and what protocol would be adopted to insure the optimum cooperation of the Atlanta Police Force and the Federal Agency. The statement makes it clear that authorities had not yet established a corpus delicti.

On his way to his regular Thursday morning foursome, Boomer turned his 450 SL Mercedes into the limestone entrance of the Atlanta Plantation Club as he had done most Thursdays during the years since old Jacobs had greased his way to membership in the Club. After passing through the guard gates, Boomer maneuvered his car into a parking space and waited while an attendant loaded his clubs into a golf cart and drove him to the first tee where a starter was waiting ready to start the four golfers on 18 holes of play. Boomer shook hands with "Bud", Edward, his partner for the day, and a partner with him in the law firm, Getty & Jacobs. He chatted briefly with Peter Coleman, a surgeon friend and Mitch Parsons, a wealthy businessman and owner of a large sum of old Atlanta money. The starter impatiently motioned for the players to start the game.

After winning the toss, Richard Boomer stepped up to the first tee and shielded his eyes against the glare of the early Georgia sun. He measured the fairway and carefully positioned himself for his first drive. "Four hundred and sixty yards, par 5," the marker read—dogleg to the right. He knew that hole well. He drew erect, bent over the ball, and sent it flying straight down the fairway.

He walked silently to his cart, replaced his driver into his golf bag and drew himself up to his full height. Taking a neatly folded handkerchief from his pocket, he wiped the perspiration from his forehead, and then ceremoniously ran a comb through his white hair. There was no smile or celebration, only a somber Boomer.

Boomer looked over the course. Fairways wide and long, carefully nourished and mowed; tall pines and mature magnolias on either side; water and sand traps placed at proper intervals. He liked the hot Georgia days and the time with his friends sipping brandy afterward in the clubhouse. It had become his favorite diversion.

Without another word the other three players hit their balls and fell lazily into their carts beginning the search for their balls. Only Boomer made the fairway. The others were in various places in the rough or out of play.

Peter Coleman, Boomer's surgeon friend, had twice hit his ball into water. He slammed his club to the ground, picked it up again and decided not to play the hole.

Boomer moved the cart down the cart path toward Bud's ball, perched precariously between two tree roots.

"Get out your chainsaw, Bud. I believe that tree may have you hooked."

Bud took out a nine iron and plopped the ball into the fairway grunting, as he always did, when he hit the ball. He staggered onto the turf, sweating and tired, and hit the ball out of play, tugging at his sagging shorts and pulling them up over his fat belly. The sun had already zapped him.

On the green, Boomer tapped the ball in, effortlessly, for his first birdie. He bowed gallantly to the applause of his partner. He motioned to Bud, rubbing his thumb against his forefinger, and reaching again for his handkerchief.

The predicted Atlanta rain had already begun to form on the golf cart windshield and players all over the course were beginning to leave, scurrying to avoid the rain.

Boomer started his Mercedes 450 SL and glided out of the

parking lot and turned toward his office in the prestigious Starks office building, his thick white hair parted by the sudden rush of rain and wind. He skillfully maneuvered the little white car, darting in and out of I-75 traffic like a teenager on his first joy ride. To him, the rush-hour traffic was more a challenge than an aggravation. A little lady, erect in her seat, her little knuckles white from gripping the wheel, stared as he sped past her. He smiled and winked, flirtatiously, as she gave him the familiar gesture of defiance.

"Gutsy old gal," he thought, as he hurried down the interstate. He loved Atlanta,. He loved his little car. It was his only folly. As he sped toward the office, he fell into deep thought, as he often did when he got behind the wheel of a car. He thought about Emily and how he had come to marry her. He thought about the twins, Troy and Edward, as different as different can be: one a rising neurosurgeon; the other a prosecutor, too smart to deal with the competition and politics in a metropolitan law firm. They didn't look like twins. In fact, they didn't even look like brothers.

"It's strange," he thought. Edward, the neurosurgeon, looked as though Boomer had spit him out. There was no outward trace of Emily in his appearance. Tall, slender, muscular; erect; hairline, almost to his eyebrows; incredibly handsome; deep, resonant, reassuring, voice. Edward could easily have modeled for an ad in the *American Bar Journal*. But, nature is perverse. Edward, like Emily, was vain; ye was often impatient and rude, a trait often found in his specialty; and he tended to be ambitious and greedy. Cold and impersonal, he seemed to live for the moment he could excise a disc or open some poor devil's skull.

Troy, on the other hand, was different. He was affable to a fault, uttering excitedly every thought that entered his balding head. Empathetic, he was the perfect advocate for an outraged victim. His voice was curiously high in pitch so every word would ring with great clarity throughout the courtroom, beating its way into the ears and mind of all present. His speech was interspersed with carefully timed "uhs' or "ahs" which gave the ear time to process the information— but never so as to be distracting. His voice would rise and fall. Both volume and inflection were carefully measured to emphasize his point. Endowed with an acute sense of right and wrong, he could have been no more zealous if he were the victim himself.

From the start, juries loved Troy. He could make a crime scene come alive. The jury was made to feel the pain of the victim and the outrage to public order. Lawyers began to say to their clients: "You've got problems, buddy. This case has been assigned to Troy Boomer. He's tough. Pack your toothbrush. You may need it." One lawyer always doubled his fees upon learning that Troy Boomer was on the other side and would make him work his lazy butt off.

The Atlanta bar took great delight in the contradiction. Richard Boomer was acknowledged to be the best criminal defense lawyer in Georgia, if not the entire South. Troy Boomer, his son, was the most capable prosecutor in town. When the conversation got around to that irony at afternoon happy hour, lawyers would speculate who the winner would be in a showdown. Boomer loved the debate. It made him very proud but Troy was embarrassed by it. Boomer never missed an opportunity to lunch with Troy or meet him after work for a drink. The conversation invariably turn to law.

On the other hand, Boomer avoided Edward when civility permitted, tolerating him when occasion demanded it. They had absolutely nothing in common. To Emily, he was "My son, Edward. You know, the neurosurgeon. He's the smart one in the family." Troy would smile and agree. To Boomer, Edward was a stranger. Emily would say of Troy, "I just don't understand my son, Troy, bless his heart. Works for nearly nothing—day and night that boy works and for what? Down there in that smelly courtroom all day. Criminals and, well, just the dregs of humanity. One case after the other. I never see him. Why, he could be making all kinds of money but he just doesn't seem to care. Poor Brenda! I feel sorry for her and little Michael and Elizabeth. Living in that little old house—won't take any help from us. Offered to buy them a house. Made him mad!"

Boomer was glad. He was proud of Troy. He admired his independence and reveled in his obstinacy. "No whore, that boy." He loved Troy's enthusiasm. He and Troy would sometimes sit outside on the warm Georgia nights, sipping brandy after dinner, while

Edward sat in the kitchen telling Emily of his latest investment, or describing one of his delicate miracles of modern surgery.

Back in the kitchen Edward and Emily would wonder, in whispered tones, why Troy had so little ambition and how he was ever going to educate his children on the poor salary of a prosecutor.

"By the way, Dad," Troy said one night. "things any better between you and Mom? Still on beef stew and cornbread? Still sleeping by yourself? I'm really sorry, Dad. I really am. I know what a life that must be."

Boomer swung his Mercedes into the parking garage attached to his office building. He looked at his Rolex, put his key into the elevator, and rode to the fifth floor where his office was located. He had plenty of time to read the memos left on his desk by his law clerk and to go over some documents assembled by his paralegal for Monday's motion hour.

By the time he had finished it was ten-thirty. He neatly stacked the documents on his desk and returned to his car for the drive home.

He should be tired from the golf game, but he was not. Bored yes. He had begun to resent the routine his life had become. At times he was acerbic; sometimes dispassionate. The Boomer of long years ago was changed. The earlier dreams of a close family with dinner on the table at six, Little League ballgames with the boys, hiking trips and scout troops—those things just never happened. Emily preferred bridge parties, daytime soap operas, and long afternoons reading.

Lately, he had begun to brood. Edward, with his studies and school activities, never had seemed to have time—nor the inclination—to do the things he had wanted to do with him. And, Boomer seemed always to have been working on some important case that required him to stay at the office through dinner.

Boomer and Troy were more companionable, fishing occasionally during the summer or skiing in the winter in Colorado. When he was in high school and living at home, Troy always had waited up for him when he worked late. Boomer would sit at the kitchen bar while Troy made him a sandwich and poured a glass of milk. They would discuss the day's events.

Troy knew his Dad was an important criminal lawyer, which made him proud. He loved to see Boomer being interviewed on the six o'clock news; or, reading about the drama of some trial in the morning *Constitution*. In the mornings, Troy was always the first one up and ready to go. While Troy perked coffee and made toast, Boomer showered and dressed.

Emily slept, never rising until late morning.

"It's my Cajun stock," she would say to defend herself.

Her mother had come from southern Louisiana and she could trace her ancestors to the first Acadian settlers.

"Everybody knows Cajuns need more sleep," she would say,or "Cajun women can't cook—Boomer you know that. Why the men do the cooking down there. What woman could stand to touch those old nasty craw daddies?" That was, of course, not true. In fact, Emily never mentioned her Cajun origins except to Boomer, and then to excuse some flaw in her personality.

Now, Boomer was a better trial lawyer than he had ever been. No matter how tough a case was, he always seemed to find a way to win. Winning was a personal and professional imperative. He could not stand to lose. If he failed to get the result he wanted, which seldom ever happened, he would brood for days—ashamed to go back to the office and avoiding lunch at the café for days, until the outcome was dead in the minds of his colleagues.

In the courtroom, his offbeat affect was hypnotic. He never began a trial without having fully and carefully examined the background of all the potential jurors. He knew what part of the city they lived in, whether they rented or owned, and where they worked, and he had at his fingertips every available detail of their personal and economic circumstance.

By the time a jury was selected, Boomer, by *voir dire* had obtained a promise from every juror to carefully examine the evidence and the instructions of the court—to hold Georgia to its burden of proof; and to acquit upon a finding of reasonable doubt. By the time he had finished his questioning, the jurors who were accepted were flattered at having passed his scrutiny and were determined to do nothing to disappoint that good man who had placed his faith in them.

By the end of the case, the jurors had reason to say to themselves: "This man likes me. If I ever get in trouble, this man will help me."

Women loved him—even the young ones. Once, after a very important trial, he got a telephone call from a young juror, who had just voted to acquit an alleged rapist, inviting him to her apartment for dinner to "further discuss the case."

"There were some things about the case I didn't understand, but I knew he didn't do that awful thing or you wouldn't represent him. He didn't do it, did he Mr. Boomer?"

"I don't know, madam," he softly replied, "I didn't ask him."

Boomer always stood before the witness box while examining a witness. At six feet, three inches, his 195 pound-frame towered over everything. His piercing blue eyes, set slightly back in his head, looked directly into the eyes of his witness who squirmed under his relentless stare. Questions flowed freely, with a cadence meant to give the quarry no time to think about his answer. After a time, the rhythm between question and answer would become a thing of beauty, with the witness yielding to Boomer's version of the incident.

Boomer could sense a witness's final surrender—a flash in their eyes—a tremor in their voice, or an embarrassed smile. Those moments of capitulation were sweet to him. From that moment there would exist a silent understanding between them, like the one between lion and fawn: "You've got me down. I'm gone. I cannot—I will not resist. Get it over with quickly."

The covenant? "I'll say anything you want me to say, within reason. In return—you'll let me leave this courtroom as soon as you get what you want."

When the occasion demanded, Boomer's strong resonant voice became tender and sympathetic. "Now Mrs. Smith, I know this is difficult for you, but there's no need to worry. Just take all the time you need. Would you like a short break?"

Or, he could be defiant—outraged at a witness' corrupt effort to criminalize his client.

In executing the closing argument, Boomer was the acknowledged master. He always began by summarizing the prosecution's case and pointing out the smallest inconsistency or any sign of bias or incredulity. He then reminded the jury that under our system of justice, the prosecution had the burden of proving guilt and that his client had no duty to prove his innocence. He would then argue convincingly that the evidence, taken as a whole, gave rise to a reasonable doubt, mandating an acquittal.

His summations were always complimentary of the work of the prosecutor: "He did the best he could with the case he had."

His arguments were eloquent and reasonable. By the time Boomer had concluded he had usually woven a web of doubt that the prosecution could not untangle. The poor prosecutor could only sit there and listen while his ironclad case slipped quietly away.

In the courtroom, Boomer was a lion. At home he was a neutered cat. "No, pussy, Don't do that pussy. Drink your milk, pussy."

At 11:00 o'clock, Boomer pulled the little Mercedes into the driveway of his columned house and put his golf clubs in the garage. He wondered what Emily had for dinner. Whatever it was, he would have to eat it too – out of the refrigerator.

He slipped the key into the lock and opened the kitchen door into darkness. He was right, again. Emily was in bed. He could imagine her with her curlers in, black hoods over her eyes, and face greased down like a car axle. Emily dreamt. Standing on the sidelines of the stadium were hundreds of cheering fans. Emily Fortune, Homecoming Queen, Louisiana State University. Her day in the sun. Boomer crept quietly to the refrigerator. Sure enough, there it was, the stew, prepared for him by the maid. He gulped a bowl down without heating it and quietly made his way to his upstairs bedroom. As he closed the door, he heard Emily call from down the hall.

"That you, Boomer? Goodnight." Boomer set the alarm for 6 o'clock. He would get to the office early.

CHAPTER 3

Boomer and Bud waited to be seated. The restaurant was full. A waitress squeezed between them, raking her bosoms against his arm. Boomer stood erect, as always, hands in his pockets and head cocked slightly to his right. The waitress smiled at him and wiggled her way through the crowd. She began to straighten a table in the corner as they waited. Boomer looked around at the assortment of eaters—lawyers, stockbrokers, and merchants—just emerging from tall, gray buildings, glad to escape their tight little cubicles and keyboards for an hour. Across the room he saw Royal Getty III, the most senior partner in Getty and Jacobs and grandson of its founder, leaning across the table, whispering to the new receptionist.

"Bastard," he muttered to Bud, nodding toward the pair. "She's what? Twenty-five? He's sixty-four. Already accused once of sexual harassment—had to buy his way out of that one to save his reputation and the reputation of the firm. He'd better keep that shriveled up old mullet in his trousers."

Bud grinned. "Don't knock it 'til you've tried it. While we're on the subject," Bud said, lowering his voice, "why don't you get out of that office and move around a little? You work your can off day and night—or at least that's what your secretaries say. I wouldn't know. I wouldn't be caught dead in the place after five. Emily quit checking on you a long time ago. Get out, man. Live a little. There's a world out there you don't know about. It's everywhere—I mean everywhere.

All sizes. All shapes. All ages. Anything you want. They call it the sexual revolution. Better join the revolt, Boomer. You're almost sixty not much time left for that at best."

Boomer was annoyed by the suggestion. In spite of his failed relationship with Emily, it had never occurred to him to really do as Bud suggested. Oh, he had seen women that he was attracted to. He had had many subtle invitations. He had wondered what it would be like to be with another woman after all those years, but he never pictured himself crossing that line. Besides, he had always been shy around women. He could stand before the Georgia Supreme Court and ask that a convicted felon go free on some technicality. But he could not bring himself to ask that attractive brunette on the commuter if she liked the book she was reading. Yet his life was as empty as the bed he slept in. In the years since LSU, his soul had slowly departed.

He looked at Bud. Short. Fat. Balding. Always grinning. Always talking, joking, poking fun. Women loved him—a big, harmless teddy bear, until he got a few margaritas down them. Then, look out.

Bud was proud of his conquests, always talking, like a big kid, about a new one. "Man, you should have seen her body. Long white legs," he would groan. "Little hot belly. Round little butt."

"Come on, Boomer," he whispered. "Look around you, man. What do you see? Beautiful, sweet little businesswomen? Huh? Know what I see? Tail! A room full of tail! Get out of that office. Get a life, for God's sake. Look at you. I never saw you wear anything but a business suit—white shirt, tie, and black shoes. My God, man, you ought to hire in as a mannequin at Burdines. Where did you get that shit? Emily? She buy that shit? Look at the shoes, Boomer. Plain toe, laces. Get some tassels, man. Get some tassels. At least do that! Emily buy you all that shit, Boomer? I thought so. That'll keep you in the deepfreeze. She knows that. Aw, heck. I'm going to give up on you." Only Bud could tease Boomer this way.

The waitress finally came to seat them.

"Mr. Boomer, your table is ready."

He heard a faint female voice behind him whisper, "Isn't that Richard Boomer?" He didn't look back.

As she led them to the table, Boomer stared straight at the waitress's hips, swishing around chairs and tables. *About thirty-five,* he thought, *Woman's golden age. Nice shape.*

After they were seated, Boomer's thoughts returned to next month's court trial and courtroom. He stood before the jury, making his opening statement, meticulously organized, every word important, every facial expression carefully rehearsed.

Bud ordered a dark beer and lifted the glass to his mouth. Boomer smelled the yeast. He thought of Marcus and his home-brew beer. He heard the fiddle, smelled the jasmine, and listened again to the excited laughter of the revelers. Emily. Beautiful, feisty, spoiled Emily. How could he have been so stupid?

"Let's see. Give me a Caesar with broccoli soup. Just water." Boomer ordered his usual soup and salad. "Got to get it back down," he said, patting his stomach.

"Bagel, cream cheese, sweetened iced tea, and a blintz for desert." Bud joked derisively, "Gotta get my blood grease up!"

Boomer's eyes moved around the room. Everybody was talking at once, excited to be away from their tight little cubicles for an hour. His eyes fell on a woman at a table next to a window, overlooking Peachtree. She smiled, acknowledging his casual glance with a slight nod of her head as though she had waited for him to look her way. Her wide, smiling eyes then turned to her young companion. She laughed, touched his arm, and replied to something he said. Then she turned to Boomer and smiled again. He flushed and looked away.

Mustn't stare, he thought. *Not polite. Something about her though. Something different.*

He lifted his spoon to taste the soup. His eyes fell again on her.

My God, he thought. *She keeps looking at me. Do I know her? I don't think so. A new secretary in the office?* No. He would certainly have remembered her.

"Come back, Boomer, come back." Bud grinned. "Can't you get your mind off that damn case long enough to have a social lunch?"

Boomer looked again toward the window. The chair was empty.

There by the cashier she stood while the young man paid. He wondered again who she was.

"What the hell," he muttered aloud.

Bud looked at him, puzzled. "See, now you've started talking to yourself. Let's get back to the sweatshop."

As they waited for the light to change, Boomer looked around him. Atlanta. How he loved it. He didn't see much of it anymore except the business district. Too busy—can't get Emily out of the house. Office, work, metro, house, Emily, bed. Then back again. He disappeared into the caverns that made up the Stark Building. Getty and Jacobs—fifth, sixth, and seventh Floors. Back to the catacombs.

That afternoon, as he was reading the final draft of his trial brief, his secretary, Mary Stavanitis, came into his office and, without a word, closed the door, locked it, drew the drapes, and, in ten glorious minutes, changed his life forever. She was the architect of a new Richard Boomer. Without meaning to, Boomer had finally crossed the line.

On his way home, Boomer turned on the radio, barely catching the tail end of George Preston's six o'clock news. He heard the familiar voice of Captain Thomas, chief criminal investigator of Fulton County. "We are out in the streets everywhere investigating every lead, but we have hit a stone wall. We need a big break, anything that will tell us if Tommy is still alive. Don't get me wrong. Atlanta's criminal law enforcement is second to none. We have technical capabilities we never had before. We are still learning how to use much of it, particularly the computer technology. Most criminal cases are solved in the same way they have been for many years. The technology is useful but it is, at most, an aid to traditional methods and investigators still pound the pavement like they always did carrying their pen and notepad."

Boomer whispered to himself, "That's right Thomas, that's right."

CHAPTER 4

Edward reached the hospital at 6 a.m. Wednesday morning. Looking at the schedule, he saw that he had a full day of surgeries beginning at nine o'clock: a laminectomy, a facial nerve reconstruction, and a cyst removal from the right frontal lobe of a thirteen-year-old boy. He hoped the cyst diagnosis was confirmed on surgery, so more invasive surgery could be avoided and he could make the afternoon racquetball game on time. If not, there were compensations. More extensive surgery, if necessary, would require an increased surgical fee.

"Get the kid in here first," he bellowed. "Who the hell scheduled him last? I have standing orders down there to schedule open cranials first, always! I don't want to split some kid's damn skull open when I am already dead tired. Takes too much out of me," he roared.

The surgical nurses all hated him. Edward—no one but Boomer dared call him Eddy—looked over the diagnostic information, refreshing his memory of the case: blood, okay; chest x-rays, fine; EKG, normal; no allergies; no medications. He pulled out the EEG tracings, which were grossly abnormal for a defect in the right frontal lobe, and removed the magnetic imaging of the affected area from their envelope to exactly identify the surgical site. Mechanically, he went through the preliminaries before discussing the surgery with the family so that he could obtain the required "informed consent," a necessary shield against malpractice suits.

Preoperative discussions with the family were distasteful to him, especially where the patient was a child. There were always so many questions to answer, so much emotion involved. He had learned a long time ago he could not deal with medicine on an emotional level and that he must, in order to be effective, remain totally objective and aloof from all emotional considerations.

There were always requests for reassurances. ("Jimmy will be all right, won't he, Doctor?") If he had a crystal ball, he would have a lock on the stock market, he wanted to say. His contact with the patient and the family was always impersonal. He would never say, for example, "Yes, Mrs. Jones, Jimmy will be fine." He would most likely say, pompously, "Well, it is a gravely serious operation anytime you go into the brain. But I believe the patient will survive the surgery," as though survival was the goal to be achieved. If the surgery was successful, the family was duly grateful to that "fine surgeon who pulled our baby through."

While scrubbing, Edward mentally added up today's take: intervertebral disc at $3,200.00; facial nerve resection at $4,800.00; right lobe cyst excision at $6,500.00—a total of $14,500.00. He reduced that by overhead costs of 40 percent for a net taxable income of $8,700.00. Even if Tommy didn't come through the surgery, Blue Cross/Blue Shield certainly would.

When Jimmy was wheeled into surgery, he was not Jimmy Smith, age thirteen, eighth-grader. All the little patient would ever be to Edward was an exposed right frontal lobe.

Edward subscribed to (and read) *The Wall Street Journal* and *Barron's*. He spent hours in the evenings pouring over Valueline, always trying to improve his portfolio of stocks and bonds. He had a financial advisor whom he consulted from time to time, but he preferred to plan his own investment strategy.

"Hell," he used to admonish his colleagues in the hospital cafeteria, "if stockbrokers know so much, why do they all live in ranch-style houses in the pissy end of town? I'm not going to turn my money over to some dumbhead to lose for me. I've been that route already." Edward, as a matter of fact, had managed to accumulate a modest nest egg by investing in various speculative securities.

His conversation was so involved in investments and other money matters that many of his colleagues avoided him, charging off in the other direction when he approached. He was regarded by doctors, nurses, and administrators as pompous, egotistical, and overbearing.

Boomer, whose investments were principally in real estate and bank stock, resisted Edward's efforts to lure him into speculative investments.

"Too slow. Real estate's too slow to generate a profit," Edward would say. "Bank stocks are a bummer—too conservative."

Boomer, however, had recognized Atlanta's destiny for growth early. Old Jacobs had advised him to invest in certain parts of the city. He began in 1970 to buy parcels of land and old buildings at favorable prices. During the 1980s his investments in real estate yielded considerable gains, making him and Emily less dependent on the income from his law practice and more able to afford the 450 Mercedes SL that he was so fond of driving and the six-bedroom Georgian house they occupied, alone. Boomer had begun to divert his holdings into trusts for the benefit of Edward's and Troy's children, freeing up funds they normally had put away for college.

Several weeks earlier, after a rare squash game, Edward had confided to Boomer that he had a large commitment to common stocks. Much of the stock, Edward admitted, was bought on credit. He had borrowed from the brokerage firm to pay for a part of the stock, pledging the stock as security for payment of the margin account.

"Isn't that pretty risky?" Boomer asked. "What if the stock goes down rather than up? Won't they make you pay up or sell the stock and recover their money from the proceeds? That would scare the hell out of me—just the thought of it."

"That's not going to happen—not the way I work at it," Edward protested. "I've found one stock, Ralston Electronics out of LA, that's developed a new process. The stocks will go crazy. It's selling for just under ten and should be sitting on thirty by this time next year. The new process will revolutionize computer processing, which should translate into handsome profits for the company. I'm going to load up on the stock." He had just talked to the bank about a large loan on his house and other assets with which to make the purchase.

"Be careful, Eddy. Don't get in over your head," Boomer cautioned, advice Edward unfortunately did not take. He got the loan and bought the stock—a lot of it.

Edward did the three surgeries. All were successful. Tommy's case was resolved, happily, when surgery confirmed the lesion to be a cyst rather than a malignancy. Chalk up one for good ole Eddy. Only time would show if the facial nerve reconstruction was successful. The disc surgery was routine, and the patient obtained immediate relief from the pain that had plagued him for so long. Edward left Grady Memorial Hospital for home at four thirty. Not a bad day.

"Edward, that you? Glad you're home. How was your day?" Mary, dressed in tennis shorts, smiled broadly. "I just got in myself from the club. Whew, it was hot out there, almost too hot to play. Here, let me fix you something. What? A bloody Mary? No, too hot. I know. I fixed some lemonade before I left. Sound good?"

Edward frowned and shook his head. "I was about to pour myself a vodka tonic."

"Here," she said, smiling, "I'll fix it for you. You just sit there and relax. Jody is at gymnastics, and Eddie is upstairs on the computer."

Edward sorted through the mail lying on the bar. He retrieved *The Wall Street Journal* and began to turn the pages. There it was! "Ralston Electronics Accused of Patent Infringement. Stock Plummets." Stunned, he quickly folded the paper. Mary placed the drinks on the bar as he stood, pale and trembling.

"What's the matter, dear?"

Without a word, Edward wheeled, went into the study, and closed the door.

"What's the matter, Edward? Are you ill?" she asked through the closed door. "Did I do something wrong? Is your drink all right, dear?"

"Go away," he shouted. "I've got some business to attend to."

He opened the paper again in disbelief. There must be some mistake, some explanation. But there it was: "Overvalued Stock

Closes at $5." He had lost it all. That must have been the reason for the call from his broker. He wished he had returned it. Tomorrow, there would be a notice in the mail from the brokerage firm demanding a large payment of cash with interest. The stock would be sold to satisfy the debt to the brokerage house, leaving him with the bank loan. He would have to liquidate his other holdings. He felt helpless, sickened. He had lost it all. How would he explain it to Mary? To Boomer?

He quietly opened the door. There was Mary, frightened and in tears.

"Come in. There's something I have to tell you." He gently took her by the arm and led her to the couch. "I'm afraid I have really messed up." He handed her the article.

"But what does this have to do with us?" she protested. He told her.

That night as they lay in the bed, Mary embraced him. "It's okay, Eddy. We'll get through this. It'll be all right, dear."

"Sure, it will," he choked. "Dad'll be there for us."

CHAPTER 5

Troy flung open the door and strolled into the office of the Fulton County District Attorney's Office, charged with prosecuting serious criminal violations of state law occurring in Fulton County, Georgia. As only one of one hundred such prosecutors, Troy had been employed by the popular district attorney for only five years, but he was known as the man to go to for advice when one of the other staff attorneys needed help on a difficult case or problem. He had already earned a reputation as a devoted public servant, and the office had learned to depend on him in more important and complex cases. "Gonna have to give that man more money, or I'm going to lose him," Billips surmised after reading his last year's performance report, probably not knowing the Harvard alumnus had been recruited by private law firms at much higher pay, including Getty and Jacobs.

"Good morning, Annie," he greeted the receptionist seated behind the information desk. He always tried to learn the names of people he saw on a regular basis. "How's the family?"

"Hi, Mr. Boomer. They're fine. My, you must have a big case today. You're all duded up this morning like you wuz going somewhere—big briefcase and all. You look like a Philadelphia lawyer."

In fact, Troy didn't look like a lawyer at all. His 206 pounds was spread ingloriously over a six-foot frame. Unlike Boomer, whose body fit perfectly into a forty-three extra-long suit, he was not well proportioned. Edward, when they were boys, had dubbed him "Mr. Short Legs on Mr. Big Feet," which he accepted with a smile and a bow. His features were pleasant, if not handsome: full lips, turned slightly upward in a permanent smile; good teeth; broad nose; jutting cleft chin; friendly brown eyes; clear, swarthy complexion; coarse, curly black hair, balding. He looked more like Marcus Fortune, though, than anybody. Though not handsome, Troy was an entirely pleasant-looking, friendly, well-adjusted, and likable man.

"Thanks, Annie," he replied, grinning. "Just an arraignment."

Troy pushed the button and waited for the elevator, humming quietly to himself. It was his tenth anniversary. He had six orchestra seats to *La Traviata* at the civic center, and reservations for a surprise anniversary dinner for Brenda at the Florencia Restaurant. Boomer, Emily, Edward, and Mary would join them at six for dinner and enjoy an evening at the opera. Brenda would love it. He had bought her a dinner ring, which he would give to her tonight. Emily had insisted they should wear tuxedos and evening wear "for such an auspicious occasion." Boomer and Edward, of course, had their own. He would have to pick his up, appropriately altered, at the rental store.

Troy left the elevator at the sixth floor, still humming.

"My, aren't we happy this morning." Marie Kegley, his paralegal, handed him the file for today's arraignment.

"I should be—it's my tenth anniversary."

Taped to the door of his office was a yellowed piece of typing paper on which he had scribbled, "Troy Boomer, Assistant D.A." *Got to get a better sign,* he thought as he had every morning for the last five years.

The office was small—barely room for a desk, a file cabinet, and a telephone stand. He flipped on the fluorescent light. It flickered for a moment, as it always did, and then struggled to full brightness. *Not the Waldorf,* he thought.

He sat down at the desk and attacked the piles of subpoenas, indictments, and case investigation reports. The size of the room didn't matter—it didn't matter at all. Indictment 95-603-Theft by Deception-set for arraignment. Assigned to Troy Boomer; Indictment 95-806-Possession of a Controlled Substance. Assigned for trial to

Troy Boomer. Eight new cases in all. Total cases, one hundred and three. Most would cop a plea.

The phone rang. "Troy, this is Marvin." Marvin Billips was the district attorney of Fulton County. "I've got a tough one for you, and it's yours if you want it. I got a call from Captain Thomas, head of the Atlanta police. They found the boy. I want you to get over there quickly before they take the body out. Do whatever you can to help them. Just observe. Stay out of the way, and make plenty of notes. I want to make sure they don't screw the investigation up. They've asked me for our help, and I want you in from the beginning. Here's the number. Call Captain Thomas, and have him send somebody to pick you up and take you over there. The kid was abducted from near his home, on his way from school, giving us jurisdiction. Report to me the minute you get back. I want you to drop whatever you are doing and get on this. If you've got a trial or a court appearance today, I'll take care of it. Okay? You with me? Get going. By the way, I don't want you to discuss this matter with anybody, okay? Nobody! The press will be hot on you. No comment, hear? No comment.

"By the way, I've been talking to the Feds ever since the boy went missing, and I get the feeling they have about decided to yield jurisdiction and let us go on with our work we've already started—what with their already heavy workload. And they know we have the resources to handle the investigation, with Thomas, Farley, and other retired federal agents on our payroll. Of course, we'll have to agree to keep them advised on our progress, which is no problem."

Troy grabbed the phone and dialed the number. Twenty minutes later, he was speeding toward the park with Captain Thomas.

Troy had seen the reports of the missing child on television. Tommy had been missing for several days and was listed as a probable abduction. The search for the youngster had been covered extensively by television, radio, and newspapers, and scores of volunteers had turned out to help in the search. The family was of modest means, so ransom was not considered a motive. Tommy had left school at three o'clock and had apparently gotten off the school bus at approximately three thirty. He was last seen playing in a vacant lot near his home with a brown spotted dog shortly thereafter.

"Who found the body?" Troy inquired.

"Some hikers," Thomas replied. "One of them left the trail to take a leak and caught a glimpse of a piece of yellow clothing under some brush. He moved closer, saw it was a body, and got the hell out of there without going any closer. I understand there were three or four of them, so it appears they just stumbled on the body."

Troy looked at his Timex. It was eight thirty. He had an appointment at the rental store for a fitting at ten thirty. He wouldn't be able to make that. But he'd call Brenda and have her pick up the closest thing they had to a 44 long, shorten the legs to 30 ½, and just hope it fit. Emily wouldn't be happy, but Brenda wouldn't mind. Not Brenda.

Troy was not sure what role he would play in the investigation. He knew it was extremely important to the case that the scene be properly secured and investigated, but he was largely unfamiliar with the accepted protocol.

"I hate to ask you this, Captain Thomas—it will show my ignorance. But what should I do when we get there?"

"Just watch, fellow," he replied. "Stay out of the way, and just watch. I want you to see this thing firsthand. And when we catch the freak, I want you to nail him good. This investigation today will come under close scrutiny. I want you to see, to know firsthand, that the work was done properly. Besides, we may uncover evidence that would require the issuance of a search warrant or an arrest warrant. If it does, I want you there, boy, in person. I don't want no technical foul-ups in this one. Know what I mean?"

Arriving at last, they confronted a group of reporters, TV cameras, and other media people. An officer had barricaded the narrow roadway, blocking their entrance to the site, and ordered them to stay behind the barricade.

"Captain Thomas, can you confirm that Tommy Perelli has been found? Is he dead?" A reporter grabbed the side mirror, hoping to stop the cruiser. Another stepped in front of the car.

"I have no comment at this time. I'll have a statement at the appropriate time. Meanwhile, stand clear of this vehicle so we can proceed. Don't block this entrance. Remain where you are. Do not—I repeat—do not attempt to gain entrance, or you will be arrested for unlawful interference with a police investigation."

Thomas moved the cruiser slowly through the crowd and proceeded up the hill to the location where the body had been found, after directing the officer to prohibit entrance by anyone other than police personnel. Troy felt his hand tremble slightly when he realized the gravity of the situation. He did not expect what he saw. No words—no description—nothing could explain the horror of seeing this nine-year-old boy, dead on the side of a mountain.

Troy watched the drama unfold. Never had he seen such care, such precision, as the scientists and technicians went quietly and methodically about their work. On their knees they worked with gloved hands, turning over every weed, examining every bush, every twig, taking samples, making casts, taking photographs, searching every square inch within an area of a hundred yards or more, preparing grids and marking the exact location of every sample taken.

The victim was moved to the morgue, where the body would undergo a complete and searching examination to determine the cause of death, the time of death, and any evidence that might link the killer to the crime. That examination would take place tomorrow. Troy would be there.

Every piece of possible evidence was properly sealed in a container, catalogued, signed, verified, and witnessed by the finders, and delivered to and signed for by a representative of the laboratory. As the investigators were concluding their work, Troy asked Dr. Adam Forest, nationally known anthropologist and head of Atlanta forensics whether the investigation had found anything of immediate importance to the case.

"Well, we found some things." Forest smiled, satisfied. "Some black marks on a rock leading down to the site where the body was. Looks like somebody slipped and fell, maybe leaving some rubber heel marks on the rock when they slipped. Not much, but we have the entire stone slab, about sixteen inches in diameter. We'll photograph it and take some scrapings to determine what kind of material it is and where it might have come from. We also found a piece of shoelace near the body—about three inches torn off the end of it—looked like it was torn off. It was fairly clean, indicating it had not been in the weather very long. Could have come from anybody—but who knows. We need to talk to the hikers who found the body and the officer who first arrived to be sure none of them fell or tore a shoelace. If not, we may have some link between the disposal site and the bastard that dumped the poor kid here. Also, we have casts of tire tracks just off the dirt roadway above where the body was found. The tread design is unique and might be important. You need to get casts of the tires on the officer's car so we can exclude that as the source of the tread marks. I don't believe any other official cars were that close to the scene, but you might inquire to be sure.

One more thing—and perhaps the most important. The body was found there, just under that rock—there under the slight overhang. Apparently, the killer tried to dig out a place to bury the kid, but the dirt was shallow, and he hit rock after two or three inches. Looks like he was scraping around with a tire tool or one of those little army trench shovels. I don't know what. Apparently, though, the bastard forgot about the rock over his head and, in trying to dig the hole, raised up and hit his head on the roof of the overhang. We found dry blood and a couple of hairs stuck to the rock. We'll do a DNA analysis for comparison in case you find us a suspect. Well, that's about it. We got a few things that might be useful, but there's still a lot of work to do before we're through."

Troy knew what he meant. The team from the medical examiner's office would examine every square inch of the child's clothing—what was left of it—and the surface of his body, looking for fibers, semen residue, hair—anything that might tie the body to the killer. They would take scrapings from under his fingernails and examine him for sexual molestation. Within a week, most of the laboratory work would be complete, and the police and the prosecutor's office would know if they had uncovered any hard evidence.

Captain Thomas looked at Forest.

"I know it's too early to tell for sure, but could you estimate about how long the kid has been dead? Could it be as long as four days ago, when he was reported missing? We need to start looking for people that might have been in the park when the body was brought here——-hikers, boy scout troops, tourists, bike riders, anybody that might have seen him in the park area."

"I would assume from the condition of the body that it was probably brought here within twenty-four hours of the abduction," Forest replied. "That's just a guess, but an educated one. They can estimate the date of death more accurately after they've done the autopsy tomorrow."

It was now three fifteen. Captain Thomas thanked Forest and called aside Troy and Detective Ron Farley, who would lead the investigation.

"Ron, the first thing I want you to do is to talk to every park employee who works here. Find out if they remember anything suspicious. Find out if there is any way to identify who visited the park—day or night—within seventy-two hours after the abduction. There probably is no way, but ask anyhow. Put whatever men you need on this, and let me know what you find out."

The investigation of the scene was interrupted, and the area was marked against intrusion.

"Let's see. Troy, I believe you need to call home, don't you? I'll drop you off at the souvenir shop. They may have a phone there. Or I could patch you in on my mobile."

"Well, I need some aspirin," Troy explained. "Besides, if Brenda got a call from the station, it might upset her."

Troy entered the souvenir shop, bought his aspirin, and called Brenda. Unconsciously, his eyes swept the store. They fell on a sign. "Free Raffle. Win a Trail Bike. Register Here."

"'Bye, Brenda. Got to go now. See you in a little bit."

Troy left the shop and climbed into Thomas's cruiser.

"Call Farley to come down here. I believe he might be interested in something I just saw inside this shop." He was right.

CHAPTER 6

That evening, Boomer and Emily arrived at the Florencia Restaurant at precisely 5:30 p.m. She stood by the entrance fidgeting, her black evening dress almost touching the sidewalk, while Boomer handed the car keys to the valet. Her square hips filled the dress, while the buttons down the front struggled to hold her breasts. Her hair, colored a raven black and stiff with hair spray, was piled on her head like a beehive. Boomer did not like to touch her stiff hair or breathe the smelly spray. Short and plump, somewhat dowdy, she bore no resemblance to Emily, the child of Chaumier du Prairie—beau ideal of fashion. He despised her adiposity. She didn't know and wouldn't care.

As Boomer reached to open the entrance door, she pulled him aside and adjusted his cummerbund, which, in the course of the drive in the little sports car, had slipped below his suspender buttons.

"I swear, Richard, you embarrass me. Look at your tuxedo. Why, it got all wrinkled up in that tacky little car, and look at my dress. That's the last time I'm getting in the thing to go anywhere. It just doesn't fit me. The next time, you can just get out the sedan." Boomer, whose love for sports cars was incurable, merely grunted. She might fit in a boxcar, he surmised.

In the early days, Boomer had tried to assert himself. He was not, by nature, dominant or dictatorial. Rather, he had considered marriage as a covenant between a man and a woman, founded on

38

cooperation and mutual respect, if not love. How naïve he had been.

Emily had proved to be a difficult partner. It started when she became pregnant with the twins. She wept. One day when she awoke, ill with morning sickness, she complained, "You did this to me, Boomer. You made me sick. You and your thing did this to me, and I hate you for it. I do. I hate you."

As the pregnancy advanced, she would stand before the mirror, naked, rubbing her round belly.

"Look at me, Boomer. Look at me. I hate it. You'll never do this to me again. I wish Marcus was here with me. He'd know what to do."

Boomer didn't know how to deal with her. At first he tried to comfort her. She brushed him away. He tried to play with her. She cried even louder. He tried to ignore her, to stay away. She pouted and locked herself in the room. By the end of her term she had grown by fifty-five pounds. The more she complained about her body, the fatter she got. By the time the twins were born, an agreeable silence had descended about them. He soon learned that the price of peace was capitulation and the penalty for assertion was war. He had become so accustomed to surrender that he hardly noticed anymore.

"Hello," Boomer said to the maître d'. "I'm Richard Boomer. You should have reservations for six in the name of Troy Boomer. Has he arrived?"

Emily picked a thread from his sleeve, dropping it carefully to the floor.

"No, sir, but your table is ready. Would you like to be seated now?"

"Humph!" Emily sighed. "Troy's never been on time in his life. I can understand Edward's being late—he's a doctor. I just hope we don't miss the opening curtain."

They had just been seated when Troy and Brenda arrived. "Hi, folks. Sorry we're late. I had a little business to take care of," Troy apologized.

Boomer stood and gently took Brenda's hand.

"Congratulations, daughter." He handed her the gold bracelet he had bought that afternoon, wrapped in silver foil. "Here's a little something for you. Troy's is out in the car." He leaned toward her and whispered quietly in her ear, "Don't tell him, but I bought him a set of clubs, hoping I could get him started back in the game."

Emily frowned and whispered to him, "Silly, you should have gotten them something for the house that they could use together." Boomer shrugged. He had screwed up again.

Brenda was beautiful. Her platinum hair fell gently around her shoulders, crowned by a silver tiara with colored rhinestones. Her pink evening dress with its plunging neckline revealed full, firm breasts and made her trim waist seem even thinner.

"You look gorgeous, Brenda." Boomer beamed, kissing her on the cheek.

Emily frowned, looking at her watch. Six o'clock, an hour and a half before curtain time. They had just enough time to eat and get to the theater. "I wonder where Edward and Mary are," Emily said. "Poor Edward, I'll bet he had an emergency. I do hope they will arrive soon. He works so hard."

"Troy," Boomer said, "I heard they found the Perelli kid. Everybody was hoping they would find him alive, but after four days, I guess they had about given up on that." Boomer shook his head in frustration.

"Hush, Richard," Emily said, frowning. "Let's talk about something pleasant."

"Well," Troy said, "you'll find out soon enough. Billips assigned the case to me. I was there and saw the body recovered. Billips told me not to discuss it, so I can't. It was awful."

Emily put her forefinger to her lips to silence Troy.

"Shhh, I'm not going to sit here at dinner and listen to all that gory stuff. It's Brenda's anniversary. Let's keep it pleasant. Brenda, how are the children doing? I never see them, seems like. With their school and my charity work, our paths don't cross." Emily's charity work consisted of one afternoon a week as a hostess at a local hospital.

In fact, Emily preferred Edward's children, Jody and Edward Jr.

"They are so much better behaved," she once confided to Boomer. "They never get into things or run through the house screaming, or get bread crumbs all over the kitchen like Michael and Elizabeth did that time—like two little Indians."

Emily loved to visit Mary and Edward at their big house in North Atlanta. She and Mary would sit and drink tea. Or Mary would make her a cup of that strong Louisiana coffee with chicory that she loved so much. If the children were home, they would sit quietly by, fidgeting slightly, waiting to be spoken to and speaking only when addressed. Boomer felt sorry for them. Edward was a stern parent who wanted his babies to act like adults. Mary was more indulgent of them, so the children soon learned to behave one way when Edward or "company" was around, and another way when they were alone with Mary or their playmates.

Emily seldom visited the duplex where Troy lived with Brenda and the children. "It makes me so sad to see the little fellows living in a shack—why, it's a shack, Boomer. No doubt about it, a shack! I'd like never to go back there." In fact, it was a rather nice three-bedroom duplex in a nice part of town.

About once a month, Emily would call Brenda to bring the children over. "I have something for them," she would say. It was usually a book, or a picture of one of their Fortune ancestors. They would accept the gift, grin as if delighted, kiss her on the cheek, and romp off again. That was the way Emily satisfied herself that she was an attentive and affectionate grandmother to all four of her grandchildren.

"Michael and Elizabeth were over here today visiting," she said to Boomer one day. "They just about tore the house down." To Boomer that meant one thing: Troy's children had played and enjoyed themselves like children are supposed to do. He was sure that they never suspected that "Gramma Emily" didn't really like them that much.

"Why, Edward! Mary!" Emily rose quickly from her chair. She offered Edward her hand, smiling broadly, and kissed him full on the mouth—something she had never done to Troy.

"Hello, Mother, Dad, Brenda. Congratulations." There was no smile. There were no presents.

"Edward," Emily said. "You look tired."

"Well, I am a little done in," he said, sighing. "Been going at it pretty hard. I didn't sleep very much last night." He didn't tell her why.

Edward sat down next to Boomer. As Emily and Mary and Brenda talked among themselves, Troy studied the menu like a freshman cramming for a torts exam. He liked to eat.

Edward leaned over and whispered to Boomer in a choked voice, "Dad, I need to talk to you. Something's come up. I've got a real big problem."

Sensing the urgency, Boomer said instantly, "See you at Perkins for breakfast, seven thirty, okay?"

Boomer picked up the menu and began to study it. He was worried. In thirty-five years, Edward Boomer had never said to him, "Dad, I need your help." He had never once said, "Here, fix this for me," or "Help me up on this limb," or "You see, there's this girl." Edward Boomer had always been independent, almost to the point of arrogance, and Boomer had long since learned to simply leave him alone. If he cut his finger and Boomer tried to examine it, he would pull his hand away and run to Emily. When they were boys, if Troy refused to give up a toy, Edward would run to Emily. "Now, Troy, don't be selfish." Troy would run to Boomer, grin indulgently, and give it up.

Troy was different. The difference was not in Boomer's mind or his attitude toward the two boys. They were just, simply, different.

"Dad, tell me about the stars," Troy would say, or "Dad, would you hold me," or "Dad, will you take me to the zoo?" Boomer had to keep reminding himself that both were his sons, that they were different through no fault of their own, and that he must love them both the same. And he did. He just enjoyed Troy more.

After dinner, as they were leaving, Edward did something he had never done before. He paid the check.

"Congratulations, brother." He put his arm around Troy's broad shoulders, giving him a slight hug on the way out.

Troy felt a chill go up his back. Edward and Troy had shared the same womb for nine months. They had shared the same bedroom, the same house, the same family, the same schools for eighteen years. They had been twin brothers for thirty-five years. Never during all of that time had Edward hugged him.

Brenda had never seen an opera. Mary had. In fact, Mary had taken voice lessons through high school and had a music degree from the University of Georgia. During her senior year, she had a minor role in one of the Verdi operas, she told them.

They arrived at the Civic Center Auditorium ten minutes before the curtain went up, which gave Mary time, with the help of the program handout, to explain the plot and tell Brenda what to look for.

Emily, of course, had been to operas many times. She saw her first one, *Figaro*, in New Orleans, when she was only twelve. She didn't particularly like opera. In fact, she considered it a bore.

"Oh, I saw where *La Triviata* is coming to Atlanta," she exclaimed to her bridge club, "and that wooonderful tenor, Venzenzo Pepperoni. Richard and I simply must go. I wouldn't miss it for the wooorld. Oh, *beaux-arts!*"

After such an enthusiastic endorsement, all the ladies thought she was an aficionada, exactly the impression she wanted to leave. She didn't really give a damn about Verdi. But she did want to let everybody know she was "cultured," a word that she often heard in Baton Rouge but never in Atlanta. "Oh, yes. I know Margaret Monahan. She's *cultured*," they would say.

The men sat there yawning as the orchestra tuned up—each with his own thoughts—quietly wishing he was somewhere else. Anywhere.

Boomer thought about Mary Stavanitis and her wonderful gift to him. He was puzzled that he felt no remorse. He'd thought he would. He looked at Emily. He resented her profoundly; he couldn't help it. He had given his life to her and his children, but she had given nothing in return. Maybe Bud was right. Time to move on. Time to get a life—getting older—take whatever you can get.

He thought about the little store where Emily bought his

clothing. She knew exactly every size. He would go there tomorrow and surprise Emily. He would look for a brown silk sport coat, then a shirt, matching tie, tested leather belt with a big buckle, pleated tan slacks, and brown-and-white shoes *with tassels!* Richard Boomer had finally crossed the line. He was glad he had.

Edward thought about the bank note. He had been a fool to mortgage the new home he had purchased with a loan from Boomer, made at Emily's insistence. ("Come on, Richard. Lend him the money. He's a doctor, Boomer, just getting started. You don't want him living in some shanty, and him a neurosurgeon—or under a big bank obligation his first year of practice, paying all that interest.") He thought about the breakfast with Boomer the next morning and the crawling he would have to do.

Troy thought about the day. The crumpled little body; the horde of reporters, like scavengers, fighting over every bloody morsel; the policemen and investigators, doing their best to avenge the atrocity; the poor grieving parents; and the sick, sick bastard that did it. He was glad Billips had assigned the case to him. He was glad he went to the scene. He was glad he was an assistant district attorney. But he dreaded the autopsy he would have to observe tomorrow.

"Just find the son of a bitch, and I swear I'll nail him," Troy said audibly, without meaning to. Emily's eyes widened. "Why, Troy. Whatever are you talking about?" Boomer smiled. He knew exactly what Troy was talking about.

That's my boy, he thought. *That's Troy Boomer. He's a prosecuting attorney, a good one. He's my son.*

The opera was finally over. When the curtain fell, Brenda jumped to her feet, applauding wildly. She turned to Boomer. "It has been simply wonderful. How happy I am. Thank you, Troy. It was a wonderful anniversary. The opera was wonderful too."

Emily agreed. "Yes, I can't wait to tell my bridge club about it."

CHAPTER 7

Boomer met Edward at Perkins Restaurant the next morning.
"I'm sorry, Eddie, I really am," Boomer said softly, gently laying his fork on the unfinished waffle. "I know how you must feel. It could be worse. I mean, I don't know all the details, but whatever they are, it's not the end of the world."

His words and tone were gentle, reassuring, with no hint of deprecation. Those platitudes were better than the scolding he had almost expected, and they made him feel much better, coming from Boomer. Edward had passed the first hurdle.

"I'm glad you came to me with this, Eddy. I'm sure it must have been hard for you. And I'm glad you didn't go to your mother with it." Boomer paused, waiting for him to respond, but he did not. He just looked away, remembering it was always Emily he had turned to.

Boomer fixed his eyes on Edward's tie. There was a long silence between them. Finally, Boomer said, "There was just—well—," he said haltingly. "There has always been a wall between us, Eddy, or a kind of miasma. To put it bluntly, I never did feel you really liked me. I never knew why." Boomer looked away, struggling for the words. "You were always so—it was like you were saying to me, 'Look, we have to live in the house together for a few years. Let's make a deal. You leave me alone, and I'll leave you alone.' "

Edward knew what he said was true. He didn't know why, but he suddenly felt a little sorry for the old guy.

Edward had lain awake most of the night trying to sort things out in his mind. What would he say to Boomer? How should he start? Should he go to Emily first, as he always did when he had a problem? Should he come right out and say it? "Look, Dad, I've screwed up bad, and I'm sick over it"? Or should he merely say he was "overextended" and had used bad judgment? He had decided he had better do a quick schuss and get it over with. That's what he had done. "Confession," he had heard Boomer say. "Confession is the first act of repentance. It brings forgiveness quicker than denial." He had said that to him once when he broke an expensive vase. What would be Boomer's reaction, he had wondered? Would he be angry? Would he scold him and tell him he had been forewarned or that he had been greedy? Here he was, a board-certified neurological surgeon, dreading the condemnation of his father. He had hoped he could conclude the terrible business of telling Boomer without losing the little pride he had left.

Would Boomer tell him it was his problem, that he must solve it himself? That was true, and he could live with that. He might have to. Maybe he should say nothing and try to work it out himself. Should he ask Boomer for help? Just a loan, perhaps, enough to pay the margin account and give the stock a chance to come back? His income was more than he had ever thought it would be at this juncture. He could pay him back. It would take a while, but he could manage it. He could liquidate his other stock and have a little left over from that; or maybe he should ask for an advance on his inheritance. No, he wouldn't do that. It would sound too much like the prodigal son.

Telling Boomer had been easier than he thought it would be. There was no anger, no ridicule, no scolding—only cautious concern, simple words carefully chosen: "I'm sorry, Eddy. I really am." He was grateful for that. He had not expected the cautious Boomer to offer to bail him out, but the soft tone was encouraging. He had gotten so far as to explain the problem in terms as direct as he could make

them. ("I just flat screwed up, Dad. Got too greedy, too cocky.") He
had chosen his words wisely.

"You know, Eddy, I've been thinking a lot about things lately—
about you and Troy and Emily and the grandchildren. You know,
I'm fifty-seven now. You and Troy are grown, gone from home, and
have your own families. (*What's he talking about now? What does
this have to do with anything?*) "Your mother and I don't have much
for each other and never have had. You know that. I'm beginning
to have some strong regrets, Eddy. Things haven't gone exactly as I
wanted them to. We can't help that. We can't do anything about that.
Christmas past and all that. Do you know what I worry about more
than anything else? What I regret more than any of it? I wish we
could have been closer. I wish we had been friends. But we weren't.
Maybe that was my fault. Maybe I failed somehow. (*What's he getting
around to?*) I wish we could have done things together—played golf,
gone fishing. You know, we never once went fishing. You've never
been fishing, have you? It's a lot of fun—there on the lake in a little
fishing boat, tossing your bait, drinking a beer, and eating crackers
and Vienna sausages. We ought to do that sometime, Eddy. Just you
and me. (*Poor guy, he's almost begging me.*) I wanted to do those things
with you, but somehow it never worked out."

Edward remembered that, as a child, he had been afraid of
Boomer. He didn't know why. He remembered a few times when
Boomer scolded him mildly, but not many. He never once thrashed
him or even threatened to punish him. He left that to Emily. He
remembered Boomer as detached and silent—always silent—
browsing in solitude among his thoughts. Boomer had spent most
of his evenings in his office, working. Edward saw him most school
days during the ride to school with Troy. That was it.

Boomer, however, had made it a point to avoid the office on
weekends. Saturdays, he worked in the flowers or did repairs around
the house. Troy liked to work with him, but Edward had preferred to
stay to himself. Boomer always took them to midmorning Mass on
Sunday and was careful to see they learned the catechism. Edward
remembered Boomer taking him and Troy to minor league tryouts,
coming home every night for a week to practice. But he didn't like

it. Troy did. He remembered once that Boomer took them boating, but he had not liked being out on the water. Troy did. Boomer was manifestly disappointed, but he never tried to push him into doing any of those things.

"Would you like to go fishing with me, Edward? Just the two of us? I could rent a cabin, buy some provisions, and we'll spend a few days together."

Edward thought of his schedule.

"The only accouterments are a pair of khakis and a cool shirt," Boomer continued.

"We might be able to do that sometime," Edward said reluctantly.

Boomer fell silent for a moment, disappointed. "Sometime" was all he heard.

"Now, back to your problem." He lifted his head and studied the ceiling. Edward had seen him do that hundreds of times, when he was thinking about something important. "I don't know what we can do about that. I'll need to see it all on paper so I can see how deep the hole is. Then, of course, with your permission, I'll need to talk it over with Emily. And there's Troy to consider. We've already advanced you a considerable amount of money, and we will want to be fair to Troy. I'm sure you feel the same way. Tell you what we'll do. Get the figures together, and we'll talk about it on the lake."

Edward thought, *The old fox. He figures I'd go fishing in the river Styx if it would get me out of this mess.*

It was nine o'clock. "Sorry, but I have to go," Boomer said. I've got to interview a witness at ten.

"My day off." Edward grinned, relieved that the conversation had ended. "I just have to make my rounds." He was satisfied with the conversation. It had gone as he had hoped.

Edward and Boomer had finished their breakfast. Boomer walked the short distance to his office, warmed by the early morning sun. Cars hurled past him, and smartly dressed downtowners, carrying their loads of files and briefcases, disappeared through cavernous openings. He thought of Edward and what he should do. Of course, he would have to help him—do whatever he could to ease the situation. *He's my son,* he thought. *Whatever I have is his and Troy's.*

Edward arrived at the hospital at ten sharp and made his rounds. He felt happy—somehow renewed. His feelings toward Boomer had changed. He knew Boomer loved him and that he ought to love him back.

The fees he would generate in surgery tomorrow were important, but they did not seem quite as important to him as they had. He took out a chart and began to dictate.

Preoperative report: This pleasant ten-year-old female, Mary "Poopsie" Evans, scheduled for surgery July 25, 2000, presents a suspected intracranial lesion in the medial cortex, provoking petit mal seizures. I have advised the parents that, while such surgery under general anesthetic is accompanied by some risk of injury or morbidity, the risk under modern surgical procedures and anesthetics is minimal and that the chances of a successful result are excellent."

"Poopsie" would be okay. He would see to that.

He replaced the microphone and winked at the nurse next to him. He looked at his watch and remembered that Eddie had asked him to take him to Little League tryouts. He would call him and tell him to wait, that his squash game had been called off. He would call and cancel.

He thought about Boomer and the conversation. He knew Boomer would offer him whatever he needed. He had made that clear without saying so. That was all Edward really needed, just the offer and Boomer's support, which suddenly had become very important to him. He would thank him gratefully and tell him everything was all right—that he would let him know if he needed it. Someday they might fish together, just the two of them. Someday. They had a long way to go to pull down the wall, but today was a good start.

He dialed home from his car. "Mary, tell Eddie to wait. I'll be there shortly to take him to tryouts. Be sure he has his glove and the doctor's certificate. How do you feel? Okay? Yeah, everything went fine. We're okay, baby. See you soon.

CHAPTER 8

Troy's eyes opened suddenly. It was Thursday, the day Dr. Molsen was scheduled to do the dreaded autopsy. He stirred a little, waking Brenda.

During the ten years since they were married, they had slept together every night except those nights when Brenda was in the hospital delivering Mike and Liz and the four nights Troy had spent in Denver without Brenda, attending a conference on forensic evidence. They had become so accustomed to each other that they slept in unison, almost as if the bed were a dance floor and they were on it. Each yielding, turning, standing close. No twin beds for them. No separate bedroom down the hall.

Troy lay there a few minutes in the crook of her body, his eyes closed, trying not to move and wake Brenda again.

His mind returned to yesterday's events. He saw, again, the horde of reporters. He saw Forest moving stealthily among the rocks and bushes, watching, looking, and singing out words of caution to his technicians. He saw the little body, shrouded in a sheet, as it was loaded into the van for the trip to the morgue.

"I want to catch the bastard, and I want to see him fry," Captain Thomas had said.

So did he. He thought about the parents, Arlene and Joe Perelli, remembering their names from a news broadcast aired while the search was under way. Good people. Decent people. Working people—going about the business of home, family, job, children. He thought of Mike and how much he loved the little fellow. He knew that while he slept that night, the Perellis did not. He would get up and take his children to St. Mary's School this morning. The Perellis would not. He would see his children disappear into the school building, under the tender care of a parish nun, laughing, carrying their books and lunch pails. The Perellis would not.

"God! What does all this mean?' It meant, he knew, that out there somewhere, living among the thousands of children in Atlanta, was a caliginous monster. His lusts were out of control. As long as he prowled the streets of Atlanta, neither Mike nor Liz nor any other child was safe. The next victim need only be in the wrong place in the wrong circumstances at the wrong time.

He wondered. What provoked the maniac? What evil had created him? Had the demon been summoned out of the pages and pictures, the filth and slime, of the adult bookstores lining the back streets? Was the killer infected by the rentals in the back room ("You must be eighteen to enter here") of Padgett's Videos? Was he driven down the path of perversion by some encounter with a neighbor or a family member, while still a child himself? Troy didn't have answers to those questions. Before the case was over, he would try to know more about the killer's mind than he knew about himself. He had to be caught. There must be no more Tommy Perellis.

He knew it would be hard. Even monsters have legal rights. The right to remain silent; the right to competent counsel; the right against self-incrimination; the right against "unreasonable" searches and seizures; the right to trial by jury; the presumption of innocence; the right to multiple appeals; the right against cruel and unusual punishment; and on and on. Every step in the state's investigation, accusation, and trial of the case would be carefully scrutinized by the defense. Any technical foul-up could end an otherwise ironclad prosecution, and the killer could be set free. It had happened before, and he must see that it didn't happen in this case. That was why he was there yesterday; why he would be there today; why he would be there in every critical phase of the investigation and arrest. That was why Billips had called him in.

He dreaded today. Above all things, he dreaded today. He had to go to the county morgue at one o'clock, sit behind a glass enclosure, and observe the dissection of a nine-year-old child. Troy was suddenly angry. He was very angry. He would get through the day somehow. The postmortem would be the worst part. After that he would suggest to Captain Thomas that they begin their investigation by employing, as soon as possible, whatever experts were required to assemble a psychological, social, and familial profile of the killer, based on what was already known of the crime. That consisted principally of the scant facts known about the abduction, the age and appearance of the victim, and the brutality with which the murder had been carried out.

Captain Thomas had been pleased that Troy had noticed the raffle advertisement. He too surmised that some visitors who registered their names, addresses, and telephone numbers might have information that would help them. Farley had immediately impounded the box and was putting a list of names together, along with the telephone numbers recorded on the registration. A list of questions to ask each of the registrants was being prepared. It was a good place to start, Farley had said. He seemed receptive to other suggestions that Troy had made, but Troy had to be very careful not to interfere in the investigation. He would know just how far to go, but he would need to feel his way along.

"Quit squirming." Brenda smiled and turned onto her back, her eyes tightly closed.

Troy looked at the clock, set for seven o'clock. It was only five thirty—too early to get up. They lay there, motionless.

"Thinking about the little boy, aren't you?" Brenda rolled onto her right side, facing him.

He didn't answer. He sniffed and reached for a tissue on the nightstand.

"Well, you know it could have been Mike or Liz, any little kid in the city."

He knew the Perellis would ask themselves over and over why it had happened to their child. Would they blame themselves, he wondered, for not being there when the school bus came, or for not keeping him in day care until Sarah got off from work? Had the Perellis not noticed that the circus had come to town and that the jackals were out of their cages? No one could guess how many or when or where one of them might strike. They must have seen the wretches daily, going in and out of the windowless stores and movie houses, near their small grocery and delicatessen.

Brenda could see Troy's sleep was over. She lifted the covers and stepped down onto the carpeted floor, at the same time putting her right arm into the sleeve of her blue negligee.

It was a quarter to six. As she did every morning, Brenda leaned across the bed and kissed Troy lightly on the lips. He reached to pull her down to him, but she squirmed away, squealing, "Oh, no, you don't, Buster. You had your chance!"

"When?" he protested. She knew he was only playing, trying to put away for a while the lugubrious sounds and sights of yesterday's events.

"Breakfast?" she teased. She knew what the answer would be. Troy always had breakfast—two eggs, bacon, toast, and coffee—and Brenda always fixed it for him.

She usually got out of bed before he did and brought him a cup of coffee. She would break two eggs into the skillet, turning only one, and flipping bacon fat on the other. That ritual was to remind her of Troy's first egg order after they had returned from their wedding trip. "Fry one on one side and one on the other," he had requested, hoping to confuse her. She put the plate in front of him, one yolk uncooked. He didn't say a word until he had eaten both.

"Those were good, but you fried one of them on the wrong side. Fry both of them on the flat side next time." She knew she couldn't get ahead of him, but she kept trying.

Troy dressed, had breakfast with Brenda, and waited for Mike and Liz to get ready for school. As he waited at a traffic signal, he saw the little store. "Perelli's Grocery and Delicatessen," the sign said.

The door to the store was open, and Joe Perelli stood on the sidewalk bending over a straw broom and sweeping away yesterday's litter as he had done every morning for fifteen years. Troy recognized him from the pictures in the local paper and his tearful appeal, made on local television, for the return of his boy. As he swept, a child passed close by him. He paused and watched him turn the corner and pass from sight. He lifted the broom from the sidewalk, took a handkerchief from his pocket, and wiped his eyes. He turned, without finishing, and disappeared through the doorway. Troy understood. He pulled his car to the curb in front of the store.

"Wait here," Troy told the children, careful to lock the door and take the key. He went inside.

"I'm sorry, sir, we're closed," Joe Perelli said.

"Hi, Mr. Perelli. I'm Troy Boomer." He reached his hand to shake. "I just came in to tell you I am very, very sorry."

Perelli choked, "I don't know who you are, sir, but I thank you very much."

Troy put his arm around Perelli's shoulder and embraced him gently.

"Here's my card, Mr. Perelli. Call me when things settle down and you feel like talking." Perelli looked at the card, nodded, and wiped his eyes.

"I will, I will," he said softly.

CHAPTER 9

After Troy left him, Joe Perelli returned to his sweeping. The news had come yesterday morning. Officer Johnson and the investigator for missing persons assigned to the case came to the house and told Joe and Arlene that Tommy had been found.

"The news isn't good," Johnson had said, trying to prepare them for the words to come. They were told Tommy's body had been found in Stone Mountain Park by a group of hikers. "No, we don't know who did it," Johnson told one of the Perelli brothers. A task force is being organized within the department, headed by Captain James Thomas. "You may be assured the Atlanta Police Department will do everything within its power to find the assailant and bring him to justice," Johnson had told the Perellis.

A call from Arlene had begun the ordeal. "Joe," Arlene had said over the phone in a worried tone, "it's five thirty, and Tommy is nowhere to be found. I've called around to his friends, and none of them has seen him. I called his friend down the street, and the last time he saw Tommy, he was getting off the school bus. No, he didn't have ball practice today, and he should be home. I've told him a dozen times he is to come straight home and stay there, do his homework, and call me or you before he goes anywhere. Yes, I left the key where I always do, and it's still there where I left it. I'll keep looking and call you back when I find him."

Arlene replaced the receiver and went next door to the neighbors'.

Timmy, the younger son, was home but had last seen Tommy on an abandoned lot, playing with a stray dog that had been hanging around the neighborhood since the day before. She went back to the house and waited. Maybe he was out somewhere romping with the pup. Maybe one of his cousins had picked him up on his motor scooter and taken him to the video game parlor at the mall. She called. None of Tommy's uncles or cousins had seen Tommy since Sunday Mass. She tried to call his Little League coach, hoping he had called a special practice and that Tommy was there. The coach was somewhere camping.

The little imp, she thought, suddenly angry. *Wait till I get my hands on him—worry me like this.*

Tommy was nine years old, outgoing and friendly. A favorite among the neighbors, most of whom knew him by his first name, he was always ready to sweep a neighbor's drive or pull crabgrass out of a neighbor's lawn for fifty cents an hour. "That Tommy is the best-looking boy in the whole family," one of the aunts had once said.

The few times that Joseph had dropped him off at school on his way to work, the nuns greeted him at the car, patted him on the back, and walked with him to the door.

Arlene had often wished she could quit her job and stay home. She didn't like Tommy's being alone between three thirty, when the bus came, and five o'clock, when she got home from work. But the business was not doing well, and they needed the income. She usually called every day to make sure he was home, and she always admonished him to stay there until she arrived. She had been too busy at work to call that day.

Arlene had waited. There was nothing else to do. She was worried, but she felt Tommy was somewhere, safe. They had bought the little house where they lived five years earlier, careful to choose a clean, safe neighborhood. The neighbors on her block were decent, hardworking people. She knew them all and felt very safe there. "A good neighborhood for kids," Joe had always said.

At six o'clock, the phone rang. It was Joe. "Let me speak to Tommy," he said, obviously annoyed.

"Tommy's not here, Joe. I don't know where he is, and I'm worried sick. I've called everybody, and nobody's seen him. I'm worried, Joe, really worried. I was just about to call you but decided I would wait until six, and if he wasn't home, call you. Well, he's not home, and I don't know what else to do—" Joe interrupted.

"I'll close early and come on home. He'd better have a good explanation."

At eight o'clock, Joe called the police. He was connected to a gentle female voice. "Have you called the relatives? You have? Have you checked with the neighbors? They haven't seen him? Has he ever been late coming in before? No? Well, I'm sure he's all right, Mr. Perelli, but so you will feel better, I'm going to send Officer Johnson right over to take a statement for our records. Meanwhile, I'm going to run a check on all the hospitals and emergency clinics to be sure there hasn't been an accident." Behind the reassuring words, Joseph sensed alarm. Joe thanked her and replaced the receiver.

"Oh, God, Joe, where's my boy? Where's Tommy? What's happened to Tommy?" Arlene's voice began to tremble. She began to sob. "He's never done this before. Did you say anything to him this morning? To cause him to run away? God, I hope that's all it is—maybe he ran away, Joe. I'll check his closets and his drawers to see if anything's missing." She ran to his bedroom, threw open the closet door, and checked the bureau. Everything was there, just as she had left it. They had waited for the officer to come.

At ten o'clock the doorbell finally rang. Officer Johnson interviewed the Perellis and, after issuing a bulletin to all mobile units describing Tommy and the circumstances of his disappearance, stayed the rest of the night. "The dispatcher has this number. If anything develops, he will call us immediately."

While they waited, Joe kept assuring his wife that Tommy would call soon, lost in the city, or at a friend's house. At midnight, family members began to arrive—the other three brothers and their wives and an assortment of cousins.

Father Boniface, smiling and optimistic, arrived about the same time. "Our father always looks after the little ones. Tommy will be all right." He was wrong.

For four days, the vigil was kept. The Perelli brothers stayed on, going to their homes in shifts to shower, fix food, and put on fresh clothing. Each hour the mood grew grimmer. Searches of the neighborhood had been fruitless. Appeals on television, in newspapers, and on the radio for Tommy's return went unanswered. It became clear Tommy might not be alive.

When the news came from Officer Johnson that Tommy had been found, it was more than Arlene could endure. She looked at Joe wildly, screamed a piercing cry, raised her arm to make the sign of a cross, and before she could complete the gesture, melted into the floor. Officer Johnson had been wise to have an emergency vehicle standing by so that he needed only to open the door and the medics would enter.

Joe went quietly to the bedroom, closed the door, sat on the side of the bed, fixed his eyes on the flowered wallpaper, and stared. There were no tears.

Louie, his oldest brother, came into the room and sat on the bed next to Joe. He looked deep into Joe's face but said nothing. He took Joe's left hand and placed his right arm around Joe's shoulders, drawing him closer. "Father Boniface is on his way," Louie whispered.

"Tommy loves Father Boniface." Joe smiled. "He will be sorry he missed him."

CHAPTER 10

Boomer leaned back in his swivel chair and looked down on the tan file folders staring up at him. He had come to think of that desk and its files as a huge mouth, its jaws opening every morning, ready to chew up his day.

He was trapped, and he knew it—locked in a dungeon he had fashioned for himself, bound to a routine of his own design. His work no longer bridged the great chasm that separates drudgery from contentment. No peace could be found in a motion for discovery, no joy in a plea to arraignment, no contentment in a motion for bail.

There were flashes of the old Richard Boomer—the drama of a trial or the pleasure of a legal coup d'état—but his transformation was almost complete. The maw and its manila-colored teeth had chewed up the gonads that had made his practice so successful and satisfying.

The rewards of his former successes had come from within. Each victory had been a tonic, an elixir that sustained him until the next swallow. The potion had long since lost its effect, and he could find no formula to replace it. He doubted he would. Victory in the courtroom was no longer enough. He needed more. . His work had become an abatis separating him from the rest of the world, and he was alone behind the barricade.

He looked at his watch. Twelve o'clock. He rang Bud. "Sorry, buddy," Bud declined. "Got to pick up my ex and go to the school—some kind of conference with Richie's teacher. Call me tomorrow, though."

He called Troy asking him to join him for lunch, but Troy's secretary told him he had already left for the autopsy on the Perelli kid, so he would have to lunch alone. Boomer picked up a file folder and retrieved a pretrial brief filed by the opposition, so he would have something to read while he ate his chicken salad and soup. He made his way through traffic to the restaurant, where he was seated at a table in the corner, next to a window. *The same table,* he thought, remembering the friendly smile and nod she had given him earlier in the week. Taking the brief from its jacket, he put on the reading glasses he had recently acquired, at some expense to his vanity, and began to read.

"Hello." He first thought the throaty voice, clear and soft, had come from the adjoining table. He didn't look up. "Hi, there." The voice this time was a little more insistent, as if to say, "Well, are you going to look up—? Are you going to answer me, or are you going to keep on reading that damn brief?"

He looked up, and there she stood—the same smile, the same quick nod of her head—holding a tray from the buffet.

"Hi, again. Are you alone? I wonder if I might join you. I went straight through the buffet thinking my friend had already arrived and had a table. He hasn't, and here I stand with a tray full of food and no place to eat it."

Boomer looked around the room. All the tables were full. He stood, feeling somewhat clumsy, as he always did when he met a beautiful woman. "My pleasure." He smiled, pointing to the chair opposite him. "I'm Richard Boomer, and—"

"I know who you are—everybody knows the famous Richard Boomer." Her voice grew theatrical. "Zealous defender of the unalienable rights of innocent, well-heeled felons. I'm Jessica Moreland. I have just taken a job as a trainee with the Centennial Advertising Agency, just down the street. I hope you don't mind my sitting here. I have an abbreviated lunch break today—have to be back at one o'clock for a training session."

Boomer looked at his watch. *She will be late,* he thought.

"You just go on reading, and don't bother about me," she apologized as she began to take the plates off her tray.

When she had finished, Boomer, still standing, took the tray from her hand and put it on the seat of the chair next to him. She sat, silent, her large blue eyes focused on the salad plate in front of her.

He looked into her face. *About thirty-eight,* he thought, *between thirty-five and thirty-eight.* No engagement ring or wedding band, he noticed.

Her dense blond hair, coarse and full, was parted slightly to the left side, exposing a slight widow's peak centered over a flat, perfectly contoured forehead, held up by generous blond eyebrows, which were bowed slightly to fit the contour of her eyes. Her features were otherwise regular. Her dimpled chin receded slightly, revealing a fullness in her mouth and neck that was, itself, pleasing.

Boomer put the brief back into its folder. She knew he was looking at her. She did not mind. She wanted him to. She continued to look down into her salad plate as if she were reading its contents: three slivers of carrots, two small tomatoes, four croutons. She looked up and smiled as if to say, "Something wrong, Boomer? Like what you see, Boomer? I hope so, Boomer. Now that you've looked over the merchandise, let's talk."

She began, "You know, I saw a news report last night where they were talking about that poor Perelli kid,—you know, they found him yesterday on Stone Mountain—and they mentioned a name, I believe it was Troy Boomer, of someone who was involved in helping to investigate the case."

"That's my son," Boomer said proudly. "He's been assigned to give legal advice to the police in the course of the investigation and to prosecute the assailant when he is caught—and he will be if I know anything about the Atlanta Police Department."

A slight look of pain and worry came on her face. "They must," she said.

"Are you a native of Atlanta?" Boomer inquired. He did not consider that question too personal. It seemed like a good way to be pleasant.

"No, I'm from Chattanooga, recently divorced after fourteen

years. Charley has remarried. Our only son died of leukemia when he was ten. There were so many memories there, I decided to leave—really nothing left to keep me there. So here I am. I sold my house on Lookout Mountain and have taken an apartment here. This little job I've taken is temporary, until I can find something better. Is Troy your only child?"

Boomer began to talk. He really began to talk. He didn't know why he talked so much. As he revealed bits and pieces of his life to her, Jessica responded appropriately with a smile, a frown, a grimace, a giggle, or a nod of understanding. He wondered how she could be as interested in the details of his life as she appeared to be.

He looked at his watch. It was one fifteen. "I'm sorry. Look at the time. I've made you late," he apologized.

She reached over to give him her check and ten dollars. "Would you pay for me—there's a line there—and I'll get my change later. Thank you for letting me sit with you and for taking care of the check. 'Bye!" Then she was gone.

His eyes followed her to the door. Her straight skirt just covered her knees, revealing small ankles and long slightly muscular calves. The skirt and white blouse covered a body that would fit well between the pages of a Victoria's Secret catalog, and he tried to imagine how she would look in that setting. *Hot damn,* he thought. *What a woman!* He hoped he would see her again sometime, but he knew that he probably would not. She already had a young friend whom she seemed to like; besides, he had a wife. Nevertheless, he could not remember a time when he had talked so freely and so openly to someone whom he had just met. And it was good having someone to talk to other than an obsessive son interested only in sending people to jail and a nagging law partner bent on sending them to hell. He rose, walked to the cashier, and paid their checks.

As he stood waiting for his change, there she was again. Red-faced and out of breath, she gasped, "I just ran back. I am all out of breath. Here, I meant to give you this." She handed him a small piece of paper folded several times and hurried away before he could speak.

He unfolded the paper and read it. Jessica Moreland, 404-463-

4691. He felt his heart pounding in his chest. His face felt flushed. He felt old stirrings in his body that he had not felt in years. He knew what it was. He looked down at his shoes. Black lace-up, six eyelets, plain toe—the same shit he had worn for twenty-five years. Then he remembered his promise to himself. He wheeled, left the restaurant, turned right, and walked the three blocks to Elhannon's Men's Store.

"Yes, Mr. Boomer. Good to see you, Mr. Boomer." Harry had provided Boomer's wardrobe for over twenty years, yet Boomer had been in the store only a few times—usually to buy a present for one of the boys or a pair of shorts for himself, but nothing else. His weight, size, and proportions had not changed in twenty years. He had worn a 43 extra-long coat during every one of those years, a tall men's shirt, 16-½ collar and 35 sleeve, a size 13C shoe, and an extra-long tie. Emily knew the sizes by heart and had Harry call her immediately when a new shipment of Hickey Freeman suits came in. Every year Harry would include in his order three suits, ordered especially with Boomer in mind. They were always the same three-button cut, the same fabric, and the same thread. He knew exactly what Boomer liked. One solid black, split down the back; one dark charcoal with narrow thin stripes, very muted; one dark blue, very muted stripe with split down each side. The pant lengths were always altered, without cuffs, by measurement.

"He wears a 34-1/4 inseam, exactly 34-1/4, no more, no less," Emily would say.

The legs when altered were always correct to Emily's liking, and he did not remember a single instance when it was necessary to return trousers for corrections. The new suits with six white shirts, matching socks and ties, would always be delivered to the house and placed in his closet. Three of the oldest suits would be removed and sent to Goodwill, along with an equal number of shirts, socks, and ties. Boomer would never know he had three new suits unless he happened to see the clothing bill, which was almost never. He simply put on the suit, shirt, tie, and socks every morning that Emily had laid out for him the previous night.

Boomer had never owned a sport coat suitable for the office. It wasn't that he didn't like them. Emily just never bought him one, and he knew better than to ask.

"There you go," she would say, "being difficult as always." Those were her favorite words, and he had heard them thousands of times regarding almost every suggestion he had to make.

"What can I do for you, Mr. Boomer? Some shorts? Some socks? I just got in a shipment of Sunspel shorts and undershirts from England that I know you like, and—"

"No," Boomer interrupted him, a little upset. Harry apparently considered him too stupid to buy anything other than garments that would be hidden from the rest of the world. "No, I want to look at your sport coats, shirts, and casual slacks. You know the sizes by now, I am sure. I don't, I'm sorry to say. I saw a sporty-looking coat in the window there—that one—that I like. Is it silk?" The coat was a three-button silk, with brown checks and a faint blue foreground.

"We have that in your size, a 43 XL. It's a Hickey on sale at $560.00."

Boomer tried on the coat. It fit him perfectly.

"It's an athletic cut and looks very good on you." He hesitated and said meekly, "Mr. Boomer, have you talked this over with your wife? I know she would definitely not pick this coat out for you."

Boomer ignored him. He left the store two hours later, having bought three sport coats with matching ties and shirts, an assortment of casual trousers, and two pairs of shoes, brown, and Cardovan wingtip loafers, with tassels. The bill came to $3,650.00. "When those are ready, deliver them to the house," he instructed Harry. "I need them tomorrow."

He was not there the next day when Emily called Harry, insisting there had been some mistake and threatening to move their business elsewhere if he didn't remedy the outrage. She might have saved herself the trouble. Boomer, after paying for his purchases by check, closed his account at Elhannon's Men's Store. He would see Harry no more. He wanted to leave the memory of those blue and gray suits with him.

He couldn't wait for Bud to see him. What would he say? It would go something like this: "Hey, Boomer, you damn dipso!"

Apparently Bud didn't know what the word meant, because he used it even to describe nondrinkers. "What the hell you got on? Emily see you in that? Wait. I know. You filed for divorce! She died? Went crazy? Your house burned? I can't believe it. You look great, just great, ten years younger—forty-seven, forty-eight maybe. Damn, I should look so good."

Boomer sat down at his desk. He looked out the sixth-floor window at downtown Atlanta. He felt good for the first time in a long while. He thought about how much the city had changed since the year he graduated from law school and how little he had changed. The new clothes. What did they mean? Why had he bought them? Was he in the throes of a midlife crisis? Did he do it because of Jessica Moreland? Did he do it to feel better about himself, to feel younger, to recapture his lost youth? He knew. It was Emily. They were a message to Emily. The clothes would tell her that Pussy had grown tired of his litter box and had taken to the streets.

He looked at his watch. Four thirty. The office had emptied out As always, his was the last. He suddenly, impulsively, rose to his feet, turned off the light, and left. He would stop by the bar across the street and have a quick beer with Bud and the others. For the first time in several weeks he would be home in time for the six o'clock news and evening meal, if there was one.

He pulled the little Mercedes into the garage. Inside, Emily had fixed herself a salad and was about to sit down and eat.

"Why, Richard, you're home early. You startled me. I just saw Troy on the early news, something about that Perelli case. I swear, Richard, I hate to see Troy mixed up in that nasty business—blood and gore and sex fiends. It just takes my breath away. Oh, well, I gave up on that boy a long time ago."

Boomer smiled sullenly. "Well, I'm quite sure he gave up on you about the same time, Mother." He called her Mother only as a gesture of derision.

She dropped her fork into the salad and rose. "See what you've done now, don't you? You've ruined my dinner."

He was glad.

CHAPTER 11

When he arrived at work, Troy was still thinking of his encounter with Joe Perelli. Joe had acted very strangely, he thought.

He turned to his daily diary to record the events in the Perelli case for the previous day. A daily log would help him to better organize his work and remind him of things he must do. He then recorded today's appointments. He would send Elsie, his secretary, to the public library for reference materials on the forensic sciences. If he was to do his job properly, he must develop an understanding of the analysis of forensic specimens. There could be no little screwups in this one. He summoned Elsie and gave her a list of reference books he would need. "Look for some books on forensic psychology too. Try to find out what is considered most authoritative and get it all to me as soon as you can. Here's twenty dollars. Take a cab."

Elsie flew out the door, knowing the errand was important. Troy turned to his events calendar, filled with the dates of arraignments, hearings, motions, and witness interviews. Several of the cases were pending pleas and sentencing based on plea agreements. Most of the rest were in their preliminary stages and could be readily transferred to another prosecutor in the office. Only a few would require his continued attention.

He called Billips. "I need to come down and talk about the Perelli case—what you want me to do in it and what I should do about my other work." He was told to come immediately and to bring a list of his cases and a copy of his calendar. Troy hoped Billips would give him free rein, at least for the first days or weeks of the investigation. He got his wish. Except for five violent offenses, Troy's entire caseload would be shifted temporarily to other prosecutors, which Troy knew would cause a loud groan on the sixth floor of the building.

"By the way, Troy, one of the reasons I wanted to see you was to give you the good news. I just heard from the Feds, and they have agreed to stay out of the case and let us handle it as long as we can show them progress, which I am sure we can do. I was also given assurances that the Feds would yield jurisdiction to our court and let us indict and try the killer."

By the time the conference with Billips was over, Elsie had returned, loaded with a box full of books. She had commandeered one of the assistant librarians, who had surveyed the computer catalogs, obtained the necessary printouts with the shelf numbers, and dispatched helpers to retrieve the books from their shelves.

Troy looked over the references briefly and found they were precisely what he needed to get started. He would scan them first to get some initial information—enough to get him through the autopsy and the task force meeting that afternoon. He could go to the library later and pick up more volumes if he felt he needed additional instruction, but right now he needed to concentrate on the autopsy of the body, since it was scheduled that day.

Troy arrived at City Hospital thirty minutes before the postmortem was scheduled to begin. He was ushered into the office of Dr. Henry Molsen, a renowned pathologist and forensic scientist. Dr. Molsen explained the sequence of the autopsy.

So that Troy would understand completely what was being done, Dr. Molsen agreed to explain each step of the procedure. Those explanations would be recorded in their entirety, serve as a permanent record of the procedure, and be used in the preparation of the final autopsy report.

Troy, who had always been very squeamish anyhow (he had once fainted when Edward had stuck a nail in his foot), reluctantly entered the cold room where the autopsy would be carried out. He looked around him. There in the center of the large room was a gurney with the small body of Tommy Perelli, encased in plastic, he speculated, but covered with a white sheet. Troy was led to a glass observation booth, fitted with headphones, and seated on a tall stool.

The coverings were removed from the body, and Dr. Molsen spoke into a microphone that hung above the table, suspended from the ceiling. "Mr. Boomer," Dr. Molsen said softly, "we are ready to begin the examination of the body. Can you hear me all right? Just nod your head. Good! Then the postmortem examination of the body of Thomas J. Perelli will begin. The subject, according to information furnished to the examiner, was born on August 25, 1991. He was in good health prior to his demise..."

On and on the voice continued, reciting what seemed to Troy to be an endless account of the victim's social, familial, and medical history, gleaned mostly from the scant medical records of City Hospital and Tommy's pediatrician.

He ended the preliminary statement. "Mr. Boomer, I know you must wonder what's going on here, but let me explain to you that, as we examine the body and particularly the organs of the subject, it is important for us to be aware of any possible preexisting medical conditions that might influence our findings. And, frankly, knowing something about the person being examined serves to remind us we're dealing with more than a cadaver. This procedure is known to you, I am sure, as an autopsy. I know it as a necropsy, since we are trying to discover facts other than the cause of death. We will determine not only the cause of death but also the manner of death, if possible, since intentional homicide certainly appears to be involved."

Troy wrote "necropsy vs. autopsy" on his legal pad. He suddenly felt a little ill. His hand trembled slightly as he wrote, and he became aware of a trickle of sweat on his forehead.

Dr. Molsen lifted his eyes and looked at Troy, seeing his apprehension. "Mr. Boomer, I want to reassure you this necropsy should not be viewed as a desecration or mutilation of the body. The surgical procedures will be performed in the same professional way as any operation."

The environment certainly looked professional. At the foot of the body was a white metal table, draped with a sheet. Located on the table were scalpels and various instruments, a scale, receptacles of various sizes, and other medical devices. Dr. Molsen and the two assistants were dressed in white gowns, and their mouths and noses were covered with gauze masks and goggles covering their eyes. They all wore rubber gloves extending above their wrists. Their manner was quiet, efficient, serious, respectful, and professional.

"We will begin with the external examination." As the assistants examined every inch of the body under magnification, and looked for any sign of foreign substances, Dr. Molsen dictated a general description of the body, which included the apparent age, sex, muscular development, state of nutrition, and other features. He then examined the body thoroughly beginning with the feet, describing in general the form, location, depth, and measurements of the wounds observed. "The body displays multiple gross contusions with accompanying deep wounds, particularly around the anterior and posterior portions of the lower torso, apparently inflicted by a sharp instrument, probably a knife. They extend also onto the upper thighs. Those wounds will be further described in the course of the regional examination. Rigor mortis is not observed, but areas of suggillation are noted, particularly on the left posterior, indicating the victim probably expired while lying on his left side. This suggestion is further supported by the presence of rigor mortis in the weight-bearing areas of the left shoulder and buttock. From photographs taken in the course of recovery of the body, it appears that the victim was found in a prone position. From the observed lividity, it would be reasonable to conclude that the victim had reposed on his left side after death for a period of at least four hours and that the body had been placed at the site where it was found four or more hours after the victim had expired. This finding is indicative of that fact but is not conclusive. The areas of wounding and lividity are being photographed in color for future development, and some of the areas of lividity are being excised for analysis."

Troy continued to record all the information as he understood it. Although it was unsettling to him, he was glad that he was there to observe the procedure. The experience would be of real benefit when the testimony of Dr. Molsen was presented at trial.

"We now begin with the regional examination. In this phase of the necropsy, Mr. Boomer, we will examine specific areas of the body and record our findings." He began by describing the texture, tone, color, and vascularity of the skin. He then tediously examined every wound, recording the exact location on a diagram, and its size, depth, and characteristics. Several rolls of films were needed to record each wound from various positions.

Dr. Molsen, over the next hour, carefully examined the victim's head, face, eyes, nose, mouth, ears, chest, abdomen, trunk, and extremities. Of particular interest to Troy was Dr. Molsen's observation that "the victim has a distinct facial expression often seen on persons who have died of extreme pain or by physical violence. The multiple bruises and deep wounds further confirm that conclusion."

After he completed the regional examination, an assistant handed him an instrument. "We will now begin the internal examination of the thorax and abdomen. Are you all right, Mr. Boomer? This will be the really difficult part for you, I am sure. I will begin by making a Y-shaped incision, beginning at the points just above each of the acromion processes, and they will be joined a short distance below the suprasternal notch …" He deftly applied the instrument to the left side of the body and began to make an incision.

Troy went cold. "Are you all right, Mr. Boomer?" Troy found himself outside the room, lying on a gurney, with a nurse gently bathing his forehead with a cold wet cloth.

"I'm sorry. I don't know what happened to me," he said.

"That's all right, Mr. Boomer," Dr. Molsen said. "It's tough, I know. No need for you to observe the rest. I'll provide a complete report of my autopsy protocol to Captain Thomas and the coroner. After you have seen it, I will be glad to go over my findings with you and answer any questions you might have. If you are all right, I'll just go back inside and finish this business. Nurse, stay with him until he is okay, and call me if I'm needed."

Troy left the hospital, glad to feel the warmth of the Georgia sun. He thought about Sunday's Mass and a scripture Father Boniface had read in the course of the service. "And whoso shall receive one such little child in my name receiveth me. But whoso offend one of these little ones, it were better for him that a millstone be hanged around his neck and that he be drowned in the depth of the sea."

He unlocked the door to his car and slid under the wheel. The tears came in torrents. "I don't know who you are. I don't know what you are. I don't know where you are. We'll find you, and when we do..."

Troy shifted the little Chevrolet into gear and pointed it toward police headquarters. It was four thirty, time for the meeting with Captain Thomas and the members of the task force.

"Okay, men. I think you all know why we're here," Thomas began. "Everybody already knows each other, except for this fellow. He's Troy Boomer, a prosecutor from the District Attorney's Office." Captain Thomas walked to Troy and put both hands on his shoulder. "We asked that he be assigned to the case early to make sure there were no mistakes. For your information, Troy was at the scene when the body was recovered and observed the forensics; and he was able to observe the autopsy of Tommy's body at City Hospital this afternoon. He looks a little pale, and I'm sure that was not a pleasant experience. To begin, let me say that this case is on the front burner. Be prepared to spend whatever time is necessary to do your assignments. You have been selected because each of you has unique qualifications. Some of you have not been on the force very long, and here you are investigating a murder already. Well, don't let that send you to the lavatory. There might be some undercover work here, and we need people who will not be recognized. Okay, here we go. Let me now introduce Ron Farley. Gentlemen, Ron will lead the investigation, and he will report directly to me. He understands that we will not be limited to any particular reporting protocol, so if you get onto something you think is important and can't get up with Ron, just call it in to me. I don't want to know what you had for breakfast, but you will know what's important. Now, for some of you that don't know him, Ron is a bullheaded, slave-driving, ass-kicking piece of mean-ass cop. He's worked some of the toughest cases we've had, and he has a good track record. Now, Ron will be responsible for putting together a plan of operation, seeing that the plan is implemented, and revising it as the investigation unfolds. I'm sure he would welcome any suggestions or ideas you might have later. I'll now turn the meeting over to Detective Ron Farley, who will bring you up to date on what has happened thus far. Before that, however, I want to make some things very clear.

First, when it comes down to searches of cars, houses, offices, people, or anything, don't take off on your own. We don't want to pick up a valuable piece of evidence and have some asshole judge kick it out on some technical ground that the search was bad. That's why Troy Boomer is here, to see that doesn't happen.

Second, keep your mouths shut. This case is our responsibility and not the business of some jackleg reporter or TV talking head. If you want publicity, sign up with the Little Theater or go into politics.

Third, we've got a piece of shit out there that wants to go around mutilating little kids, ours if he could get to them, and we've got to get him off the streets and into a straightjacket or a chair connected to about ten thousand volts. Give it all the time it needs, and let's get this business over with. Ron, it's your turn."

Ron Farley stood: a short man, five feet, six inches; full facial beard; a completely bald head; large hands, too big for his body. Full round shoulders and a chest giving the appearance of great strength; a permanent and ever-present scowl for a countenance, complemented by a deep, grave voice that belied his small stature. A veteran of the Vietnam War, he was decorated three times for valor under fire. All in all, he presented himself as fierce, abrupt, impatient, and arrogant. He was all of that and more, but he was good at what he did.

"Now, men," he began, pointing to the wall. This is, as you may recognize, a map of Atlanta and its environs. We have flagged certain locations in the city, as follows: The red pins with a red flag, marked with the number 1, tells you where Tommy Perelli lived with his parents, Joe and Arlene Perelli. The yellow flag here, marked 2, identifies the location of the school Tommy attended. The blue line here shows the route the school bus took that dropped him off from school. It ends where the bus stopped and let him off. We have marked that spot with an X. The blue flag marked 3 here is the spot where Tommy was last seen playing with a stray dog, or puppy, on a vacant lot. Now, the first thing I want you all to do is to take copies of this map, which we have made for you, start at the school, drive down the school bus route to the point of exit, park your vehicle, and locate on foot the vacant lot where he was last seen. Now, do this in shifts, four to a car. I don't want no motorcade. As you do this, I want you to observe everything right down to the piss ants crawling across the sidewalk. Get a good look at everything so you can put yourself in Tommy's place the afternoon he was abducted. Now, this ain't going to solve this case for us, but it will put you in a proper frame of mind to begin the investigation. And I don't want a lot of jaw between you on the ride. Just keep thinking of Tommy Perelli. Now, on this map, I have also indicated every location where we have had a complaint of stranger contact with a child during the last three years. Believe it or not, we already had this information on a map which we had prepared recently in investigating another case. Study that if you will. Those are indicated by a round blue dot. You'll be given a handout summarizing each of those complaints, the incident date, the nature of the contact, the accused if his identity was known, and other information. This is reference material in case you need it. Finally, we have on this map, marked with green squares, the place of residence of every pedophile in Atlanta known to us. We will hand you a rap sheet of each dung dog on this map—his name, age, a list of offenses, his MO, conviction records, and so on. There are a lot of sick-o's out there we don't know about, and a new crop is coming along all the time, but this information might help. Incidentally, these names were taken from court records of convictions, so the information is reliable. Acquaint yourselves with their names. That information may come in handy later on.

"Finally, we have marked in yellow, the color of dog shit, the location of every adult bookstore and sleaze dump in Atlanta where this turd might enjoy going. Now, some of you will be asked to infiltrate these garbage dumps, so drive by them and get an idea of where they are. Now, I guess you've got the general idea. Troy, you suggested we get a head-make on this creep by a forensic psychologist.

I agree. When we do, we'll have a better idea of what we're looking for. That's where we'll begin. We should have that in two or three days and we'll consider that in finally planning the operation. Until then, keep your eyes and ears open, your mouths shut. Make your drives, and we'll be in touch."

Troy was delighted. "Look out, rat bait. Your days are numbered," he muttered.

That night, the phone rang. "Hello, Mr. Boomer. This is Joe Perelli." His voice was weak. "You know, Joseph H. Perelli. I have the grocery store and deli. You were by there and left a card. I think it was about my boy, Tommy. We have been looking for him—night and day, we look for him—" His voice broke. "Is that why you came by the store, because you know where he is? We've got to find him. That's all there is. We have to find Tommy. He hasn't had his supper. He needs his supper. He's a growing boy. I called his coach, and he was not at practice today. I'm worried about him. If you see him, Mr. Boomer, would you tell him he don't have to mow the grass. I mowed it for him. If you see him, tell him to just come home. Thank you very much. Good-bye."

Troy hung up and fell into Brenda's arms.

CHAPTER 12

"Come on, Dr. Miller. Help me out here!" Troy's face grew red. "I'm sure you get calls every day like this. If you don't like being called, you shouldn't have written the book. No, don't hang up. Please don't hang up. Look, I'm sorry I spoke that way, but you have to understand. Tommy Perelli was savagely murdered and brutalized by a crazy mutant, and we've got to get him off the streets. The psychologist we contacted here is a cone-head himself. He can't help us." Troy waved his arms and gestured wildly.

"Pay? How will you be paid? Look, I've got a nine-year-old boy in the morgue down here in Atlanta, and you're wondering how you're going to get paid? Excuse me, Dr. Miller. I'm sorry. Please don't hang up. You do the work; I'll see you get paid. You what? You only charge your expenses? Your salary from the university where you teach is adequate, you say? Well, to begin with…"

It was Friday. Troy made arrangements to meet Dr. Andrew Miller at his office in Boston on Monday, since the preliminary autopsy report and the photographs would not be available until then. Dr. Molsen had promised to provide an abbreviated report of the autopsy within forty-eight hours, describing the wounds on the body, the nature and extent of the sexual assault, if there was one, and prints of the photographs taken; so he should be able to pick those up from Dr. Molsen on Saturday. They were delivered to him that afternoon. It remained for him to talk to Captain Thomas and Detective Farley about his conversation with Dr. Miller and the appointment.

"Look," he told them, "I'm not trying to take over this investigation. But we need a make on this sucker—a good one, I mean a good one. That's our only hope. We've got no place else to start. This guy can do it. I've read his book. He's helped nail a bunch of them, including the so-called hammer killer."

"Let's try it," Farley grunted. "Can't hurt."

Except for Sunday Mass, Troy spent the entire weekend reading the reference material Elsie had gotten from the library. Sunday afternoon he boarded a plane for Boston. He would have to spend another night away from Brenda.

"Drop the kids off at the door, watch them safely inside the school, and be back there fifteen minutes before school lets out. That way I won't worry. Promise?"

Troy arrived in Boston and checked into the hotel. The phone rang as he walked into the room. It was Miller.

"Mr. Boomer, Miller here," the voice said in the same soft English accent. "My wife and family have gone on holiday, and I'm here alone on this Sunday afternoon. I thought we might get together this evening for a little dinner and perhaps a pint, and get a little head start on tomorrow. I called your home, and your wife told me where you were staying. I would like to have whatever information you brought with you so I can study it in the morning. I always get up very early. That's the time I get most of my reading done—what with classes, you know. So why don't I meet you in the lobby, and we'll get started."

Troy was delighted. "I can be ready in fifteen minutes," he replied.

"Your description of the case intrigues me. Besides, my good man, I can't wait to meet the jolly fellow who precedes his request for unpaid assistance with invectives strange to the halls of academia."

Troy was relieved. He had worried about his outbursts and was glad to know Miller had a sense of humor. That would make him easier to talk to.

They met in the lobby and drove Miller's car to Fisherman's Wharf. Troy had enjoyed the big fresh Maine lobsters he got when he was at Harvard Law School, and he couldn't wait to tie into another one.

"So you graduated from Harvard Law School, you say? You're a prosecutor, you say? Good! Most graduates from those hallowed halls wind up in big city law firms carrying honey buckets. You do know what a honey bucket is, don't you? It's those little buckets you see on either side of a long pole, positioned behind the neck of a Chinese peasant, on the way to placing the fecal matter inside the buckets around his okra." They both laughed heartily. "Anyhow, tell me about your case, Mr. Boomer."

Troy paused, wondering where he should begin. He started with Tommy's abduction and went on for fifteen minutes, giving Miller every bit of information he had.

"Well," Miller said, "I must assume you have no good suspects, or you probably would not be here. I can tell you right off what you already know. You are dealing with a very complex and psychotic personality, perhaps dual or multiple personalities. Fortunately for your investigation, but unfortunately for these poor victims—and there will be more if he isn't apprehended—their thought processes, sexual attachments, and sexual behavior fall within recognizable patterns and have similar developmental sources. Therefore, they can be described in profile—not always so accurately, but often amazingly so. And their future conduct can sometimes be predicted with similar accuracy. In a case like this, we can learn a lot about our quarry by reviewing the type of damage he did to the poor lad, the locations of wounds on the body, and the apparent malice with which they were inflicted. These and other factors will provide a vague theoretical, albeit helpful, road map through his psyche, which may well give you a better idea of the kind of person you are looking for."

"Dr. Miller, I've had barely enough time, with everything else that's going on, to scan your book on forensic psychology. What I understood of it, I found very interesting and impressive. If you don't mind, sir, first of all I'd like to take back with me, or have you mail to me, your curriculum vitae for my records and so I can have something to show Captain Thomas and Detective Farley.

Miller unzipped a small leather satchel and handed him a thick package containing his academic achievements, professional affiliations, scholarly writings, and other information.

"Here," he said, smiling indulgently, "I hope this will do."

"Indeed it will," Boomer replied, stuffing the large package into his own, larger briefcase, which held Dr. Molsen's preliminary report and photographs showing Tommy's wounds. He handed Dr. Miller those documents.

"Here is the information you asked for. I would not suggest you view the photographs before dinner," he cautioned. "To tell you the truth, I haven't yet been able to bring myself to look at them."

The waiter served their dinners—whole Maine lobsters with drawn butter, pasta on the side, and a large baked potato. At nine o'clock they moved to the pub and began drinking mugs of Guinness stout. Questions poured out of Troy, questions he must have answered in defense of his own humanness.

"How does a human being get to be so cruel?" "Does every human being have in him the capacity to do such a thing?" "Do these guys worry about it—do they have feelings of guilt, remorse?"

Troy went on and on searching the mind of the great scholar, trying desperately to understand how this thing could have happened, how it could have been prevented, and how to set traps for the perpetrator. Finally, Dr. Miller looked at his watch. It was eleven thirty.

"Well, Troy, this has been a most interesting and a very provocative night for me. I am intensely interested in your case from a professional standpoint, but I must say, you have done a very good job of elucidating the human considerations in the case, and I thank you for that, too. Your zeal, quite frankly, is infectious, and I find my own adrenalin flowing. You must be a hell of a prosecutor. I will get on this the first thing in the morning. In view of our conversation tonight and the information you gave me, there really is no reason for us to meet tomorrow. I'll just use this time to begin my work."

"Good," Troy replied. That would enable him to catch an early flight and be back in Atlanta by early afternoon.

"I should have something in the mail for you to look at within a fortnight."

Troy's face showed his disappointment. Two weeks. The investigation would be virtually stalled for two weeks?

Miller read the disappointment in Troy's face. "Yes, yes. You're right. Tell you what I'll do, old man. I'll get someone to do my class work for me, delay some writing I had planned, and put off my holiday for a couple of days. That should permit me to work the profile in quite well. What, say three days? It's set then," he said without waiting for an answer. "I'll send it down by Federal Express, then, within four days, and it should be there by Friday."

Troy smiled happily. "Dr. Miller, you're the greatest!"

On the ride back to the hotel, there was a studied silence between them. Each knew what the other was thinking. No words were needed. It had all been said.

"Good-night, Dr. Miller."

"Good-night, Troy ... and, Troy, I hope you nail the son of a bitch."

Those words didn't come from the hallowed halls of academia either, Troy thought to himself. *They came from the gut.*

Troy tried to sleep, but he couldn't. Sleeping without Brenda was like trying to sleep without a pillow, or on the floor. He missed the sound of her breath, the soft warmth of her body. He missed Mike, Liz, even the parakeet fluttering around in its cage. He turned on the television.

"This just in," the voice said gravely. "Authorities report that they have discovered the body of little Mary Ann Wilson in a shallow grave alongside State Highway 67..."

He buried his head between two pillows.

Back in Atlanta the next afternoon, Troy presented Dr. Miller's curriculum vitae to Captain Thomas and Detective Farley.

"Look at this. Did you ever see such credentials?" Troy said proudly. "He's gonna help us—gonna drop everything, send it by

Federal Express by Thursday so it will be here Friday. What do you think of that?"

They nodded their approval.

"Look, fellows," Thomas said gravely "we're getting bombarded with calls. The whole town is in an uproar, demanding results. We've had over a hundred calls from people claiming they know who did it. One guy said he had positive proof that a city commissioner did it. The press is giving us pure hell. All we can tell them is that we are giving the case top priority but that we have no suspects. Arlene Perelli is out of the hospital. Her sister flew in from Denver to look after her. They had to take poor Joe to Georgia State for observation. He refuses to accept that Tommy is dead, and he was wandering around on the streets asking everybody he met if they had seen Tommy.

"This thing is bad, boys, bad! We need to do something, but I don't know what. We're going through the calls and checking every one out that looks even remotely credible. But what can you do? Knock on a door and ask some postal worker who gave some kid a bar of candy if he killed Tommy Perelli? 'Give us some blood, baby. Drop your drawers.' There's not a helluva lot we can do but wait for this Dr. Miller to give us his report and plan our operation around that."

"Look," Farley interrupted, "the way I see it is this: We've got the forensics. This asshole left a hole you could shove an elephant through—heel marks, broken shoelaces, blood, hairs, maybe tire tracks. Who knows what else we may find at the place where the crime took place or in the vehicle he used to transport the body. The analysis of the rest of Tommy's clothes, if we find them, may give us some fibers or hairs off the killer; there may be seminal residue for DNA. As I said, who knows what else? I tell you what we need, boys. We need a suspect. We need a suspect or a whole bunch of suspects real, real bad. When we can locate the creep, if we can get our hands on him, we'll have plenty to nail him with."

"I agree," Troy interposed. "But you've got some problems even then. If he has a car with tires to match the tire cast, that doesn't convict him. Every car of that make and thousands of others will have the same tread pattern. Besides, as the captain has said, you can't just walk up to a man and say, 'You're a suspect. Gimme some blood and a few pubic hairs,' without a court order based on probable cause. You can't go into his house and take a shoe or some article of clothing without a search warrant. That takes probable cause. No, I'm afraid we need more than a suspect. We also need enough evidence to show there is probable cause to believe the suspect has incriminating evidence among his possessions or has committed the crime. We need to remember to look for evidence that will establish sufficient probable cause to examine that suspect and search his premises."

"So what the hell good is the profile?" Farley countered, already knowing the answer. He already knew everything Troy was saying was true.

Troy smiled. "Once we know who he is, we'll get him. Let's take first things first."

"By the way, Farley," Thomas inquired, "have your men talked to the workers there at the park? Any leads?"

"No leads. We talked to all of them and didn't get anything remotely helpful. We also impounded the raffle box and got 350 names. Damn near everybody must want a trail bike, or maybe they just want something that's free. According to the manager of the gift shop, the raffle box was put out three days before the abduction, and we've got to call them all. The registration cards weren't dated—just names, addresses, and phone numbers. I've had eight people calling them. A lot of the people are from out of state, but we're calling them all anyhow. I started another bunch calling last night, since I'm sure a lot of the people who don't answer work during the day. I checked the reports today. We've contacted over 260 of them, and, so far, nobody saw anything out of the ordinary. I'm sending personnel out to the houses in Atlanta that don't answer their phone and telling them to leave notes to call us. We should finish most of the calls tonight and wrap it all up by tomorrow afternoon—all the ones we can get to. We'll keep a list of the ones we can't reach and keep working on them until we have talked to them all. Looks like a dead end, but who knows."

Troy was disappointed. He had hoped the names in the raffle box would provide a lead.

"Well, guys, looks like we've done about all we can do," Thomas said, rising to leave. "Keep on making the calls, and report to me when you finish. See you boys Friday."

"Troy," Farley said as they walked through the door, "you can check with me about three tomorrow. We should have all the calls made by then."

Troy went immediately to his office and reported to Billips.

"Okay, Troy," Billips said after Troy had finished his report. "By the way, Troy, you've been going at it pretty hard. Take the rest of the week off—go somewhere, do something, get a little rest. Keep me updated on the investigation."

Troy phoned Boomer at his office after the talk with Billips. "Dad, look, Billips gave me the rest of the week off. How about a couple of days on the lake. Think you could make it? It's been a long time since we did that. You still have that old fishing tackle at home? It's in the attic? What say, you want to oil it up and get out of here for a couple of days?"

If Troy had called and told Boomer he had won the Florida lottery, he would not have been more pleased.

"Sure," he said gleefully. "Look, I'm going to call Eddy. Maybe we can make it a threesome."

There was an uncomfortable silence as Troy thought about Edward. He had wanted some quiet time on the lake with Boomer, just like it used to be when he was a boy—just the two of them. He knew if Edward went, they would have to hear about his surgical miracles and listen to how well his investments were doing.

"That would be fine, Dad," he said after a moment, knowing that Edward would probably decline. "It's all set then. You oil up the gear and get it ready, and buy the provisions, and I'll arrange for rental of the houseboat and fishing boat and motor. Let's make it Wednesday and Thursday." Troy wanted to stay in town the next day so he could meet with Farley and go over the final results of the telephone canvas.

"I'll call Eddy now," Boomer said excitedly. He placed the call but couldn't reach Edward, who was with a patient.

Shortly after, the phone rang. "Hello, Dad, this is Eddy. I got your message you wanted me to call." Boomer was stunned. In the thirty-five years he had known his son, Edward had never referred to himself as Eddy. He had always hated that "corruption of his name," as Emily called it.

"Uh, Eddy, I just got a call from Troy. He has the rest of the week off and wants to go to the lake Wednesday and Thursday. We thought you might like to go along. He's rented a houseboat with three bunks, a kitchen, a refrigerator, a stove, and everything, and it would be very comfortable. I'll take care of everything else." There was a pause. Boomer waited for him to decline.

"Dad," Edward said, "I've meant to call you about that conversation we had last week. I spoke to my broker, and the stock is better than a wash. It regained two points, so I'll have $200,000 there. I sold my other stock. The proceeds from that, along with the $200,000 from sale of the Ralston stock, will pay off the bank note. So I'm even-steven. I won't be needing help after all. But I do appreciate your willingness to help. It meant a lot to me. This thing has been a real shock to me, and I guess it made me realize that I might have had my priorities screwed up. I've been thinking about the things you said. You were right. I guess I never really thought about it. About the fishing trip. I'd love to go. Wednesday and Thursday are fine. That's day after tomorrow and the next day. I'm off every Wednesday anyhow, and I'll just move Thursday's appointments around."

Boomer was very pleased. Eddy had solved his problem and had agreed to do something he had always hated.

The plans were formalized that night. Boomer happily cleaned and oiled the fishing tackle, put new lines on the reels, mounted them on the rods, and tied a swivel to each line. He was glad to see the old equipment in such good condition after so many years in the attic. He went to the market and loaded the Bronco with charcoal and starter fluid, crackers and Vienna sausages, pretzels, potato chips, and beer, lots of beer. He would buy the steaks, eggs, bacon, bread, and other provisions on the trip to the lake.

Troy went back to his little office. He got out the files on the other cases he was responsible for and tried to do some work on them. He couldn't. His mind kept returning to the Perelli case. He felt a little guilty about leaving for two days, but there really was nothing for him to do except to check with Farley on the calls to the raffle people, which he would do tomorrow, and wait for Dr. Miller's work to arrive.

The next day at four o'clock, he went to Farley's office.

"Not a damn thing," Farley said. "Not a thing. We reached all but ten people. Two of those live in Tennessee, one lives in Chicago, another in Louisville, and the rest in Atlanta. We've sent cars to check out the ones in Atlanta, with instructions to check back every hour until they reach them, and then have them call the office. We contacted the authorities in Tennessee, Louisville, and Chicago, where the others live. They're going to try to contact them and let us know. When we've gotten them all, I'll give you a call."

"Wait a minute." Troy reached into his billfold and pulled out a folded slip of paper. "I'm going fishing tomorrow and Thursday. Here's the number of the boat rental place. We'll be coming into the dock from time to time for bait and provisions. If anything else comes up that I need to be here for, I'll come immediately. I'll make arrangements with the dock to come out on the lake after me if it's an emergency. I'll let them know where we're anchored."

CHAPTER 13

The next day, Wednesday, Boomer pulled out of his driveway at 5:00 a.m. and steered the Ford Bronco toward Troy's house. He was dressed in a pair of old khaki trousers and a short-sleeved khaki shirt. Emily shook her head and frowned when she saw that was all he was taking, but she didn't offer to pack him a bag. He had thrown a pair of underwear and walking shorts and his toilet bag into a brown paper sack and stowed them in the Bronco with the groceries.

"Get in here, boy" Boomer said to Troy when he arrived at his house.

Brenda came outside with him and kissed him good-bye as tenderly as if he were going off to war. He, too, was dressed in khaki. She handed Boomer a plastic mug of black coffee and two large egg and sausage biscuits wrapped in plastic wrap.

"Here, I made these for you. Here's a sack for Edward. You all have a good time, and be careful. It's dangerous out on that lake. Anything can happen."

Edward was already outside waiting. He deposited a large suitcase in the Bronco. Boomer wondered about its contents. Edward had on white cotton trousers and a white short-sleeved shirt with nautical embroidery on the shoulders. Perched on his head was an officer's hat with gold decoration on the bill.

"Get in, Admiral," Boomer teased, before he remembered whom he was talking to. Edward smiled and ignored the jibe.

"The next time you plan a trip, try to give a man a little more notice."

He had enough notice to buy that damn silly sailor suit, Boomer thought. He was glad he had taken the trouble, though. It showed an interest in the trip.

"Damn, you suckers stir early," he groaned.

He took the passenger seat in the front of the Bronco that Troy had reserved for him and smiled broadly as the Bronco pulled out of his driveway. "Feels good, though."

Edward turned in his seat and faced Troy.

"How's it going Mr. Short Legs on Mr. Big Feet?" That was the first time he had called him that since they were in middle school. "Brenda okay? The kids? Mary wants you all to come over for dinner next week if you can make it. And you and Mother, too," he said to Boomer.

"Great!" Troy nodded.

An agreeable silence prevailed during much of the trip to the boat dock. The usually serious Edward told a couple of lawyer jokes he had heard at a recent deposition, laughing heartily as though the jokes were on them.

When they arrived at the dock, the attendant loaded their provisions onto the long metal houseboat, instructed Boomer on its operation, and tied the fishing boat and motor to its stern. Boomer steered the boat away from the dock. He needed no map of the lake. He already knew the exact spot where they would anchor and the general area where they would fish. They would steer into the main channel of the lake, turn east and go about three miles, turn up Walden's Branch, and dock just inside the mouth of the Branch. That location would put them near what Boomer used to know as the best fishing on the lake.

Boomer had prepared trotlines to put in the water late that evening and bought three pounds of cubed unsalted pork for catfish bait. Once they were in the channel, Troy began to unload the provisions onto the kitchen shelves and to examine the fishing gear that Boomer had brought along. The sun was now full in the eastern sky, and it was beginning to warm up.

"It's going to be a hot one today," Boomer predicted.

Both sons nodded. He looked at them standing there together at the front of the boat. He thought again how different they were. Yet that day they seemed somehow alike.

Edward suddenly put his right arm on Troy's shoulder. Troy turned to him, smiled, and lifted his face toward the sky. He bellowed at the top of his voice, "This is going to be fun, man. Fun." The two faced each other.

"Gimme some skin." Troy extended his hands, palms up. Edward slapped both palms clumsily, and Boomer knew that was the first time he had ever done it. Edward smiled broadly at Boomer.

Damn, he's enjoying himself. He really is! Boomer thought.

Boomer steered the houseboat close to the bank, just out of the main channel, and signaled for Troy and Eddy to drop the makeshift anchors, one on either end of the boat, to steady it in position.

"Let's take a spin up the lake," Troy said excitedly. Eddy went pale.

"No, let's wait on that," Boomer said, sensing Eddy's response. "We'll fish close around here for a while and get used to the boat and motor—make sure it's okay. I don't want to get five miles up the lake and get swamped or have the motor quit."

Troy understood. Boomer wanted to get Edward into the small fishing boat and ride him around close to the houseboat until he got used to it. They stepped into the boat and positioned themselves.

"Let's troll these banks," Boomer called, over the roar of the motor. He knew Eddy would not know how to cast his bait or snag and retrieve a fish if he had a strike. Trolling was something anybody could do, even a child. Again, Troy understood and agreed. Boomer, at the rudder, snapped a lure on his and Eddy's lines and maneuvered the little boat close to the bank.

"Now, just put the bait into the water and let the line out a little bit at a time," Boomer instructed Eddy. "The bait will crawl about eight feet beneath the surface, where the water is cooler. There's where the fish ought to be. Then we'll see how it goes."

Eddy dropped his bait into the water and let the line out gradually. When the lure was about fifty yards from the boat, Eddy applied the brake to the reel as Boomer had shown him. He sat holding the rod with his thumb on the spool. Boomer slowed the motor to trolling speed and had just begun to let his own line out.

Troy was still looking into the tackle box for a lure when, suddenly, whhhhhhhrrr! Eddy grabbed the handle of the rod with the other hand and began to tug fiercely. The rod bent so that he thought it would snap at any moment. Both Boomer and Troy thought his lure had become entangled in a snag or wedged between rocks at the bottom. Boomer killed the motor, hoping he might save the lure. The rod straightened for a moment, and then, whhhhrrr, the old reel screamed under the weight of its adversary.

Boomer maneuvered the little boat so the fish and line were perpendicular to the side of the boat and reached for the net. Whhhhrrr, the old reel sang as it struggled. Finally, after fifteen minutes of combat, Eddy managed to bring the tired old fish close enough to the side of the boat that Boomer could put the fish's head through the hoop holding the net and draw it into the boat. Eddy was trembling.

"Son uv a bitch!" Troy hollered. "Son uv a bitch! I never saw a bass that big. Son uv a bitch, Eddy, that's a big one. If I were you, I'd put that on my wall, man."

Eddy looked at him, his eyes full of the fire of conquest.

"I will! I will!"

The morning's fishing ended abruptly. Boomer, without returning to the houseboat, pointed the little craft toward the dock, thirty minutes away. As they were nearing the dock, Troy held the big fish aloft. The people on the dock began to gather, pointing toward the boat and talking excitedly as Boomer tied up.

"Where'd you get it?" "Whatcha gonna name it?" "Damn, what a whopper." "What kind of lure did you catch him on?"

Eddy proudly stepped over onto the dock, with Troy right behind him. Troy suddenly leapt into the air and came down with his arms around Eddy's chest, forcing him to the deck.

"You lucky asshole. You lucky asshole."

Eddy, with surprising strength and agility, flipped Troy aside and rolled on top of him, pinning his arms to the ground.

"Now, take this, dog breath." Boomer fell on top of them both, laughing hysterically.

The rest of the morning was spent measuring and weighing the fish, posing for pictures for the local paper, and taking the catch, packed in ice, to a taxidermist.

Before going back to the houseboat, Troy called Farley and got the bad news.

"We've talked to all of them but two. When we call, they all get excited and think they won the damn bicycle. Well, none of them saw anything unusual, so we got no help there. The one in Louisville is somewhere in Canada fishing. He gets back Monday, so we'll call him then. Nobody knows where the guy in Chicago is. He's new in the neighborhood, and we can't get a make on him. We'll keep trying."

That night after supper was over, the dishes were washed, the trotlines were set, and everything was put away, the three sat drinking beer and fishing for crappie by kerosene light. They talked about growing up, remembering only the funny times. ("Remember when Aunt Bessie got her dress tail caught in the car door and the car tore her dress off right on Main Street? Busted up her knee."). They breathed in the clean smell of the lake and listened to the frogs croaking their coarse songs.

"You know, this has been great," Edward said. "Let's do it again real soon."

"You bet," the others answered in unison.

The next morning, Boomer and Eddy ran the trotlines, fixed an early breakfast, and prepared for a day of fishing. The lake was hot and still.

"Now, Eddy, you can't get impatient. Sometimes you go for hours like this and not get a strike. It's not every day you can leave here with a record bass to your credit."

After six hours of casting their bait in the hot July sun, without a single strike, the trio decided it was time to pack up and go home. The end of the day found three tired, but happy, Boomer men home in their beds, glad they had the time together. Troy had enjoyed the time on the lake, but he was glad to be back with Brenda and the kids.

Tomorrow was Friday. Somewhere between Boston and Atlanta, sealed tightly in a red, white, and blue envelope, was a profile of Tommy's killer. At about ten o'clock the envelope would arrive at his office. He would pull the tab, open the envelope, and meet him. Then the search could begin.

CHAPTER 14

riday, the package was delivered. Troy's hand shook as he opened it and spilled the contents on his desk. He searched through the contents until he found the seven-page profile. He began to read:

Hon. Troy Boomer
Assistant District Attorney
County of Fulton
162 Peachtree Avenue
Atlanta, Georgia 40504

Re: Psychological Profile Of Unknown Assailant

Dear Mr. Boomer:

At the request of your office, I have reviewed the preliminary necropsy report of Dr. Henry Molsen, forensic pathologist, performed on Tommy Perelli, together with the several photographs of the body of the young victim taken where the body was discovered and at the post-mortem examination. I have also reviewed the notes that I took at our recent meeting in Boston, when you related the circumstances of his abduction and, of course, your investigation to this point.

My purpose is to give you my best judgment of the kind of person you might find once your search is over and the assailant is taken into custody. I was interested to learn that the authorities have surveyed the child's neighbors, kinsmen, and acquaintances and have identified no suspects among that group. This, of course, leads me to conclude, for purposes of this profile, that the assailant was probably a stranger who either selected the victim randomly or stalked him for a period of time awaiting an opportunity to abduct him. I was also interested to learn that a review of the criminal records has found no crimes closely resembling this one having occurred in the area within the last sixty months. This could mean that the assailant was a transient who moves about committing his crime, or it could mean that this is the first time that he has been impelled to act on his sadistic passion.

The report went on several pages describing the offender types found among human predators, the inferences he would draw from certain observations and the kind of assailant that would commit such atrocities. Troy moved on through the report to the seventh page:

Conclusions

Observations, Predictions, and Recommendations:

1. Because of his interest in young children, the assailant would probably enjoy hanging around playgrounds, swimming pools, and other areas where young children might congregate to play. Any unaccompanied adult male found to be observing unorganized play activities in which such children are involved should be regarded with some suspicion.

2. In view of the time when the abduction occurred, your search should consider that the assailant might be unemployed or a transient. If he is, indeed, an idle person, he might be inclined to frequent adult theaters or other places of entertainment that pander to sexual deviancy.

3. Pedophiles are notorious collectors of child pornography. The assailant can be expected to make efforts to gain access to such pornography and will tend to gravitate to adult book stores or other locations where such child pornography might be acquired. Such establishments would be a good place to look for your quarry.

4. I believe the assailant is somewhat younger, yet I would concentrate my efforts on possible suspects up to the age of thirty. Considering the passion with which this crime was carried out, I don't believe that the assailant (assuming that he lived in Atlanta throughout his life) could have suppressed his lust long enough to have reached a more advanced age. I believe he would have acted before now.

5. Look for, and expect to find, that the assailant has retained the knife or weapon for use again, since he will doubtlessly associate it with sexual pleasure. It will be a source of great pleasure to him. When found, it will be among his possessions where he can get ready access to it in order that he may use it in feeding his sadistic fantasies. Indeed, he may even be a collector of knives.

6. The interval between this crime and the next one (and there will be another owing to the recurring compulsion and paroxysmal sexual desire) may be somewhat long, provided this is the first, and I believe it is. The intervals between other crimes will become briefer after the second assault.

7. You can expect that his conduct will be quite normal until the next paroxysm.

8. You may expect the assailant to return to the crime scene or to the place where he deposited the body in an effort to relive the sexual thrill he got from the killing.

9. In trying to identify the assailant, you may assume that the child was taken by forced abduction, rather than being seduced. From what I have been told of the child, he engaged in several forms of athletics and would have struggled with the assailant rather than submitting readily to the abduction. Someone may have witnessed such a struggle and considered it horseplay.

10. This profile is very tentative and should be reviewed every moment a new piece of evidence is received that sheds further light on the assailant's profile. I should be glad to hear from you if I can be of further help in catching this nasty fellow.

Very truly yours,

Andrew Miller, PhD

"Good old Dr. Miller. Wait 'til Thomas and Farley see this." He grabbed his jacket and plunged through the door, almost knocking Elsie to the floor.

"Oh, excuse me, Elsie. Call Captain Thomas and tell him to get Farley in his office right away. Tell him the package from Boston is here and that I am on my way down there. By the way, don't schedule any appointments or court appearances for me until I tell you otherwise. I won't be around here a lot during the next few days."

When Troy arrived at Thomas's office, Farley was already there.

"Fellows," he exclaimed, "it's all here, or as much as we could possibly expect. Some people might think these profiles are so much voodoo, but, fellow, this guy knows his stuff. I swear to you, I believe old Miller has tagged our man. At least he has given us something to sink our teeth into!" He handed the report to Thomas, who rang his secretary.

"Here, make us three copies of this, and be sure any reject pages get shredded. Get it back to me as quickly as you possibly can."

"Troy," Farley said after the secretary had gone, "we've talked to all of the raffle people but one. We haven't been able to reach this guy, Jonathan Prentice, in Chicago. Here's his name and telephone number." Farley handed him a slip of paper and continued.

"None of the others remember seeing anything unusual or suspicious. I am really disappointed, but I guess we've struck out there. I've taken my people off that duty entirely, but I'll keep trying this number myself and get up with him yet."

"He'll have to come home sooner or later, I guess," Thomas volunteered. "I don't think he's a suspect. I don't know who would have been stupid enough to do this thing and then sign up for a raffle."

"Forest called me this morning," Farley continued. "The crime lab finished the analysis of the piece of shoestring and the black mark on the rock. The string is of the type commonly used on hunting boots, hiking boots, and outdoor footwear, so that is not much help to us. He says if we can come up with the rest of the lace, the lab can make a connection. We were right also about the scuff marks on the rock. Forest says it is a neoprene material, common to an assortment of footwear. Again, he said if we could come up with the boot or shoe that made the scuff marks, he has tests he can make that can connect the two with a high degree of probability. So, unless we can find the boot or shoe, the torn shoelace and scuff marks aren't very much help to us. Of course, we got a good mold of the tire track, but every mile that tire has traveled, the less that it is worth, even if it was made by the killer's car."

Farley took a document from his briefcase.

"The blood on the rock was, let's see, type A. The lab analyzed the hair. A couple of the hairs had follicles still attached for DNA analysis, and Forest said the hair had concentrations of trace elements that were unusual and would help tie the hairs to the killer."

"The medical examiner's people, during the autopsy, found two kinds of fibers on the shirt and on his body that they have analyzed. The ones on his shirt look like they might have come from a blanket, and the ones on his body probably came from a carpet or car mat of some kind. By the way, after we left up there, Forest went back with some of his men and cut out a piece of the rock that was under the place where he tried to dig a grave. They had found some tool marks and some paint they believe came from a shovel, tire tool, or something. Anyhow, they have made pictures of the tool marks under an electron microscope, and they have analyzed the paint residue. This man didn't leave his ID for us, but he might have left enough to tie him to the Stone Mountain site if we ever find him."

Troy shook his head.

"Other than the tool marks and the paint, the other things could have been left there by almost anybody. Am I right?"

"Yes, you are," Farley replied.

"How should we go over Miller's report?" Thomas asked, handing them copies of the report. "Troy, why don't you just read it through for us, and then we will go back over it paragraph by paragraph and discuss it."

As Troy read through the report, both Thomas and Farley would nod agreement from time to time and Farley would occasionally intone, "Yes, yes!"

"Fellows," Thomas said after Troy had read it through, "I believe this is our man. I swear to God, I believe this is him. Now let's figure out how we're going to get him."

For the next two hours, they talked, going back over the report, discussing each paragraph and posing questions to each other.

"I have some questions," Thomas began. "Let's say Miller is right, that this is a forced abduction rather than the kid being seduced. I agree with Miller that is probably what happened. Here this freak is with a kid in his car. Is Tommy just going to sit quietly and let him take him wherever he wants to? I don't think so. He's going to have to restrain him some way. Did he hold him down to the floorboard until he got to where he was going? I doubt it. There were no marks on his body to indicate that. Did he drug him? The medical examiner found no evidence of drugs in his body. Did he tie him up? Probably.

There was plenty of evidence on his body that he had been bound up. If he tied him up, where did he do it? Did he stop in the middle of the street somewhere? He could have, but I doubt it. Okay, he's got him restrained; where did he take him? Did he stop in front of his house and carry him in kicking and struggling? Where in the city of Atlanta could this creep take this child where he wouldn't be seen? I mean, right in broad daylight. Remember, he got him before five o'clock, and it won't even get dark until nine. That's four hours. It seems to me he would have to drive his vehicle into a closed garage or warehouse, a barn, or a building of some kind if he was not going to be seen—or take him to a remote place somewhere. If Miller is right, and the killer lives with his parents, he certainly couldn't take the kid there. No, I am more inclined to believe that this creep took this kid out in the boonies somewhere to a cabin, barn, or someplace outside the city where he wouldn't be seen and did this thing." Thomas frowned, took a sip of coffee, and continued.

"I think we need to keep these questions in the forefront, because we need the crime scene, where the killing took place. There's going to be a lot more evidence of who did it at the crime scene than there is at Stone Mountain. It might be easier to make the connection between the assailant and the location where he carried out the homicide than it would be to tie him to the Stone Mountain site."

"I agree with that." Farley nodded.

"The next thing I have to ask myself is, did he act alone? If there were two of them, it would have been easier to restrain him, in which case we would have two screwballs out there instead of one. I don't know the answer to that, and I won't until we solve the thing. Miller apparently feels that he acted alone, and I believe he did."

"I believe that," Farley said.

"Finally, I ask myself why he chose Stone Mountain as a place to leave the body. I agree with Miller that indicates the killer is familiar with the Atlanta area. The shoelace and scuff marks on the rock where he slipped might mean he is a hiker who knows the park and goes there from time to time. Hikers are usually younger people, and that would tend to support Miller's assessment of age—his being a younger person. Now, I don't have any answers to any of these questions. They must be answered in the course of this investigation. Those questions would be much easier to answer if we had a line on who he is."

"It's an enigma" Troy offered. "You reach and get a piece and try to fit it in. If you can't, you lay it down and reach for another one. It takes a lot of time, but if you stay at it, you wind up putting it all together."

"Well," Farley said, smiling, "we can't search every barn, warehouse, and cabin in Fulton and Dekalb Counties. You are right, Captain, we need a suspect, and the only way I know to get one is to start beating the pavement. Miller says we are dealing with a pervert. He has told us how this pervert thinks, what turns him on. If you are looking for a buzzard, you won't find him at a banquet. You find you a piece of carrion. That's where we will find this buzzard, hovering over a piece of carrion. Somehow, we have got to smoke him out. That's what we'll do—smoke him out."

"Smoke him out," Troy echoed.

"Here's what I propose to do," Farley continued. "I think we ought to park a cop in a private vehicle, unmarked, at every grade school in that area between three and four o'clock when the children are boarding the school buses. No uniforms. No cruisers. Anybody hanging around there that doesn't belong will be observed, and his identity will be established through the car license, if possible. I'm going to start that stakeout Wednesday after I've had a chance to formulate the whole plan of operation, and we'll meet with the task force on Tuesday. I'd like to keep that going for the next thirty days and maybe even beyond that. They will report any suspicious people to the task force coordinator immediately, who will cross-match them and see who, if anybody, we come up with. Even if we don't come up with anything out of this, it will make us feel a lot better knowing that we are keeping an eye on these kids."

Farley took a deep breath and continued.

"Next, we'll get some of our boys inside these porno shops to see what they have. We'll assign one man to each one and have him to drop by every day or two and spend an hour or so—see if he can't get to know the operators, try to gain access to some literature involving minors, and try to worm his way into the network. I understand these creeps have an organization to promote sex with children and swap their dirty literature among themselves—"

"God, I can't imagine anybody that sick," Troy intoned. They agreed.

"Finally, we have got some of these kooks on the string in some court cases and others on probation. By and large they are fondlers, or they have been convicted of nonviolent stuff. Maybe one of them can point out the really bad ones in exchange for some leniency. Maybe we will get some leads there. Other than those things, I don't know what else we can do other than to hope for a break. Maybe somebody will come forward with a lead or something. We'll keep checking all of the calls we get, even the crank ones. But those have begun to slack off now."

"What about you, Troy?" Thomas looked at his watch. "You have any further ideas?"

"Well," Troy replied, "it looks like it's going to take some real digging. I suggest that we get the task force together again as soon as possible. If you think it will be helpful, I will see if Miller can fly down and talk with them next week. He can explain in person who they're looking for and answer any questions they might have. I keep thinking about what Miller said—that sooner or later the guy is going to need another jolt. That could be sooner than we think, so I believe these stakeouts at the schools are wise. Who knows, the creep might have stalked Tommy all the way from school. So we ought to have men watch out for cars that might try to follow the buses from school. I'd like to interview the bus driver. These guys are pretty alert to traffic, and we need to ask him again if he had noticed anybody hanging around or following the bus on its route. Another thing—this stray dog Tommy was playing with. You know, we've got some pretty strong dog laws in Atlanta. You don't see a stray dog for long. We need to check with the Humane Society or dog warden to see if they have made any pickups. They probably won't lead to anything, but you never know. I think they keep strays for a period of time before snuffing them, so the dog might still be around if they got it. I mean, this is not going to solve the case. I just want to know everything I can know about that day, right down to the brand of bubblegum Tommy was chewing. If there were any pickups of dogs and they are still alive, we can have the kid next door to look at them and see if he can identify the one Tommy was seen playing with."

Troy looked over at Farley.

"I believe your idea of getting into the porno shops is a good one. According to Miller, these people are notorious collectors of pornography, and they should be drawn to the porn shops like maggots to a graveyard. We've got to find some way to separate this vermin from the other two million people in Atlanta—narrow it down to a few perverts to concentrate on." Troy looked away for a moment.

"Now, fellows," Troy concluded, "I don't want to interfere with your investigation, but I want to be helpful. If you want me to go back and talk to the bus driver again, give me his name and telephone number and I will. And I can check on the dog. Farley, I tell you what else I will do. Just so you won't have to worry with it, I'll keep dialing this Prentice guy until he answers—tie up that loose end for you. If there is anything else you want me to do, just let me know. I've made arrangements to be out of my office for as long as I need to be, so just call me anytime."

"Let's leave it this way," Farley said, rising. "I'll take Monday getting organized, putting the final touches on the task force plan and reducing it to some kind of written form so that you can shove it upstairs. I want to interview every man on the task force again to be sure he is the right man for his job. Then we can have our orientation session on Tuesday, make our final assignments, and get the men out on the streets."

"Okay." Thomas rose. "Let's leave it at that. Let's try to get together Monday and see what Farley has come up with by way of a written plan and get ready for Tuesday's meeting."

Troy left the building and went directly to his office to call William Fentrell, the school bus driver. He got out the copy of the map Farley had prepared and made arrangements to interview Fentrell at his office the next morning. Elsie agreed to come in early and record the interview. He called the Humane Society and made arrangements to meet with a representative immediately after lunch. It was 11:30 a.m. Troy grabbed a sandwich and a Coke and proceeded to the offices of the Humane Society.

"Let's see here ..." The clerk began to peck on the keyboard. "This street where you say the dog was last seen. It doesn't look like we took any animals anywhere near that immediate area the day you say the child was reported missing. Let's see, now—for that week there were three pickups within that five-block area. One mutt was picked up the day before, so you don't need that one. The other two were picked up two days later. Let's see, all three of these dogs were scheduled for euthanasia if nobody claimed them. You know, we have room to keep them only so long—there are so many strays out there. Looks like the one that was picked up the day before is a mixed bitch. No, wait a minute. That dog was adopted out. The other two were picked up together. So there were two of them. I am sorry. The computer shows they have already been disposed of. Here is a printout of the record for that week, giving the dates and locations where all of the dogs were picked up in that area for that week, as well as descriptions of the dogs."

Troy took the paper, put it in his briefcase, thanked him, and left. He was not terribly disappointed. He hadn't expected to find anything of value anyhow, but he was glad he had checked it out. It looked like the dog had strayed into another area of the city or had been picked up by the owner.

He checked his watch. It was two o'clock; there was time enough to go by Tommy's school and observe the boarding of the school buses. He would follow Tommy's bus to the corner where he got off the day he was reported missing, just as Farley had instructed the other members of the task force to do. That would help him to prepare for the interview with Fentrell the next day.

As he watched the children boarding the buses, laughing and pranking, glad to escape their confinement, he thought of Tommy Perelli and the senselessness of it all. He went to bus number 5, introduced himself to Fentrell, and explained that he would be following him as he delivered the children to their homes, so that he would not be alarmed. Fentrell drove the bus skillfully, giving each child time to exit the bus and be well out of the traffic before he pulled out. Most of them waved to him after stepping onto the curb.

After the bus reached the spot where Tommy got off, Troy turned his car toward home, happy to lay aside the business for a few hours. As he pulled away from the curb, Troy noticed a man mowing the vacant lot where Tommy had last been seen. He stopped and learned that the man, William Mathis, lived next door, and that he kept the lot mowed in order to keep insects down.

"Yes," Mathis said he knew Tommy Perelli and had seen him playing on the lot from time to time with other children. "Yes," he had seen Tommy on the vacant lot a few days ago. Mathis had been mowing his own grass and had briefly observed him playing with a dog.

"He was there one minute and gone the next." Mathis neither saw nor heard anything unusual.

"No," Mathis said he did not know the date, and he had not yet been interviewed by the police. He had left town for a few days and had not learned of Tommy's disappearance and death until returning to Atlanta yesterday from a fishing trip in Minnesota.

"Yes," he could be reached at anytime at home. He was a retired civil engineer, and his telephone number was listed in the directory.

After interviewing Mathis, Troy realized the abduction probably had not taken place at that location—certainly not in full view of Mathis. There really were no places near that spot where it might have taken place unseen. To Troy, as it was to Thomas, that was the biggest mystery of all—how the abduction took place in broad daylight, in the middle of the afternoon, and in a subdivision, without somebody seeing it.

Saturday morning, Troy went to his office to interview William Fentrell.

"Come on in, Mr. Fentrell. Good to see you again. This is Elsie Conklin, my secretary. Elsie, this is William Fentrell, a school bus driver from the school that Tommy attended. Mr. Fentrell, may I call you Bill? Good! We have a lot of territory to cover, so if it is all right with you, let's get to it. Elsie has a recorder, and she is going to be recording your statement to be sure she gets everything down. She will type the statement up, and we will give you a copy if you will agree to keep it confidential. I want to state on the record that your name is William Fentrell, your address is 1642 Westside Drive, and you have appeared here today voluntarily to give your statement and help us in any way you can to solve the murder of Tommy Perelli. Am I correct in that statement?"

"Yes, you are," Fentrell said solemnly.

Troy began his questions:

Q   "Well, first of all," Troy began, "tell us something about yourself, your age, where you were born, who your parents are, your education, where you live, that sort of thing."

A   "Well," Fentrell began, "I am twenty-seven years old; I moved to Atlanta with my parents and baby sister the year I graduated from high school. My daddy moved his business in that year—he had a small computer software business. I now live with my wife, Zelda, and our seven-year-old son, Collins, at 1642 Westside Drive. After moving to Atlanta, I enrolled in college at Emory under an athletic scholarship. I was a pretty fair catcher—majoring in accounting. When my daddy became ill, I quit school and started helping him in his business. Unfortunately, my dad died. I didn't know the first thing about computers, so I had to close the business. That was in 1995. It has remained closed since that time. After that, I worked at various jobs until I landed this one as a custodian and school bus driver—that was 1996—and I have been there ever since. Zelda, my wife, works in the home. She is a seamstress and does drapery jobs and alterations. I guess that is about it."

Troy continued with the questions:

Q   "Mr. Fentrell, how well did you know Tommy?

I knew him pretty well. I picked him up every morning and delivered him home every afternoon for almost two years." Fentrell paused and looked down at his folded hands. A tear fell from his cheek, and he took a tissue out of a box on Troy's desk. He paused for a moment, regaining his composure. "He was on the minor league team that I coach every year. He was my best pitcher. Our practice field is near the school, so Tommy usually walked over to the field for practice while I drove the bus. When I got back and got the bus situated in the bus garage, I would drive my car over to the practice field. We would finish our practice, and then I would usually drive him home or to his father's store when practice was over. It was on my way anyhow."

Q   "Bill, I know this is hard on you, but it is important. I want you to try to remember everything that you can about that day."

A   "Well, Tommy's mother called me the afternoon that he was reported missing, and the police called me again about one o'clock in the morning—some officer named Johnson—and asked me a lot of questions. I told him I didn't remember anything unusual happening that day. I told him that Tommy got on the school bus like he always did when school was out. I dropped him off at his house like I always did. He hollered back, "Good-bye, coach," when he got off, like he always did, and he turned around and waved as I pulled away. He was really a nice kid, never rowdy, never smart, always pleasant, always smiling and kidding around."

Q   "Did you see where he went? Was he walking toward his house?"

A   "I don't believe I noticed that."

Q   "Did you see a dog around, like a stray pup or something?
     One of the neighbor boys said he saw him playing with
     a stray dog in the vacant lot near his house the day he
     disappeared."

A   "Yes, I do. I do remember a dog. I had forgotten about
     that. There was a mutt there when he got off. Tommy
     reached down to pet it, and it jumped up on his legs. I
     had forgotten about that."

Q   "Well, that confirms what the neighbor kid said about the
     dog. Had you noticed any strange people hanging around
     the school, any cars parked around while the buses were
     being loaded that didn't belong there, or any vehicles
     following you, or anything?"

A   "I have been asked that several times. And I've thought
     a great deal about it. *No*, I can't say that I ever noticed
     anything like that during the time I drove the bus. If I
     had seen anything suspicious, I would have reported it to
     the school authorities or I would have told them myself
     to blow off."

After another hour of questions, Troy concluded:

"Okay, I guess you are getting tired of answering the same
questions over and over. As you can tell, we really don't have very
much to go on. I do appreciate your taking Saturday morning to
come down here to talk with me.

"This will conclude the statement of William Fentrell in the office
of Troy Boomer."

Troy was disappointed. He had hoped something new would be
divulged, but it was not.

CHAPTER 15

It was Friday morning. Boomer hadn't seen Jessica since the day she had invited herself to sit at his table. He had gone to the same café every day at noon hoping to see her. He had thought about calling her number, but he couldn't decide what to say. Should he call her Jessica? Should he ask how she was and how she liked her new job? Should he suggest that they get together somewhere for a drink, maybe lunch or dinner? If they were seen together, he could always claim she was a client from out of town. That deception would bother him a great deal, he knew.

Then he saw her come through the door. She didn't stop to be seated but proceeded directly to his table with the same young man following her.

"Hi, again!" She stood smiling down at him. "This is Jacob Downing. He works where I do. Our lunch breaks are at the same time. Jake, this is the famous Richard Boomer. He was kind enough to let me sit with him the day you didn't show up and I was left standing with a tray of food, but no table. Jake, you go on over to that table. I want to visit with Mr. Boomer for a few minutes. Then we can go through the buffet." She turned to Boomer.

"Sit down, please. I want to ask your advice on something if I may." They were seated and Boomer waited, wondering what kind of advice she might need.

"What do I have to do to get you to call me? Since I saw you the last time, I have sat by that phone almost constantly, waiting for it to ring." Her face suddenly reddened with embarrassment.

"Well, I have to go now. That is a beautiful coat. Makes you look distinguished—handsome. If I don't hear from you soon, I'll know you're not going to call. In case you were wondering, Jake isn't my boyfriend."

She looked at him, smiled, and took his hand and squeezed it gently. As she turned to leave, Boomer felt a flush of pleasure. *No problem*, he thought. *I'll call tonight.*

Emily was leaving that afternoon for New York for a week with three members of her bridge club. Since his trip to Elhannon's, Emily had apparently started a diet. He had overheard her tell the neighbor.

"I didn't realize it until I got on the scales last week that I am up to 160 pounds! And with me only five foot three. That's too much, Margaret. I've got to lose at least forty pounds, and I don't know how I'm going to do it. I like to eat so good! But I've already lost three pounds in less than a week, and I'm just so thrilled. It's going to be tempting in New York, all that good food, but I'll just have to be strong, I guess. I swear. I don't know how Richard does it He never gains a pound."

Boomer left the restaurant and went directly to the parking garage He would drive to the house, load the sedan with Emily's things, and drive her to the airport. She would board the plane and fly to New York. She would call and leave word with his secretary that she had arrived safely. The next time he heard from her would be the evening before her departure, when she would call to make sure he knew what time to pick her up and what flight she would be on. Emily didn't like to fuss with the luggage or summon cabs or ride limos. Boomer would learn about her trip—where she had eaten, where she had shopped, and what plays she had seen—by looking at the credit card receipts when the bill arrived the first of the month. Emily would tell him about how hard it was to get a cab or how dangerous the streets were—anything that made her uncomfortable—but that was about all.

Boomer helped Emily check her baggage at the entrance and

waited with her until the other travelers arrived. Then, with a great show of affection, Emily hugged and kissed him, sighing as if she were having to tear herself away from him.

Back in the car, he breathed a sigh of relief, glad to have a break from the tension that always followed Emily wherever she went. He thought of Jessica and the café.

"What do I have to do to get you to call me?" she had said.

The words thrilled Boomer like he had not been thrilled in a long time. His mouth felt dry. He would call her tonight—early. Should he suggest a drink, at her place or his? A dinner at some out-of-the-way place where they would not be seen? No, let her suggest it. She probably had already thought about it. He could just say, "I thought if you weren't doing anything this evening, we might get together." If she agreed, then he'd ask her if she had any ideas. She was smart enough to know they had to be discreet.

Boomer drove straight home. It was four o'clock. He wouldn't call her at work. He would give her time to get home and settle in, and then call about six. That would be early enough to make plans and give her time to get ready. He put on his garden clothes and began to trim back the shrubbery and mulch the azaleas. He kept looking at his watch every five or ten minutes, planning again and again what he would say.

He thought to himself, *This is silly. I'm acting like a high school freshman trying to get up the courage to call my first date. I'm a fifty-seven-year-old man. If this thing bombs, it's not the end of the world. Just relax. Be yourself. Let matters take their course. After all, it's her idea. Let her take the lead. That's what I'll do. That's the way I'll handle it.*

"Hello, Jessica?" Boomer's deep, resonate voice spoke into the phone. "This is Richard Boomer, of course. How are you? How was your day? Well, I see you got home all right."

She interrupted, sensing his confusion. "Richard. Oh, I'm so glad you finally called. I wondered if you would. Listen, Richard, I hope you don't think I'm pushy or too aggressive, or—well—that I'm some kind of slut chasing around after every man I see. Because I'm not. As a matter of fact, and this is the truth, I haven't had a single date since my divorce eighteen months ago. I just haven't been interested in going out. At least not until I saw you and decided I had to meet you. I guess I knew if I didn't make the first move, I never would—you know—get to meet you. Look, I know your situation. You didn't see me, but I saw you with your family the other night at Florencia. I saw your wife. A real little toewaddy. Cute, though, in a way. So, I know you are married, and that's something I'll have to live with. So, what do you say? Want to give it a try?"

Boomer quickly said he wanted to see her and suggested they get together at eight o'clock.

"Richard, I'm so sorry. I've already made plans for this evening. I promised a girlfriend at the office I would go with her to the Civic Center to an antique show. I'd call and cancel, but her car is in the garage and I am her transportation. Oh, I'm so sorry. Look. How about coming over here tomorrow night for dinner if you can sneak away. That way, I can have time to get my hair fixed, buy some wine, get steaks, straighten up a little, and plan the dinner. Good! Say, seven thirty? Just pull your car into space number 63, and I'm apartment 63. I'll leave word at the gate you're coming. Here's the address. Look. I have to go now, get ready to pick up my friend. Good-bye, Richard. And, Richard, I'm so glad you finally called."

Boomer thought a moment before answering.

"Let me bring the wine. How about a good Bordeaux? That is good with beef. Well, then, I'll see you tomorrow at seven thirty. Incidentally, I'm by myself this week, so no problem there. Is there anything else I can bring? Okay, then, see you tomorrow evening."

Boomer dialed the florist and ordered flowers.

"Deliver them tomorrow after five. If nobody's home, just leave them at the door."

Boomer went to the cellar and chose a bottle of Château Lafite, 1980. He wondered what he should wear. Should he wear a dress shirt, tie, and coat? Or should he be more casual—a pair of slacks and maybe a sports shirt? He went through the closet, finally selecting a dark gray turtleneck, which emphasized his muscular chest, trim waist, and broad shoulders. He decided on a pair of white trousers, pleated in the front. Then he did something he seldom did. He locked the doors, put on his pajamas, turned down the bed, switched off the light, and went to sleep. It was seven o'clock. That night, Richard Boomer slept the night through for the first time in a long time.

He would rise early Saturday morning and know he was alone, that Emily was not there. He would dress and go to the office, since there was nothing else to do, open the mail, dictate a few letters, do some legal research, and straighten his desk. He would leave the office in the early afternoon and make a dry run by Jessica's apartment so he wouldn't have to look for it later. He wanted to be on time.

At seven thirty sharp, Boomer stood at the door of apartment 63 and rang the doorbell. In his hands were the bottle of wine and a box of fresh Danish pastries he had bought, thinking Jessica might like them the next morning.

"Richard! The flowers just got here. They're beautiful—a spring bouquet. Thank you. I put them on the dinner table, and we can enjoy them while we eat." She raised up on her toes and kissed him on the cheek. "Come in. Here, let me take the wine. My, my, this is rare, I'm sure. I'll open it now so it can breathe a little; been cooped up in that old bottle for almost twenty years, hasn't it?"

Jessica was stunning in a sheer black skirt and white blouse. Richard looked around the apartment. It was not what he had expected. He had been impressed with the private, guarded entrance and the layout and landscaping of the development. Inside, the apartment was spacious and tastefully decorated. His eyes surveyed the furnishings. He could see the apartment was furnished with antiques and artful accessories.

"Very nice," he said, continuing to look around. "I see you like antiques."

"I do," she said, nodding. "Do you?"

"Well, I like them, but I don't know very much about them."

She moved toward the bar. "Here, let me uncork this, and I'll take you on a little tour. What's in this box? Oh, breakfast pastry. Were you planning to be here for breakfast?" she chided.

"Well, I came prepared," he said, surprised at the boldness of his rebuttal.

"Mama was an antique dealer," she began. "She opened an antique business in Chattanooga after Daddy died. She used to make buying trips up East and to England in the fifties and sixties when antiques were still available at reasonable prices. She sold in Chattanooga and had a lot of customers—decorators and collectors—in other parts of the country. Mama had an incredible memory and a discriminating eye. She did a lot of studying and did real well. When she came across an oil painting, a piece of furniture, a good Georgian silver piece by a good artisan, pottery, ceramics, or porcelain or just anything special, Mama would take it home to keep. So she developed a large collection of antiques and artwork she had bought. She would sell the ordinary things and keep the good. When she died five years ago, I had each item appraised and valued. I sold a lot of it but kept the good things—the things I really liked. Mama taught me to value and love old things."

Jessica led him to the living room and two paintings on the wall above the sofa.

"For example, these two oils are by Turner—*the* Turner. Mama loved them and told me I should never sell them, that they would become progressively more valuable. This table is Irish Chippendale. It has the original finish, a very fine honey-colored patina. It is about 1720. This clock is a tall case clock, all original, that was made in Connecticut in 1734 by a very famous American clock maker. See here, the case as well as the works are signed."

Jessica spent the next fifteen minutes pointing out the interesting pieces in the collection, dating each piece and telling him where "Mama" had acquired it.

"My favorite things, though, are the china and silver."

She pointed proudly to the dinner table, already set with china, silver serving pieces, and linens.

"The china is Flight and Barr. It's about 1810. The candelabra is early Georgian by Anthony Nelmes, crafted in 1688. The epergne is by another Georgian era silversmith. Mama was clever and resourceful, and I loved her very much. I value these things almost as much as I do my own life. Now I want to look up your wine. I always enjoy wine more if I know exactly what I'm drinking. I know it has to be good, and very expensive because of the winery. But I want to look up the vintage."

She drew a book from behind the bar. "Let's see. It's Château Lefite Rothschild, 1990. Here it is. Let's see, the comment is 'vintage year, exquisite Bordeaux. Very rare, very expensive. Price range, where available, $600–$800 per unit.' "Excellent!"

Boomer was surprised. He had bought five cases of the wine for $30.00 a bottle in 1985. He had tried a bottle ten years ago, had found it to be very good but had not corked any since.

"Mr. Richard Boomer. I'd say you have done better than middling in selecting the wine, and I congratulate you."

She walked to where he had seated himself, leaned over, and kissed him firmly on the forehead.

"Okay," she said. "I have to go to the kitchen and finish dinner. You sit here and entertain yourself. It should be ready soon. Here's the TV remote. Turn it on if you'd like, and here is a magazine I enjoy on archeological digs around the world. I'd offer you something to drink, but dinner will be ready shortly, and I want to begin with a glass of that wine."

Boomer settled back. He laid the magazine on the coffee table, walked to the secretary-bookcase, and opened the old glass doors. There on the shelves were several anthologies of English and American poetry; old classics by Theodore Dreiser, Steinbeck, and others; and references on antiques and artworks. He wondered if these were part of "Mama's" collection, or if Jessica had selected them for herself. He took a thick blue volume from the lower shelf. *The Sea* was the name of the book. He opened the cover. "A Volume of Exquisite Sea Poems by Rising Poet Jessica Moreland." He returned to the sofa and began to read the first poem, "Sea Dawn," inscribed, "This poem was written in July 1998 on a trip to Bar Harbor, Maine, with my husband, Charley, and son, Jamie."

SEA DAWN

Gathered life in patterned growing,
Life to life in pointed role.
Time on time, the time-felt blowing,
Slow-felt making of the soul.

As gray clouds stand in pale dimension,
Shoreward trails the dawning light,
Shape-on-shape in slow ascension,
Dawn clouds robe the waning night.

As seabirds turn to greet the morning,
Tide songs sound the endless flow.
Sea-strewn lights on growing waters
Dance as shore waves meet the tow.

Seamen watch in senseless rapture
And cast their boats upon the bay,
While earth and rock and sea waves capture
Sea songs of the coming day.

As he read the last four verses of the poem, Boomer could feel chills of delight climb up his spine and into his neck.

"Jessica," he said as she entered the room bearing a platter of food. "This poem is delightful. I'm surprised. I really am."

"Oh, do you like poetry, Richard? I do hope so, because I love it."

"Frankly, I don't read much poetry," he continued, "but I sometimes write it for my own entertainment. I never keep it—just write it, get whatever it is out of my system, and toss it. I love the sea. I'd like to read some more like this, and I will if you'll let me."

"Why don't you sit here." She pulled a chair out from the table.

He seated her in the chair to his right and then took his own seat. He poured a small amount of the deep red wine into a wine goblet, first smelling the cork and then tasting the wine to be sure it was good. It was.

He poured the wine for both, lifted his glass to toast, and said, "Here's to Jessica Moreland, who prepared and served this meal; here's to Mama, who furnished the fine porcelain from which we will eat it; and here's to those circumstances that, happily, have brought us together in this place. I toast the two of us and Mama." Jessica laughed, delighted.

For the next hour, they slowly enjoyed the salad, soup, steak Diane, and berries that Jessica had prepared and served so skillfully. They finished the bottle of Bordeaux and moved to the sofa, where Boomer picked up the book again, not knowing exactly what he should say or do at that point. He felt clumsy, slow, almost tongue-tied.

Jessica sensed his uneasiness. She gently took the book from his hand, smiled, and rose.

"Come with me," she said.

He followed her to a darkened patio. She touched a switch, which lit an underwater light in a small enclosed pool. Without a word, she pulled a band from her hair, letting her blond hair fall around her shoulders. She loosed her skirt, pulled it down over her hips and let it fall, revealing her full naked hips and smooth brown legs. Never had Boomer seen a woman so beautiful, standing there in the near darkness, silhouetted against the glimmering light of the pool. As she removed her blouse, revealing the rest of her body, he felt an excitement engulf his body. She walked slowly toward him, cupped his face in her hands, and kissed him gently. He felt her smooth sweet lips and smelled the quiet, clean perfume.

As she began to tug at his belt, she whispered, breathing quickly, "Come into the water."

He awakened the next morning at seven o'clock. It was Sunday. He turned gently onto his side and looked into her face. She breathed slowly, quietly. From time to time, she would smile slightly and move her lips as if to speak, but he knew she was asleep. He had never seen a face so beautiful. His body felt different, refreshed, and he marveled that only twenty-four hours ago, he hardly knew her.

He would get up, quietly dress, and slip away without waking her. He would leave a note ("I'll call you this afternoon"), drive home, go to early Mass, and then get out his garden clothes and do some repairs around the house. He would wash his little car, go to the athletic club and work out, and be back home by two o'clock. Then he would call her. He would thank her for a wonderful evening and tell her how much he enjoyed it. He knew he should tell her that it was something that just happened and should not happen again. But he would not. He would see her again, no matter the risks and no matter the cost. He knew that last night was more than an encounter. In one evening she had managed to awaken his sleeping soul.

He had just walked in the door when the phone rang. It was Jessica.

"Are you alone? Good! Why did you leave? You're not angry, are you? You're not sorry—tell me you're not sorry. I couldn't stand it if you said you were. Oh, Richard, you make me feel so good! You make me so happy! I thought after Charley, I could never feel again, but I do. I wanted to wake up with you and make some coffee; I was going to fix bacon and eggs and lay out the pastries you bought and have breakfast on the patio. It's Sunday, Richard—Sunday morning. We have a whole day that we can be together—that is, if you want to. Why don't we get in the car, pack a lunch, and drive somewhere. We can pack our clubs, find a course somewhere, play eighteen holes, and be back tonight."

Boomer thought for a moment. He looked at his watch.

"It's nine thirty. Be ready at eleven. I'll shower, gas up, and be on over."

They packed their clubs into the little car. She handed him a picnic basket and cooler and suggested he put the top down. He would wait until they got out of town. As they passed the gate, out onto the road, the black gate attendant smiled and waved them through. Boomer thought of Baton Rouge, Chaumiere, and the old Negro attendant. He thought of family and that day over thirty years ago.

He was happy, very happy. All that day and every night for the next week he was with her. Quiet dinners at her apartment, followed by hours of intimacy or quiet reflection. At times, he could feel her eyes staring at him. Then without a word, she would smile broadly or giggle happily, glad to be with him. It seemed they could not get enough of each other, that the twenty-two years that separated them did not matter. It was as though the seasons of their lives had vanished, merging into inseparable time. The one time he had mentioned it, she brushed it off, laughing.

"Come on, silly, what does that matter? I'm April and you're August. So what?" It really didn't matter to her. He felt that.

The day before Emily was to return from New York, Jessica called him.

"Look, I won't be able to celebrate your birthday with you Saturday. I called and got reservations at this little place I know in Chattanooga. It's a lot of fun. They have a little combo on Thursday nights, and we could have dinner, drink a little wine, and dance. It takes an hour and a half to get there, so we won't see anybody we know from Atlanta. I have a little surprise for you."

"I have reservations for eight o'clock in the name of Jessica Moreland," she said when they arrived.

They were seated at a table in the corner. Boomer looked over the patrons and saw no one he knew. After dinner, Jessica pulled a package from her purse and handed it to him. He read the title: *Petals: A Second Volume of Poems by Jessica Moreland.*

"I didn't tell you this had been published because I wanted to surprise you. I just got it yesterday. I didn't autograph it for reasons known to us both. Here, open the card, please." Inside the card she had written,

Happy birthday. I have loved this week and the time we have had together. I wish it could last forever, but I know it can't. I don't want to cause you any trouble, so I won't call or try to see you. That does not mean I don't care. I do. I care too much. If you sometimes want me or need me, you know where I am.

Love,

Jessi."

Boomer looked at her, tore the card in half, and handed it back to her.

"You won't get rid of me that easily," he said, leaning over and kissing her on the cheek.

He suddenly rocked back in his chair.

"Edward! Edward is over at the bar! He's looking straight at us. Just get up slowly and go into the powder room there. Give me a few minutes before you come out and meet me at the car."

As she rose to leave, Edward took a sip of his fresh drink, paid the check, waved to his companions, and quickly left. Boomer was suddenly angry. Had he followed him there? Then he remembered that Eddy had told him he was to be installed in an office in the Southern Neurological Society at a convention to be held in Chattanooga. That was probably why he was in town.

Boomer called Edward the next morning.

"Eddy—he began.

"Dad," Edward interrupted. "I was in Chattanooga last night at a medical meeting, and I saw this fellow. He was a dead ringer for you—had this younger gal with him."

Boomer had expected questions: "Who was she? What were you doing with her?" There were none. Boomer could see he was not going to tell Emily. Whatever his reason, Boomer was grateful.

He called Jessica at work.

"Look, Jessi. I called Eddy. Don't worry. Everything's fine. I'll call you soon."

Jessica leaned across her desk and smiled at Jacob Downing.

"That was Mr. Boomer. He thinks everything is fine. What do you think of that, darling?"

CHAPTER 16

Buck Hinkler pulled his Jaguar into his driveway. He was glad it was Friday. He had spent a long, grueling week negotiating the sale of his family-owned bank to a large, multistage bank holding company. The deal, if consummated, would double his wealth and leave him in charge of one of the largest and best-capitalized banks in Atlanta. The bank lawyers at Getty and Jacobs had prepared the preliminary commitment papers outlining, generally, the terms of the acquisition. He was very anxious to complete the transaction, but he had found that the negotiators on the other side of the table were interested as much in the bank's personnel structure as they were its capitalization, operational systems, and the condition of its loan portfolio. "We won't go into detail, but he'll have to go. Our group is very interested in its public reputation, and the board chairman insists that every manager type be free of any private or public controversy that might affect his work with the bank, and especially the confidence the public has in us."

Hinkler had employed Remerick seventeen years earlier and had promoted him to the position he held. They had become friends through the years.

"I was not aware he had problems, but I certainly agree that all our employees must be above reproach. I will take care of that matter as soon as the preliminary documents affirming the sale have been executed," Hinkler had said.

He knew Remerick would have problems finding other employment because of his age and the fact that he had been terminated, but he would comply with the suggestion that he be fired if that was what it would take to make the deal work.

Hinkler opened the garage door with his remote. In the kitchen he found his wife, Mary Rachael, sitting at the table, her eyes red from crying.

"What's wrong, Mary Rachael? Has something happened to Billy?" he asked, referring to their twenty-four-year-old son.

She went to the kitchen sink and began to wipe mascara from her eyes and cheeks with a wet paper towel.

"Buck," she began, suddenly angry, "Billy is here. He came in this morning. I didn't call you, because I knew you were in those negotiations and I didn't want to worry you with it. I've never seen him like that. He was drunk as he could be—staggering around, eyes glazed over. He couldn't talk—I mean, he was real bad. Wouldn't answer me or even act like he knew who I was. He had a frightened look on his face and kept brushing his clothes off, screaming, 'Get the spiders off me. Please get them off.'"

"How did he get here?" Buck asked, taking off his coat and laying it across a chair. He had not seen Billy's car or the old Range Rover four-wheel in the driveway.

"I saw them bring him in. A whole carload of them. A bunch of trash, if you ask me. They pulled into the driveway in this old wreck of a car, opened the door, pushed him out in the grass, and simply pulled away without a word. I don't know how they got by the guard at the gatehouse. I managed to get him into the house and tried to clean him up, but he wouldn't let me. He's upstairs in his room, stretched across the bed. Every now and then he will let out a bloodcurdling scream. I hate for you to have to see him. He's just like he was when they brought him in. He smells awful, like he has been lying in a sewer. His clothes were wet, and his shoes are muddy like he had been outdoors somewhere. I'm at my wits' end. I thought he was doing better, but this is the very worst, the last straw. What are we going to do with him? He's twenty-four years old. All he wants to do is to drink and take those drugs. I went through his pockets and found two bottles with some kind of pills in them."

Buck climbed the steps and opened the door into Billy's bedroom. There he lay sprawled on the bed. Buck couldn't believe what he saw. He was exactly as Rachael had described him. Billy stirred slightly, put both hands to his head, and began pulling at his hair as if to rid himself of some imagined invader.

It had all started when Billy was sixteen. A freshman in high school, he had decided to enroll in public school after finishing the eighth grade in parochial school. Buck wished he had not given his approval—maybe things would have been different

Billy had been a good son—obedient, respectful, and never contumelious. Then one day as Rachael was changing his sheets, she found a sandwich bag. Inside was a package of cigarette papers and a small quantity of marijuana. He denied it was his, claiming it probably belonged to the maid or had been left there by one of his friends who sometime spent the night with him. She knew that Buck would be furious, but she believed Billy. He persuaded her not to tell his father, and only later did Buck learn of the incident. At that time, she began to make frequent searches of his room but found nothing. But Billy changed. He became irritable and surly. He would sometimes go to his room, lock the door, and stay there for hours, complaining of any intrusion.

"It's just a stage," she assured Buck.

It was then that things began to disappear from the house. Rachael first noticed a pearl necklace was missing from her jewelry box, but she thought she had just misplaced it. Once, she missed a ring Buck had bought for her birthday. She let the maid go, suspecting she had taken it. From time to time, she would leave currency around the house, only to find someone had taken it. She never suspected Billy of any of the thefts.

By his senior year, Billy's grades had fallen, and he had failed so many courses that he would not graduate with his class. They noticed his friends had stopped coming around.

On the night of Billy's senior prom, Buck got a call from the Atlanta police, telling him Billy was in custody for driving under the influence. When he went to the police station to arrange bail, he found Billy was too drunk to walk to the car. The turnkey suggested Buck take him to see a doctor. A search of his car had revealed a quantity of marijuana, a substance that was thought to be LSD, and a bottle filled with what the police thought were amphetamine tablets.

Billy was released to the custody of Buck, who drove him to the hospital. Upon arrival at the emergency room, he was taken directly to the intensive care unit, where it was learned he had ingested a possibly fatal mix of alcohol and amphetamines. For twenty-four hours he hovered precariously between life and death. The drugs and alcohol had depressed his central nervous system, requiring a respirator.

After two days he was released for further treatment to a substance abuse facility. That episode began a long trail of arrests for drunken driving, assault, and possession of controlled substances. Buck managed to clear him of each of the charges, but always in exchange for a promise he would "get back in school and stop this foolishness," promises that were never kept.

Over the next six years, Billy lived at home, sinking deeper and deeper into alcohol and drugs, unable to control his habit. A week before his twenty-fourth birthday, after Buck had bailed him out of jail, he told him on the ride home, "Look, Billy, you're not a kid anymore. You're a man. We've done everything we can for you, and we'll do anything we can to help you lick this thing, but you don't seem to want to help yourself. Mother can't take this anymore, and neither can I. You're making a wreck out of your life and ours too. Now I want you to pack your things and get out of the house. If you ever decide you need help and want help, you just call us. If it takes it, I'll spend every dollar I have."

Billy had packed his things into the old Range Rover and moved to the cabin Buck owned near the foot of Stone Mountain. That had been six months ago.

"Look," Buck had told him, "I'll keep paying the utilities on the cabin, and I'll give you some money until you get squared away.

But I'm not going to keep on feeding that damn habit any longer. I'm asking you. Don't come to the house ever—unless you call first and let us know you're coming. And, Billy, come sober, son, dead sober."

Buck had wondered, as Billy pulled away, if he was doing the right thing by moving him out. He knew it was harsh, and he didn't want to do it. But they had done all they could do, and he finally realized it was something Billy had to work out for himself.

Billy pulled the old Range Rover they always kept at the cabin into the garage and carried his belongings into the cabin. He knew he was now on his own. He opened his bag, pulled out a bottle of vodka he had taken from the house, and, over the next hour, drank himself into oblivion.

During the next six months, Billy complied with Buck's orders to stay away. He returned to the house only twice during intervals when he was too sick to drink, telling them both times that his drinking was under control and that he had stopped using drugs. He was looking for work, he told them, raising hopes that he was finally bringing his life under control.

Each time, Buck put money in his pocket.

"Here, son, is a little something to tide you over until you find work."

The last time Buck had driven to the cabin to visit him, he found two old cars in the driveway and heard loud cursing inside the cabin. He left without going in, because he knew what he would find. Before today, Buck and Rachael had not heard from him for nearly a month.

Buck smelled the stench of Billy's clothing as he entered the bedroom. He walked over to the bed, put one arm around Billy's waist, and pulled him gently from the bed onto his feet. His legs crumpled under his weight. Buck loosened his hold and let Billy fall gently to the floor. He leaned over him and began to remove his clothing, hardly able to stand the stench of it, and took it outside to the garbage can. He ran a tub full of warm water and lifted Billy's limp body into it. Billy began to chatter wildly, complaining that the water was burning him. Buck bathed him carefully, lifted him from the tub, and dried him roughly with a towel, trying to bring him to consciousness. He then put him, shivering, between the covers of the bed and went to the phone.

"This is Buck Hinkler. Let me speak to Dr. Stevens, please. Well, interrupt him. This is an emergency. Just tell him I'm on the phone and it's about my boy, Billy."

During the next fifteen minutes, Buck made arrangements with Dr. Stevens to admit Billy to the Norton detoxification and substance abuse facility—the same one they had used before. He knew now that Billy couldn't do it by himself. He resolved never to throw him out again.

After Billy had been loaded into the ambulance, Buck climbed in between the driver and orderly. He knew Billy would complete the detox program and enter into the therapy gratefully and voluntarily as he always had. He would leave the facility, promising to stay away from the people and places that fed his habit. He would get a job, with Buck's help, and stay around the house at night reading and watching television—for a while. Then one night he would fail to come in, and it would start all over again. At least that was the way it had always happened before.

The ambulance arrived at the substance abuse facility. Billy, trembling and thrashing about, was taken to a room where he was restrained. The nurse placed an oxygen tube in his nose and introduced medication and fluids into his dehydrated body through an IV. Billy began to calm and sank into a deep sleep. Buck signed him into the facility, made the necessary financial arrangements, and had a brief conversation with the psychiatrist on duty. He returned to the room where Billy lay sleeping. Pulling a chair close to the bed, he took Billy's limp hand and sat, weeping. He swore to himself that, no matter what happened, Billy would never be left alone again.

The next day he drove to the cabin to get Billy's things and move them back into his house. He would bring Billy home when the treatment ended and again try to help him get hold of himself.

The cabin was located on a remote road near a branch coming from the watershed of Stone Mountain. Buck had bought the twenty acres eighteen years ago when Billy was seven years old, so they would have a place out of the city where they could go to hike, picnic, cook out, ride trail bikes, and enjoy the quietness of the place. He and Billy had used the cabin several times a year when he was a youngster. Buck would hike with Billy, pointing out and naming birds, small animals, trees, and other things they came by. Billy had loved those days and the cabin.

As Billy got older, he would bring three or four boys to the cabin to camp and spend the weekend alone. He had always kept two trail bikes and a four-wheel-drive vehicle at the cabin for access to the more remote parts of the area. After Buck had collected Billy's things, he would leave the bikes, Billy's sports car, and the Range Rover at the cabin as he always did, locked in the garage, until Billy got better. They would be safe there, he thought.

He reached the gate leading into the compound and found it open. The hasp had been broken, and the lock was on the ground. He opened the gate and drove to the front of the cabin. He got out and paused, as he always did, standing for a moment looking at the mountain that towered behind the cabin. It was a beautiful and tranquil sight. He reached into his pocket and searched for the key to the cabin.

As he climbed the steps leading to the porch of the cabin, he saw that the front door was already standing open. He looked again around the grounds and noticed for the first time that the Range Rover was out of the garage, resting on the paved drive. From where he was, he could see a pool of oil under the front end. He walked back down the steps and went over to the vehicle. As he walked around it, he saw that the door on the passenger side was so damaged from some collision that it would have to be repaired and replaced. Buck wondered how Billy had damaged the vehicle and hoped he had not hit another vehicle or a pedestrian on one of his drunken sprees. Buck found the doors unlocked and the key in the ignition. Without starting the vehicle, he locked the car doors. He would send a tow truck to get the vehicle for repair of the body damage and what appeared to be a ruptured oil pan. He checked the sports car, which was in the garage, and found it was locked and undamaged.

Buck again climbed the steps and went into the cabin. He couldn't believe what he saw: ash trays full of cigarette butts; kitchen sink full of moldy dishes; empty bottles all over the floors; and what appeared to be soft drink stains on the carpets. He went into the bedrooms and found the beds striped of covers, the mattresses soiled with stains. He left immediately to escape the smell of alcohol, stale cigarettes, and rotting food.

Buck picked up a newspaper as he left and read the headline. "Body of Boy Found on Stone Mountain." He laid the paper on the kitchen counter and left, locking the door behind him. He would bring a crew to clean the house next week, take up the carpets, haul off the mattresses, and give the cabin a general cleaning and sanitizing. After getting a chain and a new lock from the garage, he drove to the open gate, wrapped the chain around the post, and snapped the lock in place.

As he drove toward Atlanta, he wondered what had gone wrong. With the opportunities available to him, Billy should have graduated from college and been well established in a job in his bank by now. Billy should be married with children. He should be, but he was not. He was in an institution drying out, as dependent on Mary Rachael and Buck as he had been the day he was born. For the first time in his life, Buck was faced with a situation he could not handle. He had failed so far, but he would keep trying.

Billy began the long and already familiar road back, with Buck constantly at his bedside. The sedatives placated his mind's demand for oblivion, while the fluids and nourishment began the tedious process of restoring his strength.

"Unfortunately, we have no medication for the soul, the will," Dr. Parker had just told him. "We can help him regain his strength and get him off the drugs, but whether he stays off depends entirely on him." Billy's eyes were closed and he slept, calmed by the sedatives from the IV.

The spider danced across the web as Billy tried desperately to free himself. Its long orange body reared as it reached to seize him. He looked into its face. He saw no compassion. He waited to be devoured. Then, suddenly, it scampered away. Billy bolted upright, blinked his eyes, and looked at Buck.

"Hello, Dad. What day is it?"

"It's Sunday, son. Sunday morning."

Billy lay back and closed his eyes. He wondered if it would come back for him. He wondered, but he didn't really care.

CHAPTER 17

Detective Ron Farley leaned back in his chair and put his feet on the already scarred desk. He folded his hands on his stomach. Outside were ten offices awaiting their final interviews and assignments. On his desk were the files of each of the men whom he did not know personally. He had already read each file and had outlined the investigation he had in mind.

Detective Roy Martin would be assigned to records, remaining at headquarters. He would search the computer records of sex offenders throughout Georgia and compile a list of offenders in the Atlanta area to be interviewed as possible informants. He would assemble and assimilate reports from the other officers involved in the investigation, and serve as liaison between the captain, Detective Farley, and the other officers. He would consult the National Crime Data Bank for reports of similar crimes, looking for evidence that Tommy might be the victim of a serial killer. He would also consult the postal authorities in an effort to identify anyone in the Atlanta area known to receive pornography involving children through the U.S. mail.

Detective Dan Marshall would coordinate the surveillance at the schools during loading of the school buses and transportation of the children to their homes. He would oversee the activities of the seven rookie officers who would be used to infiltrate the adult bookstores, looking for suspects who might fit Dr. Miller's profile of the killer.

Detective Bill Marion, the remaining member of the task force,

would begin anew the task of examining Tommy's life, his day-to-day
activities, his neighbors, and every shred of information that could be
gathered in an effort to reconstruct the day of his abduction.

Detective Farley would monitor the entire process and direct the
investigation into different areas as new information came to light.
Every other day, the members of the task force would meet with
Farley and Captain Thomas to share with each other the results of
their work and to offer suggestions how the investigation ought to
be expanded.

Farley knew the measures they were taking would not end in an
arrest without a major break in the case, but he also knew the plan
was the most they could do for now.

He interviewed the seven rookie officers again and found them all
to be acceptable. He then told them to report to Detective Marshall
for their assignments. They were admonished again that the operation
and their assignments were not to be discussed with anyone outside
the task force.

Farley spent the rest of the day reducing the plan to an eight-page
conspectus and sent it up to Captain Thomas for his review and
approval. He then phoned Troy.

"Dr. Miller will be in Atlanta on an early flight," Troy advised
him. "I'll pick him up and have him there in the large conference
room at ten o'clock."

"It's all set then," Farley growled.

"By the way, I've called the guy in Chicago twenty times," Troy
said. "Still no answer. I'll keep trying."

The next week was full of disappointments. Detective Roy
Martin had not been able to produce a similar offender profile from
the central files of Atlanta or the State of Georgia. Nor was he able to
find any possible connection to the commission of serial killings.

Detective Dan Marshall's surveillance of the bus-loading sites
found nothing unusual. The recruits had begun to infiltrate the adult
book stores but had been met with anger at any request for literature
involving children. Only one officer had received a referral to such
a publication.

"You ought to read *Alice in Wonderland*. I understand Carroll liked little girls. Or maybe you ought to read the Constitution. I hear Ben Franklin was a pedophile."

Detective Bill Marion had interviewed the school official in charge of transporting the school children and had obtained copies of the routes and stops for each bus by child, street, and house number. He was beginning the sensitive task of interviewing each child passenger of school bus number 5. He had twice interviewed Arlene Perelli about Tommy's activities, his interests, his associates, and his habits. There were no further leads. At Troy's suggestion, he had talked again to Mr. Mathis but got the same report he had related to Troy.

A week had gone by without the development of a single lead. Still, the investigation ground on. Troy was disappointed. Every day that passed, the trail grew colder. It appeared more and more likely that the case would not be solved. Then another week passed. Nothing.

"Hello," the voice spoke roughly into the phone. Troy was startled. He had dialed the Prentice number what seemed like hundreds of times without an answer. Thinking he had dialed the wrong number, he asked, quickly, "Is this the residence of Jonathan Prentice? It is? Mr. Prentice, this is Troy Boomer—from Atlanta. I've been trying to reach you for three weeks. You see, I'm an assistant prosecutor in Atlanta, and we have a homicide we're investigating—a nine-year-old boy. We found his body in Stone Mountain Park."

Prentice interrupted, thinking it was a joke.

"Well, I was in Stone Mountain Park with my wife and kids, but we didn't kill nobody." After he was assured the call was authentic, he said, "My company sent me to Saudi Arabia on assignment, and my wife and kids went to stay with her mother. I just got in. Matter of fact, I was asleep when the phone rang."

Troy understood.

"Well, that's the reason we haven't been able to reach you. Could I ask you a few questions? I know you are probably tired and all, but this is very important."

"Shoot, he replied, "but please make it quick. I'm expecting a call from my wife. She's coming in tomorrow, and I need to get her travel plans."

Troy learned the Prentice family had visited the park two days before Tommy's body was found. Prentice knew because his vacation ended two days later. They were on their way home from vacation when they stopped to camp at the park near a rock formation Prentice knew as "Face Rock." They had arrived late in the afternoon, set up camp, gone for provisions and a tour of the park, and returned to the campsite after dark. The next day they broke camp and started again for home.

"No," he did not remember having seen or heard anything out of the ordinary. "Yes," he would take Troy's name and number and call him if he recalled anything that might help.

"Did you say it was a nine-year-old boy?" he inquired. "Damn shame. I hope you catch the bastard that did it."

Troy thanked him and hung up. He then called Farley.

"Well, I finally reached Jonathan Prentice. He's been in Saudi Arabia. No. Nothing. Nothing at all."

"Well, that finishes that one," Farley groaned. "It's like everything else in the case. But we'll just keep plugging."

Troy pulled out a map of Stone Mountain on which he had marked the spot where Tommy had been found. He ran his fingers along the road beside it. At the end, he saw the words, "Face Rock Camping Area." Prentice had driven by the spot at least twice. He wondered if Tommy's body was already there that night. He figured it was. He was about to leave for Billips's office when the phone rang, startling him.

"Hello, Mr. Boomer? This is Prentice again. My wife called after we hung up—you know, I was expecting her call? Well, she called and I told her about somebody killing a kid and about how you had called me. I was still half-asleep when you called, and we got to talking. I don't know if this will help you—but we remembered something that might. You see, on the way back to the camp, I rounded this curve—gosh, it was late—and my lights fell on this four-wheel vehicle, a green Range Rover with its lights off. We figured it might have been some kids necking or something—you know how that is.

Anyhow, when our lights fell on him, it was like he gunned it and slid over against a big rock there on the side of the road, and it hit the rock and bounced up and down. I believe it went over a big rock, bounced on a big rock underneath, and when he finally straightened up, he went by us flying—I mean, flying! I had to get my camper all the way off the road—there was a wide place there—to keep the fool from hitting me. I'm sure it was a green Range Rover, because my brother-in-law has one just like it, only it doesn't have a big antenna on it like this one did. And I believe this one had a decal or place where the front license goes with some kind of an insignia on it My wife remembers that; I don't. I'm going to guess it was a '96 model by the looks of it. That's what my brother-in-law's is, but the body styles might be the same for several years. I don't know. But it was a green Range Rover. I know that."

"Could you identify it if you saw it again?" Troy asked.

"Well," he said in reply, "the only way I could identify it positively is by the antenna and the plate on the front. My wife remembers that. If you find it, it'll be damaged on the right side where it hit that rock, and it might even have a bent frame where the underneath hit that big rock while it was bouncing up and down. It hit it pretty hard. I couldn't see the driver. It all happened too fast, and I was trying to get out of the way. I know one thing—he was trying to get the hell out of there as fast as he could."

Troy thanked him excitedly and requested that he call if he thought of anything else or if he planned any more trips.

"Farley, come over here. Bring Thomas. I can't move. I'm shaking all over, man. We've got our break, I believe. Prentice just called back. We may have a make on the vehicle the bastard used to transport the body."

Farley and Thomas hurried to Troy's office.

"This had better be good," Thomas said, smiling indulgently.

Troy blurted out the conversation as he remembered it.

"Damn! That might be the break we need." Thomas clapped his hands together. "Let me get Chicago and have them get over there and get a statement from that sweet man. Meanwhile, we'd better get back up there and find that rock he's talking about. There might be some paint and metal residue on it. Farley, get Forest and his crew up there to meet us. Tell him to please drop whatever he's doing, that this might be important; and tell the state police to get their team and van up there."

By the time they got to the scene, a team of crime scene investigators from the crime lab had already arrived and were waiting. Forest drove up shortly afterward, as did the van from the state police with its team.

The group began inspecting the roadside, starting at the location where the body had been found and proceeding down the hill. They were only a few minutes and a short distance into the search when one of the team exclaimed, "Here it is. There's green paint all over this rock. See, here." He pointed. "And look here. Here's a whole sackful of paint flakes where it hit. Look at this rock on downhill a little ways. Something's scraped it pretty good. And look here where oil has puddled. Somebody's lost an oil pan on this one. He couldn't have driven far."

For the next hour the teams carefully, meticulously, gathered every flake of paint they could retrieve. Using a masonry saw from the van, they cut large slabs of rock, preserving the paint stains intact. Curiously, Troy thought, they took shovels and dug up every trace of oil they could find.

"Well, we've got plenty of everything." Forest grinned. "We'll analyze the paint, and I'll be able to tell you exactly what kind of vehicle it came from. If the oil can be properly separated from the dirt and you find the vehicle, we can make a positive linkage by the motor contaminants that are unique to each vehicle. Boys, I'd say if that was the vehicle that transported the body, you're well on your way to getting your man."

The next day, Forest called Troy.

"I just finished talking with Detective Farley. He said I should call you too, so you could hear it directly. Your man from Chicago was dead right. We matched our sample of paint with the manufacturer's index, and it's a perfect match. That paint came from a Range Rover, no doubt about it; the paint mix was used by the manufacturer only in the year 1996. Looks like you're closing in, fellow. Farley's giving you all the credit—you know that. By the way, we got a good separation of the oil laid down when the oil pan apparently ruptured. It should be plenty good enough to make a match with the vehicle when you find it. Congratulations to you, fellow."

"Thanks," Troy said gratefully.

Troy rang Farley, who told him, "Detective Marion is in touch with motor vehicle registration. They're running a computer search of the owners of all Range Rovers in Georgia. The colors aren't listed on the registration, but the dealer here thinks he can fax the serial numbers to the manufacturer in England, and it can tell you which vehicles were burberry green. They only have to check the '96 models. We've got a crew calling all the body shops in the area to see if they had a green '96 Range Rover in for repairs. Hold on a minute." Troy waited.

"Troy, I was just told that the local Range Rover dealer got a call this morning from a Buck Hinkler to pick up a 1996 with a ruptured oil pan and a damaged door on the passenger side. Sounds like our boy."

"Buck Hinkler?" Troy shouted into the phone. "I know him. He owns one of the largest banks in Atlanta."

"I don't care if he owns the Omni," Farley remonstrated. "I'm sending Forest and his crew down there, impounding the vehicle, getting a search warrant, and having the crime scene people go over every square inch of it."

By the end of the day, the examination of the vehicle was completed. Samples of paint and metal were removed from the passenger door; the oil remaining in the crankcase was drained; the floor mats were ripped out and taken to the crime lab; and the inside was dusted for latent prints. Pictures of the vehicle, showing a long antenna and front plate with a rebel flag decal, were developed and flown to Chicago by police courier for Jonathan Prentice to view.

The evidence was taken to the crime lab, where it was quickly but thoroughly analyzed. The results were not long in coming. The paint matched perfectly. The oil found on Stone Mountain, without question, came from the crankcase of the impounded vehicle. Fibers from the floor mat matched fibers found on Tommy's nude body. The tire treads matched those found at the park.

Together, the evidence pointed, inexorably, to the 1996 green Range Rover as the vehicle used to transport Tommy's body to the Stone Mountain site. Added to that evidence was evidence provided by Jonathan Prentice, who had immediately identified the vehicle from among other photos exhibited to him.

Captain Thomas, upon learning of the findings, quickly called a meeting of the mayor, the chief of police, and the principle investigators. The prominence of the vehicle's owner prompted the group to act with caution. It was decided that one person, a civilian, should contact Mr. Hinkler at his place of business, so the press would not be alerted. Troy was designated to be accompanied by Captain Thomas.

"Mr. Hinkler, this is Troy Boomer. How are you today? Listen, I need to come see you about a very private matter—a very sensitive matter—and I wonder if I might come down now and if we could talk privately. Fine. Thank you, sir. I'll be right down."

Upon arriving at the bank, they were ushered directly into Hinkler's office.

"Why, what's the trouble, Troy?" Hinkler said, seeing the grave look on his face.

"Mr. Hinkler, I'm here on police business. In fact, it's on the Tommy Perelli investigation."

Hinkler looked puzzled.

"What could I possibly have to do with that unpleasant business?" He laughed as though he thought the whole matter was a sordid joke.

"I'm afraid this is very serious, sir. I'm sorry to be the one to tell you this. I was sent here by a group who are interested in saving you all the embarrassment possible. Sir, the investigation of Tommy Perelli's death has established without any question whatever that the Range Rover that you sent in for repairs to the right passenger door and oil pan was used by whoever killed Tommy Perelli to transport his body to Stone Mountain."

After Troy had fully explained the findings, the astonished Hinkler began to redden, realizing the seriousness of the situation.

"Of course, if what you tell me is true, I'll cooperate fully in the police investigation. I appreciate the consideration you have shown me, Troy, in coming here to break the news to me rather than hauling me into the police station like a common criminal. That was very considerate."

"By the way, Mr. Hinkler, the driver of the tow truck has led one of the police officers to your cabin, the location where he picked up the Range Rover. That officer has made the site secure against entry, and I believe crews of crime scene investigators armed with a search warrant are on their way there now to conduct a search."

"The place is a mess," Hinkler said. "I had people lined up to go out and clean it tomorrow. I pity anybody who has to spend very much time in that stinking place."

Forest and a crew of crime scene investigators from the state police sifted through the cabin and the grounds. They worked two days, leaving with a large collection of latent prints, and with samples of carpets and mattress covers that preliminary tests had shown contained blood stains of the same type as Tommy's.

The following day, after a long interrogation of his father, they learned that Billy Hinkler had possessed the vehicle and cabin during the period of Tommy's disappearance. Billy Hinkler was placed under hospital arrest under heavy guard for murder. The newspaper reported the arrest: "Banker's Son Charged with Sex Murder. Assistant District Attorney Troy Boomer Credited with Detective Work Leading to the Arrest."

That afternoon, Hinkler received notice that negotiations for acquisition of his bank were at an end.

Richard Boomer was sitting in his office pondering the headlines when the phone rang. It was Buck Hinkler.

"Boomer, I'm sure you know already they've charged Billy with killing the Perelli kid. It looks real bad for him. I don't know what his involvement was, but I want you to represent him. I want Troy off the case too."

"Buck," Boomer said calmly. "I'm sorry, I really am. Under other circumstances, I'd help. You know that. But this puts me in a really bad spot. Troy is being credited with the arrest, and he's prosecuting too. I can't ask him to withdraw from the case. It would destroy his career. Besides, if I know Troy, he'd tell me to kiss his ass. Get Billy another lawyer, Buck. Go get Walter Robinson. He'll do him a good job."

"Dammit, Boomer, I don't want Robinson. I want you. If your firm wants to keep the bank's business, you'll get your butt down there and see after my boy. So, don't ask Troy to get off the case. I'll go along with that. I don't expect miracles. Just do the best you can."

"I'm sorry, Buck. I'd like to help you, but I just can't."

That afternoon there was an emergency meeting of the partners in Getty and Jacobs. Boomer was told Hinkler had directed the managing partner of the firm to begin transferring its files and cases to a competing firm. He was told that the loss of Hinkler's business would be catastrophic and might result in "realignment of the firm." He knew what they meant. "Could you not," they asked, "consider obtaining a written waiver of conflict from the client and proceed to represent him?"

Boomer had no choice but to agree. He prepared the necessary notice to the examining court, prosecutor's office, and police.

"This will notify you that this firm, through the services of Richard Boomer, makes its appearance on behalf of defendant Billy R. Hinkler and will represent him throughout these proceedings."

"Dad, are you crazy?" Troy phoned him, enraged by receipt of the notice. "I can't believe that you would represent Hinkler and make a fool out of me, yourself, and everybody else we know. Listen, Buddy," Troy said before hanging up on him, "I respected you. I thought you were a cut above the other money mongers in the criminal law profession. But I see you're not. Do what you have to do, but stay the hell away from me. And Boomer, get this! I'm going to kick your sweet ass up between your teeth."

"Troy, you can't talk to me that way!" Boomer said just before Troy hung up.

Boomer called Buck Hinkler.

"Buck, this is Richard Boomer. I want you to know going in what you did was pretty shoddy. Now you've got me crossways with my boy, and you almost got me kicked out of the firm. Look, I'll represent Billy, but I've got to have a written waiver signed and notarized by him, waiving any conflict of interest that might arise because of my relationship with Troy. Considering the notoriety of the case, the public clamor, and the difficulty of the case, my retainer will be fixed at $500,000.00. That's my minimum fee, and it will buy you exactly one thousand hours of my time. Law clerks, paralegals, investigators' fees, and case expenses will be billed separately every month. And, the bank's business stays with Getty and Jacobs—agreed?

"Boomer," Buck answered, "I don't mean to be a jackass, but that kid down there in the hospital is my boy. I've got to give him his best shot; and, Boomer, you're Billy's best shot. I know that. I appreciate very much your helping Billy and me, and I realize the situation this puts you in. As far as the fee is concerned, I'll have a check on your desk by early morning. You send me the necessary form, and I'll get Billy's signature. I've already explained things to him. They're going to move him to the detention center first thing tomorrow morning. The arraignment is day after tomorrow at one o'clock. I know it's a tough case, but do the best you can. Spare no expense, and, Boomer, if you need anything at all, just get it."

That was it then. He was committed.

Over the next several hours, as he mapped out a strategy in his mind and thought about the case, Boomer felt the juices begin to flow. The case had all the ingredients it took to corral his energies and send them off, like a laser, in a single focused direction toward the target.

The case would be a challenge and would require him to marshal all his legal prowess. Indeed, the newspapers had made the evidence against Billy appear to be such that whatever results he got, short of the death penalty, would be considered a victory. Then there was the accused, a physically and mentally weakened prisoner whose very life depended on him. He would not wait for the waiver or the fee to get started.

First, he would need his own team of investigators. That would be Hugh Jones and his assortment of slouches, who, in spite of their appearance, never missed a lead or a clue. Then he would need a psychiatric examination of Billy, paid for by Hinkler and privileged against discovery by the prosecution, pending a possible plea of insanity.

He would assemble the best research lawyers in the firm to research and prepare motions for discovery, motions to suppress evidence seized in the search of Billy's automobile and the cabin he inhabited, and any interim appeals that might become necessary. He knew the defense of Billy Hinkler would be a difficult and time-consuming business, but he had learned in other cases to assign the drudgery of research brief preparation and document assembly to the weevils Getty and Jacobs had found nesting in the ivy of Harvard and Yale Law Schools.

There would be plenty of time for the psychiatric examination. He would save that until the indictment was handed down. Preparation of motions to suppress the evidence seized in the searches of the vehicle and the cabin could proceed once the search warrants and affidavits were obtained and the details of the searches were known. Informal requests for discovery were out. He couldn't leave the impression that Troy was cooperating with him by voluntarily furnishing information about the state's case—so formal requests for information, filed with the court, would be prepared for submission at the appropriate time.

Captain Thomas in his press interviews had said enough to tell him much of what the investigation had revealed—so he had that to begin with. But that was not enough. That was only the prosecution's theory of the case. To develop a defense for Billy, he must conduct his own investigation, setting his hounds on an already cold trail. He could not, and he would not, accept any of the findings of the state's investigators. He had to convince himself, through his own inquiry, that Billy had, indeed, committed this horrible crime.

With those thoughts, Boomer began his journey down the long road to the courtroom.

Boomer called private detective Hugh Jones. "Hugh, I've got something for you."

"I know, Boomer" Hugh said darkly. "I just heard—the Perelli thing. Sounds like a mean one. You and Troy, huh? From what the papers say, he might just stomp your butt."

"Sounds like you've been talking to him. That's exactly what he told me."

They laughed.

"Look, Hugh, do you have any problems getting in this one? I mean—".

"Boomer, I've already got my street shoes on and was just waiting for your call."

"Then meet me at the detention center at one o'clock tomorrow," Boomer said. "We're going to talk to the client and see what he can tell us. I'll meet you outside the west entrance."

It was four thirty. Jessica was home by now, he thought. So was Emily—down, she said, to 155 pounds. She had asked him to come home early so he would be there.

"I wanted to surprise you," she said when he arrived home. "A kind of a belated birthday dinner. I called Troy, but he declined. And Eddy (Did she say "Eddy"?) had an emergency—said he might be over later. So I guess it's just the two of us."

She ushered Boomer straight into the dining room.

"I got some crawdaddies, fixed Cajun style at the deli for starters," she said excitedly. "I know how you love them. I've fixed a Caesar with that good dressing you like. Let's see, we have capons, basted with butter sauce, and, oh, I opened a bottle of that good wine that's been in the cellar all those years."

What is going on? Boomer thought to himself.

He had expected the usual beef stew and corn bread. The sight of the gleaming porcelain, which he had hardly seen in twenty years, the linen napkins, tucked lightly in their little silver rings, and the candles were strange to him in this house. He found the idea of sitting down to a formal meal alone with her somewhat disturbing.

"Oh, Boomer," she said excitedly as he began to eat the crawfish she had served him, "I had the best time in New York. We'll have to go there someday ..."

Through the salad and into the capon and asparagus, she described what seemed to him to be every detail of the trip, some of which she made quite amusing. He hardly said a word.

The dinner ended with a lemon parfait and then coffee. As she began to collect the dishes, he moved to the den, leaned back in his lounge chair, put his feet up on the ottoman, and fell asleep.

"Wake up, Boomer, wake up now. It's ten o'clock. Come on, let's go up to bed now."

He staggered to his feet, wearily climbed the stairs, undressed, and climbed into bed. That night, he dreamed of fat little chickens running down the driveway toward Chaumiere, wearing little pink panties, while Rooster Jack Napier played a funeral dirge.

CHAPTER 18

Hugh Jones raised up in bed, reached and got his watch off the nightstand, and peered at the dial. It was eleven thirty. He got up and pulled the drapes, letting the hot morning sun pour into the room. He walked again to the nightstand, took a cigarette from a Camel pack, and lit it. He took a long, deep breath of the smoke, exhaled, and began to cough fitfully. At forty-five, he was already showing the signs of dissipation that accompany too much alcohol too often and a three-pack-a-day cigarette habit.

He put on his old leather house shoes and terry cloth robe, went to the door, got the morning paper, and went into the little kitchenette. Pulling a quart of milk from the refrigerator, he turned it up and took a deep swallow, breathing a sign of satisfaction.

He perked a pot of coffee, sat down at the table, lit another Camel off the first, and looked at the headline. "Richard Boomer to Represent Hinkler." The article, covering the upper one-fourth of the front page, recounted all the events leading up to the arrest of Billy Hinkler, beginning with the account of Tommy's abduction.

The article began, "Many Atlantans have expressed shock, and even outrage, upon hearing that well-known criminal defense lawyer Richard Boomer has agreed to represent accused sex killer Billy Hinkler. Richard Boomer is the father of Troy Boomer, whose detective work was largely responsible for Hinkler's arrest."

At the end of the article were the pictures and statements of five persons who had responded to the question, "How do you feel about Hinkler's choice of lawyers?"

All five were critical of the Boomers, both Richard and Troy.

"The fix is on," one person replied. "If you've got enough money, you can buy yourself out of anything."

"Poor Richard," Hugh murmured. "Poor Troy," he added.

Hugh fixed a bowl of cornflakes, poured a shot of Early Times in his coffee cup, gobbled it all down, and went for a shower. It was good to be working again. Business had been slow for several months—just a surveillance every now and then for a jealous wife—a search for a missing relative or heir—nothing of real importance since the last investigation he did for Boomer. He could use the money the case would produce.

He must tell Boomer his hourly rate had increased to $100.00 per hour, or $600.00 per day; and the rate for his helpers was $50.00 each, $25.00 for him and $25.00 for them. Old Hinkler could afford it, and he could catch up on his bills on this one. He must include in the arrangement a bonus payment at the end of $50,000.00 if he was able, through his investigation, to uncover evidence leading to exoneration. He must also remember to hit Boomer up for a $1,500.00 advance to catch up on his rent, buy gas for his car, and defray other expenses until his first bill was paid.

Hugh dressed, took three packs of Camels from a carton on the kitchen counter, and started for the detention center. His 1986 Chevy started, choked, and finally caught, propelling him forward. "Been a long dry spell," he moaned. *Got to get something coming in. Maybe this case will bring a little rain. Maybe we'll have to do Boomer a little rain dance.*

"Hello, Boomer."

"Hi, Hugh."

The two shook hands and entered the detention center. Inside, they were led to a small bare room containing only a counter with a wire screen to separate them, and benches on either side. The room was lined with yellow ceramic tile, which seemed to amplify every sound.

Billy was pale and pasty, his voice weak and trembling. His eyes danced in his head, and he kept sniffing, incessantly sniffing, as though he had a terrible cold.

Billy was thin. In the short-sleeve prison shirt his very thin arms looked like straws sticking out of a soda cup. Boomer could see scars on his naked arms, which he surmised were caused by needles.

Boomer had not seen Billy since he was very young, but he did not remember him being so physically unattractive. His features, though regular, just didn't seem to fit together. The distinguishing features on his face were his ears, which were small, cupped, and simian-like. His complexion was badly scarred from bouts of acne suffered when he was a teenager. Boomer knew Billy's appearance would not favor him before a jury. He would have to give some thought to whether his appearance might be used to provoke sympathy or understanding from the jury.

"Hi, Billy. I'm Richard Boomer, a lawyer and friend of your Daddy's. He has asked me to represent you in this business and I have agreed to do so, subject, of course, to your approval. Let me ask you right off. Do you approve? Do you want me to represent you? Very well, then. You do understand that my son, Troy, is the prosecutor and he will be trying to convict you and send you to jail or worse? You do? And, do you understand you are charged with a capital offense, punishable by life imprisonment or death by execution? You do? Very well, Billy. I understand you have signed a waiver so we can proceed to try to help you." Boomer continued.

"Billy, this is Hugh Jones. Hugh is a private detective. He will be helping us in our investigation. I just wanted you two to meet. He won't be here as I interview you, because I don't want to jeopardize the privilege that attaches to communications between us as lawyer and client. He will step out of the room, and we'll talk briefly. Then we can call him back in if he is needed. I can supply him with whatever information you give me that I think he might need."

When Hugh had gone, Boomer looked directly into Billy's eyes.

"Let me ask you a question, son. Did you kill and mutilate Tommy Perelli, or do you know who did? Your answer, please understand, won't leave this room."

Billy sniffed several times, looked down, cupped his hands on his forehead, covered his eyes, and answered simply, "I don't know. I mean, I don't think so. I don't think I did, but I don't know. You see, Mr. Boomer, I had been tripping on LSD, angel dust, crack, pills, liquor, thump bugs—anything I could get my hands on—for more than a month. I don't know where I was, who I was with, or what I did during that time. I have flashes of being at the cabin or in the car driving somewhere, but that's all. Really, to tell you the truth, it scares me what I did during that time. They tell me I'm different then, and it scares me that I might have done that. I mean, it was my Range Rover and all—so I don't know."

Boomer believed him.

"Let me ask you something else, Billy, straight outright. Do you like children? I mean, are you sexually attracted to children? Did you ever want to touch them in a sexual way or fondle them, or anything like that?"

"No, Mr. Boomer. I never have been around children much, being an only child. But I like children. I mean, I like to watch them play, hear them talk, roughhouse with them. But as far as any sexual feelings, I mean, I never had any that I know of; except when I was ten I tried to get Jill Brock to go into the garage with me and lay down on a blanket I had spread. She was ten also But, no. I never did."

"Another question, Billy. Do you ever buy or have you ever seen, or had, or possessed any child pornography—magazines depicting children in sexual situations?"

"Lord, no, Mr. Boomer. Why would I want to do that?"

"One more question, Billy. Have you ever felt a need to injure or hurt other people, to inflict pain on them, or have somebody do the same to you?"

"No," he answered.

"If I understand it, you don't know if you did what they accused you of or not?"

"Mr. Boomer, I can't see myself under any circumstances hurting anybody. I never had any desire to hurt anyone, and I never had a need to. The only people I ever hurt in my life were myself, my mother, and my dad."

"Billy, I'm going to leave now. I want you to keep your spirits up the best you can. There is no need to apply for bail, with the mood of public opinion and all. It would just be denied. We'll get started on this thing and check back with you from time to time. In the meantime, I don't want you to talk to anybody about anything. If they put you in a cell with another inmate, don't talk about any of this. Nothing. Do you understand? It's very important, and I want you to think about this and think very hard. I want a list of all your drinking buddies—boys and girls—who they are, and where we can reach them. I want to know where you get your booze and your drugs, and how we can reach them. We're going to have to find out what you've been doing the last thirty days and whom you've been doing it with. I'll be back here in the morning to pick it up."

"Let's get a cup of coffee," Boomer said as they left the building.

Hugh lit a cigarette as they walked to a coffee shop.

"I've got a real dilemma here, Hugh. When I asked him if he did it, he said he didn't know—that he was out of his gourd for weeks on booze and drugs—but he doesn't think he did. I believe him. Did you ever hear anything to beat that? We start out on a cold trail, without a clue as to what happened here, and we have a client that can't give us any help at all. He says during the time frame here, he doesn't know where he was, who he was with, or what he was doing."

"That's tough." Hugh shook his head.

"Now, here's the way I figure it. I believe the state's case is circumstantial. It may be mostly forensics. I don't know what all that is, but we'll find out. Some of what they have may not tag our man and might even point to somebody else. I mean, even admitting this Range Rover was used to haul the body doesn't necessarily mean Billy was the killer or even the driver of that vehicle. Especially considering he was out of it and they apparently don't have an eyewitness. When you get right down to it, the big thing Troy's got is Buck's ownership and Billy's possession of the vehicle and occupancy of the cabin. We'll just have to keep digging, beyond what the police have done, and come up with the other players in this thing—anybody who had the opportunity and the means to carry it out. Troy's no dummy. Possession of the Range Rover and occupancy of the cabin might get him to a jury, but he knows that's not going to be enough to get a conviction unless he has direct evidence connecting Billy to the murder. I don't believe he has that, at least not yet."

"Then why would they authorize the warrant?" Hugh asked.

"Do you know what I think?" Boomer replied. "I think there was so much public clamor for an arrest that Billips and the police commissioner jumped the gun on this one. If that's true, you can expect them to go on with their investigation and try to establish a personal link between Billy and the murder. For that, they're going to need an eyewitness to the abduction, which I'm sure they don't have; or they're going to need someone who can connect Billy to the actual murder or disposal of the body; or they'll need forensics that will do it. Of course, we don't know what they found at the autopsy. They could have found semen, or hairs, or blood on the body that matches Billy's on DNA testing, but I doubt it. If they do, we're cooked. If they don't, we may be all right. Anyhow, we'll have to forge ahead, hope for the best, but expect the worst."

Boomer took a breath and finished his coffee.

"Now, here's what I want you to do. You get that bunch of jokers of yours together and get started. I don't want a rock—no, I don't want a pebble—left unturned. I want to start with the Perelli kid the day he was born. I want to know what time he got up in the morning and what time he went to bed, if I can, and I want to know what he did in between. Interview every neighbor within a three-block area; talk to his teachers; talk to the school bus driver, the dispatcher, or whatever; and talk to every kid you can that was on that bus the day he was abducted. Follow every lead, take nothing for granted, and let's find something to take some of the pressure off Billy."

Hugh asked for a $1,500.00 advance.

"Why don't we make that $5,000.00 so you won't nickel and dime me to death. I'll take it out of your weekly billings in $1,000 increments. Bill me on Fridays for you, your crew, and your expenses. I'll have your checks cut on Monday.

After collecting and cashing the $5,000.00 advance, Hugh called his crew together for a meeting at his apartment. They were an interesting assortment:

Bobby McKnight: A forty-year-old graduate of Michigan State with a master's degree in chemical engineering and an interest in forensic science.

Melvin Jenkins: Regularly engaged as a pool shark and professional poker player; devoured every murder mystery he could find; was especially useful in assimilating information and turning superficially random facts into meaningful information.

Larry Ball: The real genius in the crew. He seemed always to be at the right place to get the rebound and go in to score; seemingly hopeless investigations seemed to somehow suddenly break wide open with just a small jab from his remarkable and incisive mind.

"Bobby"—Hugh held his hand up for silence—"I want you to interview all the neighbors in this three-block area that will talk to you. You know what to ask. Write up a short interview report in a tablet. Here are all the newspaper reports going back to Tommy's abduction. Now, there's a lot of good background there, so read it before you start."

"Melvin," Hugh said, pointing to him. "I want to know everything there is to know about that school Tommy was going to. Classes, bus schedules, routes, passengers, times, drivers—everything there is to know. I want to know who Tommy's friends are, what he usually did after school, the whole thing."

"Larry," Hugh said, smiling. "I just want you to hang around. Poke around until you find something to do—and you will."

"Now, fellows, we meet here every morning at eleven thirty to share information. Okay? See you tomorrow."

CHAPTER 19

oomer arrived at his office at eight o'clock to prepare for the one o'clock arraignment. He hoped Billy had completed the list he had asked for. He took a cab to the detention center, where he found Billy more relaxed, responsive, and anxious to cooperate.

Billy passed several sheets of paper to Boomer on which he had scribbled the information Boomer had asked for. As Boomer rose to leave, Billy said, "Mr. Boomer, I appreciate what you're trying to do for me, and I know you will do all you can. You asked me yesterday if I killed that boy. I can tell you this. The Billy Hinkler you're looking at today didn't do it. But I honestly can't tell you what the other Billy Hinkler might have done."

Boomer returned to his office and prepared a written plea of not guilty and a request for a preliminary hearing. Since Billy would not be seeking bail, he asked that the hearing be postponed for ten days to give him time to prepare.

As he was reviewing the paperwork, a courier arrived from the district attorney's office with a motion signed by Troy. The motion and accompanying affidavit asked the court to order Billy Hinkler to submit to the extraction of blood from his person; to provide hairs with attached follicles from his head and pubic area; and to provide a urine specimen. The affidavit filed in support of the motion, also signed by Troy, after reciting the circumstances giving rise to Billy's arrest, revealed that blood and hair had been discovered at the Stone

Mountain site that he said were believed to be the blood and hair of the accused. The affidavit explained that samples of blood and hair from the accused were needed for DNA testing. The motion was set for hearing at one o'clock, the time of the arraignment.

Boomer was stricken. The evidence against Billy might be even stronger than he had thought. He knew the request would be granted, so there was no need to resist. The affidavit did not state where the blood and hair had been found, but Boomer might worm that information from the prosecution when the motion was heard. And he might convince the court that he was entitled to a copy of the results of the analysis.

Troy knew a direct DNA match of the samples would link Billy directly to the Stone Mountain site. That, and the matchup of the paint and crankcase oil, would decimate any alibi defense he might offer.

At the arraignment he would simply offer his plea of not guilty, get what information he could about the discovery of the blood and hair, and ask to be provided with the results of the testing. He would also ask to be furnished cuts of the discovered blood and hair. Maybe Troy would agree.

The arraignment was perfunctory. After accepting Billy's plea in a small courtroom filled with news reporters, the court sustained the state's motion for production of the blood and hair samples but denied Billy's motion for cuts of the discovered samples and the results of the testing. The court also ordered Boomer to be present when the blood and hair samples were collected.

"Mr. Boomer, I can certainly sympathize with your desires, and even your needs in this matter. I am sure you will be entitled in due course to what you are asking for, but this is an examining court, and I find nothing in the rules giving me the authority to order discovery. Perhaps the state will agree. Will you, Mr. Boomer—Mr. Troy Boomer?"

"We will not agree, Your Honor," Troy replied.

"The little shit," Boomer muttered to an associate. "The little asshole. I'll find out what the results are at the preliminary hearing."

If the state failed to introduce the results, he would know they didn't have a match. He would then bring the subject up on cross-examination as dramatically as he could.

After the arraignment, Troy marched out of the courtroom, avoiding any contact with Boomer. As Billy was being led from the courtroom, the reporters fell on Boomer.

"Mr. Boomer, what is your reaction to this latest development in your case?" one of them asked.

"We'll see," was all he could say.

"Were you aware of this evidence?"

"No, I was not," he replied.

Boomer left the courthouse with a ten-day delay. That request had not been opposed, causing him to believe Troy was not yet ready to present his case on probable cause. Perhaps he wanted to wait on the results of the DNA testing or had other leads he wanted to follow up.

The delay would give Hugh and his boys time to get into the case, and, perhaps, come up with some sort of alibi evidence.

Boomer wished he had more information about the state's investigation—what they had found and what they had not found. He had been in old Judge Lamprey's court before. He knew he would be allowed wide latitude in cross-examining the investigating officers about their investigation at the preliminary hearing. He knew the judge would find probable cause to hold Billy to the grand jury, unless Hugh came up with a miracle. Boomer would use the hearing to find out everything he could about Troy's case.

Back at his office, Boomer sat at his desk, looking out his window at Atlanta. He thought of Jessi and the week they had together. He looked at his watch. It was four thirty. She was just around the corner, probably putting her work away and getting ready to go home. As he thought of that first night in the pool, he felt her firm breasts against his body as she held him close, her warm mouth caressing his shoulder. He heard again her voice as she whispered, "Richard, take me, please take me." He felt the now familiar stirrings in his body, passions he had thought dead.

He felt also her youth, her vigor, her beauty.

"I'm April and you're August," she had said. "What does it matter?"

He wanted her, he knew that. He wanted her with him now. He wanted her always. He must find a way to see her, to be with her, to have her—whatever the cost. Nothing else mattered; all that mattered was he could not get her out of his mind. He opened a drawer, pulled out a legal pad, and knowing of her passion for the sea, wrote:

Winter Wine

I know where
There's a secret place—
A place known only to me.
Where endless strands
Of soft, warm sands
Look out on a summer sea.

Come down with me
To that summer sea.
Look out on the waning tide.
Look out and smile, and
For a little while,
Run down to the sea and hide.

I have built us a house
By the side of the sea.
Summer is by the sea.
Come, bring the spring
With its April dream,
And spend some time with me.

Come dream, or I
Will dreamless be
In our house by the side of the sea.

Though summer is past,
The Dream still will last
In our house by the side of the sea.

I built our house
Near the water's edge,
With wood from a fallen tree.
Whose gentle arms,
In a raging storm,
Once furnished a shelter for me.

Nearby the water's edge,
There stands a garden wall.
There sing a song
To the waiting dawn—
To the sound of a seabird's call.

Sing your song,
And dream your dream,
And fill your April heart.
All your songs
And all your dreams
To the waiting sea impart.

We'll gather there
The summer grapes
From off the garden vine.
For, from those summer grapes,
The vintner takes
The taste of his sweet winter wine.

Come down with me
To my summer sea—
To my garden by the sea.
Bring along
Your April song,

And spend some time with me.

Come sing, or I
Will songless be
In our garden by the sea.
When April is gone,
There'll still be the song—
The song you sang for me.

Then the pleasures of
That sheltered place—
The sand, the rocks, the garden too,
The garden wall,
The seabird's call,
The sturdy house I built for you.

All my hopes,
All my dreams,
All my seasons through,
All my life, and
All my love,
I'll give them all to you.

All I am, and
All I was, and
All I can ever be;
I'll lay them all
By the garden wall
By the house by the side of the sea.

There we'll sing our songs
And fill the years
With dreams of every kind;
And fill our glass
While seasons last
With the taste of our "sweet winter wine."

He had to have her. He knew that now.

He thought of Emily, waddling around in that house of horrors. He resented the attentions she had started to give him.

Too late, he thought. *Too damn late.*

It was six thirty. Emily had asked him to be home by eight, if he could. She would have dinner ready, she said, and they could watch a special on geriatrics and the secret to aging gracefully, beginning at nine.

"Jessi." He did not know why he whispered when she answered. "I had to call you. I miss you real bad. I think about you all the time. I want to see you, soon. I have something for you, a poem. Tomorrow night? At seven thirty? I'll be there."

When he walked into the kitchen from the garage, Emily reached up to kiss him. As he leaned forward, reluctantly, she put her arms around his neck, embracing him.

"Hug me, Boomer. Hug me."

He pulled her arm from around his neck.

"I'm tired, Emily, real tired."

That night, after dinner, served again in the dining room by candlelight, Richard Boomer, age fifty-seven, spent two hours watching television, learning about the inevitable demise of the male and female endocrine systems; the wearing away of the joints and the development of arthritis among persons past sixty; the incidence of heart disease and cognitive disorders in advanced age; and problems society would face in dealing with an aging population.

"It does give a person something to think about," Emily mused after the program had ended.

"Yes, it sure does," he replied.

"Yes, it does," she echoed again.

It makes you think old Bud was right—get it while you can and forget all that other shit.

He knew there was a silent message in that program from Emily to him. She did not have to say it. He knew what it was:

"Just remember, Buster, you're fifty-seven. It's about over for you. You're over the hill, Richard Boomer, and don't you forget it. All the silk sport coats and tasseled shoes in the world are not going to change that."

He thought again of Jessi. If he was to die tomorrow, he wanted only one thing today—all of her he could get.

"Oh, Richard," she said the next evening. "It's beautiful! I love it! Oh, I accept! I accept!" She read the poem again, this time out loud. That night they joined in raptured silence. No words passed between them, only an unspoken passion, too sweet for expression.

As he drove toward home, he felt an overwhelming need to give her something very special, a gift to consummate the wedding of souls that had taken place in that bedroom. He would see to it tomorrow after Billy's blood and hair had been collected for the crime lab and Boomer's own DNA analysis.

Bobby called Hugh the next morning.

"I started doing my interview of the neighbors and went by that vacant lot—you know, the paper said Tommy was last seen playing with a pup or dog before he was abducted. Well, I stopped by the house next door, and this fellow, William Mathis, was outside trimming his hedge. He said that Troy had already talked to him. Well, he did see Tommy playing on that vacant lot with a dog. He said he was mowing his grass, and this little brown spotted dog crossed his yard. It squatted, so he figures it was a bitch. He later looked over and saw Tommy in the vacant lot playing with it. I asked him if that was the day Tommy was reported missing, but he said he didn't know, that he left town that night to go fishing in Minnesota and didn't know about Tommy until he got back a week later. I asked him to be more specific on the dates, and he remembered his lawn mower breaking down on that day. He took it to the dealer for repair that same day so it would be ready when he got back. He got out the repair ticket where he took it in and, you know, they wrote on there what was wrong with it. So—now get this—that was the day *before* Tommy was reported missing. I got that date from the newspaper articles you gave me. But this kid next door to Tommy—he's about nine years old, too—says he saw him playing on the lot the day he was reported missing—after the school bus dropped him off! Now, Hugh, somebody's wrong. Maybe the repair shop put the wrong date on the ticket, but Mathis has a credit card receipt where he bought gasoline the night he left—in Chattanooga—and it has the same date on it as the repair ticket. Now, what I want to know is, do you want me to follow up on this or go on to something else?"

"No, don't go on to something else. Follow up on it, you dummy," Hugh scolded him. Bobby laughed.

"Well, I can check around the neighborhood and see if anybody else saw the dog or maybe owned it. The paper called it a stray. I can go by the pound and see if they picked up a brown spotted mixed breed like the one Mathis described to me in this area."

"Okay, do the best you can with it. Remember what Boomer said. Follow every lead to wherever it takes you. It's his money, not mine."

Bobby found there were over twenty-seven dwellings in the three-block area. He began knocking on doors asking questions. The occupants were by and large friendly and cooperative, seemingly anxious to help any way they could. Bobby explained that, while they represented the accused, they were, after all, just "searching for the truth" as to who killed Tommy.

In the course of his interview of the neighbors, Bobby took the names of the children in each household that attended the same school that Tommy attended and rode school bus number 5. He found only three. One of the children, Robbie Wilson, was twelve years old, a very bright, outgoing, and gregarious youngster.

Bobby learned that Robbie had ridden the same school bus on the same run for four years. The bus had been driven by an older gentlemen until his retirement two years ago, when the route was taken over by Mr. Fentrell, who had driven it since. Most of the children seemed to like Fentrell, but Robbie hadn't liked him since he scolded him several weeks earlier for being slow to get off the bus.

"Quit playing and get on off, you little fart," Fentrell had said.

Robbie had been the last one to get off the bus that day, so nobody heard the exchange.

Shortly after that, Fentrell began to take a different route, which enabled Robbie to get off the bus and get home a little sooner. He was grateful for that, but he knew Fentrell didn't like him. Bobby made a note to himself.

"Have Melvin show me the bus routes when he gets them."

Nobody he interviewed had seen a brown spotted stray in the neighborhood, and he could find no one who owned such an animal. The mystery of the missing dog intrigued Bobby. The riddle probably had nothing at all to do with the case, but he had to have an explanation for the conflicting dates. If indeed, the neighbor child was wrong and what he related to the police had actually occurred the day before, the case would take on a different complexion. Of course, it could be that the dog was in the neighborhood both days, but that was unlikely, because of Atlanta's strict dog laws and the zeal with which they were enforced. Still, that was the most likely explanation for the conflicting evidence.

Bobby worked two twelve-hour days going through the neighborhood, not counting the time spent at the daily conference. The third day he scheduled a meeting with the dog warden.

"Let me ask you something," the dog warden said when Bobby had made his request for information. "Isn't that the same dog the prosecuting attorney came in here asking me about three or four weeks ago?"

Bobby smiled.

"It may be. The last time the Perelli kid was seen before his disappearance, he was playing with a brown spotted stray dog or pup. That was on April 15. It probably was a bitch. I'm looking to find dogs answering that description that were picked up near his residence from, say, April 10th through April 20th."

"Let me look here." The warden operated the keyboard. "We had one on the fourteenth, the day before. A brown spotted bitch pup. She was picked up near Keeton on Monrose at six thirty on the fourteenth. The other one was on the sixteenth. Those were two males, picked up together. Both of them were black. That's all for that period."

"What happened to them?" Bobby inquired.

"Well, the bitch was adopted out. Here, let me pull the file on that one. Let's see, she went to a family in Marietta. Here's the name and address," he said, writing the information on a slip of paper. "By the way, here's a picture of the dog. We took that for adoption purposes—sometimes we advertise in the paper. Here's the negative strip. Must have been in here by mistake. We won't need that."

Bobby was elated. He held the negatives up to the light and saw that the picture of the dog was among them. He thanked him for his help and delivered the negatives to the printer, who produced eleven-by-thirteen enlargements of the dog.

Bobby showed the picture to William Mathis, who readily identified the picture as the same dog he had seen playing with Tommy the day he left for Minnesota. Bobby then walked down the street and showed the picture to Tommy's neighbor, Timmy, who also identified the dog.

He drove to the address he'd been given and asked the new owner to see the dog. Thinking Bobby was from the Humane Society, the new owners advised him they would not be able to keep Spotty after all, because their daughter was allergic to dog dander. They placed Spotty in a dog Pullman, and Bobby drove off to Mathis's house for an eyes-on identification.

After giving Boomer the good news about Bobby's find, Hugh asked Boomer the next day, "Boomer, what am I going to do with the damn dog? It's pissing all over my floors. We've got to figure out someplace to keep her. What about taking her over to the kennel and boarding her for a while? If we keep her too long without telling the prosecution about her, they may try to say we've switched dogs on them."

Boomer suddenly had an inspiration.

"You bring Spotty over here to the office at five o'clock. I'll take care of that problem."

"Look what I brought you, Emily," Boomer said when he got home. "Isn't she nice? I thought you might need something to keep you company during the day when you're here by yourself."

Just as he set Spotty down on the floor, the dog squatted and made a puddle on the carpet.

"We can't keep her, Richard. No, please! We can't keep her," Emily protested.

"Well, we have to see that she has a good home. Troy's kids have been wanting a dog. Have Brenda bring them over tonight to see Spotty. I'm sure they will like her."

Relating the story to Hugh the next day, Boomer roared.

"And that's how Troy Boomer, assistant district attorney, came to be the custodian in loco parentis to one spotted brown bitch dog, 'Defendant Exhibit No. 1.'"

Melvin went to the school and introduced himself to the administrator.

"I'm a part of the team investigating the death of Tommy Perelli. We're interested in finding out who is really responsible for his death. I am interested first, in talking to the person in charge of transporting boys and girls back and forth to their homes. I'd like to get schedules, drivers' names, routes, passengers—the whole thing. I'd like to see anything you have related to the drivers—any personal data. Then I may want to interview some of your administrative personnel, teachers, and maybe even some selected students."

The administrator smiled.

"I'm sorry, sir. For reasons that should be obvious to you, the information you ask for with respect to bus transportation cannot be disclosed. Furthermore, I cannot and will not permit you to interrupt our instruction by interviewing either our personnel or the students. If I turned you loose interviewing the children, the parents would have my head by dark."

Melvin reported the conversation to Hugh, who in turn passed it on to Boomer.

"What do you want us to do now?" Hugh inquired.

"You have Melvin down here first thing in the morning. I want him in a suit and tie, hair combed, clean-shaven, ready to present to the governor if necessary."

The next morning, Boomer introduced Melvin to Father Boniface.

"Melvin needs to look into bus transportation at the school, and they won't let him. Can you help us with that? Go to the bishop if you have to?"

That afternoon, Boomer got a call from the administrator advising him that the school bus dispatcher was in charge of transportation and that he was available to talk to Melvin at any time. He or his representatives would have access to any records related to transportation he wanted to see. Boomer asked him to keep the nature of the inquiry completely confidential and to refrain from telling anybody on staff of Melvin's review.

The next morning Melvin began what became two full days of meetings with Caesar Potts, school bus dispatcher. Potts had been with the school as dispatcher for fifteen years. He had established the transportation policies and procedures to be followed in transporting the children to and from school.

Melvin learned the fleet consisted of ten buses and ten regular drivers, with two alternates in case a driver was absent. All the drivers were part time and worked at the school as teachers, custodians, or other employees. Each driver was responsible to see that his bus was regularly washed and parked in the garage at the end of each trip. The buses were identified by numbers 1 through 10, and a regular driver was assigned to each bus. Each driver and bus were assigned a particular route, beginning at the school and proceeding along an established route. Each child had been designated a number, beginning with the number 1, and if a pupil joined the bus, he or she would receive both a number and letter designation (i.e., 15(a), 15(b), etc.). The pupils would exit the bus in numerical order and in accordance with the established route so that the same delivery sequence was maintained at all times.

Melvin obtained a copy of the established route of school bus number 5, beginning in 1997 and reflecting all changes that had occurred during that interval. He also obtained a pupil manifest, which included the name, street address, and pupil number for each of the same years.

Finally, he was shown the personnel records for each school bus driver who had driven the number 5 bus during the years after 1997, including substitute drivers. He was permitted, under a vow of confidentiality, to copy Form 161, Application for Employment, of each of those drivers and any other documents in their files he deemed relevant.

When Melvin left Potts, he took with him two catalog cases of information to digest before he returned to the school for further interviews.

Melvin closeted himself in his house for three days. He obtained aerial photographs from a friend in the city engineers division, which he had enlarged so that they covered the walls in his poker room. He laboriously traced the designated route for the current year in the color red, marking any changes in the route—which, as it turned out, were few—in a different color. Having defined the routes, he flagged with street and number each pupil's residence (or stop) and marked that residence with a pupil name and number.

The residence of Joseph Perelli was approximately 4.5 miles into the route and about 0.5 miles from the final pupil's stop. It was designated as 1416 Keeton Street, Tommy Perelli, Pupil No. 53.

Melvin was able from his map to memorize the names of all the pupils transported on bus number 5, the children's transportation numbers, their street addresses, and the order in which they were discharged from the bus.

For four days, Melvin sat at the curb across the street, observing the loading of bus number 5. He observed the driver as he helped to herd the children onto the bus and to maintain order and discipline. The first day, he noticed a person parked on the opposite curb, observing him. He wondered who it could be. As the school bus pulled out, he followed closely, stopping at each stop and noting on his list the distance each child traveled and the exact time that had passed since the bus left the school. The car followed him. Melvin repeated his surveillance three more times. According to his calculations, Tommy should have left the bus at 4:06 p.m.

On the third trip, he observed flashing lights in his rearview mirror. He soon found himself facing Detective Ron Farley, who finally released him after confirming with Boomer that Melvin was in his employ.

"Damn, Mr. Boomer. Are you sure? This dude's been busted for gambling so many times it would make your head swim. Besides that, he's not licensed."

"I know, I know," Boomer replied.

Melvin interviewed each of Tommy's teachers. They were all anxious to cooperate, but no leads were developed. Finally, Melvin interviewed William Fentrell, the driver. Fentrell repeated essentially the same thing he had told Troy. Only this time, he volunteered, "And when Tommy got off the bus, there was a mutt there. Tommy reached down to pet it, and it jumped up on his leg."

"Is this the dog you saw?" Melvin said, handing him an eleven-by-thirteen picture of Spotty, given to him for his files by Hugh.

"Yes, that's the dog. That's the dog I've been talking about. No doubt about it. No doubt about it at all," Fentrell said emphatically.

"Could there have been two spotted dogs?" he wondered.

Larry had spent the last few days trying to run down the coterie of alcoholics, cokeheads, mainliners, and whores from the list furnished to Boomer by Billy Hinkler.

"Well," he told Boomer. "They're all as strung out as he says he was. I can't get any sense out of any of them so far. "Hey, man," Larry mimicked, "How's my man Billy? He send me anything, man? Tell him send me sompin next time. Har, har, har!"

Larry told them about Melissa, a frequent companion of Billy who he had interviewed and who seemed to have some useful information. She was reluctant to discuss the case with him but he intended to get back with her soon, tomorrow or the next day. She did tell him, "Billy didn't do that thing they said he did," she had said. "Not Billy. I've seen him strung up the rafters, freaking out on LSD, angel dust, the whole thing. I've never in all that time seen Billy hurt or try to hurt anything or anybody."

Larry would continue to press the group for information to use in establishing an alibi, but he doubted he would get any.

Hugh reported the findings to Boomer.

"Not much, but a start," he said.

Boomer went to the detention center the next morning and observed the taking of blood, hair, and urine from Billy. Afterward, he walked out of Tiffany's with an eighteen-carat gold filigree pendant with a four-carat emerald center stone and five carats of oblong baguettes. The eight-thousand-dollar cost seemed reasonable. He knew Jessi would like it.

CHAPTER 20

Melissa unlocked the door to the furnished apartment she rented. As she entered the kitchen, she saw a roach run down the sink drain. She would remember to buy some more powder to put around.

She went to the refrigerator, took out a diet drink, and sat down at the kitchen table. Reaching into the pocket of her waitress uniform, she laid a handful of crumpled bills and change on the table and began to count. Thirty-five dollars and fifteen cents, added to her wage of forty dollars. She put the tips in a coffee can and put it in the freezer compartment of the old refrigerator. She added the day's tips to the tally already in the can. She had a special use for that money. Another two hundred dollars, and she would have enough to pay the tuition for the six hours of courses she planned to start at Emory in the fall.

She reached into the cupboard and pulled out an envelope. Inside were grade reports for the two three-hour courses she had just finished. She had successfully completed her GED and had decided to pursue a degree in accounting, since she had always been good at figures. She knew it would take a long time to finish, but she hoped, eventually, to be able to pursue a degree full time with grants and loans. First she wanted to satisfy herself she was capable of doing the work; and she had an immediate problem that would have run its course. The two *A*'s she had gotten were encouraging, but they were easy courses in English composition and sociology.

A tall, willowy blond, Melissa had a good body, a good complexion, and a nice, pleasant face. Born in Anniston, Alabama, she was gentle, quiet, loyal, and smart—very smart. At school, taking the evening classes, she had been approached several times but preferred to remain apart. She wasn't ready yet for relationships. The young men in her classes seemed somehow shallow and immature, and she knew how to turn them away.

Melissa took a cigarette from a pack on the table, put it between her lips, and struck a match. She hesitated, took the cigarette from her mouth, and threw it in the garbage can. She had stopped smoking three months earlier. Her job as waitress, waiting tables at a restaurant, did not give her time to smoke. Besides, she had another reason for quitting when she did. Each time she was tempted to smoke, she went through the ritual of putting a cigarette in her mouth, lighting a match, remembering how hard it had been to quit, and discarding the cigarette without lighting it. It seemed to take away the craving, which she still felt occasionally.

Melissa had learned to drink early in life. Both of her parents were alcoholics. They blew most of their income from public assistance on alcohol, saving little for anything else. Melissa took her first drink of alcohol at age eleven. Her mother and stepfather, Harry and Pauline, were sitting around the kitchen table drinking when Harry poured a small amount of vodka into a water glass, diluted it with water, and called her. "Come over here, girl. Here, take a taste of this. You might as well try it. You've seen enough of it already." Melissa had found the effects of the vodka very much to her liking.

Shortly afterward, Melissa was taken from Harry and Pauline and placed in foster care. For the next three years, she was moved from shelter to foster home and back to shelter again. The moves always grew out of some problem within the agency or the foster home itself. At fifteen, and already fully mature physically, she determined to escape the wrenching pain that each move had brought. Just as she got used to a foster family or a situation, the order would come to move again.

She quietly slipped away one night and hitched a ride from Anniston to Knoxville, where she found employment in a nude dance club, lying about her age. She became an instant favorite of the patrons. The job required her to dance at tables, almost nude, and to sit begging the customers for drinks, which she usually got in exchange for quick feels of her body. Her drinks were always diluted, but she would sometimes switch drinks with a customer who was often too drunk and excited to realize the difference. She would leave the club at night, wobbling, with three or four hundred dollars, which she always managed to give or throw away.

Fortunately, she did not fall into a drug habit. She had smoked a little pot a few times and snorted cocaine, but alcohol became her drug of choice. She began having dates with customers after hours and was fired from the job when the owner was arrested for promoting prostitution.

She moved to Atlanta, where, after several arrests for delinquency and prostitution, she met Billy Hinkler at a downtown bar. Billy invited her to go with him to his cabin, after finding out she had been evicted from her apartment and had no place to stay. She had lived there with him for almost three months, finally entering the treatment center and then moving to the apartment where she now lived.

Slowly sipping the diet drink, she thought of Billy and their time together. Most of it had been spent in a state of stupor, but there had been good times, also, sitting on the screened porch, listening to the sounds from the mountain and talking about how it would be when they "got to normal again." She thought of the booze and drug parties, which sometimes lasted for days and were not always peaceful.

She remembered one occasion, shortly before she left. Billy had run into a man he called Ralph Hensley, one of Billy's classmates whom he knew slightly, but had not seen in several years. He had stopped by the cabin with his girlfriend. Hensley suddenly rose from the sofa and began beating the girl in the face with his fists because of some remark she had made. Melissa treated the girl's injuries and drove her home in Billy's Range Rover after Hensley had left, leaving her alone and injured.

"Billy this is the last straw. We're going to quit this, or I'm getting out. You know, this isn't getting us anywhere, is it? I mean, here you are and here I am. You're always flipped out on drugs, and I'm down on the booze. I don't want this anymore. Look, you're the best friend I ever had. In fact, you're the only friend I ever had. And I care for you. I mean, I really do. But I want better than this for you and for me too. You get off the drugs, and I'll get off the booze. Deal?"

Billy had agreed. At least for three days he agreed. During that three days, Melissa sat with him almost day and night, trying desperately to help him through withdrawal. She tried to get him to agree to go with her for help, but he insisted he could deal with it himself.

One afternoon, Billy got up, dressed, and slipped away, determined she would not be there when he got back. As she left the cabin, she wept bitterly. It was the nearest thing to a home she had known. *Will I ever find a stopping place?* she wondered. She walked to the highway carrying her suitcase, hitched a ride to Atlanta, entered a treatment center, and began to put her life together. She needed desperately to call Billy, to tell him something very important, but she could not.

As she sipped the soda, she thought of the conversation she had with the detective. She wished she could have been more helpful, but she had told him all she knew. She knew some of the names on the list Billy had given Boomer, but she did not know where any of them could be found. She knew one thing for sure. Billy Hinkler didn't kill Tommy Perelli. Billy couldn't do that.

The phone rang. It was Larry, the detective.

"Melissa," he said, "this fellow Ralph Hensley. I can't seem to get a line on him. All I have is the description Billy gave Mr. Boomer, but there are thousands of people in Atlanta. I've talked to everybody on Billy's list except Hensley, and nobody else knows who he is. I've called about every Hensley in the book, but nobody ever heard of a Ralph Hensley matching the description. Do you remember anything special about him?"

"Listen, here's the way I remember him," she replied. Melissa gave him a description that differed in many respects from what he had already been told.

"Well, if you happen to run into him, or think of anything else, please call me. I've run out of ideas."

"Poor Billy," Melissa whispered to herself after hanging up. She suddenly felt an urgent need to see him—to talk to him, to tell him something he needed to know. She dialed the detention center switchboard and got the visiting hours. The next day on her afternoon break, she took a taxi to the detention center.

"Sorry, ma'am," the man told her. "He's in maximum security. Restricted visitation; no visitors except upon prior approval."

She went to the bank where she knew he worked and asked to see Mr. Hinkler.

"I'm sorry, Miss, but he's in conference. May I help you?"

"Yes, please," she said. "Would you give him this note, please?" She scribbled a note, folded it, marked it "private" on the front, and handed it to him. "Mr. Hinkler," it said. "I am a good friend of Billy's. Please call me at this number after five o'clock. I have something to tell you."

At six o'clock, the phone rang. For the next thirty minutes, Melissa told Buck of her relationship with Billy, her attempts to get him off the drugs, and her efforts to care for him. Buck at first was annoyed, but as she told him familiar things about Billy, the cabin, his childhood, and other personal things, he grew more interested.

"Mr. Hinkler, I went by the jail today to see Billy. I know how he must feel and what he's going through. I didn't want to bother you with this, and I would never have called you or Billy, either, if this awful thing had not happened to him. And I won't call you again, ever. I know they will let you in to see him. The next time please tell him Melissa called. Tell him I love him very much. And if you think it is appropriate and will maybe help him or at least not hurt him, tell him I'm carrying his child."

There was a long silence. Finally, Buck said in a choked voice, "Young lady, where are you now?"

"Please, Mr. Hinkler, I have to go now. I can't talk anymore." Her voice broke as she said, "Good-bye, Mr. Hinkler."

Buck didn't know where to find her. He didn't even know her last name. He took Mary Rachael into the study and told her what he had just learned.

"We must find her, Buck. I must talk to the girl and find out if it is really true."

"How?" he asked.

He thought a moment and then dialed Boomer. Maybe he would know who she was and where she could be found. Emily told him Richard was still at the office. He phoned.

"I don't know who she is," Boomer told him. "Wait a minute; give me ten minutes. I'll see what I can do. Is there something I should know about?"

"Maybe later," Buck replied.

Boomer called Hugh, who remembered that a girl named Melissa was included on the list of people Billy had provided.

"I'll call Larry—he's handling that—and have him give you a call." In fifteen minutes Boomer called Buck.

"I just talked to Larry. He interviewed a Melissa Stokes yesterday. It may be the same one. Her telephone number is 843-6092."

Buck looked at the number she had left at the bank.

"That's her, Boomer. Do you have an address?" Boomer read off the address Larry had given him. An hour later, Buck knocked on Melissa's door.

"How did you find me?" she asked.

He looked down, seeing that she was beginning to show.

"Come with me," he entreated. "My wife, Mary Rachael, wants to meet you."

Melissa looked frightened, confused.

"Oh, no, Mr. Hinkler," she finally gasped, "I just got off from work, and—"

"Now, don't argue with me, young lady," he interrupted. "You look fine."

The Jaguar pulled into Buck's driveway. Melissa's eyes widened in disbelief. *So this is where Billy lived,* she thought. They went into the house.

"Hello, Melissa. I'm Mary Rachael, Billy's mother. So nice to meet you. Won't you come into the parlor? Would you like some tea or coffee? Buck, you will excuse us, I'm sure. We girls have a lot to talk about, don't we, dear? And, Buck, please close the door, won't you?

Buck sat in the study and waited. *She's a pretty girl,* he thought, *kind of refined in a way—out of a good family from the looks of it. Probably a little wild—got messed up maybe. Who knows?"*

An hour later he heard the parlor door open and Mary Rachael say, "It's all set then."

Buck met them in the hall.

"Buck, Melissa is going to come visit with us for a while, just until we can find her another place. I've convinced her it's better for her, considering the neighborhood where she's living. Here's the key to her flat. Have Roger and Mavis go there in the morning and bring her things here. Come, dear. I'll show you to your room. I'll bring you some pajamas. They'll be a little large, but you can manage until you get your things. And, Melissa, we'll be so glad to have you with us for a while."

"But my job," Melissa whispered. "How will I get to my job?"

"You can phone them in the morning, dear, and tell them you won't be in," she answered firmly. "There are pastries in the fridge if you get hungry during the night, and we'll be in the next room if you need us."

"Really, Mary Rachael, do you think it is wise?" Buck asked after Melissa had closed the bedroom door. "We don't really know anything about her."

"Buck, this child is telling the truth. I know. Just trust me."

Melissa lay in the bed looking up at the pleated canopy. She had never seen such a room. She lay awake wondering how it had all happened; wondering also, if she had done the right thing by calling them and by agreeing to stay. The soft down mattress caressed her body, and she smelled the sweet aroma of potpourri. She remembered the foster homes she had been taken to and the strange beds she had lain in—always for only a little while. Then she was packed up to move again. She wondered where Margaret, her little sister, was. *In the streets,* she thought. She felt suddenly alone.

It was only eight o'clock, too early to go to bed, but she was tired from waiting tables all day. Melissa closed her eyes and dreamed.

It was Anniston, she thought, but she was not sure; she didn't know the neighborhood. It was getting dark, and Melissa was walking home. She felt someone following her close behind. She didn't know where she lived or what the house looked like, but she knew it was a large, beautiful house and she must find it or spend the night alone in the dark while the rest of the city slept. She ran from house to house, knocking on doors. No one answered. Suddenly, as she ran, crying, the earth opened up under her, and she fell, screaming into darkness.

"Melissa, Melissa. Wake up, dear. You were dreaming." Mary Rachael put her arms around her and rocked her gently. "It's all right, dear, it's all right. We're here. I'll stay until you go back to sleep." It was only ten o'clock.

As Melissa slept, Boomer, still in his office, went over the motions to quash the search warrant and to suppress what the young lawyers had prepared. They would be overruled, but the issues would be saved for the trial court and for appeal if Billy was convicted. He called Jessica to tell her good-night. "Yes, the case is going well," he told her.

Hugh opened his third package of Camels and read the notes Bobby had given him of the interviews with Mathis and the dog warden. He was pleased with the progress so far. The dancers were out shaking their rattles, chanting calls.

Melvin sat in his poker room, staring at the walls, studying the routes and addresses as if they were tarot cards.

Billy Hinkler folded his hands behind his head and lay back on the narrow bunk, wondering what had happened to bring him to this place. He wished Melissa was here. He was scared.

Troy studied the lab reports of the most recent analysis. He didn't understand. The blood and hair found on the roof of the overhang didn't match the blood and hair taken from Billy Hinkler. The blood samples were of a different type, and the hair samples had different trace elements in their composition.

There was no match. He was stunned. He had depended on that analysis to lock up his case. He had been given credit in the press for developing the evidence that led to Billy's arrest. He knew if the case blew up on him now, he'd be the laughingstock of the Atlanta bar. Somehow, he had to keep the results under wraps long enough for Farley to develop other evidence. He could agree to bail, provided the defendant waived the preliminary hearing, but the public would view that as a sellout. He could agree to release the results to the defendant, provided they would remain confidential. Boomer, he knew, would see through that. He had only one choice: to not mention the results at the preliminary hearing and hope Boomer would forget or be afraid to ask about it. That was what he would do.

Don Farley reviewed the reports compiled by the task force members. The operation had developed no further evidence in the case against Billy Hinkler. He wished Billips and the commissioner had not moved so quickly in making the arrest.

Joseph Perelli, back home on trial leave, rubbed oil on Tommy's baseball glove.

"He'll need a good, soft glove when they play that team from the south side tomorrow," he told Arlene.

Atlanta began to shut down. Doors were locked, lights were out, and the children put safely in bed. The death of Tommy Perelli and the case against Billy had moved to the back page for a while, waiting for some new, dramatic development. The city was beginning to calm, but it could not forget.

Ralph Hensley rose quietly from his bed, careful not to disturb his wife, went to his locked gun cabinet, and took out the hunting knife with its gleaming blade. He smiled, remembering the special pleasure it had given him. He wrapped it and the extra key to Billy's Range Rover in a face towel and returned them to the cabinet. He felt a stirring inside, but he would have to wait.

"Time to get up," Mary Rachael whispered to Melissa. "My, it's nice to have a young person in the house again. After you shower and dress, we'll have some breakfast. Your things have arrived, and

I'll have Mavis bring them up right away so you'll have something to put on."

Melissa looked at the clock on the nightstand. It was ten o'clock. Mary Rachael opened the door leading to the garden, and Melissa heard the soft sounds of the Atlanta rain.

"Oh, my gosh! I've overslept. I meant to call and tell them I won't be in for work."

She knew they would be shorthanded, so she had planned to ask Mr. Hinkler if she could ride into work with him and give them time to hire a replacement. She would have to apologize later.

Melissa bathed hurriedly in a grand marble tub with gold faucets shaped like a swan. She wished she could take her time and soak in the warm water, but she knew Mrs. Hinkler was waiting breakfast for her.

During breakfast, Mary Rachael inquired, very tactfully, about her past.

"Are you from Atlanta, dear?"

Melissa liked the word. Nobody had ever called her "dear." It was reasonable for the Hinklers to want to know what kind of person they had invited into their home.

"Mrs. Hinkler—"

"Now, now, Melissa. You must call me Mary Rachael. Everybody else does."

Melissa looked away for a moment and then turned her eyes toward her and began.

"I'm going to be perfectly honest with you. I guess I have not been a very good person ..."

Over the next hour, Melissa told her everything—Harry and Pauline, the foster homes, the arrest, everything.

"I don't guess you ever knew anybody like me, did you?"

"Don't be so sure," she replied.

"Anyhow," Melissa continued, "I've been off the booze now for several months. That's under control. I've been going to Emory, taking a few hours. And, you know, for the first time in my life, I feel good about myself. I'll never go back to that life again. All I want to do is find my little sister, Margaret, get my degree, and forget all those bad times."

"I believe you will, Melissa. I believe you will."

"Now," Mary Rachael said, apparently unchanged by what she had heard, "we have a little shopping to do. You're going to need maternity clothes and a few accessories, and I took the liberty of setting a hair appointment for both of us. We'll have an enjoyable afternoon together. Tomorrow, we'll go see Billy." The next morning they did.

"Billy," she said, crying. "I'm sorry I haven't been here sooner. I wanted to, but I didn't know if you would want to see me."

"Melissa," he said, smiling broadly, "I knew you would come—at least I hoped you would. And then Dad told me yesterday you had called and that you were staying at the house. It's great! How have you been?"

"I'm dry, Billy, really dry," she said proudly. "I have a job, or at least I did have. And, Billy, I'm enrolled in college part time. Can you believe that? Billy, I'm sorry I left. I had to. But I'm here for you now, and I will be here for as long as you want me."

She did not tell him about the child. Somehow it didn't seem to be the right time.

CHAPTER 21

Boomer had forgotten it was "Emily's anniversary." He had always called it that as a way to separate himself from it. When he got home that afternoon, Emily was dressed for dinner.

"You forgot, didn't you?" she said, slightly annoyed, as he took off his coat and laid it across the sofa. "I knew you would, silly. With that old case and all. I bought this new outfit today, and I thought we would go out for dinner tonight if you're not too tired."

Boomer looked at her trying to figure out what she was talking about.

"And I went to the hairdresser's and got a new style. So do you like it?"

Her hair had been shortened so that it fell straight to her shoulders, covering her ears and curling upward slightly in the front. The stiff hair spray was gone, and her hair had been skillfully colored.

"Very attractive," he said truthfully.

Anything was better than the bird's nest she had worn on her head for so many years.

"All my other clothes are too big for me now that I've lost that ten pounds," she said proudly. "I saw Mary Rachael Hinkler at the stylist. She had some young girl with her she said was visiting. I never did understand who she was."

Emily took Boomer's coat from the sofa and started for the stairs.

"Why, Richard, what's this?" she said, taking the package from the coat. "You didn't forget, did you? I can't wait to open it, but I'll save it for after dinner. My, isn't it wrapped up pretty. It must be jewelry. You devil you. I thought you had forgotten," she said again.

"Damn," he said as he shaved. "Damn it, damn it, damn it."

He had meant to lock the pendant in the glove box, but he had forgotten and left it in his coat pocket.

That night after dinner, Emily got the surprise of her life.

"And it's from Tiffany's too. How charming." She leaned over and pecked him on the cheek.

"Boomer, are you ill? You've barely touched your dinner."

"I'm not hungry tonight," he muttered sardonically, glancing at the anniversary present hanging lazily against her bosom. Emily had won again.

"Richard, I probably shouldn't mention this on a festive occasion like this (festive?), but I wish you hadn't gotten into this Perelli thing. Charlene Poynter got me off in a corner at the garden club and told me everybody was talking about it. Apparently, word has gotten out about your fee—I don't know what it is, you never tell me things like that—but she said everybody was talking about, well, you and Troy, and all that mess—and how could you represent a child killer—and hoping you would lose the case and that he would be executed—well, it just took my breath away—all she said they were saying about you. It's got me about ashamed to show my face. But please understand I'm behind you 100 percent. The boy must be innocent, or you wouldn't represent him, would you?" He sensed uncertainty in her tone.

Boomer had already begun to notice it. During last week's golf game Pete Coleman had asked him, "Boomer, I noticed you were representing Hinkler's boy in that Perelli case. How can you stand to be in the same room with somebody like that, much less represent him? I mean, he killed that kid for no reason, man. Everybody that can read knows that."

The three waited for his answer.

"Well, you see, Pete—and you of all people should know this—we can't send people off to prison or execute them on the basis of street talk. Everybody has a right to counsel, and Billy is no exception; or maybe we should close the courthouse and go back to lynchings. Besides, I happen to think he's innocent."

"Yeah, he's innocent all right," Mitch Parsons said sarcastically. "Not from what I read in the papers."

Boomer looked at Coleman, angered by what they were doing to him.

"What if he came down with appendicitis, Coleman? It's ruptured and he's dying. Would you take his appendix out if he paid your fee?" Boomer asked pointedly.

"Hell, no. I might take my scalpel to his prick."

They laughed.

"Well, you're not much of a doctor then."

He replaced his club in his bag, started the golf cart, and drove to the clubhouse, leaving Pete standing with his nine iron in his hand.

"Screw that bunch," he whispered to himself as he drove away.

Boomer had even noticed a decided change among the parishioners at Sunday Mass. The Serafinis, who usually sat in the same pew beside him, had moved to the other side of the chapel. Even the priest looked at him queerly as he took Communion, hesitating for a moment before finally putting the wafer in his mouth. Even Bud noticed it.

"Everybody's giving you a hard time in this Perelli thing, aren't they, buddy?" he had said. "To hell with them. You do what seems right to you, no matter what the rest of them say. What do they know? Just hang in there, pal." Boomer had not known just how bad it was until Bud had offered that advice.

The thing that bothered Boomer most was Troy. He could live with what the others said, but Troy had been the thing in life he was proudest of. He missed the hurried lunches, the almost daily telephone calls.

"Big Boomer," Troy would say, "this is Little Bummer. How about buying my lunch today, old deep pockets?" Or, "Let me tell you a funny one. I was in Judge Lamprey's court this morning doing an arraignment—you know he's eighty years old—and right in the middle of my argument, he let out a big one. I mean, thunderous. He just looked at me and said, 'Excuse me, Troy. Go on—get to the point. I'm ready for a recess.' "

Boomer missed those calls. He missed Troy. He missed him terribly, and he was sorry people felt the way they did. He hadn't asked for the case. He had tried to refuse it. But he couldn't put that in the newspapers.

The next morning, Hugh called Boomer.

"As I told you earlier, old Larry talked to everybody on the list Billy gave you—you know, his so-called friends? Well, everybody but one—a Ralph Hensley. He's looked for him for four or five days. He's checked everything there is to check—phone, utilities, tax records, the whole smear. Well, he decided as a last resort to check court records for the third time. Now get this. He found a Ralph Hensley in the traffic computer, about the right age. Somebody had filed it under Hensley. You know, they keep those in the computer for so long. He gave an address that turned out to be a nursing home. Now, this was three weeks before Tommy was abducted. Hold on to your hat. Hensley was driving a 1996 Range Rover, plate number the same as Billy's, when he was stopped. He told the trooper he had "borrowed" the car. He was charged with speeding and no operator's license. Larry went back and checked the ticket and talked to the state police officer—this happened near the cabin, just on the main road—and he remembered Hensley having a girl with him but nobody else. Hensley established his identify with an outdated Illinois driver's license. The officer wrote him a warning ticket. The officer remembers this one because Hensley gave him a hard time and he started to take him in for drug testing. Apparently, this Hensley had access to the Range Rover. At least he did that night. Big problem, though. From that point the trail goes cold again."

Boomer was delighted. He could now show that the vehicle used to transport the body was driven at times by someone other than Billy. That was important evidence they had not had up to now. He would have to decide whether to save the information for trial or offer it at the preliminary hearing and go for bail.

CHAPTER 22

Boomer drove directly to the detention center to meet with Billy. He told him what they had learned and asked, "How did this fellow Ralph Hensley get the keys to your Range Rover? He obviously was driving it, and you weren't with him. Did you ever see any evidence it had been hot-wired? Did you let him use it or the cabin?"

Billy thought a minute.

"No," he replied. "Nobody had a key but me and Dad. We had the only keys. The Range Rover always stayed at the cabin with a '91 Chevy I had. We only used it off the main road. I don't guess I've started it three times in the last six months, and then only to see that the battery was up. Wait a minute! I remember something that might help. You see, I had met Ralph Hensley in a history class at Emory. I mean, we weren't friends or anything. Just talked some between classes. Well, I was in this bar downtown, and he came in and sat down. I told him he looked familiar, and we got to talking and remembered where we knew each other. We started drinking more and talking, and we met these two girls. We took them to the cabin. He drove his car, and I drove mine—not the Range Rover, the other one. It was in the garage at the cabin. Well, the next morning, after Ralph and the girls had gone, I started looking for my keys to the cabin and the two vehicles, and they were gone. I knew I had them in the house the night before, because I used them to unlock the cabin. I always put them on the kitchen counter. I looked everywhere but couldn't find them. I found an extra set in the Chevy and forgot about it, thinking they would show up or that one of the others had picked them up by mistake. The only other time I saw Ralph was when he showed up on Saturday afternoon—Melissa was there—and he had some trouble with the girl he was with and he left. I haven't seen him since. I didn't think to ask him about my keys. After that, I just stayed spaced out. I would stay sometimes at the cabin and sometimes with friends, drinking and tripping. I was away from the cabin a lot, I guess. But I always drove the Chevy—never the Range Rover."

Perfect, Boomer thought. He called Hugh.

"Look, this Hensley fellow may be the key to this whole case. Let's find him. Tell Larry to get over to Emory and do whatever he has to do to get into Hensley's school record and see if we can find out something about him. I want to avoid having to subpoena the records, because I don't want to tip off Troy or Farley."

Larry knew Emory would not permit him to look at Hensley's file without a court order. He figured the records going that far back were on microfilm or were computerized. He would have to begin by developing an understanding of how Emory's records were kept. He picked up the phone and called the registrar. He was given over to an assistant who was very cooperative.

"Mrs. Jones, I'm Bob Hendrickson with Calvar College in Tupelo, and I have been asked to make a survey of how other colleges and universities deal with records of graduated or discontinued students. My survey has found that some institutions maintain their records in original form; some use microfiche; some have computer programs; and some have a combination of those. What is Emory's preference?"

Jones explained their procedure.

"I see. And when do you purge a record from your active files, and what provisions do you make for storing the inactive files?"

She said that inactive files were purged after three years and put in storage.

"I see. Are those inactive files maintained in-house, or are they stored elsewhere?"

They were stored at a separate location, two buildings away at the archives.

"I see. Then they would be readily accessible if the need arose? Listen, you have been more help to us than you will ever know."

Larry had the information he needed. Hensley's file would be among the purged files. He knew now where to find it—if he could gain entrance. He did so by the method most familiar to him. He bribed a custodian.

Hensley's record contained only his high school transcript from Waukegan Township High School and one semester of failing grades at Emory. Nothing else. Some fool had left the application for admission out of the file. He hurriedly searched the files of the other Hensley students hoping it had been misfiled, but he could not find it.

"Damn it," he muttered, closing the file and replacing it in the file cabinet. "Another dead end."

"Hugh, I bombed out again. Yeah, I got into it. Nothing but a high school transcript from a high school in Waukegan, Illinois, and a semester at Emory. Okay, I'll keep digging."

He called Waukegan High School admissions and was told that the school maintained only the grade reports of each student, which contained only the full name of the student and the date of graduation. Yes, they might find a yearbook, but it might not have more than a group picture of Hensley and the rest of the class. A picture of Hensley! That was what he needed.

He flew to Chicago, rented a car, and drove to Waukegan and the school library. There he found a dingy photograph of Ralph Hensley with full beard and shoulder-length hair.

Larry tore the page out of the book, put it between the pages of a magazine, replaced the annual on the shelf, and made the rounds of teachers. The ones who remembered Hensley at all recalled him as surly, insolent, and a very poor student—an "underachiever." His high school transcript had shown that.

Larry flew back to Atlanta, armed with a picture of a bearded Ralph Hensley and nothing else.

"This guy's as elusive as a handful of snot," he told Hugh.

Larry took the page from the annual to a photographer and had it enlarged to an eleven by thirteen. He took a negative to an anthropologist at the university and asked him to remove the beard and shorten the hair. Without the beard and long hair, Hensley looked very much like any other high school senior. Larry took copies of each photograph to Boomer, Bobby, and Melvin, who placed them in their files. Larry retained the negative in his file.

"I just can't go any further with this bird," Larry told Hugh. "I've been everywhere but Jerusalem looking for him. I don't know why—or even if it is intentional—but this guy hasn't left a clue as to his whereabouts. If the trail didn't go all the way back to Waukegan and his high school yearbook, I'd swear to Caesar this Ralph Hensley's name is an alias."

"Okay, Larry, you've done a heck of a job getting this far," Hugh said. "We have our suspect at least. We may have to get to him through the back door."

Melvin racked the balls, chalked his stick, placed the cue ball behind the two diamonds, and broke the rack of nine balls. He had bought the pool table eight years earlier and had it set in his poker room for practice. It had been a very good investment, indeed. Through practice he had become one of the best nine ball players in the South, winning tournament after tournament. He had been able to make a very good living traveling to remote towns, letting the suckers win a few games to get their confidence up, and then walking away with a roll of bills, always playing barely well enough to win, by letting the suckers win enough to keep their nerve up. As his reputation grew, the suckers slowly disappeared, and he was relegated to tournament play and recreation. He deftly pocketed the nine balls in rotation, beginning with the one ball.

Melvin laid the cue on the table, walked to the kitchen, and took a beer from the refrigerator. He had finished his assignment at the school and had contributed nothing to the investigation. His interviews of Tommy's teachers had produced nothing. The busing routines were regimented, and Fentrell had followed the routine faithfully on the four days he had observed him.

Still, something bothered him. Something kept him going back, time after time, to the routes and the pupil drop-off points. He had gazed at the streets and stops posted on his walls until he had memorized them. "1042 Richards Street, Student No. 1, Jenny Wilburn, distance from school, 2.6 miles, time ten minutes... 1062 Mapother Street..."

According to his observations, Tommy should have exited the bus between 4:15 and 4:20 if the routine was followed and all the scheduled stops were made—unless of course, there were delays. He was intrigued by Bobby's discovery that no one had, apparently, seen Tommy after he had gotten off the bus. Maybe that was not so significant, but it did leave his whereabouts between 4:20 and 5:30, the time his mother had arrived at home, to conjecture.

Surely somebody in the neighborhood would have seen him. They knew he hadn't gone home, because, according to the newspaper accounts of the abduction, the house key was still hidden in its usual place. He wondered how Tommy could have been abducted without somebody in the neighborhood observing it. And what about this fellow Hensley and the Range Rover? Where did that fit into the picture? Somewhere in all this there must be an answer. He didn't' know what it was. He didn't have a clue.

CHAPTER 23

"Hi, Pop. How's it going?"

It was the first time Boomer had talked to Eddy since the episode in Chattanooga and Boomer's call to him the next day. He clearly had said nothing to Emily, or Boomer would know it. He had been afraid Eddy was angry, but he sounded friendly enough.

"I'm sure you've heard about Troy by now," Boomer said. "He's very angry with me, and I guess I understand why, but that doesn't keep me from being disappointed. He doesn't know all the circumstances, and he didn't give me a chance to tell him. I didn't really want to get into the Perelli case, but I didn't have a choice."

"I don't know the circumstances, and I don't need to. I'm sure you had your reasons for getting into it. When he thinks about it, Troy will come around. He loves you, Pop, like I do. Maybe he's afraid of you, like I used to be—a little anyhow—afraid you'll whip his arrogant little ass in that case."

Edward hesitated a moment.

"I guess you know there's a lot of shitty talk going around about a sellout. They're saying you got a $2 million fee from Hinkler and that you and Troy are going to split it. Shit like that. A friend told me about it. Things have quieted down some, but there's still an awful lot of anger out there over this case, and I guess they're taking some of it out on you."

184

"Well, that goes with the turf, I guess," Boomer said gravely. That cliché didn't make him feel any better. "But you know, Eddy, I can't let that worry me. This is what I do, and if people don't like it, I guess that's just too bad. Billy Hinkler is a pitiful little fellow. He didn't do this thing. I know he didn't. Don't tell Troy or anybody—I can't give you any details—but there have been some developments in this case that convince me they've charged the wrong man. Billips and the police might have gotten in a hurry and jumped the gun just to placate the public. They've given Troy credit for the arrest so if the case bombs, he'll have to take the heat. Anyhow, in spite of the talk—and you'll hear more of it—I'm glad I'm in this case."

"Well, whatever happens," Edward said, "I wanted to call and let you know I'm with you all the way. And I'm going to call Troy and tell him he ought to be ashamed of himself."

"How's Mother?" Eddy changed the subject. "She told Mary about the anniversary present. Pretty nice from what I've heard. A little gift straight out of the conscience, I'm sure," he said, laughing. "Be careful, Pop."

If there had been any doubt that Edward had recognized him in Chattanooga, it was gone. "Thanks," was all Boomer could say.

"The other reason I called was to invite you and Mother to dinner tomorrow night. It's been a while since we've seen you two, and, besides, Mary thought you could use a little break."

"Thanks. We'll try to be there."

"By the way," Eddy concluded, "I wanted to tell you I got that little problem with the stock all straightened out, and I wanted to thank you again for your offer to help."

Boomer was glad Edward had called. Without Troy, there really wasn't anyone to talk to in a personal way except for Jessi. That was different. Bud had been in a long trial, and he didn't even have him to talk to.

Damn, life is perverse, he thought, hanging up the phone. Eddy had called to comfort him—to let him know he was behind him. Troy was out there with his butt hanging out—all swelled up. Life was a bitch, no doubt about it. He went back to reviewing the three written motions he would file at the preliminary hearing tomorrow.

Boomer would have been amused if he had known about it. Troy was called to Billips's office that day for a report and discussion of tomorrow's hearing.

"Troy, the preliminary hearing is set in the Perelli case tomorrow, and, with the election coming up next year, I thought the exposure might be good for us. I wonder if you might need a little help in handling it. I'm not suggesting taking the case away from you; please understand that. But you know the talk that's going around about you and Boomer. The public just doesn't understand. It's a very high-profile case, and I thought it might help if I participated. It would let the public know I was keeping an eye on the case. I thought it might take a little of the pressure off you. I want you to think about it for a few minutes while we go over our case."

Troy could feel the blood flow into his cheeks. He was stunned.

"Mr. Billips, if you have any doubt about my ability to handle the hearing, or if my representation of this office in the case is causing you any concern or is hurting our case, I should be happy to withdraw."

Troy was aware of the ugly rumors Billips had alluded to. He had not wanted to bring the charges against Billy solely on the strength of the evidence obtained from a search of the cabin and the Range Rover. In fact, he had urged Billips not to approve the warrant for Billy's arrest until Farley had a chance to look for evidence connecting Billy directly to the murder. Besides, they knew Billy was undergoing treatment and all they had to do was to put a hold on his release from the treatment center as a material witness and place a guard at his door. Captain Thomas had agreed but was overruled by his superiors.

Troy and Thomas had been right. Almost three weeks had gone by, and the police had not found any further evidence linking Billy to the crime. Troy knew the evidence against Billy was tenuous, but he was hopeful that the Range Rover evidence was enough to hold Billy to the grand jury, where the proceedings could be delayed, giving Farley more time to develop the case. He was not sure it was strong enough to sustain a denial of bail, if the motion was made.

"Before we decide whether I'm needed tomorrow, why don't we

go over the case a little bit," Billips said, leaning back in his chair and putting the tips of his fingers together. "Troy, I think the … what was it, a jeep?"

"A Range Rover," Troy replied.

"Range Rover, yes, Range Rover. I think that evidence is pretty strong, don't you? I mean, the crime lab's analysis of paint and oil puts the vehicle at the place where the body was dropped. Then there's the witness from Chicago who saw it. And the fibers from the floor mat matched those taken from Billy's body. I mean, is she strong? Then there's the cabin where Billy lived. I mean, the DNA stuff shows that Tommy was killed there. Add that to the Range Rover stuff, and bingo, you've got your killer, Billy Hinkler."

Troy tried to conceal his annoyance.

"We have all that, but it's not that simple. Let's look at it the way Richard Boomer is going to argue it. Assuming both the Range Rover and the cabin were possessed by Billy and were under his control, does it necessarily follow he was the killer? Sure, he had keys to both and used them both. But so did Buck Hinkler. And we don't know who else. You can be sure Richard Boomer is trying to find that out. The vehicle is registered to Buck, and title to the cabin property is in Buck's name. So who's guilty? I mean, I know Billy killed this boy. I'm convinced of it. But we have to prove it. The big problem is we can't put Billy in that Range Rover when the body was dropped off, and we can't put him in that cabin when Tommy was killed. We can't tie him to the abduction. We can't establish any relationship between him and Tommy. We don't have the murder weapon. We have no evidence showing Billy had the propensity to commit such an act or that he had the opportunity to do so. We have no statements by him against interest. And we certainly have no eyewitnesses. All we have are the Range Rover and the cabin and a few pieces of forensics that we can't tie to Billy yet. You see, I haven't told you the worst. I just learned the blood found at Stone Mountain was not Billy's type, and the hair was not a match. If the killer is the one that hit his head on that rock, then we've charged the wrong man."

Billips thought a minute.

"Troy, it looks like you've got the case pretty well in hand. I didn't know there was that much to it. I was going to cancel some very important appointments to be there tomorrow, but I'm convinced you don't really need me. I know you will do a splendid job representing this office, as you always do."

Troy went to his office and began going through reports from the crime lab, preparing for tomorrow's hearing and Forest's testimony. He had a feeling he had not had in any case he had ever handled. It was kind of a dread—a feeling of impending embarrassment. He had told Boomer he was going to kick his ass. It was beginning to look like he would have to climb a ladder to do it.

Just then a courier arrived, carrying a sealed manila envelope from Farley's office. He opened the package. Inside were eight reports from the Federal Bureau of Investigation of the examination of latent prints taken from the cabin and three reports of prints taken from the Range Rover. The bureau had identified three of the prints taken from the cabin as belonging to Billy Hinkler, Atlanta, Georgia; Marty Hightower, Atlanta, Georgia; and a Ralph Hensley, Waukegan, Illinois. Marty Hightower had been incarcerated in the detention center during a period beginning three days before Tommy's abduction and ending two days after his body was found. The investigation had been unable to find Ralph Hensley in the Atlanta area.

Only two of the prints found in the Range Rover matched prints on file with the bureau. They belonged to Billy and to Ralph Hensley. Hensley had been fingerprinted following his arrest in 1984 in Waukegan for unlawful sexual contact with a minor under twelve.

"Damn," Troy barked into the telephone. "What does all this mean, Farley?"

"It means we may have another suspect," Farley replied. "We could have the wrong man, or maybe there were two of them. We did a pull on a Ralph Hensley. He's in town somewhere—picked up just a few weeks ago for speeding, driving Billy's Range Rover. He gave a false address—a nursing home, I believe. Didn't have a current driver's license either."

Sometime in the course of the case, Boomer would make a motion for discovery. Troy knew that. The discovery order would require Troy to produce all exculpatory evidence in his file that might tend to prove Billy innocent. Included in Troy's compliance with the order would be the print evidence showing that at least one other person, a Ralph Hensley, had been inside both the Range Rover and the cabin. If he asked Farley the right questions tomorrow, he would even get the information then. Boomer would have a heyday with that, and so would the press. It was certainly exculpatory. Anybody could see that.

Troy's secretary came into the office with another large envelope, delivered by courier from Getty and Jacobs. He opened it. Enclosed was a motion, supported by a thirty-eight-page legal memorandum, attacking the searches of the Range Rover and the cabin and asking that all articles or other evidence be suppressed and excluded; a motion for an inventory and full description of all articles or other evidence seized during the search, also supported by a long memorandum; and a motion for bail, arguing that the offense, based wholly on circumstantial evidence, was bailable, and asking that bail be fixed at fifty thousand dollars.

Troy expected his first two motions would be overruled. He hoped the judge would also deny bail. If Billy was released, it would cause an uproar and would signal to the public that there was something wrong with the state's case.

"Damn it," Troy said audibly.

He had planned to go home early and get some rest before tomorrow's hearing. Now he would be in the office law library with his secretary most of the night getting up responses to Boomer's motions. He knew without any question whatever that Boomer, by serving the documents at the last minute, had planned it that way.

Boomer made his way through the crowd and into the Fulton County courtroom, laid his briefcase on the table, and nodded to the clerk and the court reporter.

"Good morning, Ms. Elliott. Good morning, Ms. Price."

Both women spoke coolly, turning their heads away immediately. Boomer felt their resentment. Shortly thereafter Troy arrived, making a point of not looking at or speaking to Boomer. Then the bailiff brought Billy in, his hands and feet shackled by clanging chains, and directed him to sit down between Boomer and Boomer's law clerk.

"Take the shackles off my client," Boomer ordered the bailiff.

He complied, signaling to the guards in the rear of the courtroom. The room, already full, began to buzz like a swarm of wasps. Boomer heard somebody in the audience behind him.

"There is the jerk." Boomer didn't know if he was pointing to him or to Billy.

The courtroom grew suddenly quiet as the door to Judge Lamprey's chambers opened and the Bailiff announced, "This Fulton County court is now in session. Honorable Judge Lamprey presiding. Please be seated."

Judge Lamprey sat erect behind a mahogany bench, pulled his chair forward, and peered toward the counsel table to confirm the presence of the accused and his counsel, and the prosecuting attorney. He looked then to the audience packed into the small courtroom. Some he knew, and some he didn't. There was the crime writer from *The Atlanta Constitution*. He recognized him. Then there were the TV reporters from three of the local stations. He had seen a van parked near the courthouse with the name and logo of a TV network, and he understood reporters were arriving in town to cover the hearing from various news outlets around the country and from wire services. They sat in their seats with their notepads on their laps and pencils poised, ready to write.

The case could hardly have escaped notice by the national press. It had all the ingredients for a major and ongoing news story: "Handsome Child Murdered and Mutilated by Banker's Son." He had wondered how long it would be before the attention of the country was focused on the case. Added to that was the unique and somewhat suspicious confrontation between father defender and prosecutor son.

Lamprey calculated that half the courtroom was filled with newsmen and newswomen. Most of the rest, he speculated, were blood and gore freaks. Also, there in the front row were Buck Hinkler and his wife, Mary Rachael. He recognized her from pictures he had seen on the society page of the *Constitution*. Lamprey knew how difficult it was for them to be there—an old Atlanta family, highly respected in the community, not a breath of scandal around them anywhere, until now. Here they were, their only son accused of a heinous crime, the quietude of their lives shattered, perhaps forever.

He wondered if it was true what they were saying—that Buck Hinkler had paid Boomer a two million dollar fee. He guessed it was probably true. That was more than he made in twenty-five years.

He looked also for the Perellis. They were not there, spared the ordeal of reliving the tragedy. They would spend enough time riding the hard spectators' benches in the trial court and listening to endless contention and bickering, Tommy's memory lost in the sea of motions, objections, arguments, and rulings.

Having absorbed the drama and gravity of the moment, Lamprey looked at Troy, who was flipping pages of scribbled notes on a legal pad. He appeared nervous and apprehensive.

"What says the State of Georgia?" Judge Lamprey inquired.

"The State of Georgia is ready, Your Honor," Troy said in a firm, high voice.

Lamprey looked then at Boomer, sitting there calm and erect, a slight smile on his face. His short-cropped white hair gleamed in the light from the window beside him, almost luminescent.

"Gentlemen, Mr. Hinkler is charged with the capital offense of murder in a warrant procured by the State of Georgia. Let the record show Mr. Richard Boomer appears in behalf of the Defendant and Troy Boomer appears representing the State of Georgia. This is not a trial. It is a preliminary hearing. We are here only for the purpose of determining whether there is sufficient evidence to believe defendant is guilty of the offense he is charged with and whether he should be held to answer to a Grand Jury; also whether he is entitled to bail. The Court can and does take judicial notice that Troy Boomer is the son of Richard Boomer so we must determine whether either of you is disqualified under the Rules from representing your clients in this preliminary hearing. Let the record show that Richard Boomer has filed a Waiver signed by his client, waiving any disqualification which might arise because of that familial relationship which I find to be sufficient. Turning now to Mr. Troy Boomer and his representation of the State of Georgia in this case. At times under the Rules, because of such familial relationship, a prosecutor may be disqualified. I find in the record no motion by him to recuse. Does either party desire to file such a motion either orally or written? Let the record show that both parties answered "No." In that case, we are now ready to proceed. If either party wishes to demur to the representation, let him then raise the question in trial court which seems to me to be the more appropriate forum in view of the state of the record."

Both parties having announced ready, Judge Lamprey turned to the court reporter.

"Then we will be on the record in the case of the *State of Georgia v. William J. (Billy) Hinkler.* Let the record show the defendant is present and represented by the Honorable Richard Boomer of Atlanta, and that the State of Georgia is represented by the Honorable Troy Boomer of the district attorney's office. Before we begin with evidence, gentlemen, let's dispose of a couple of matters that need to be addressed. Mr. Richard Boomer, I have read your very scholarly and erudite motions and briefs to quash the search warrants under which the Range Rover possessed by the defendant and the cabin he occupied were searched. You also ask in that motion that all evidence seized in those searches be suppressed under the authority of *Map v. Ohio* and other cases. I received those only this morning, but I have looked at them briefly. Mr. Troy Boomer, I have read your equally scholarly and erudite briefs in opposition to the motions. Frankly, gentlemen, I'm no constitutional lawyer, but I am enough of a judge to recognize a close question when I see it. I will overrule the motions to quash and to suppress without further argument from either party. I also overrule the motion for inventory along with it, for now. The accused will, of course, have an opportunity to raise these issues again in the trial court, which will have an opportunity to give the issue more careful attention." He paused and poured a glass of water.

"Now, the defendant, through counsel, has filed a motion for bail," he continued. "I will not rule on that motion until I have heard all the proof each of you has to offer at this hearing. In other words, we will use this as a bail hearing. Let me set some parameters. I begin by reminding you the warrant charges a capital offense, punishable by life imprisonment or death. Mr. Richard Boomer, if I find that the evidence presented by Georgia, taken as true, raises a reasonable probability that the defendant committed the crime charged, I will deny bail. If, however, Georgia's evidence is only slight—even if it is sufficient to hold him to the grand jury—I may allow bail, unless he presents a danger to the community. As you both know, gentlemen, bail is a discretionary matter, and I will try in exercising that discretion to do it fairly, taking into consideration the presumption of innocence. Gentlemen, this may not be black-letter Georgia law, but it's the law in Judge Lamprey's court, so I need not hear arguments from counsel on the issue of bail. I have considered the fine briefs filed by both of you on this issue, setting forth Georgia law, but I will be guided in my decision by the rules I have just articulated." Judge Lamprey leaned back in his chair.

"Now, are there other matters to be taken up—any motions, anything, before we get started with the evidence?"

Both counsel shook their heads.

"How long do you anticipate this will take?"

"The state's case will be brief, Your Honor. We have only two witnesses, Detective Ron Farley and Dr. Forest of the state crime lab."

Boomer stood.

"Whether we offer evidence will depend on the state's evidence. If we do offer evidence, it will be brief and should not take over forty-five minutes to an hour."

Lamprey again looked across the room.

"Let me explain to those present that this is not a trial. It is a preliminary hearing only. Its only purpose is to see if there is sufficient evidence to even hold the defendant to answer the Fulton County grand jury. And, in this case, to see if he should be admitted to bail. If I hold him to answer the grand jury, that doesn't mean I think he is guilty. That decision is up to a jury."

There was silence.

"Very well then. Let the State of Georgia call its first witness."

"Georgia calls Detective Ron Farley of the Atlanta Police Department," Troy announced.

Boomer leaned over and whispered to his associate, "This guy Farley's a real hothead. You could fry a turkey egg on his bald head in January. He's arrogant and tough."

Farley took the stand. When Troy asked his name, Farley answered in a quiet tone. His description of his duties with the Atlanta Police Department was monotonous and halfhearted. Boomer whispered again to the associate and to Billy, "Something's going on here. That's not the Ron Farley I know."

For the next thirty minutes Farley, in the same subdued manner, related how the Atlanta police had received the report that Tommy was missing. He described the four-day effort, joined by groups of private citizens, to find Tommy. He told of the discovery of Tommy's body at Stone Mountain Park on the fourth day after he disappeared. He did not, Boomer noticed, describe the work of the crime scene technicians on the first day the body was discovered or the blood, hair, and other forensic evidence discovered that first day. Boomer whispered again to the associate,

"No mention of blood or hair. Means one of two things. Either there was no match, or Troy expects to bring it in through Forest."

Farley also described the later discovery of paint and oil from Billy's Range Rover at the Stone Mountain site and the search of the vehicle, which contained fibers matching those found on Tommy's body. Boomer noticed there was no mention of fingerprints on the vehicle.

Detective Farley then told of the search of the cabin, which revealed blood identified as coming from Tommy Perelli, but, again, he made no mention of fingerprints. Boomer knew Billy's fingerprints must have been found in both the vehicle and the cabin unless they had been wiped clean. He wondered why Farley had not mentioned them. He surmised there must have been other prints of third persons in one or both places that the state was not yet ready to tell him about. Maybe they'd found fingerprints of a third person, such as Ralph Hensley, and didn't want to alert that person for fear he might flee. He didn't know what, but something was wrong with Farley, and something was missing in Troy's case.

Boomer settled back, relaxed, and listened to Farley drone on and on as Troy struggled to put his case on without revealing the results of the blood and hair analysis or the fingerprint reports from the bureau, which Boomer knew he must surely have. Boomer knew he now had his weapon. He could use it in this proceeding and in the press interviews he knew would come after the hearing. He could argue to the judge that the analysis of blood and hair was exculpatory and that it showed Billy was not the assailant. If the fingerprint reports showed other people driving the Range Rover, that was exculpatory evidence also. His hopes for bail for Billy were much better than they had been before the beginning of the hearing. He must, however, proceed very cautiously. He didn't want to spook the real killer.

As he was finishing with Farley, Boomer looked over at Troy. His shirt collar was wet with perspiration, and he repeatedly swabbed his forehead with his handkerchief.

"So, you're going to kick my sweet ass," Boomer whispered to himself. *Well, old buddy, you're the one that's going to get his ass kicked,* he thought, angered for an instant by the memory of those words.

As he watched Troy deftly trying to conclude the testimony of the subdued Farley, sweating profusely, his voice high but strong and piercing, Boomer's mind suddenly turned from the case. He saw Troy, his eyes red from crying, in the top of the apple tree in the backyard of the house where they once lived.

"I can't get down, Daddy," he had said tearfully.

Boomer climbed the tree, took his trembling body in his arms, and helped him to the ground. Troy was up that apple tree again today. Somehow he had to help him down. He knew if the analysis of the blood and hair were revealed to the press, all hell would break loose. He could see the headlines.

Troy knew it too. He knew he would be mortally injured in the eyes of the public. Maybe that was why Farley was so quick to give him credit for Billy's arrest.

Troy finished, and Boomer stood. He knew what he would do.

"Judge, Your Honor, defendant, with your leave of course, would like to forego cross-examination of this witness, subject to recalling him for cross in the course of our evidence if we present any."

"Hearing no objection by the state, your motion is *sustained*."

If the judge granted bail, there would be no need to recall Farley for the information. That would avoid the risk of alerting the real killer to the presence of evidence exculpating Billy and, at the same time, help Troy out of that apple tree. Boomer already knew there was not a match of blood and hair and that the Range Rover probably contained fingerprints other than Billy's on the driver's side of the vehicle. He had not seen the evidence, but he knew it was there, unless, of course, Forest brought it out. He did not.

After Troy had finished with Forest and announced finished with his presentation, Boomer rose again, knowing what he would do.

"Your Honor, before cross-examination, we wish to renew our motion for bail. If I may, I would like to say a few words of argument in support of that motion."

"Your request is granted. The court will hear from both parties."

"May it please the court," Boomer began, "let me start by saying the state's case against my client is wholly circumstantial. It is based entirely on the fact that the cabin usually occupied by my client was the location where the crime was apparently committed and that the Range Rover, which remained at the cabin for use by the Hinklers off the road, was used to transport the body to Stone Mountain. Now both those facts are probably true from what I can tell. At least we can assume that for purposes of this argument. But that doesn't mean my client killed this child. There is not one scintilla of evidence placing my client, personally, at the cabin when the murder was committed. No eyewitnesses. Apparently no forensics; otherwise, we would have heard about them. Nor is there any witness who will place Billy in the Range Rover at the time the body was taken to Stone Mountain. Again, no eyewitness and no forensics that we are told about. The state's case against Billy is based entirely and completely on the fact that Billy sometimes drove the Range Rover; that it was parked at the cabin where he lived; and that the crime was committed at the place where he usually resided—that is, the cabin. Under court rulings, which we need not cite, there can be no legal presumptions of guilt based purely on remote ownership or possession of the instrumentalities used in commission of a crime." He paused and then continued.

"Using the standards already articulated by you, we submit the state has failed to sustain its burden of showing, with reasonable probability, that Billy committed this awful crime. We, therefore, ask that the accused, based on the state's evidence, be freed upon a failure to show probable cause or, in the alternative, that he be freed on fifty thousand dollars' bail or such other bail as you deem appropriate. Let me conclude by saying there is no evidence that Billy is a risk to society. While Billy has a history of substance abuse, he has absolutely no record of violent behavior."

Troy argued, emotionally, that while the evidence was indeed circumstantial, it gave rise to a reasonable implication that Billy was the assailant. He argued that the public had an abiding interest in protecting children from such heinous acts, and he insisted that it would be dangerous to release Billy from custody and "put him back on the streets, where he may kill again."

"Gentlemen, I have heard your arguments," Judge Lamprey began. "I have concluded that the evidence offered by the State of Georgia is sufficient to hold the accused to answer to the grand jury. I do not find from the state's evidence, however, the necessary quantum of evidence to hold the defendant without bail. I am concerned, however, with the public safety. I will fashion what I believe to be a reasonable alternative to customary bail. I will put restrictions on his release. I will order bail in the amount of one million dollars. As a condition of release, I order that the defendant undergo psychiatric examination and that he enter a rigid program of psychological surveillance by a certified psychiatrist, who will report to the court in writing every ten days. The defendant will bear the cost of that. I direct as a further condition of bail that he refrain from the use of alcohol or drugs and that he be tested by the appropriate agency at least weekly for the presence in his blood of alcohol or drugs. I further order that the defendant be confined to the residence of his parents during the hours from 6:00 p.m. until 7:00 a.m. and that one or both of his parents be present with the defendant, in or out of the home, at all times during the day or night."

Boomer stood. "Your Honor, in view of that ruling, the defendant will forego the presentment of evidence."

"Very well," the Judge stated. "Is there anything else, gentlemen? If not, this hearing is adjourned."

The courtroom was in pandemonium.

"Damn, what guts," Boomer said to the associate. "This judge is going to catch pure hell for letting Billy have bail, and he knows it. I believe that's the most courageous thing I've seen a judge do in my thirty years at the bar. Somehow, we've got to vindicate this judge and that decision, and the best way to do it is to prove Billy is not guilty. We can start, Buck, by making sure every condition of bail is met. Don't let this man out of your sight. If he is caught somewhere without one of you, he will go back to jail and the judge will have shit on his face."

Boomer packed the files again in his briefcase, turned and shook hands with Billy, and received a warm hug from Mary Rachael. He looked at Melissa.

"I don't believe I know who you are."

"We'll tell you all about it soon." Buck grinned as he took Melissa and Mary Rachael by the arms.

"Billy, I'll be back down this afternoon to post that bail as soon as Boomer makes the arrangements and tells me what to do. Son, you'll be in your own bed tonight."

Boomer made his way through the crowd as the bailiff once again shackled Billy. On the outside of the courthouse he saw Troy being interviewed by the news people who had gathered around him. Boomer imagined they would ask for his reaction to the allowance of bail, and what Judge Lamprey meant when he said there was not such a reasonable probability of Billy's guilt to justify the denial of bail. Troy was definitely on the defensive. He was up the apple tree, but he was old enough now to know how to get down on his own. If he panicked, Boomer would be there to set him on the ground again.

Boomer knew the press people would be waiting for him, waiting to hear the rooster crow. He would have something to crow about. He could even rub it in a little. It would be sweet after what Troy had said to him. But he would not. He turned and went back into the courthouse. Buck, Mary Rachael, and Melissa were coming out.

"Come on," Boomer said. "Let's go out the back way. The dogs have a young fox at bay. I don't want to be there for the kill."

"Boomer," Buck said as they reached their cars, "see why I had to have you? Listen, Billy's going to be home tonight, and we're planning a little welcome home party. Nothing fancy—no drinks, of course. We want you and Emily to come over. We want you there if you can possibly make it. You wanted to know who Melissa is. Well, you'll get to know her tonight if you come. She's been at our house for a few days now. We love her—best thing that's happened in our home for a long time."

"I'll talk to Emily. She might have plans already, but I'll be there even if I have to come by myself."

"Go to the Hinklers?" Emily recoiled. "Go to the Hinklers' home to a welcome home party for Billy? Out of jail? How trashy. How tacky. Richard, you can get these people you represent out of jail, but don't expect me to jump in bed with them. Hinklers or no Hinklers, I'm not going. Not on your life."

Boomer laughed indulgently.

"Back to your normal form, I see. I knew all this sweetness shit couldn't last."

Boomer was surprised when he arrived at the Hinklers'. There were more than thirty people there—most of them friends who just dropped by after hearing the news of Billy's release.

Boomer had been right. The lead story on the six o'clock news began its coverage:

"New Doubts Raised in Perelli Case."

A somber-looking reporter, standing outside the courthouse, summarized the preliminary hearing and Billy's release on bail. After a brief interview of Troy, she concluded the report.

"Today's events raise questions, frightening in their implications: Is Tommy Perelli's killer still out there? Could it be that the wrong man has been arrested and charged?"

Troy reached his tiny office and slouched back into his chair. He was tired and embarrassed by the outcome of the court proceedings and Billy's release on bail. He had given the case all that he had but that was not enough. He comforted himself by remembering that the case to that point was wholly circumstantial and that his opponent, Richard Boomer, was probably the best criminal lawyer in the State of Georgia. But there had been no giants slain in the court room that day.

Troy found a letter in the mail from Dr. Andrew Miller. He had written Dr. Miller telling him of Hinkler's arrest and providing to him such information as he had which related to Hinkler's life and asking him how the arrest might affect his profile. Troy opened the envelope and read its contents:

Mr. Troy Boomer
Assistant District Attorney
County of Fulton
162 Peachtree Avenue
Atlanta, Georgia 40504

I am surprised to learn of the arrest of Billy Hinkler for the brutal killing of young Tommy Perelli. Thank you for the information you sent of the accused. As you may apprehend from my report, there are certain accepted markers that are considered to be of help in identifying a violent predator. Those are shared with you in my report beginning with page six, Conclusions, Paragraphs 1, 3, 5 and 8 with other aberrant conduct also listed therein.

Without evidence of such behavior a diagnosis of violent pedophilia would be difficult if not impossible to make. You mentioned no such evidence in your letter. I have reviewed what information you have provided to me relating to Billy Hinkler. I can find nothing in those papers leading me to believe that Billy Hinkler is a violent pedophile inclined to commit such barbarities or that he has any one of the other.

I might say that criminal profiles are best utilized as an aid to identify suspects that have not yet been arrested. As you know, they're not admissible as evidence in criminal trials.

"That's the end of that," Troy murmured. He must remember, when things calm down and he has more time, to write and thank Dr. Miller for his help.

People kept coming up to Boomer and congratulating him on the "victory." He really had done little to bring about Billy's release on bond, other than to make a short argument pointing out the deficiencies in Troy's case. He came out of the hearing encouraged. He had ammunition in his arsenal that he didn't know he had before going into the hearing. He was totally and absolutely convinced of that. Barring some unexpected development, he knew now he would win the case of *State of Georgia v. William R. (Billy) Hinkler*. But Billy's release on bail was only the first step in the long and arduous journey to total exoneration. The Rain Dancers—Hugh, Bobby, Melvin, and Larry—would shake their rattles and do the dance they did so well. He couldn't depend on deficiencies in the state's case. He still must be prepared to offer strong defenses, pointing to Billy's innocence, in order to overcome the natural reluctance of any jury to free any man accused of such an atrocious act.

Boomer knew that really the only way out of all this—for Billy, for himself, for the Hinklers, for Troy—was to apprehend and convict the real killer. Only then would the public's hunger for vengeance be satisfied. There would always be those, even among lawyers, who would say that Billy was guilty, but lucky enough to have parents rich enough to buy him out of trouble; that Troy had used his law license to cleverly put a killer back on the streets; or that Troy was impetuous, incompetent, neglectful, or just a crook who sold out to the Hinklers. No, it would not be enough just to acquit Billy. The rain must come down in torrents and wash away all vestiges of this sorry business for total justice to have its way.

Boomer was standing by the punch bowl getting a cup of juice.

"Hi, Pop." The familiar voice startled him. He turned around and faced Eddy and Mary. "Congratulations, Pop."

Hinkler had called Eddy, knowing that Troy could not be there and that Emily probably would not come. He had noticed the melancholy that overtook Boomer near the end of the hearing. Hinkler wanted Eddy there. Boomer needed him, he knew. And he was right.

"Where's Mom?" Eddy asked. "No, don't tell me. I think I can guess."

CHAPTER 24

Boomer went into the restaurant, Bud waddling along beside him, talking excitedly and throwing his arms in wild, emphatic gestures.

"You did a helluva piece of work yesterday. Only Richard Boomer could have persuaded an elected judge to turn Billy out on bond. I'm sure you have read the editorial in today's paper, giving the judge hell for—how did they put it?"

Boomer interrupted.

"The editorial said, 'Finding enough evidence to hold him to the grand jury but releasing him on bond was like letting a rabid dog run the streets, foaming at the mouth, while waiting to bite somebody.' Well, Billy Hinkler's no rabid dog, and he's not foaming at the mouth."

Boomer had hoped Billy's release and Judge Lamprey's statements approving bail would soften some of the sentiment against Billy and against him as his counsel. The opposite had been true. He noticed after the hearing that the clerk and court reporter had shown their disapproval by looking at Troy and lifting their eyes toward the ceiling in disbelief. At motion hour this morning, the chickens had gathered around him, pecking at his wounded flesh.

"Well," Robinson had said jealously, "there's Merlin. Pulled the rabbit right out of the hat, didn't you, Slick? I just hope little Billy stays out of trouble."

"Go screw yourself, Robinson, and tend to your own cases," Boomer had said, grabbing the spongy Robinson by the lapels and drawing him closer.

As the waitress led them to the table, he heard someone whisper, "That's Hinkler's lawyer." There was no hint of admiration or awe in the voice.

Suddenly, Boomer felt like every eye in the restaurant was on him. It was the same embarrassed feeling he always had when he lost a case or failed to achieve the result he thought he should have, as if every person in Atlanta knew about it. This was the first time he had been embarrassed by a win. Until the Perelli business died down again, he would do what the always did when he got those feelings. He would have his lunch brought in, stay in his office all he could, and avoid for a while any social engagements. Or he might take a week and leave town "on business." The case was now in repose for a while, waiting on the grand jury to convene. Hugh and his men could go on with the investigation, which was now focused on locating Ralph Hensley. He could call in from time to time and check on their progress.

He called Jessi at work.

"I've decided to go away for a week," he told her. "Can you get away?"

"Where did you have in mind?"

"I had thought about the Caymans," he offered. "The firm has a client there, and I could arrange to go down on business."

"Let me check the boss, and I'll call you right back."

She called in five minutes.

"I can leave after work Friday," she exclaimed excitedly.

"Good, I'll make all the arrangements, and we'll fly out Saturday morning."

Boomer told Emily of the planned business trip.

"Richard, I just may plan to go with you. I haven't seen the Caymans in a while, and I always said I'd like to go back."

How perverse, he thought. Many times he had asked her to go with him on trips earlier in the marriage and while there was still hope the situation might improve. She had refused. He had long since quit asking her. Damn if she was going to ruin this one for him.

"I think not, Emily. I'm going without you."

"Well, I never ... Is there something going on here I don't know about?" she said angrily.

"Go to hell, Emily," he said, turning to walk away.

"Richard, you've never talked to me that way," she bellowed.

"Maybe that's the problem, Emily. Maybe that's the problem."

The next morning, Boomer called Jessi. He had the travel reservations and the accommodations confirmed. He would go to a ticket agent and buy the tickets. He would meet her at the departure gate at 7:30 a.m. They would each get in bed early Friday night so they would be rested for the trip. Two days—a little less than forty-eight hours—and they would be on their way.

He went by the jewelry store and bought Jessie another gift. He would take it by the apartment tonight and surprise her. He went to his car, locked the present in the trunk, and returned to the office, where he would work until he had brought his correspondence up to date, rearranged appointments, postponed appearances, and satisfied himself that his responsibilities for the next week were seen to.

He didn't leave the office until ten that night. He drove to Jessi's apartment. Space 63 was taken—probably somebody visiting another tenant. He pulled his car into a spot three spaces down, turned off his headlights, and started to open the door. Suddenly Jessi's door opened, and Jacob Downing emerged. He stood in the doorway facing her. She stood there in a robe, her hair falling around her shoulders, just as he remembered her that first night. Jacob took her by the shoulders and pulled her to him. He kissed her long as she held onto him, her arms around his shoulders. Boomer sat there for a moment, not believing it. He was suddenly very ashamed, feeling the pain of utter betrayal. The words of his mother, heard over forty years ago, came back to him. "There's no fool like an old fool."

"I'm April and you're August. What does it matter?" she had said. He had believed her. He had wanted to.

As the door closed behind him, Jacob walked to space 63, started his car, and drove away. Boomer wondered what he should do. A great sadness—an almost unbearable hurt—had seized him. He could knock on the door, but what was there to say?

He started the car and went through the gate. Let her pack. Let her drive to the airport. Let her wait at the departure gate until the plane left—wondering if she had written the wrong gate number, or if something had happened to him. He would go by the ticket agency in the morning and get his money back. He would call the travel agent and cancel, forfeiting the deposit.

Then she would call. He would tell her something had come up and he couldn't get away, and he had tried to call. He would apologize.

On Tuesday, Hugh reported to him.

"As far as I can find out, Jessi Moreland never owned a house on Lookout Mountain. She was never divorced from a Charlie Moreland in Hamilton County, and neither she nor a Charlie Moreland has had a phone listing in Chattanooga in the last five years."

She had made it all up.

Boomer, without giving his name, called the frauds section of the Atlanta Police Department, alerted them to the presence of Jacob and Jessie in Atlanta, described their appearance, something about their methods, and suggested they check the national crime files.

The following Monday at eleven o'clock, the phone in his office rang. It was Jessica.

"Richard, there are some men here from the police, and they have come here to arrest me. I'm here at work. Could you come over here and see about this for me?"

Boomer voiced outrage.

"I'll be right there."

He went to the parking garage, started the Bronco loaded with provisions, and drove directly to Eddy's house, passing Jessica's workplace just as they were putting her and Jacob into the police van.

What a waste, he thought. *What a waste.*

As the two of them left for the lake, Boomer turned to Eddy.

"My mother once said something to me that you should hear. She said, 'There's no fool like an old fool.'"

Eddy smiled. He knew the pretty blond in Chattanooga was history.

Boomer and Eddy spent the rest of the week at the lake, the rented houseboat anchored, again, in the same place. Eddy couldn't get enough of fishing. He hadn't hooked that big fish on the other trip. It had hooked him. He rose early each morning and ran the trotline they had placed the night before. He had learned to start the motor in the small fishing boat and would cruise the area investigating the banks and waters.

During that week, Boomer often thought of Jessica and the Caymans. In spite of what he knew, he still felt an emptiness—a vague longing for her. She had been a painful disappointment, but she had taught him something about himself: August was not December. He was still alive; he could feel; he was still a man.

They missed Troy—both of them did. Eddy knew Boomer was grieving for him.

"He'll be back, Dad, soon as the Perelli business is over. We'll be closer than we ever were."

"I hope so, Eddy. I hope so."

Jessie was gone now. That dream and all it had brought him was shattered. He thought about the four people he had most trusted with his feelings. Emily, Troy, Eddy, and then Jessica. He wanted to cry, but he knew August never cries. December, maybe, but never August.

When he wrote the poem, he had expressed tenderness and warmth he had never felt before. He wondered if she showed it to Jacob. She probably did, and they had a good laugh. He suddenly felt a surge of shame. The staid, serious, self-confident Richard Boomer was, after all, a silly ass. Pussy had seen the streets. Time now to go back inside.

When he and Eddy got back to Atlanta, his secretary brought his mail. There on top was a pink letter marked "Personal." It bore no return address. He opened it and read a single paragraph.

Dear Richard:

I tried, but Jacob wouldn't let me go. I truly love you. I know I will never see you again, but I will never, never forget. Thank you for the lovely poem and the times we had together. Thank you for loving me. I will lock the memory of you in my heart forever.

Love,

Jessi

The writing blurred as tears formed in his eyes. Oh, well, time to get back to work. He climbed once again into the maw and felt again the yellow teeth begin to chew on him.

CHAPTER 25

After he ate supper, he took the tent out of the closet of the modest house where he lived and kept his gear. It had been several weeks since he had been camping and he was feeling an urge to get away. He had begun to experience the feelings of entrapment the marriage and child had brought.

The week's vacation he requested had been approved and he was already planning the venture. The pressures and feelings inside him would not be denied.

The anger seemed to grow day by day making the job stressful to him, and the pay was poor—barely enough to pay the bills, with nothing left over.

The last time he went, the rain had almost ruined it for him. He had made elaborate plans and had set up his tent near Billy Hinkler's cabin when the rain came. The set of keys he had stolen from the cabin the night he and Billy had been out drinking might be useful. He had remembered to bring them home. He had gone there twice before with girls he had picked up, and he had found Billy gone. It had been a perfect place to take the girls without his wife, Zee, knowing about it. Both times the place was a mess. On one occasion, his car ran out of gas near the gate to the cabin. He had tried one of the keys in the ignition of the old vehicle parked in the garage and had used it to go for gas.

Taking most of the gear out of the closet he began cleaning and setting some of it aside: the tent, two kerosene lanterns, some rope, a trench shovel, blankets, and an inflatable mattress. Things that would not be needed were returned to the closet. He wouldn't be doing much cooking, so he wouldn't need the gas stove and oven.

The gear was placed on the screened back porch, where it would be easy to get to. Then he went to another room, unlocked the gun rack, and took out the leather-handled hunting knife. After running his thumb down the sharp side of the blade he wrapped it again in the face towel. Going through the back door, he opened the trunk of his car, and put the knife in the tire well. He knew who it would be. That had been decided days before. With Billy Hinkler now out of jail, it would be easier.

Going to his desk, he pulled out the paper saved from the week before. "Evidence Raises Doubts—Hinkler Released on Bond." He read the article again, as he had done so many times. There was no mention of his name or anything remotely connected to him. Billy would have to take the heat again.

Hinkler's release had been a surprise to him. The state's evidence against Hinkler seemed clear. He had been amused when Hinkler was charged and jailed, but he was more amused that he had been released. It was proof, he thought, that the police were confounded.

He had wondered what he should do. Should he stay in Atlanta and risk discovery? Or should he move his family to another location—maybe Waukegan—and begin again? Or should he simply pack his bags and leave alone? Even if he decided to stay and ran into Billy, it wouldn't matter. If Billy recognized him, he would simply shake hands, tell him he was sorry about his troubles, and move on.

For now he decided to stay for a while and wait. There was no reason to leave that he could see, and he didn't want to deprive himself of the pleasure he got from reading and hearing about it. If he did decide to leave, he would simply disappear, leaving Zee the furniture and the rest of their meager belongings. It might be nice, he thought, to get away from the job and his obligations and be free to go wherever he wanted to. He had tired of Zee and her bouts of apprehension and depression. It had become increasingly hard to deal with her and their situation calmly. The last time they had argued, he lost his temper, threw her to the floor, and came very close to choking her. The bruise on her neck could still be seen. Only the screams of their small son had brought him to his senses. Such incidents made him feel better and seemed to assuage the anger that had built up inside him, waiting to erupt.

The next morning, he showered and started to put on his clean work trousers. "Zee," he bellowed, "get the in here, and find my brown belt."

She scurried into the bedroom, opened the top drawer of the bureau, and handed the belt to him. She did not dare tell him that she always kept his belts in that drawer.

"It's six o'clock, and I'm running late. Fix me an egg sandwich and a cup of coffee to take with me."

She was relieved when he pulled out of the driveway. It was the same feeling that comes when a tornado passes close by, leaving you unhurt.

After he had gone, Zee waited awhile and then went out to the detached garage, which stood a few feet from the house. It was used to store the lawn mower, tools, old magazines and newspapers, and an overflow of discarded furniture and other things they had decided they could do without. It was a perfect place to hide something.

Yesterday, she had begun to clean and straighten it up. As she was going through a stack of old magazines, she discovered two that contained disturbing pictures of children in various poses. She was appalled. Looking at her watch, she saw she didn't have time to go through them, since he would come in from work soon. She had replaced the stack of magazines on the shelf and gone to the house, intending to examine them more closely the next day. She was sure they had been left by a previous tenant or by the landlord.

After looking again, she knew that was not true. They were his. The magazines she found so offensive were between other magazines addressed to them and bore publication dates after they had rented and moved into the house. She carefully replaced the books on the shelf, being sure to leave them exactly as she had found them. She left the garage, went into the house, sat at the kitchen table, buried her face in her hands, and wept.

"My God, who have I married?" she said over and over.

She wondered why he would want such filth. Then she remembered something. He had come in the morning of his last camping trip, gone straight to the washer, placed some red-stained clothes and washing powder in the washer, and punched in the wash cycle. When she asked about it, he told her he had fallen and hit his head on a rock and that he had bled on his clothes. She took him to the bathroom, gently washed his hair, and applied ointment to the wound. She thought about it all day, wondering if she should call someone and who she would call. She knew he was moody and sometimes violent, but she never had thought of him as a murderer. Still, she seemed to recall that his last camping trip was only three or four nights before the body of Tommy Perelli was found. After looking at her diary and rereading the newspaper printed the day after Tommy was found, she knew it.

She knew what she must do. But could she do it? She feared her husband. He had shown her during the four years of their marriage that he was capable of extreme cruelty, directed against both her and their child. She lived in constant fear and dread of him. He had told her repeatedly that if she ever left him, he would find and kill her, the son, and himself. She was convinced that he would. Should she call the police? Who, then?

At about three o'clock the same day she dialed: "May I speak to Richard Boomer, please? I'm sorry, I can't give you my name. This call is very confidential. Just tell him it concerns one of his clients, and I believe he would want to speak to me."

"Hello," Boomer spoke into the phone. "May I ask who this is?"

"I'm sorry, but I can't give you my name," she said in whispers. "And I ask you not to try to record me, or I'll never call you again. I understand that you represent Billy Hinkler, the man accused of killing the Perelli boy. I have information that might help you in your case."

Boomer sat up straight in his chair. He suddenly felt a chill run from his shoulder, through the back of his neck, and into the top of his head. For some reason, he grew very nervous. Something about the voice caused him to believe she was serious.

"I certainly am very interested in your help in Billy's case," he said in a subdued voice. "What can you tell me?"

She told him about finding the magazines; about the camping trip and the bloody clothes; about her husband's collection of news articles about the Perelli case; about his frequent trips at night to the gun cabinet; and about his threats, his abuse, and her fear for her life and the life of their son.

Trying to conceal his excitement, he said, "Yes, I would like very much to talk with you personally. First I need to know who you are and where you are calling from."

He took a pad and pencil to record the information.

"Mr. Boomer, if my husband knew I called you, he would kill me. I'm so scared, I was afraid to call you from home. I'm on a pay phone. I can't give you my name or where I live. I swear, I'd like to, but I can't. Now, I'd be glad to call you or whoever you want me to if I learn anything else I think might help you."

"Miss," he said, moving up to the edge of the seat. Afraid she would hang up, he said, "Let me tell you to begin with, you can give me whatever information you want to anonymously, without giving me your name, or where you live, or anything. You have my word and solemn promise I won't try to find out who you are, or record you, or try to trace your calls. When you want me to know who you are, you'll tell me. Meanwhile, if you have any information whatever about who killed Tommy Perelli, I want to hear it under whatever terms you might impose. But I do need to be able to contact you—to talk to you confidentially from time to time."

Boomer suspected her husband might be the one they were looking for. He was afraid to ask, afraid he might cause her to hang up. But how could he be living in Atlanta with a wife and child? Larry, who was spending time looking for him, would surely have found him by now.

"May I ask only one question? Are you calling from Atlanta or from out of town?" Boomer asked.

There was a silence. He wished he had not asked the question, afraid she would hang up.

After a long pause, she said, "Mr. Boomer, I'm going to go now. Would you like for me to call you directly the next time or someone else?"

Boomer thought a minute, reaching for his address and telephone book.

"Miss, please call the number I'm going to give you and talk to Larry. He's a private investigator. I'll tell him about our arrangement, and I promise you he will abide by it. May I tell him when you will contact him so he will be there to receive the call?"

"Tell him I will call him again in three days at this number you gave me and at this same time. Good-bye, Mr. Boomer."

Boomer was excited. He was very excited. Could this be the break he had been looking for? He reached Hugh and Larry.

"Both of you get over here as soon as you can. I got a call just now that I want to tell you about. It may be a crank call, but I don't think so. If it's on the level, it might blow the state's case all to hell and clear Billy completely."

The three of them met an hour later. They talked for two hours about how the caller might help them.

"Larry," Boomer began, "I made some promises to this woman I want kept. Don't ask her any personal questions—who she is, where she lives, or who her husband is. She's already scared shitless. I've got a feeling she's the real McCoy."

Larry thought a minute.

"Let's think about what we need. What would it take to tie this fellow in, assuming he's the one who did it? Let's say he's our man. We already have him driving the Range Rover when he was stopped for speeding. That shows he had a key to it."

"Boys," Boomer offered, "I believe Farley's people found fingerprints other than Billy's in both the cabin and the vehicle. It would be nice if he had this man's prints to see if they match any of those found. Forest is a friend of mine. We're usually on opposite sides, but I can get him to do a matchup for me on a confidential basis. I can just give him a sample and ask him to compare them to any others they're interested in. If this man's prints turn up on either the vehicle or the cabin, that's a valuable link."

"Okay, then," Hugh said. "We need her husband's prints."

Boomer spoke again.

"I also believe from the way that hearing went that Troy doesn't have a match between Billy and the blood and hair Troy talked about in his motion for production. If we had a sample of blood or hair or both from this guy and it matched, that would ice the cake and we would know he is involved. I doubt if he's going to let his wife draw any blood, but she might get us some hair if she wants to."

Hugh said again, "Blood and hair. "

"You know," Boomer said, "if she still has those clothes he washed and they haven't been worn again or washed several times, they might have residue of blood in them—enough for DNA. Maybe she could get those to us. No, we won't ask her to do that—too risky. Damn, I wish I knew the rest of what Farley has by way of forensic evidence. There might be other stuff we could look at. All we know about now are blood and hair found at Stone Mountain and the possibility of other fingerprints in the cabin or on the vehicle. So I guess that's all we can look at now. If we get these things from her and any one of them matches, I can go to Captain Thomas, tell him what we have, and maybe get them to go in with a search warrant, if she will tell us who he is."

"Okay, then," Larry said, getting out of his chair, "blood, hair, fingerprints. If she calls like she said she would, I'll try to set it up with her."

Larry continued his search for the elusive witness. By using Boomer's name he learned that no tax return had been filed with the State of Georgia in his name ; no unemployment applications had been received anywhere in Georgia bearing his name; and no applications for driver's licenses, public assistance, or food stamps had been filed. He had become convinced that he had moved from the area after flunking out of Emory and that the occasions when he had appeared in Atlanta were visits to the area made while he lived in another place. Now he wasn't so sure.

He even spent several nights in the bar where Billy had seen him that first time, hoping to run into someone who knew him. All he got was a crunching headache from the loud music, the thick cigarette smoke, and the loud mutterings of a bar full of drunks. .

Larry was home when the call came in from her. He had arranged to be there two hours prior to the time of the expected call, in case she was early, and two hours afterward, in case she called late.

"Hello," he spoke softly into the phone as if he thought he might frighten her. "Yes, this is Larry. Thank you for calling again. You called exactly when you said you would. Let me begin by telling you something. I've talked to Mr. Boomer, and he told me what your arrangement was, and let me assure you I will honor that to the letter. Now, what do you have for me today?"

"I really don't have very much more," she said whispering. "The only thing I noticed, and I've been noticing this for some time, is he gets up every night when he thinks I'm asleep and goes downstairs and stays for fifteen to twenty minutes. Three nights ago I went to the door and heard him unlock the gun case where he keeps his hunting rifles. I'm always afraid he's going to get one of those out and shoot me. I'm deathly afraid of him. I really am."

"Let me ask you something, Miss. I need to get something of his. I need two things right now that might tell us what we want to know and possibly set your mind at ease—or get you out of a very dangerous situation. Do you think you might get me some hair from his head?"

"No!" she said emphatically. "What do I do? Walk up to him with scissors and cut a patch off his head? He'd kill me."

"Does he use a comb or brush on his hair?" Larry inquired.

"Well, he uses a stiff hair brush," she answered. "His hair has started to fall out pretty fast, and he makes me clean the hair out of the brush every few days and wash it. He won't let anybody else use it or any of his personal items."

"I wonder if you could clean the hairbrush tomorrow, put the hair in an envelope, and let me get it from you tomorrow. I can meet you anywhere you want to meet—maybe a grocery store where you shop—anyplace. Or if you would feel better about it, you could just mail it to me. Here's the address," he said, giving her his full name,

216

post office box, and zip code. "Another thing, we need something with fingerprints. Anything, like a piece of paper or a dollar bill. Does he give you money to shop with, or a check? Maybe you could find a bill or check or anything he has handled and get that to us also."

She agreed to secure the items he had asked for, and arrangements were made for the two to meet the following day at a supermarket, which, he assumed, was close to her home. They would see each other at the location where the dishwasher soap was displayed. She would have a pair of earrings with blue stones, and he would be in short sleeves with a tattoo of a leopard on his forearm. In twenty-four hours he would know if the caller was for real or if the whole thing was a hoax or a sordid joke.

The following afternoon she was there pushing a grocery cart. A frail, frightened creature, she glanced in every direction, looking for someone who might be watching. He saw bruises that looked like handprints on her neck.

He put her at ease by speaking gently to her and telling her that he had three other private detectives in the store, fully armed and ready to protect her at a moment's notice. He suggested that, in order to be absolutely sure of her safety, she should permit them to take her and her child, whom she had left in the car, to a place of refuge. Whatever the connection between her husband and the Perelli murder, she should commence proceedings to protect herself and the child under Georgia's spousal abuse laws. She declined, saying if her husband was not involved in the Perelli murder, she would stay with him.

"Miss," Larry said gently, "won't you tell us who you are and what your husband's name is? You know, I could have you followed when you leave here and find out, but we will honor our commitment to you."

She shook her head and turned to leave. Larry stayed in the store until she had passed through the checkout counter and driven away. He placed the two envelopes containing the items she had brought him in his inside coat pocket and left the store.

"I've got it," he exclaimed to Hugh, Melvin, and Bobby, as happy as if he had discovered a sunken Spanish treasure.

CHAPTER 26

Melvin had returned from the nine ball tournament in Orlando with the trophy. He had found it hard to concentrate on his game, because his mind kept going back to an earlier game when one of his opponents had pocketed two balls out of rotation, with combination shots. Looking at the table, he had seen the original nine balls, except for the seven and eight. He suddenly remembered what Bobby had said at one of their meetings about the child, Robbie Wilson, pupil number 55, next to the last pupil to be discharged from the bus under the transportation plan. He had something he wanted to check out when he got back to Atlanta after the tournament.

After he arrived at the airport, he went directly to the car rental agency and rented a black compact car of common make. He had one more run he wanted to make. He parked the car midway of the route of school bus number 5. As the bus went by him, he pulled in behind and followed it until it had discharged young Wilson. As each child got off the bus, he wrote the child's name, his student number, the address, and the time of day. After the bus had discharged the last pupil, Robbie Wilson, Melvin went back to his apartment and began to work. He had found something curious. He called Caesar Potts to see if there had been a change in the route. There had not.

After leaving the store and the woman he believed to be the wife of the man he was seeking , Larry took the two envelopes to Boomer, who had cut short his fishing trip to meet him.

"I called Forest and told him I thought we had something he should see," Boomer advised. "He was very interested. He promised to keep the information confidential and agreed to conduct the analysis and comparison of the hair and comparison of the prints after hours tonight. By the way, we guessed right. He told me that the blood and hair found at the Stone Mountain location did not match the samples taken from Billy. He said I'd find out anyhow, so he told me. Old buddy, if the hairs or the fingerprints we got from this lady match what they found at Stone Mountain, we've not only won our case, we've probably found the son uv a bitch that did this."

Boomer and Larry went to the café around the corner and had an early dinner, waiting for six o'clock and the visit to the crime lab. When they arrived, Forest was sitting at the entrance in his car.

"If you assholes ever let this out that I'm doing this, my name is shit—not only here, but all over. This creates an ethical problem for me of immense proportions, but I saw that kid lying up there on Stone Mountain, and I'll do anything to catch the one that did it. So let's go."

On into the night they worked.

"Encouraging," Forest said after the first, preliminary analysis of the hair. By midnight the verdict was in. "Comparing the trace elements in each sample," Forest said solemnly, "I find that the two hair samples match with a probability reaching into the millions."

Comparison of the fingerprints was encouraging, he ventured. "These prints seem to match one of those found at the cabin and in the vehicle, and which the bureau identified as belonging to their query. But, now, that's just a highly educated guess. You need a fingerprint man to verify that."

When they left the lab, both Boomer and Larry were elated.

"I'm reminded of the scripture," Boomer said as he and Larry drove back to the office. 'Let judgment run down as waters, and righteousness as a mighty stream.' You made it rain, Larry. You and Bobby, Hugh and Melvin, and whoever that sweet little bruised-up woman is."

"We've got to find her, Boomer. She's living with a maniac. I hope to God she calls me soon."

Boomer arrived home at one thirty. When he pulled into the driveway, he saw lights on in the house. When he entered the kitchen, Emily was seated at the kitchen counter.

"Well, I never," she said, smiling. "I've been waiting dinner since seven. Get your coat off, and go into the dining room. I'll just heat it up, and we'll have our supper. I'm sure you've had a hard day."

Boomer was astounded. After dinner, he turned on the television and sat there for a few minutes, thinking of the events of the day and waiting for the tension from the day to subside. He went upstairs to bed and found his pajamas folded neatly on the chair and the covers turned down. Emily emerged from the bathroom, wearing a peignoir.

"Richard," she said, taking his hands and holding them to her. "Do you think you could ever forgive me? I know I've been such a shit."

He looked at the pendant on her neck with its gleaming emerald and thought of Jessi.

"Well, Emily, I've been somewhat of a shit myself. Now, paddle off to bed and let me get some sleep. I'm bushed."

CHAPTER 27

Melvin pulled the picture that Larry had torn from the Waukegan yearbook and scanned it with a magnifying glass. He studied it closely, concentrating on the eyes and lips. He took out the group picture he had gotten from Caesar Potts, looked at each face, and finally settled on one. He moved the glass back and forth between the two faces for a long time, and then he phoned Larry.

"Look, who was the guy that took the beard off the picture of his face and made enlargements? Pretty good, isn't he? I need his name and telephone number if you have it."

Larry asked him what he was doing.

"Never mind what I want with it. Let it be my little secret. Just tell me." Larry gave him the information, wondering what he was up to.

He waited for another call from the wife of the man he thought to be the person they were seeking. It didn't come. They were so close to finding him—maybe just a phone call away.

The phone rang. It was Hugh.

"No, she hasn't called. Better not tie this phone up. Good-bye."

The phone rang again. It was Boomer. Same conversation. He waited. For hours he waited. He paced the floor, wondering when she might call—knowing she was in imminent peril. It was five thirty. He was probably home. She wouldn't call today.

The phone in Boomer's office rang. It was Buck Hinkler, screaming into the phone.

"They've been here. The police. They've taken Billy into custody again. Searched the house. The outbuildings. Wouldn't tell me anything. Just took him and left with him. What's going on? We've followed the judge's orders. Billy hasn't been out of our sight for a single minute. Please find out what's going on, and call me back as soon as you can."

Boomer hung up the phone and dialed Troy.

"What the hell's going on?" he shouted at him. "Why have they arrested Billy again? Has he broken the conditions of his release?"

"Now calm down, Dad." They were the first words Troy had spoken to him directly since the beginning. "There's been a report of another kid missing from the same neighborhood—same thing again. His name is Robbie Wilson. He wasn't home when his parents got there at five thirty. They called immediately. I called Judge Lamprey and told him what had happened, and he thought we ought to place Billy in protective custody. He said he was going to issue an immediate order effective today at six o'clock and that I should call you and tell you of our conversation and his order. I was just about to call you."

"Well, you damn sure waited long enough. Buck is foaming at the mouth, and I don't blame him. The next time you call a judge in a case I'm in and ex parte him, I'll drag your little ass before the bar association—son or no son. And let me tell you something else. You tell them down at police headquarters that they had better not try to interrogate Billy out of my presence, or I'll send their heads rolling down Spring Street from the steps of the federal courthouse. My client has nothing to do with that missing child."

"Calm down, Richard. Just calm down, Pop, while I tell you something. You know, and I know, our case against Billy is in trouble. You don't know this yet, but Billy's blood and hair analysis didn't match those we found at Stone Mountain."

"I knew that! I knew that, damn it. You think I'm a fool, Troy? I knew that when you didn't bring it up at the preliminary."

"Why didn't you ask Farley and Forest about it at the preliminary hearing then?" Troy asked.

"Figure it out for yourself, Troy. Figure it out for yourself. Hold on a minute. I've got some messages."

Boomer left the line for a long time. Troy wondered if he would ever come back.

"Look, I just received word that one of my investigators has got a line on our person of interest —you know, you got his prints off the Range Rover and out of the cabin. I assume you've been looking for him too. I've asked all my boys to get up here so we can put our heads together. You call Thomas and Forest and have them here at seven o'clock. We need to confer real bad and trade information especially in view of the disappearance of the Wilson boy. We may be able to nail this sucker and get this kid back."

"Well, I guess they can spare the time," Troy said, hesitating. He knew there wasn't much to share from his side of the case.

"Look, Troy, it's your sweet ass that's on the line now, not mine. I'm going to break this case tonight and get this kid back if he hasn't already been harmed. You can be in on it if you want to. It's your decision."

Boomer abruptly hung up.

Troy thought about the situation. He had been given credit for Billy's arrest, and he was sorry he had. He knew the state's investigation wasn't going anywhere and that Billy was not guilty. The focus of Farley's investigation had shifted to this one man, as Boomer's apparently had. Boomer had said they thought they knew where he might be. If he was indeed the assailant, there might still be time to get the Wilson boy back. He thought about what he had said to Boomer and wished he hadn't said it.

"Farley, where are you?" Troy asked after being patched into his car.

"Where the hell do you think I am? We're doing everything we can to find the Wilson boy. It's like Tommy Perelli. He's dropped off the face of the earth. No witnesses, no nothing."

"Listen. I just got a call from Pop. He says he knows where Hensley is. He wants to meet you and me and Thomas in his office at seven o'clock. I think we ought to go and hear what they have. It might be the kid's only hope."

"Roger," Farley barked. "If you say so, I'll be there. We've hit a dead end anyhow."

"I'll call Thomas and Forest and try to get them there too," Troy said.

At seven o'clock they were all there. Boomer and his four investigators were seated on one side of the conference table, while Troy, Forest, Farley, and Thomas were on the other.

"I'll start," Boomer said unceremoniously. "Here's what we already know. Some of you don't know this yet, but the blood and hair you found at Stone Mountain came from the same person. Don't ask how I know; just trust me. Second, we know you found his prints in the Range Rover and in the cabin. Again, don't ask me how we know that, but we do. Third, we know he lives right here in Atlanta and that he has a wife and child. We know because we've been talking to his wife. Fourth, we know he's a brute who gets his kicks beating other people. Fifth, we know he's a dirty slug that collects child pornography. Now, we know all that, and I'm certain that's a helluva lot more than you do." He looked straight into Troy's eyes. "Am I right?"

"Come on, " Thomas interrupted, beginning to anger, "let's not waste time. Tell us where we can find him. You've talked to his wife, so you must know where to find him."

"That's a problem," Larry volunteered. "She's given us very valuable evidence and other information, but this guy's brutalized her for years and she's scared to death of him. She wouldn't tell us where they lived, what name they were living under, or where we might call her. Said she was afraid he'd find out and kill her. I can see her reluctance to do that without knowing for sure he was the killer. We haven't heard from her in several days—not since she gave us some hair samples out of his hairbrush, which turned up a perfect match; and the fingerprints, which also matched. So right now, she doesn't know she's living with the probable killer. If she did, I'm sure she'd tell us where we could find him."

"So, what's the bottom line here?" Troy asked. "Where do we find this guy?"

"From this point," Boomer said, "I'll turn it over to Melvin. I haven't heard it all. He was just telling me before you all came in."

"Gentlemen," Melvin began judiciously, "I'll do this as quickly as I can. Here is some work a fellow did for me that you'll find interesting. Now, here on this screen is an enlarged picture of Hensley taken from his yearbook, showing him with full beard and long hair. Here is the same picture with the hair all removed. Here is a line drawing my man did, showing his facial outline and bone structure. Now, I'll lay those aside and show you these. Here is a picture of the driver of school bus number 5, enlarged from a group photograph to the same dimensions as the first ones I showed you. I am sure you can see the distinct similarities in the eyes and lips. Now, look at this! I take this drawing of the facial outline and bone structure of Fentrell, reconstructed from the enlargement of the group picture, place it on top of those made from Hensley's high school picture, and you can see they match almost perfectly."

"Are you saying Hensley is Fentrell?" Troy exclaimed.

"You bet your sweet ass he is," Melvin answered, grinning.

"That's impressive," Farley said, "but I'd hate like hell to go to court on that one."

"Farley, you are exactly right. The similarity that this shows probably never would pass muster in the courtroom, but that doesn't mean we can't use it for investigating purposes in trying to find Hensley, who is our apparent killer, as being one and the same as Fentrell," Troy replied.

"Hear me out," Melvin continued. "I went by the school this morning and handed Fentrell a picture of my nephew and asked him if he had ever seen the man before. I took the picture to a friend of mine who's fully qualified in fingerprints. He lifted Fentrell's thumbprint from the picture and compared it to the ones we got from Hensley's wife and, behold, they are the same. Fentrell is Hensley. After he flunked out of the university, he took the name

Fentrell from his stepfather, I guess, to get away from his record. He used whichever name suited him. To those who knew him before as Hensley he went by Hensley. To others he was Fentrell. Pretty handy, don't you think? No doubt about it. Fentrell killed Tommy Perelli. No doubt about it."

"How did he do it? There were no witnesses to the abduction. Nothing!" Thomas exclaimed.

"Well, that bothered me, too." Melvin smiled. "You see, Tommy Perelli was student number 53. He was supposed to exit the bus while three passengers were still aboard. Robbie Wilson, student number 55, was supposed to get off next to last. Without telling Caesar Potts, Fentrell changed the route in such a way that Tommy was the last student on the bus the day he disappeared. The way I figure it, Fentrell changed the bus route slightly. He let everybody else off and then drove Tommy on to the bus garage, tied him up, waited 'til dark, and took him to Billy's cabin, where he killed him. Yesterday, I followed Fentrell without his knowing it. He changed the route again. Yesterday, he let Robbie Wilson off last, even though he was passenger number 55 and should have exited the bus with one passenger still on the bus, if Fentrell had let them off in the required rotation. Now, Troy, you're saying to yourself that Timmy next door saw Tommy Perelli playing with a dog on a vacant lot near his house the day he was abducted. That happened the day before. We even have the dog—rather, you have her, Troy. Spotty, we call her."

Troy reddened, realizing what they had done to him.

"As I told you, I followed the bus yesterday. Fentrell didn't know I was behind him, and he changed the sequence again. Yesterday, Robbie Wilson was the last one to get off. I'm sure he did the same thing today. He left him on 'til last and took him on to the garage rather than letting him off. He's probably waiting for dark to come so he can get him out of there and not be seen. Another thing I found out. Fentrell is the last bus in, and he is the one responsible for seeing the garage and gate are locked and secured."

Boomer reached for the telephone book. "William Fentrell." He found the number and dialed it.

"Mrs. Fentrell, this is Richard Boomer. Is your husband home?

He's gone camping ? Do you know where he camps? I see. I'll tell you later how I knew where to call you. Listen, ma'am, you are in real danger. There'll be some officers over there soon. Get packed and be ready to go with them."

Boomer hung up the phone. "Well, that ties it all together. Melvin's right. It's Fentrell. That was the wife we've been talking to. No doubt about it." Boomer grew excited, taking command: "Now that we know for sure that Fentrell is our man, we can zero in on him. There are only so many places that he could hide with Robbie and we will cover them all."

"Let's divide into two parties. Thomas, you take Farley, Hugh, Melvin and Bobby and run by Fentrell's house. If you don't find him there, leave some officers to stand guard while you get over to the cabin and search it and the grounds. Stop all traffic into the Stone Mountain Park and cruise through the park for him." Thomas frowned as if to complain of Boomer's instructions taking over the operation, but Boomer continued, "Thomas, I think this is the place where you will more than likely find him. The rest can come with me. We'll head for the bus garage. And Thomas, get some officers out to the school garage pronto, but I want them to come in quietly, no sirens. We don't want to spook Fentrell if he's in there. He might harm the boy if he hasn't already. And, Captain, have an officer, take Mrs. Fentrell and her child to my house. Tell Emily to take care of them until I get in."

Boomer grabbed a revolver off his desk, took out a box of .38 cartridges, pushed six into the cylinder, and headed for the elevator.

"Troy," he said on the way to the school, "I want you to stay in the clear, here. You've got Brenda and the kids. We can handle this. If he's in there, we've got to sneak up on this bastard and get him before he knows what's happened and before he gets a chance to hurt the kid. I hope he hasn't already. I believe he's in there, and I don't want a bunch of people crawling all over the place screwing everything up."

When they arrived at the transportation area, they found that the gate in the cyclone fence was locked. Larry got a tire tool from the trunk and easily twisted the lock off. Once they were inside the compound, Boomer signaled Larry to go to the rear of the building.

The doors to the garage were down, and Boomer assumed they were locked. Running back to the car, he started the engine, and began to coast onto the lot, shutting off the engine after getting the car moving. He stopped beneath a window, high above the blacktop surface, and climbed onto the top of the car. He jammed the pistol beneath his belt, pried the window open and let himself down. He hit the floor with a thud that reverberated throughout the hollow steel structure. Then, another thud as Troy followed him through the window and made his way to the entrance door, opened it letting the others in.

As he turned again, he saw Fentrell emerge from school bus number 5, looking directly at him and wildly waving a knife. Boomer signaled for Troy and the officers with him to remain where they were, fearing that Robbie Wilson might be injured in a shooting and hoping that Fentrell would submit peaceably. He pointed the revolver at Fentrell's head, seeing that he wasn't going to submit.

"Stop. I'd like nothing better than to blow your head off."

He knew Robbie Wilson was somewhere inside the bus. Suddenly, Fentrell lunged, laughing maniacally. Boomer fired a shot, striking him in the left shoulder. Fentrell screamed with pain. He reached Boomer before he could fire a second shot, knocked the gun to the floor, and began to slash at him with the knife. As he raised the knife to stab Boomer, Troy jumped between them. Fentrell plunged the knife into Troy's arm. Boomer seized Fentrell by the throat, threw him violently to the concrete and began kicking him in the face.

"Please, please, no more," Fentrell cried, burying his head in his arms.

Boomer stopped kicking him, grabbed the pistol from the floor, and placed his foot on his neck.

"You damn scumbag. You low-life bastard, I want you to think about Tommy Perelli and what you did to him. Get yourself a good deep breath. It'll be your last. I am going to blow your brains out."

"Don't, Pop," Troy screamed, running back. "He's not worth it. Let's let the law take care of him." Boomer's finger loosened as reason returned. Troy took the pistol from his hand and said, "Don't move. You are under arrest." Several of the other police that were waiting outside entered the garage, taking the dazed Fentrell into custody from Troy. Boomer and Troy ran to bus number 5. It was dark inside.

"Anybody in here?" Boomer called.

"Humph," the muffled sound greeted them.

"Thank God," Troy sobbed as he picked Robbie up in his arms and took the gag from his mouth, ignoring his injured arm. He could see Robbie was only shaken.

The frightened Robbie was delivered into the arms of a police officer as Boomer took off his tie and fashioned a tourniquet for Troy's injured arm.

"Kick my sweet ass, you say?" He turned Troy around, planted his foot gently in his rear, and sent him sprawling, bleeding arm and all. Troy got up, laughed, and bowed as if he were grateful.

"Now, does that make us even, Pop?" he asked.

"Yes, I guess it does." Boomer smiled, knocking the dirt from his trousers. "Come on now, let's get you to the hospital."

When Boomer awoke the next morning there was Emily standing with a tray of Louisiana Ham, eggs, bacon and fresh southern biscuits. There was no mention of Billy Hinkler, Stone Mountain Park or any of the other events of the last several days.

"Try to get home early. I'll get us one of those fillets you like so well and make us some blue cheese dressing that you used to love. We'll have our own litle party. I'll get a bottle of that good wine from the cellar and let it breathe for a while if it is still there. I had Ressa dusting and saw that somebody had helped themselves to a bottle of it." Emily handed Boomer the remote and he clicked the TV over to WLAK just in time to get the weather and morning news.

"Today's weather for Fulton, Cob and Dekalb Counties calls for a continuation of Atlanta rain throughout today with clearing skies tomorrow, beginning in the early morning hours with rising temperatures to eighty-five degrees by tomorrow noon. It looks like all that rain might be over for a while. The time is now eight o'clock. Stay tuned for the latest news from WLAK."

"Good morning! This is George Preston with the morning news. Atlanta Police have arrested Ralph Hensley alias William Fentrell and charged him with the kidnapping and murder of Tommy Perelli, nine-year old student, whose body was discovered by hikers in a shallow grave at Stone Mountain Park. Hensley had also been charged with the kidnapping of Robbie Wilson, another student who was freed at the time of Hensley's arrest. Captain Thomas, Chief Criminal Investigator for Fulton County expressed his appreciation to several people who helped bring about the arrest, including Troy Boomer, an Assistant Atlanta Prosecuting Attorney, who was credited with taking Hensley into custody under a citizen's arrest."

As he reached for the remote, he heard George Preston conclude the broadcast:

"According to a U.S. News and World Report just released, crime rates have dropped nationwide over the last two decades and are expected to continue to drop. That is encouraging news to Atlantans! But, it might be too early to rejoice. Overall crime rates in most metropolitan areas throughout America still give us plenty of reason for concern.

ABOUT THE AUTHOR

Eugene Goss, who practiced law in Harlan County, Kentucky, for over fifty years, has developed a passion for writing. This is the second book Mr. Goss has completed this year.

Made in the USA
Lexington, KY
05 March 2013

Video Power

TOM SHACHTMAN
and HARRIET SHELARE

VIDEO
POWER

/// A Complete Guide
to Writing, Planning,
and Shooting Videos ///

HENRY HOLT AND COMPANY   NEW YORK

Published by Henry Holt and Company, Inc.,
115 West 18th Street, New York, New York 10011.
Published in Canada by Fitzhenry & Whiteside Limited,
195 Allstate Parkway, Markham, Ontario L3R 4T8.

Library of Congress Cataloging-in-Publication Data
Shachtman, Tom, 1942–
Video power.
Bibliography: p.
Includes index.
Summary: Explains the use of videotape equipment and gives
instructions on developing a script, planning and shooting
a video, editing, and finding a market for the final product.
1. Video recordings—Production and direction.
[1. Video recordings—Production and direction]
I. Shelare, Harriet.   II. Title.
PN1992.94.S53 1988   791.43′0232   87-23681
ISBN: 0-8050-0338-X
ISBN: 0-8050-0414-9 (pbk.)

First Edition

Designer: Victoria Hartman
Printed in the United States of America
10 9 8 7 6 5 4 3 2 1

Photograph page 8, bottom, by "Year Look" Enterprises.
All other photos by Tom Shachtman and Chuck Saaf.

ISBN 0-8050-0338-X

ISBN 0-8050-0414-9 (PBK.)

For our boys, Noah and Daniel

ACKNOWLEDGMENTS

The following individuals and organizations were of help to us in putting together this book. We would like to thank:

The cast and crew of "As the World Turns," a Procter & Gamble Production taped at CBS's Broadcast Center in Manhattan, Kenneth L. Fitts, supervising producer. Our special thanks to production supervisor and good friend Jim Picinich.

The students of the Lakeland-Yorktown Mass Communications Project, Yorktown Heights, New York, for letting us visit two school video productions. Special thanks to Project Coordinator Nadine Koval, whose enthusiasm has sparked her students toward careers in broadcasting.

Welby A. Smith of Development Communications Associates, Alexandria, Virginia, for technical review and general help with the manuscript.

Lisa Sloan of New York University's Undergraduate Film and Television department for information on video festivals.

Photographer Chuck Saaf.

Year Look Enterprises of Durham, North Carolina, Bob Levitan, president.

All of these people's efforts notwithstanding, any errors in the book are our own.

Tom Shachtman and Harriet Shelare
New York City, July 1987

CONTENTS

/// 1 ///

Welcome to the Video Revolution

We live in a television age. Television informs us, brings out our emotions, sells us products, gives us role models and affects us in many other ways. Television is the most important communications medium in today's world.

Just consider these facts:

- There are television sets in more than 85 million homes in the United States, nearly every home.
- More people learn about the news each day from television than from newspapers, magazines, radio, or word-of-mouth.
- Forty million American families, or more than two of every five, own video cassette recorders (VCRs) on which they play recorded programs or copy those being broadcast.
- School-age children spend over 1,000 hours a year watching television—more time than they spend in academic classrooms.
- More than one-quarter of the homes in the United States now are able to receive cable television in addition to commercial channels.
- Over one million families now own video cameras, and 100,000 schools now have video systems.

1

The use of television is expanding so rapidly in the 1980s that it's fair to say we're in the midst of a video revolution. As a result of a new generation of camera and recording technology, the making of television material—what we call videos—is no longer restricted to the major television networks and television producers.

The showing of videos has expanded, too, far beyond the networks and local stations. Now we have cable television and VCRs in our homes, video jukeboxes, closed-circuit broadcasts in schools, and training tapes for business and industry. And now, almost anyone with access to a camera and recording equipment can make videos.

But most people still believe that television is just something to watch and hear, not to use. Evidence of this is the fact that many of the home, school, and community facilities for making videos are underutilized. The equipment and facilities are just waiting for someone with imagination to do terrific things with them.

For you, the video revolution can be an opportunity to enjoy and use a creative outlet that's inexpensive but can reach large audiences. This book is here to help you do just that.

The basic techniques for writing, shooting, and editing a video are well within your grasp. The technology has been made as simple and as foolproof as possible, so that everyone can work with it.

While mastering the use of cameras, microphones, recorders, lights, editing machines, and other equipment is important, knowing the hardware is only part of the process of making videos. This book will help you learn how to use the equipment, but, even more important, it will help you focus on what you want to accomplish in making a video. In the following pages we'll take you through the steps that will encourage you to find good video ideas, structure those ideas into workable concepts, and enable you to translate those concepts into well-produced videos.

Along the way we'll give you some tips on avoiding common mistakes and let you in on some of the methods—and tricks—that television professionals use every day. Using video to communicate your ideas ought to be, and can be, as simple and as basic for you as reading, writing, and computing.

Compared to film, its nearest competitor, video has many advantages. Home or school video equipment is low in cost and fairly easy to use. There are no costs for developing, as there are with film, and videotape can be erased and re-used, which brings the cost of video down further.

Most small video cameras come with built-in microphones that record images and sounds simultaneously on the same tape. Perhaps the greatest advantage, technically, is that video equipment allows you to instantly play back what you have recorded; you don't have to wait and wonder whether your exposure was correct or if an actor's expression was what you wanted it to be. You see the results of your work right away, so that if you don't like it, you can do it over again.

Video is one of the most powerful tools available for your imagination. It is unmatched for creating a feeling of immediacy, the sense of "being there," participating in a news event, a science experiment, a dramatic story, an evening of song or dance. Because we most often watch television in the privacy of our own homes, video can be the most intimate of the media, even when it is being broadcast simultaneously to millions of people.

What you've seen all your life on television are impressions of the world—selected, edited, and interpreted by other people. Now it's time for *you* to use video power, to make choices and decide what images to invent, record, edit, and transmit back to the world.

It's the responsibility of the artist to entertain and interest the audience; to do so requires planning and thought. The motto of this book is "think before you shoot"—and we're going to help you do that thinking.

/// 2 ///

From Conception to Completion

News Item:
The Muscle Spasms, a rock group that has been near the top of the charts since it was formed eight years ago when its members were in high school, is splitting up. Artistic and personal difficulties were cited as the cause of the band's demise. Lawsuits are expected over the $2.5 million in royalties owed to the group by Sloppy Disks Records.

Suppose you saw something like this brief paragraph in a newspaper or magazine, or heard it on a news program, and decided to make a video program about the life and death of a rock band. What are the steps to take your initial impulse from conception to completion?

In professional broadcasting the producers, directors, and writers come up with most of the ideas. For simplicity, let's call the person with the idea to make a video about the Muscle Spasms the producer. He or she will take the project through all the stages of its creation: overseeing the writing of the script, the choosing and preparing of locations, the directing of the actions of the crew and "talent" during the actual shooting of the scenes, the editing, and, at last, the selling or showing of the program.

In big-time television, a program is produced by one or

several persons, written by several more, directed by at least one. On a smaller, nonprofessional level one person usually wears a number of hats. For your own videos in many instances you'll be producer *and* writer *and* the one who paints the scenery *and* gets the cup of water to quiet the actor's cough. But the functions of producing, writing, directing, and other aspects of making the video are the same, whether on a large or small scale.

The first stage of production happens long before "shooting," and is called *preproduction*. Perhaps the earliest task is defining the concept of the video. Is it to be a documentary about the Muscle Spasms or a fictional story about the rise and fall of a group that may resemble the actual Muscle Spasms? For the moment, let's assume you choose the latter.

Having decided to make a fictional piece, there are many more decisions to be made. What will be the actual story? How long will it be? How much will it cost in terms of time, equipment, and money to make it? Music will be important—who'll do that? Could you use a special location? How many days should be allocated to shooting, and how many more for editing? Maybe you've got some friends in a rock band who could play the lead roles and also record the music; that will make your life as a producer a bit easier, but it won't answer all the questions. For more precise answers to the others, you'll need a script.

You may want to do the writing, or work with another person or team of writers. Often a producer has an idea or part of a story line but feels someone else can do a better job of "fleshing out" the plot, characters, and dialogue. After a full script is written, there's still work to be done to turn it into a shooting script. That document also includes scene descriptions, suggested camera angles for each shot, visual and sound transitions, and screen directions. Then the shooting script is broken down into lists of what's required in each scene—props, set, actors or other talent, camera angles.

Analyzing the shooting script and deciding how to realize it is part of the process of directing a video. A director's function is mainly interpretive—to take the concept and the words on a page and make them into a completed video.

Other tasks include assembling the cast, selecting locations, making sets. To determine when and where and how to shoot, you'll take into account what equipment is available or may have to be obtained. For instance, to properly do a murky night scene, you may decide that shooting in reduced daylight with a special filter might be better than having to rent special lights to actually do it at night. Or you might decide that it will be best to shoot all the outdoor scenes one day, and, on another day, several indoor scenes that have the same backdrop but that take place at different times in the script.

During this preproduction phase, every detail must be ironed out so that the shooting will go as smoothly as possible. Preproduction often lasts three or four times longer than the shooting schedule itself.

After all the preproduction work has been done, the actual *production* or shooting phase can begin. This is the time when the director and crew function as a team to try to make everything go pretty much as planned.

A good minimum number of people on a crew is three— one for the camera, another to handle sound, and someone to direct both camera and sound. On small productions, you may be your own director, camera- or soundperson. On a larger production, a crew may include assistants for camera and sound, as well as lighting technicians, and people to handle the set, props, wardrobe, transportation, even the feeding of everybody who's along on the "shoot."

Once production is completed, there is an extended period called the *postproduction* phase. The major task to be done in "post" is editing. In editing, you put together the sometimes jumbled scenes, make sense out of many bits and fragments of sound and picture in the process of assembling a final piece of tape that reflects the work that has gone into all phases of producing a video. Simple cutting together of pictures and sound taken at different times in different locations takes many hours. If you are doing more complex editing—adding music tracks or putting in "special effects" such as dissolves or wipes between scenes—postproduction can last three or four times as long as the production phase.

/// 3 ///

Where Do Ideas Come From?

Ideas and Audiences

Ideas can be a dime a dozen—plentiful and of not much value. Good ideas, though, are harder to find and more durable once found. Some people are brimming with good ideas; others aren't, and believe they can't find anything to "spark" on. Even if you're one of those who has lots of ideas, you may need tips on thinking a project through so that it becomes more than just an idea. For example, who knows if the life and death of a rock 'n' roll band would really make a good video? Not all newspaper stories will work as fiction, and some rock songs are better heard than seen.

How do you decide whether an idea is good for a video? First of all, it must have a strong visual component. Despite the fact that television comes equipped with sound, video is essentially a visual medium. If the emphasis is wholly on the sound, maybe your idea is for radio. Second, the idea probably ought to be one that needs more than a single picture to tell the story—that is, it's about people, events, or circumstances that vary or change over a period of time. If you can express your idea with a still picture, maybe it's better for a magazine piece.

The notion that a video subject ought to change over time

does *not* mean, however, that a new image must appear on the screen every few seconds: an intellectual discussion can be quite gripping if the subject is treated in a lively or compelling way, even if the shots used don't change that much during a half hour. The third criterion for a video idea is that it must engage the audience as much as possible.

Know as much as you can about your audience. For whom, exactly, are you making this video? Let's take a new example—a TV news story about teenagers at a local bowling alley. If your audience is going to be other teenagers, you may focus your video on the bowling alley as a place to exercise and to meet people. If the audience is parents, you could focus on wholesome entertainment that won't get kids into trouble. And if your audience includes all people interested in the subject of bowling, you might incorporate both of the above viewpoints and information about the number of alleys in the country, how many people bowl, why they like it, etc.

Ask yourself questions about your audience. What is their age level? Educational level? Previous knowledge of this particular subject? Under what circumstances will they watch your video? What are they expecting to see and hear? If you're only going to be able to present your video during a five-minute break between classes in school, and what your audience usually sees at this time is instructions for ordering school yearbooks—there's no sense in showing your ten-minute documentary about bowling alleys. Save it for a more appropriate time and place, and a properly expectant and appreciative audience.

In addition to knowing your audience, you need to set goals for what you want to accomplish with your video. A video for a biology class will naturally be quite different from one that translates your favorite song into images. Also, making a music video is not as simple as setting pictures to music. Your objective might be to:

- make the audience want to dance
- create rhythmic patterns that echo the music
- convey the meaning of the lyrics
- show the interrelationship of the band members

The list could go on and on. Naming goals or objectives will take quite a bit of thought, but the more specific you can be, the better your video will turn out.

Sources of Ideas

Ideas may come from anywhere. To help you find them, here are some good sources to spark your imagination.

Newspapers and magazines contain literally hundreds of stories about events and people that can be the basis for interesting videos. You can find the subject matter of a documentary, or a fictional version of the events, or even a character whom you could place in another situation. With a headline like "Fullback Breaks Leg in Skiing Accident; Future Scholarship to College in Doubt," you could imagine:

- a documentary portrait of a teenager agonizing over whether he'll ever be able to go to college or play ball again
- a feature nonfiction piece about people who ski without adequate instruction
- a love story about an injured young man and the physical therapist who gets him back into shape

Read newspapers and magazines often; clip out or copy items that interest you and keep a file of them.

Some people call history "yesterday's news." History books, encyclopedias and similar compilations of fact are great treasure houses of interesting material. Events and people that are years or even centuries old can be relevant to what's happening today. Example: What would happen today if the United States were taken over by a totalitarian enemy, and a small band of rebels met to write a declaration of independence?

Facts are all around us, but you've got to use your curiosity and imagination to evaluate and shape them. If you happen upon a scientific fact which you find particularly amusing or amazing, why not build a video lesson, a fictional story or even a game show around that fact and others like it? Example: Why are a cat's eyes yellow? Couldn't that be a terrific question on "The Great Biology Jackpot"? (First prize, a free ticket to the science fair.)

Your own memories, or those of family or friends, may provide extraordinarily interesting, sad, or funny moments that echo the memories of other people and result in videos meaningful to a wide audience. Even partial impressions taken from memory can be used to augment other stories. Example: to "flesh out" and give more insight to the character of a young man in a story you're inventing, you make him part his hair the way your grandfather did—and that makes him look silly even though he's really quite intelligent.

In your dreams your mind may run in far more imaginative pathways than it does when you are awake. Dreams don't seem to conform to the logic of the everyday world, but through their use of symbols and connections which we don't notice when we are awake, they give us interesting notions. Psychologists and artists consider dreams to be very important sources of knowledge about people's hopes, fears, pleasures, and sorrows. They can also suggest an interesting idea for a video.

Almost any image or impression that strikes you as interesting may be the touchstone from which a story may spring.

In the introduction to his book *Four Screenplays*, Ingmar Bergman writes, "A film for me begins with something very vague—a chance remark or a bit of conversation, a hazy but agreeable event unrelated to any particular situation. It can be a few bars of music, a shaft of light across the street. . . . These are split-second impressions that disappear as quickly as they come, yet they leave behind a mood—like pleasant dreams."

A person's character—who he or she is, how they relate to others, what they've done or wish to do in life—can be the source of many stories, both factual and fictional. Drama often springs from contradictions in a person's character— the six-foot-eight bookworm who hates basketball; the girl who feels ugly but who can't keep the boys away. Try combining two or more people whom you know or have heard about to invent one entirely new character.

Building on the Past

In coming up with an idea it's sometimes helpful to start with a story, a situation, or a format that already exists or that has been tried before by other people. Now you can't just simply use material—or even people's names and lives— without obtaining permission, but there are many ways to build on the past, to utilize a structure that others have previously found worthwhile or interesting.

Formats are types of programs or genres. Some examples are soap operas, quiz shows, documentaries, variety shows, music videos, instructional programs, and half-hour situation comedies. The audience for the quiz show we've called "The Big Biology Jackpot" has a head start on knowing what to expect from your video—and you, as the creator, have a lot less explaining to do. Everyone will understand the categories of easy, medium, and hard questions, even of the bonus tickler and the idea of prizes. Choosing the structure—or format—makes ordering the contents much easier for the videomaker.

Certain formats recur quite regularly. Detective shows, family situation comedies, and soap operas are far from new, yet there are "new" ones every year on the TV networks. "Twilight Zone," a staple of television in its early years, has spawned many similar shows, such as "Amazing Stories." If you have a mystery plot, deciding whether to take it in the direction of a detective story or a fantasy adventure may depend on which format you find more comfortable or challenging.

And then, of course, there's the trick of re-using old stories themselves. Shakespeare lifted the basic love story of *Romeo and Juliet* from earlier writers, and, 350 years later, the creators of *West Side Story* took Shakespeare's version and translated it into modern dress, idiom, and music. Don't be ashamed of working from existing sources, but do be careful to obtain permission to adapt copyrighted material, or else use stories that are now in the "public domain"—in general, material published prior to 1900.

Focus, Focus

Everything we've said just above about sources of ideas, formats, and the like is to help you along the road to focusing your video. How do your choose your focus? By experimenting in your mind with various points of view on a subject until you find the one that best conveys your interests.

For example, suppose you'd like to do something about skateboards, which interest you, but you don't know exactly what you'd like to see on the video screen when you're all finished. Here are a few permutations on the "idea" of skateboards:

Focus One: A documentary, which emphasizes:
1. how exciting skateboards are to ride and how much fun you can have riding them,
2. the number of people who use them, and
3. the ease or difficulty of becoming an expert rider on a skateboard.

Focus Two: Another documentary, which emphasizes:
1. how dangerous the boards can be, not only to users but to people on the streets and sidewalks, and
2. safety equipment which must be worn while on skateboards.

Focus Three: An instructional video, which trains people:
1. how to ride a skateboard, and
2. how to be a responsible skateboarder.

Focus Four: A fictional video about a teenager on a skateboard who glides down the street so effortlessly that he is soon lost, gets into trouble, and then has to make a wild escape.

When you're working with an idea for a video, try to make it as visual and as interesting as you can. Identify your audience, work out clear objectives and goals for your video, and choose among the formats to further refine your idea until it has a clear focus. Then you'll be ready to *write*.

/// 4 ///

Nonfiction Videos

S cripts for videos can be divided into those that are fictional, and those that are not. The concept of nonfiction encompasses a wide variety of subjects, formats, and degrees of objectivity. Most nonfiction video falls into one of the following five categories:

1. Live coverage of events
2. Tape-to-time programs
3. Taped highlights or excerpts
4. Edited news
5. Documentaries

Ranked this way, the categories are points along a line that runs from simply presenting an event (live coverage) through reporting on it (the next three) on to interpreting the event (documentaries). Another way of looking at the continuum is to see it in terms of editing, to say that it runs from the direct broadcast of an event in "real time," or as it's actually happening—without editing—down to a highly edited, carefully composed, and purposefully slanted version of some event that happened in the past.

Live Coverage

"Live coverage" means exactly what it says—the actual broadcasting of an event as it takes place. It could be the launch of a new space shuttle, a performance from the Metropolitan Opera, a big league baseball game, or a Congressional hearing. The basic purpose of this sort of broadcasting is to enable many people in scattered locations to be "present" at an event while it is happening.

Most young videomakers think this sort of broadcasting is difficult to do. Technically, it's not. Many school video systems have the capacity for "going live," but seldom use it, which is a shame, because working live sharpens your ability to think while "on your feet."

Consider a high school football game: The Middleburg High football team is playing in the finals of the state championship for the first time. The game is going to be at the home field. Because of the great interest in the game, tickets to get into the rather small stadium have been sold out for weeks. To accommodate friends, relatives, and fans, the high school's video club is going to be shooting the game with its entire complement of video cameras. The administration has set up several TV screens in the school gymnasium so that people can watch the big game even if they're not in the stadium.

Now, the problem: How to structure the coverage so that people in the gym will get a better view of the game than those actually in the stadium's seats.

The key is preplanning. Before the game begins, you determine the set-up of the coverage. You decide how to best communicate the information about the game. Are the sportscasters going to be partisan (that is, root for the home team), or will they try to be scrupulously fair and simply report what's going on during the game? Do you have just a single camera or several? Where will these cameras be positioned?

What about camera angles? One camera must follow the action. This will probably be best accomplished from a high vantage point, similar to that which you'd get if you were a spectator in the stands. A second might focus on a specific player, most likely the quarterback and whoever carries the ball. If there's a third camera, you might concentrate it on the defense. A fourth might pick up the coach walking along the bench, or the quarterback's mother seated in the stands, or the cheerleaders urging on the home crowd. This "roving" camera is used essentially for reactions to the game.

Tape-to-Time

Now, let's consider the same subject treated with a bit more editing. Suppose your school video system included some fast playback equipment which you could use for showing "instant replays." Or you might consider using the playbacks during a time-out on the field to relive some earlier moments, or to show what one of the "isolated" cameras saw but which you didn't previously have room to broadcast. Or maybe you want to show a previously taped interview with the coach. If you are using any of these elements, then you're dealing with tape-to-time.

Like live coverage, tape-to-time uses video to communicate information that is recorded. Unlike live coverage, though, tape-to-time involves playing back that information, unedited, "on air" rather than broadcasting it as it is happening.

The elements described above, the "instant replays," etc. were previously recorded, *not* edited, and broadcast when they were needed during the live coverage of the game. Those, however, are only one aspect of video that is tape-to-time. The more common use is in programs that must be recorded at one time and broadcast at another and where the budget (both time and money) precludes editing, which is the most time-consuming and (in professional terms) the most expensive part of a production.

Even in an environment such as a school where editing doesn't really cost anything, many video projects benefit from being taped-to-time, because taping a half-hour show in just half an hour requires a lot of planning, and planning is the key to making good videos.

What projects are right to tape-to-time? We'll use two examples of twenty-minute videos: a performance of a band, together with an interview of the band's lead singer; and a science project which takes two hours to complete, and which has many charts and slides to accompany it. How can you capture the band's quality of performance and uniqueness in only twenty minutes of air time? How can you condense a two-hour experiment into twenty minutes without editing?

In tape-to-time, it's essential to locate and ready your elements. In the first example, prepare your interview questions for the lead singer well in advance of any taping. When the band comes to the studio, tape a ten-minute performance; this can be used as a "package" which you can insert into the longer interview. If you like, it can function as a visual and muted audio background for the conversation with the lead singer.

Another sort of preparation is needed in order to condense a two-hour science experiment into a twenty-minute program. In this case, ask your scientist to do the experiment well before taping, and to isolate materials that illustrate the important stages of the experiment. Mount these on slides or easels, and shoot them during the taping; they'll serve to bridge the time between different stages of the experiment.

Study your elements. Time them all in advance of shooting the show. Know how long each stage of the experiment takes, how long your band performance is going to be, how much time you can allocate to the topics being discussed with the lead singer or scientist.

It's also essential to make a "rundown" of your show, in advance. A rundown is an outline which lists segments and how much time each will take. A rundown will give you an idea of pacing. To keep viewer interest high throughout, a show must move along quickly. Capturing spontaneity is as important as keeping a production on schedule, but being in firm control of your elements before you tape increases the chances of keeping your program focused and continually interesting.

Tape-to-time producers think in terms of blocks to build a program. For example, both a "talk" show and a game show would share these common elements:

1. An *opening*, which may be a preproduced package such as an animation, tape or film. It could even be a slide accompanied by the voice of an off-camera announcer. Some shows have a "tease," which shows or says something provocative to keep viewer interest high.
2. *Guests* who have been pre-interviewed before they arrive on the set for taping.
3. *Program purpose*. In a talk show, the discussion; in a game show, the playing of the game.
4. A number of *breaks* or interruptions in the program. Though we tend to think of commercials in this regard, there are also breaks on public broadcasting and cable programs, too. This is the time for a producer to coach the participants on what to do in the next segment, or repair the make-up, or simply to take a break from the intensity of being on camera.
5. A *summary* and/or *closing*. The closing is usually a pre-produced package. On a talk show, the host can review the important points that have been made; during the closing segment of a game show, the grand prize can be awarded.

Here's a rundown for a talk show featuring two guests, one who is pro an issue, and the other who is con, or against, it:

1. Preproduced opening.
2. Host introduces both guests and sets topic.
3. Host questions first guest.
4. Break 1. (Makeup.)
5. Host questions second guest.
6. Break 2. (Producer tells host to ask a certain question in next segment.)
7. Host questions both guests and they argue with one another.
8. Break 3. (Nature calls!)
9. Host summarizes discussion, thanks guests.
10. Preproduced closing.

Taped Highlights or Excerpts

Since most of us aren't present at every event and can't always watch them "live," we rely on taped coverage and, more precisely, on highlights or excerpts. Instant replays or portions of sports events, small "bites" from a speech or an interview—these are the mainstays of news and information programs. Structurally, a highlight is nothing more than a visually and topically self-contained moment that can be counted on to create an impact on the viewer. Effective highlights are usually brief and summarize important aspects of the event, or illustrate the interviewee's point of view.

Edited News

The basic purpose of any news-gathering effort is to communicate facts and to put these facts in context, that is, to make them more readily understandable. "Middleburg High School won the state championship football game on Saturday" (fact). "It was the first state-wide victory ever to be won in the history of the school's athletic program" (context).

A picture is worth a thousand words, they say; if so, then video images, with their sense of immediacy and participation, must be worth tens of thousands. Indeed, video has dramatically increased the ability of news organizations to present information in ways that go beyond the mere recitation of facts.

Most television news relies on structured and edited presentations of fact and context, rather than live broadcasts of an event while it is in progress. A news broadcast consists, generally, of many taped "packages" that are connected by a correspondent in the studio. The "package," then, is the essential unit of edited news. For example, a "package" covering the Middleburg High School championship game might have the following elements:

1. *Location Pictures.* General shots of the place where the story is unfolding—in this instance, the playing field, the crowd, cheerleaders, people coming and going.
2. *Action Pictures.* The action as it unfolds. Usually this means moments in the story of high interest—such as described in "Excerpts." For example, the winning touchdown, the fumble that blew the lead, the quarterback accepting the Most Valuable Player award.
3. *Interviews.* The reporter (on camera) talking with key players, coaches, celebrities, also on camera. This includes reverse shots, or angles in which the reporter listens to what the interviewees have to say.
4. *Discussion.* A review of the game's highlights with both the opposing coaches.
5. *Stand-ups.* The reporter, at the location, making opening,

closing, or bridging remarks. (Bridges are passages that tie different segments of the story material together.)

6. *Voice-over.* The reporter's recorded comments, which are used in conjunction with action or location pictures.

7. *Graphics.* Supporting visual materials such as charts, logos, and subtitles.

8. *Natural Sound* and *Music.* Location sounds, often recorded "wild," or not in conjunction with the pictures; music added to heighten moods.

From these elements, we can sketch out a sample news report on the game:

VIDEO	AUDIO
1. Stand-up Open Reporter at scene on camera (OC)	Reporter headlines the story of the game and establishes his/her presence on scene
2. Action Shots/Highlights	Reporter voice-over (V.O.) and location sound
3. Location Shots Cheering crowd, school band	V.O. continues as reporter introduces key game interviews
4. Interview, Quarterback	Quarterback and reporter talking
5. Location Shots Crowd going home	Reporter V.O. sound bridge to intro discussion with coaches
6. Discussion begins Two opposing coaches	Coaches' discussion
7. Action Shots, more highlights	Sound of coaches' discussion continues through
8. Graphics	Reporter V.O. about chart which shows regional standings

9. Stand-up Close   Reporter sums up story
                                     school band music rises to full
                                     cadence and report ends

Documentaries

Documentaries are generally longer than edited news pieces, take more time to make, and are less tied to the present moment. Although they are prepared with the same elements as edited news, they differ markedly because these elements are put to a different use. Documentaries are visual essays that use journalistic techniques to consciously comment on the meaning or impact of events. They emphasize context over content—in general, the better defined the context, the more effective the documentary—and are the most subjective and personal of all the nonfiction forms.

As in-depth analyses of subjects or events from an individual perspective, documentaries are the most heavily edited of the nonfiction forms. They are structured to promote a specific editorial point of view, and present only carefully selected information about a subject. Edited news aims for reportorial objectivity and impartiality, but documentaries try to interpret things and strive to sway the audience's emotions and intellect.

To illustrate how documentary treatments might be focused, let's go back to our earlier example of the Middleburg championship football game:

Outline 1. The New Player. A portrait of a nervous new guy who has never played on a high school team before, as he's on his way to take part in a championship game.

Outline 2. How's It Going, Coach? This deals with the relationship between the coach and his players—what has happened during the season, and what happens as they approach and then play the big game.

Outline 3. The Long Road to Victory. This one concentrates on the heroic struggle in which an underdog team, whom nobody came out to see, surges on to the state championship game. It would detail the relationship of fans to the team.

Outline 4. Rah, Rah, Rah. This chronicles the moods of the crowd, and how they affect the playing of the game. It would take a look at cheerleaders, and at fans of both the winners and the losers.

Outline 5. Behind the Scenes. The people who set up the schedule, handle the tickets and the concession stands and the equipment, and get the field in good playing condition, but who are so busy that they hardly get to watch the game.

These are just a few of many possible documentaries that could be made about the game. The basic information—who played, who won, who lost—may be the same in all the outlines listed above, but nearly everything else changes from one to the next. Each one has a different focus and a different story to tell. Each one portrays the thoughts and feelings of a different cast of central characters. Each one has a unique "slant" that reflects the producer's opinion of the events taking place. And each makes a statement that is expressed through the careful editing of content, the pacing of action, and the overall composition of visual and factual elements.

To sum up, when creating a nonfiction video, you'll need to make a series of decisions to come up with the format, subject matter, and focus. Here are some of them.

- *Determine who your audience is.* Are you preparing a video for young people, your parents, your teachers, your adversaries?

- *Determine the editorial purpose of your video.* Are you recording, reporting, or interpreting an event?
- *Find what you want to say and how to say it.* Does your subject lend itself to visual presentation? Does your format help convey its essence?

And remember, there are no hard-and-fast rules for what makes a good video presentation. Experiment to find what works best for you.

/// 5 ///

Fiction Videos

Fiction differs from nonfiction in that it is, strictly speaking, not true. Even so, fiction often can convey important impressions of our world in ways that nonfiction cannot. That's because fiction has methods of affecting our emotions that go beyond what nonfiction can usually accomplish. However, all fictional stories, no matter how wild, have roots in the real world of human emotion. A video set in the fourteenth century, about a man who tames a dragon, draws upon the same basic emotional impressions as does a video of a contemporary teenager who has to contend with uncaring parents. The impact of a fictional piece doesn't depend on how closely it mimics today's world, but, rather, on how insightful it is and on how it stirs our emotions.

Dramas and comedies both have stories to tell that require plots and characters. What's the difference between them? More important, how do you decide which form you want to use?

In general, the decision rests on what kinds of points you want to make with your story. In the fifth century B.C. Aristotle wrote that tragedies dealt with people who were noble and high-born, and comedies with those who were low-born and ignoble—but today there is plenty of nobility in the common man, and silliness in the upper classes.

Since the word *tragedy* is much abused today, we'd rather

call the opposite of comedy a serious drama. That is a story in which the people and actions deal with important matters in a thoughtful, serious way. The characters are usually well-defined individuals and the action in such a drama is usually resolved only after it has cost a major character something.

Comedies generally have more exaggerated characters—types, rather than individuals. Think of the denizens of "Night Court," who are comic caricatures, as opposed to those in "St. Elsewhere," who, although they may have their funny moments, are basically realistic individuals involved in serious dramatic stories. The plots of comedies tend to depend on absurd circumstances or coincidences, involve physical action that makes people look silly—slipping on a banana peel, getting a pie in the face—and are resolved happily at the end.

Many stories now cross the lines of comedy and drama—there are adventure comedies, fantasy dramas, and comedic treatments of such serious subjects as abortion, homosexuality, and nuclear war. However, all comedies and dramas have stories with beginnings, middles, and ends, and present characters caught in difficult or interesting situations.

A third type of fictional piece is the hybrid known as a "performance" video. Performance videos have emerged from contemporary rock music, a musical idiom in which the theatricality of a live performance is often as important to the audience as the music itself. The video is supposed to be more of an experience for the audience than simply seeing the performer in concert.

Usually, the actual recorded performance is augmented by other images—generally multiple, fragmentary, quick-cut montages that give such videos more of the quality of abstract paintings than of film.

Rules for such videos are hard to come by; the major criterion is that they must be exciting for the audience, and, generally, the more strikingly visual they are, the greater their impact. Although most performance videos don't have stories, a subspecies known as "concept" videos do have stories and intriguing characters who star in them—for example, Michael Jackson's "Thriller" or the narrative poems in song form told by Billy Joel.

What's in a Story?

Any good story has some insight into the human condition, or, as we'll call it, the "truth" of the story. That's the first element for you to think about—what's your story going to say to people about the world? Insights need not be something grand, and should never be overtly expressed in the actual dialogue of a story, but they must come alive for the audience. "Life is difficult, but rewarding" may sound like a cliché, but if that's the insight that an audience draws from a story which deals with teenage suicide, the impact could be substantial.

The second element is "plot"—the basic story of the video—and the third is the "milieu" or surroundings in which the story takes place.

Visualize the relationship among these elements by imagining a ball which has an inner core (the "truth"), a large middle section around that core (the "plot"), and an outer covering ("milieu") which is its surface. When we make our video and show it, if we've done our job properly, the audience will be entertained by the plot and milieu, and will come to understand that core of insight or truth.

"Milieu," a French word that means "in the midst of," is the place where the action is happening. Your story could be set among motorcyclers, or among poor students at an ultra-academic high school, or among the half-men, half-robots in the mechanized world of the twenty-third century. In each case the milieu provides the physical setting, but also suggests specific notions for costumes, modes of speech, and even the previous histories and backgrounds of the characters. People in a story about Australian Olympic swimmers are going to look, feel, talk in different phrases and come from a different sort of background than those in a story about the inmates of a Soviet prison camp.

In novels and short stories, where the action often has to do with a person's inner thoughts, character usually is more important than plot. In the visual media, this is generally reversed. A visual medium has to deal with what the eye can see, and, most often, this means externalized action—what people do, as opposed to what they think—one man pursuing another, rather than sitting at a desk solving a puzzle.

A plot is the sum total of all the actions in a story, and the operative word here is *action*. Action is a concept that is often misunderstood. We tend to think of action dramas as shoot-'em-ups, but real dramatic action has to do with conflict, physical or mental. We can define a dramatic plot, then, as one that shows a conflict. Most often, that clash is between what a character wants, and what prevents that character from achieving his or her desire.

Every plot must have a clear beginning, middle, and end. In the visual media, we usually begin a story when the action is quite far advanced. Example: when writing about the break-up of the band, it wouldn't be necessary to recount the long history of the band's formation, its struggles to get to the top, and so on. We could start the story at the point where the band is at the height of its popularity but signs of strain are showing.

When does the middle begin? That question has thrown a lot of people, but the answer is that in the middle, circumstances are usually different than they are at the beginning. The middle of the story is thought of as a long period of struggle by the characters to achieve their goal. When one band member institutes a lawsuit against another, the beginning of the story is left behind, and we're smack in the middle.

Circumstances have changed so much that the band members can't go back to the relationships with one another that they had at the outset of the story.

In dramatic terms the end of the story is when the conflicts are resolved. The period of struggle is brought to a close. Things may or may not continue to be difficult for the characters from here on, but the audience is left with a clear feeling that important issues have been attacked and solved.

Each action in a story must follow logically out of the one that precedes it. That may seem like a Chinese riddle, but it's not. Each event that happens in a story ought to bear some direct relationship to the events that came before it. Remember the old saying, "for want of a nail, the shoe was lost; for want of a shoe, the horse was lost"? That sort of cause-and-effect interlocking makes for good stories. Also, it's a good idea to write stories in which the actions are in proportion to one another. If a man leaves the cap off a tube of toothpaste, his wife shouldn't murder him because of it—her action would then bear little relation to what he had done.

A plot must be interesting and suspenseful. Most successful plots put the main characters in jeopardy, in danger of losing something or someone important to them as a consequence of actions they're taking (or are reluctant to take). Suspense is maintained so we'll keep watching to "see how it turns out."

A plot without believable characters seems empty and mechanical—as if the players were cartoons, caricatures, or robots incapable of a wide variety of human emotions.

The only rule for characters in a drama is that they must somehow be of interest to us. So—how does one create a character?

Visualize yourself working from the outside in—go from a description of the physical attributes to a description of the inner, mental attitudes. Decide what the character looks like. Consider age, sex, size, intelligence, handicaps, or particular strengths. Is the person handsome? Does the character wear terrible clothes, or have hair that is too long by current fashion standards?

Next, consider the character's background—upbringing, financial status, educational level, religious beliefs, particular incidents in the past which could have some bearing on the story. (As you list these, you'll find your mind jumping with ideas that may help you shape your plot, as well.)

It's really important to set down some of the character's ways of dealing with people. Some young men can talk easily with other young men, but are tongue-tied in the presence of women. Other people take everything anybody says to them as an insult. Both modes of behavior could be used for dramatic interactions in a story.

It is just as important to consider conflict when creating a character as when constructing a plot. People who are easy-going and whose relationships have no strain in them are generally not "dramatic." Suppose the character wants to be rich, but is quite lazy; that conflict in his/her personality could be part of a dramatic story. Characters that are not completely wonderful in all aspects of their personality are more human, and more likely to have to struggle continuously against themselves and against many elements in their world—and are fit subjects for drama.

Of course plot, characters, milieu, and all the other concepts introduced in the preceding paragraphs are flexible ones. Writers often break the rules. Use the rules only as a sort of guide or checklist for yourself, and break them if you have to. It's really up to your imagination.

Script Format

There are many different formats for fictional scripts. Some list every cut or shot; others describe master scenes and leave the precise shots up to the director; still others give the dialogue and very few physical action descriptions. In general, you should put into a script what you want the audience to see, and shouldn't put in what cannot be seen. For example:

Exterior, day. The Beach House.
MARY walks along the water's edge on a blustery day, wearing her usual sweatsuit. She spots something in the water, though, that terrifies her, and crouches down, afraid.

This description of the action shows us what Mary was thinking, but doesn't tell us *why* Mary was afraid; we don't put in that her fear stemmed from a bad childhood experience, because we can't *see* that. Also, in this description, the precise "shots" the director might use are not indicated—that's because there may be many ways of shooting and editing the scene, and what the writer must convey is the mood, the tone, the action. The rest is up to other people on the creative team. If it were essential for the script to tell us that we understand Mary's terror by a close-up of her eyes, wide with fear, then we'd put that in, but there are many ways of conveying her fright and the close-up of the eyes is only one of them.

A format adapted by many writers has the script page divided approximately into thirds. For dialogue, characters' names are centered on the page, and the dialogue is put into paragraphs below the name; the margins are one-third of the page in from the left, and one-third from the right, so that the dialogue occupies a column along the middle third of the page. In these descriptions, action words are put in capital letters, as are the names of characters. Where necessary within the dialogue itself, additional stage directions are enclosed in parentheses.

In the following script sample we've tried to illustrate some of the principles of plot and character construction discussed in this chapter, and we've also put the script in a good format. The example is taken from the rock band story.

---

1. Sidewalk in front of skyscraper. Exterior, afternoon.

location?
interior or exterior?
time of day?

BARRY (long-haired, with fringed denims, cowboy boots, tall and skinny) is WALKING NERVOUSLY toward the camera with DENNIS (short hair, horn-rimmed glasses, briefcase, three-piece suit).

Descriptions of the action, and stage directions, are put into paragraph form and are flush left.

> BARRY
> I don't like it, man. It's as if I'm getting divorced, and we've never been married!

DENNIS STOPS BARRY's motion on the street and PULLS HIM AROUND so they face one another.

Direction for the actor.

> DENNIS
> (Low-volume voice)
> Do you want to lose $350,000 because you hate fighting?

> BARRY
> (Thinks)

The director might want a close-up here, but it's not essential for the writer to say so — that would clutter up the script.

> DENNIS
> (Lighter)
> Leave the arguments to me. That's what lawyers are for. Musicians don't fight, they harmonize.

> BARRY
> They used to, anyway.

writer thinks camera direction here is needed to understand the action. Conveys idea of "entering" the building.

The two men RESUME WALKING, and GO INTO the skyscraper. Camera remains outside and TILTS SLOWLY UP the building.

Some writers put "cuts" in, others do not.

CUT TO:

2. Elegant conference room. Int. Day.

abbreviation of "interior"

writer is saying the lawyers ought to look alike.

SAM (three-piece suit, dark hair, dark eyes, goodlooking) LOOKS OUT the window while SALLY (short hair, round face, earrings, black leather pants outfit) SITS at the conference table, STARING blankly at her hands. SAM COMES OVER from the window, KISSES HER gently on the cheek.

A visual clue that they may have an intimate relationship as well as a business one.

SAM
They'll be here in a few minutes.

SALLY
(Intense)
Barry's never made it to a recording session on time; why would he start being different, now?

SAM
This is supposed to be a negotiation, not a mud-slinging contest.

SALLY SQUEEZES HIS HAND, smiles.

SAM
I'll get you some coffee.

SAM LEAVES the frame, and the camera CLOSES IN on SALLY until we ...

DISSOLVE TO:

3. School band room. Int., late afternoon. (Ten years before.)

SALLY, younger and less punk-looking, is UNCOVERING a set of drums in this typical band room. There's no one around to see her.

She SITS DOWN at the drums and STARTS TO PLAY. We can tell that she's good at this. She gets very involved in the rhythm she's beating out.

We CUT TO a side door of the large band room where BARRY (younger, too, and less cocky) APPROACHES THE DOOR from outside to discover who's making the sounds. He WATCHES SALLY for a moment. Then his face brightens, and he BACKS AWAY from the door and GOES OUT of frame.

We CUT BACK TO SALLY, at the drums. After a moment, and in rhythm with the drums we and she HEAR an electronic guitar chime in with chords.

SALLY LOOKS ABOUT, but can't see who's making these sounds. Since they're in rhythm with hers, she CONTINUES her drumming.

BARRY STEPS OUT of the shadows in the back of the room and WALKS TOWARD her, play-

---

Handwritten margin notes:

Is this necessary? If the lines are written well enough to tell the actress how to say them, then such directions aren't needed.

Information required by the audience to know what's going on. Also we see (lawyer 2) calming his client as I did: the writer is making an observation about lawyers.

Here, again, is information the audience needs to know — and to see *in action*.

Sally's impression of Barry's character tells us as much about her as it does about him.

This screen direction is necessary so the writer can say how to make the transition between scenes. A dissolve often indicates the passage of time.

A visual image says it better than the dialogue could.

This second set of images could be written down as a new scene, but the writer understands it as part of the "master" scene.

A little mystery adds fun to the scene. And the audience knows something the character doesn't yet know.

ing—and now he's doing melody, not just chords.

They NOD at each other, and we understand they've never met before. But they're playing well together.

Intercuts of kids LOOKING IN at the half-windows on the band-room doors. BARRY and SALLY CONTINUE PLAYING. One kid OPENS the door and COMES IN.

Twenty kids GATHERED AT THE EDGE of the bandroom to hear the duo. BARRY and SALLY FINISH with a flourish, and the kids BURST INTO APPLAUSE.

                    BARRY
          Fantastic!
              (Pause)
          My name's Barry.
                    SALLY
          Sally.

They REACH OVER TO SHAKE HANDS. Camera COMES IN rapidly for a close-up of the hands being SHAKEN as we

                    MATCH DISSOLVE TO:

4. The conference room. Late afternoon. Int.

MATCHED SHOT of SALLY and BARRY SHAKING HANDS in the conference room. PULL OUT to reveal they're older than in previous scene, and not grinning much, anymore.

The "business" of this scene is to tell the audience how they met. The idea is conveyed through action, not dialogue.

These "intercuts" show time passing, also.

In a match dissolve the image at the end of one scene is similar in size, proportion and placement within the frame to the image at the start of the next scene.

At the end of the sequence we should feel how much has changed since Sally and Barry met, years ago.

In a video, good scripts are essential—but they are also only a beginning, a foundation upon which the members of the creative team can build. Scripts provide a guide for those in front of and behind the cameras. During the early stage of a production, the script is the only concrete vision of what will come into being when everybody's work is done and the video is completed.

/// **6** ///

The Video Hardware System

For several chapters we've been discussing ideas and how to develop them. To make your ideas into videos, you need to work with the mechanical components of the video hardware system.

Video systems come in varying sizes and are distinguished from one another primarily by the width of the magnetic tape they employ. The wider the tape, the more information it can carry, and, therefore, the better its quality of detail. Two-inch or one-inch wide tape formats are called "broadcast standard" because they are accepted for broadcast on one of the big TV networks or its local affiliates.

Smaller format tape systems, if not always up to "broadcast standard," are really quite good, and they're getting better every year due to technological advances. In fact, network and local news divisions shoot and broadcast in ¾-inch mode which uses video cassettes rather than bulky reels to store recorded images. There are also ½-inch systems and 8 mm. "camcorder" size tape systems. Schools, homes, and community facilities generally have the smaller format systems, which are more than adequate for most purposes.

In fact, smaller systems have the advantage of being portable and needing less light added to a scene to obtain reasonably good pictures. And they're easier to operate and more fun to use.

The Tools

The four main components in any video system are the camera, the microphone, the recording device, and the playback device. In many video cameras, that unit also incorporates a microphone and a cassette on which the information is recorded, so there are fewer separate elements—but all four components are necessary to have a complete system.

The video camera is the artist's most important tool. However, such a camera is not an independent piece of equipment, like a still photographer's camera. It is useful only when combined with the recorder and/or playback device.

To demonstrate how the system functions, let's contrast audiotape, videotape, and film recording systems. In a "tape" system (whether audiotape or videotape), information goes through several transformations before it is seen or heard by an audience. Information must be received, and generally recorded and stored before being played back. To process images, a video camera receives reflected light from an object and transforms it into electrical energy. The microphone similarly transforms sound into electrical impulses.

These electrical impulses—both from the images and the sounds—are then used to rearrange the magnetic orientation of oxide particles on magnetic tape, a process we call recording. The tape is not visibly altered, but, rather, stores on its surface the impulses in the form of magnetic energy.

In contrast, reflected light enters a film camera and causes a chemical reaction on a treated piece of celluloid. This transforms blank film into film that has images permanently etched into it. To be viewed, the film must be chemically treated so that further exposure to light will not alter the images. Film is actually changed by images, tape is not.

To play back film, light is projected through it and you see shadows on a screen. To play back an audio or videotape means recalling electrical impulses from the magnetic tape;

they are "read" by devices which retransform them into sound or light waves. The light waves are used to make the phosphors on the surface of a television screen glow—and we see that glowing image.

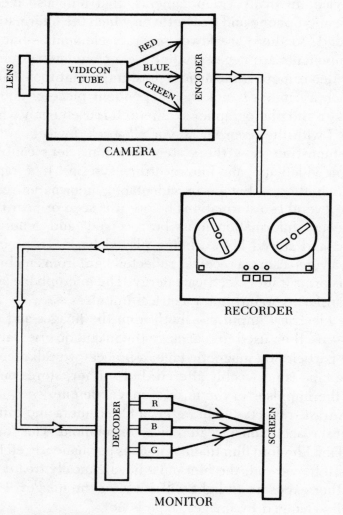

THE VIDEO SYSTEM

This is a schematic drawing of the basic video hardware system. Information comes in through the camera's lens and is processed several times before it reaches the monitor's screen.

What You See Is Not
Actually What You Get

Video images are really an optical illusion. If you were to tremendously enlarge and stop the image, you'd see row upon row of small dots that are combinations of the three primary colors red, blue, and green, and which were produced by shooting light onto the screen with a device that has the rapid-fire repeat action of a machine gun.

When a TV screen is "on" it is criss-crossed by several hundred "lines" along which these red, blue, and green dots are being placed. The lines fill the screen going from left to right and from top to bottom at a rate much faster than the eye can distinguish, so that what you see appears continuous even though it's not. Most systems produce 525 lines every 1/30 of a second. Although 1/2- and 3/4-inch systems have the same number of "lines of resolution" as the larger systems, their pictures are often less clear and distinct.

To use your video system properly, you must become familiar with it. By reading the instruction manual for your system and by testing the equipment under controlled conditions, you'll learn what it's capable of doing. Try exploring these parameters:

Minimum Illumination Level. Find and test the minimum illumination level of the system. A camera needs more light to "see" than the human eye does, and your video camera won't function well without lots of light around. Use the camera and a monitor screen to find the minimum amount of light you'll need in order to produce an image. Check this by means of a light meter. Make a practice tape noting varying levels of light and what sort of images they produce.

Gray Scale. This is a key to how many gradations from white to black, light to dark, your camera can distinguish. A sample gray scale is often included with a new camera, or one can be obtained from a professional supply store. A good chart has thirty or more gradations. Set it up in front of your camera, aim lights at it, and count how many gradations your camera can discern; a good camera, whether black-and-white or color, should pick out twenty or more. If your camera finds less, add more light to the scene, which will allow the camera to separate bands which in lower light might seem to be the same color and density.

Phosphor Trails. See how quickly you can move your camera without creating a phosphor trail. The inside of a cathode-ray tube (video monitor) is coated with phosphors which glow for about 1/60 of a second after they are hit by light. If you move the camera too quickly, or move an object too swiftly through a camera's field of view, the result will be a phosphor trail, streak, or ghost. These "glitches" occur when the camera is unable to shift quickly enough from one intensity of light on an object to another intensity of light on a second object. Practice moving with the camera slowly and steadily, giving it enough time to change from a darker image to a lighter one, until you develop a feel for doing it without creating problems.

The next three parameters involve adjusting the record/playback parts of the system as well as the camera. Since some are controls that are also present on regular television sets, you may already be familiar with them.

Color Adjustment. Because electronic impulses are separated into red, blue, and green, in color cameras and recorders there are separate controls for all three colors. Experiment with these controls to see how each color affects the others, then fine-tune your camera so that the images on the monitor most precisely approximate the colors of real life. Before shooting—each time!—use a colored bar graph to "balance" your reds, blues, and greens.

Contrast and Brightness. Controls for these are also on cameras and recorder/playback machinery. Brightness has to do with the overall light level of a scene, and how the camera is perceiving it. Contrast has to do with the differences in light levels between various parts of the scene. Boosting the light level poured into a scene will raise the brightness but may not affect the contrast. If the contrast is low, everything looks murky. Contrast is heightened (made more acute) when the differences between one part of the scene and another are emphasized, when one part seems light and another dark.

Horizontal and Vertical Hold. Horizontal hold prevents "rollover" in which the top and bottom portions of a picture appear to have exchanged places. Vertical hold prevents the picture from slipping into diagonal lines in which the image is distorted. The holds are both functions of the "lines of resolution." Adjust these controls until your picture on the monitor remains steady. Again, this is something to be done before each shoot, and during technical breaks.

Reverse, Fast-Forward, Scan, Frame Advance. In reverse and fast-forward the tape moves through the player too quickly to allow viewing the actual image. Frame advance moves it forward a small fraction each second, and scans, at six times the normal forward speed—fast, but not so fast that the image can't be understood visually. Experiment with these playback controls until you are quickly and easily able to locate portions of previously recorded material. This will facilitate the editing process.

/// 7 ///

The Camera

All cameras, whether still, motion picture, or video, utilize a principle of physics whereby light that is reflected from the surface of an object (a tree, a bicycle, a person) is used to capture and record an image of that object.

A video camera uses several basic elements to focus and record images. As with all cameras, a video camera has an *aperture,* or variable opening, through which reflected light enters the body of the camera. The aperture can be widened or narrowed, depending on the brightness or darkness of the subject. (Bright subjects require a smaller aperture than do dark ones.) The second element is a *lens*—or, often, a series of lenses—that enables the camera to focus on a single point within the field of view. The "focal length" of that lens is sometimes adjustable. The third element in the camera is the device which captures the reflected light that has been brought into the camera by the aperture and lens. In the video camera, this is called the *vidicon tube.* This is a photon collector which traps, separates, and transforms the light energy into electrical impulses. These impulses are then transmitted through the rest of the video system.

The vidicon tube is extremely sensitive to light—so much so, that you can "blind" your camera by inadvertently pointing it at a bright light. Once, on an Apollo lunar mission, the astronauts pointed their portable TV camera directly at the sun—and, as a result, there were no pictures from outer space on that voyage. They had burned out the vidicon tube.

From the vidicon tube, the light enters a refraction device that separates the light into the three primary colors, red, blue, and green. Each one is electrically encoded, and then the three streams of electronic signals are mixed and transmitted to the recorder.

The Lens System

A video camera generally has two lenses, one outside the camera (which can be changed or varied), and one inside it. These control the *focus*—the sharpness of the image. As you know from using your own eyes, if you focus on an object a few feet away from you, objects much farther away will appear fuzzy, and those much nearer to you will also be blurred. Only one part of the entire field of view is usually so sharply defined that we can say it is "in focus." To shift focus requires that the eye's lens—or the camera's system of lenses—change configuration. This is done in a camera by altering the distance of the lens from the recording medium—in the video camera, the distance of the lens from the receptors of the vidicon tube.

There are four types of lenses: *normal, wide-angle, tele-photo,* and *zoom.* A normal lens most closely mimics the eye's usual perspective. A scene viewed through a normal lens will look to a viewer substantially the same as if they were looking at it themselves. A wide-angle lens distorts the image by including in the frame a much wider range of objects and surroundings than is usually seen by the human eye. A tele-photo is the opposite of a wide-angle lens; it enables us to capture a portion of the field of view that is very far away, by making it appear as if it were very close. Like the wide-angle lens, the telephoto introduces some distortion of the "normal" image. This "long lens" tends to "flatten" the image, that is, to eliminate from the picture those clues which usually enable us to separate an object from its background. Zoom lenses are those capable of changing focal length, from normal to telephoto, back to wide-angle, and so on—all inside a single structure.

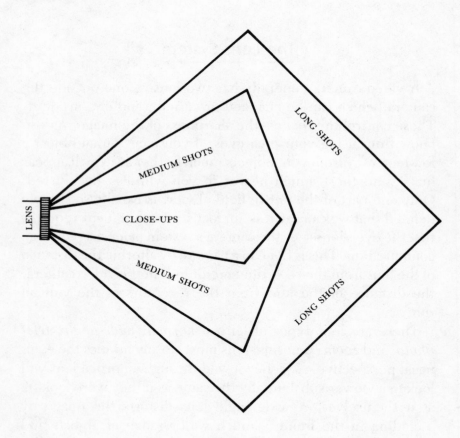

A hint about using lenses. When a cameraperson or a director uses anything but a "normal" lens, the shot calls attention to itself because it is different from our normal sight. Excessive use of telephoto, wide-angle, or zoom lenses usually distracts viewers, and takes away from their enjoyment of the video they are watching. So use these special lenses carefully.

Camera work

In his classic book *The Five C's of Cinematography* (1965), Joseph Mascelli outlines the principles of camera work for motion pictures. The principles of video camera work are much the same as those for feature film work, and the five Cs are a good way to remember some basic needs for camera work.

The five Cs are:

- camera angle
- composition
- continuity
- close-ups
- cutting

Camera Angle. By camera angle, we mean not only the placement of the camera within the scene but also the relative size of the images.

To choose such things as camera angles, one must first have a well-defined point of view. That point of view is not simply the province of the camera operator, but must be developed in conjunction with others who are concerned with the artistic conception of a project, such as the director, the writer, even the actors and actresses. Here are a few types of viewpoints:

- sympathetic to a particular character
- objective—viewing all characters equally
- subjective for one character

Suppose you're doing a dramatic scene in which a boy and girl are breaking up. If the point of view is objective, you might set the camera back far into the room, away from the characters, and look at what is happening to them from there. In this view we might see them both, full-length, sitting on chairs, talking.

If the point of view is sympathetic to both characters, you might want to use a lot of close-ups as well as camera movements that would help convey to the audience how difficult this moment is for the people in the scene. And if the point of view is subjective for the boy, we might see the scene from his eyes, looking only at the girl, or down at his hands. If the boy were thinking of the girl as heartless or cruel, we could place the camera near the floor or at some other angle that would distort the image of the girl on the screen.

To help envision the various possible camera angles, imagine five people sitting on various pieces of furniture in the living room of a house. A "master shot," or "establishing shot," shows us all the people and furniture in the scene. It allows the audience to know where in time and space these people are. Master shots are often shown at the beginning of a scene, and sometimes not used again.

A "medium shot" would show a few but not all of the people in the scene, either as full-length or half-length figures, about as we would see them if we were actually present and in the midst of the room ourselves.

"Close-ups," or "tight" shots, are isolated details in the room—faces, hands, small objects—which we can expand by using our telephoto lens until they take up an entire screen.

All other camera angles are variations of these first three.

There are high angles, low angles, all sorts of side angles.

A script might request a "two-shot" which favors one of the two people; this means that the person favored is usually depicted closer to the camera, but favoring could also be accomplished by having that person be more brightly lit.

An "ECU" is an "extreme close-up." Suppose we began a shot on an ECU of a boat in a painting on the wall of the living room; this might be the starting frame of a "zoom-out." Such a shot begins with a small detail and uses the camera's zoom lens to steadily widen the view and see progressively more and more of the room.

A "zoom in" does the reverse, that is, begins with a long-shot of all the people in the room and steadily narrows the focus until it is fixed on a small detail. In "rack focus," the zoom lens is used to shift the audience's attention from, say, one person in the room to another who is closer or further away from the camera, without physically moving the camera.

The other important shots involve actual physical movement of the camera. In a "pan" shot, the camera is swiveled along a horizontal axis from a focus on one person or object to another. A "tilt" shot is much the same, only on a vertical axis. In a "trucking shot," the whole camera—usually on wheels—is moved toward or away from the scene. These shots are most often attempted while the camera is on a tripod to steady it.

Composition. Composition is the art of arranging people and objects within the frame—the frame of a painting, or of a still picture, a motion picture or a video picture. Good composition helps to make a scene interesting, and bad composition can detract from the audience's enjoyment of the scene.

There are many rules of composition. The major idea behind all of them is to use the eye's natural inclinations to enhance the viewer's understanding or enjoyment of what he or she is seeing on the screen.

Here are just a couple of rules for composition.

Brightness. The eye is naturally drawn first to areas within a frame that are brighter than others. If you want to stress a particular object or person, highlight that in contrast to its surroundings. (This will be discussed in more detail in a subsequent chapter about the art of lighting.) Conversely, if you want to draw attention away from an area, you can darken it.

Rule of Three. We see things in groups of three, or in thirds. Use this natural inclination by placing objects or people within a frame so that there is one point of interest in each third of the frame. One of these three will become the "focal point" of the frame, as if a triangle were drawn between the three points of interest in the frame as a whole, and this one point was at the apex of the triangle. When the audience looks at a frame, a viewer's eye usually jumps from the apex to the two other points and back to the apex.

Good composition usually means a frame is arranged so that it is "dynamic" rather than "static" or motionless. To be dynamic a frame does not have to have something moving in it at all times; rather, to be dynamic means that the picture must not be too dull and ordinary.

When most of the focus is drawn to the exact center of the frame, and/or the screen is filled with objects in medium-shot, or with "objective" shots, things will get dull. Varying the placement of the focus, the size of the objects in the frame, and the sensitivity of the point of view will give you dynamic frames.

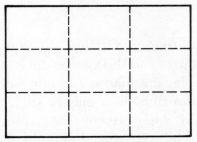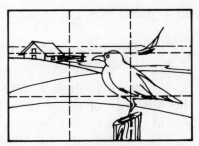

We tend to see in thirds. This frame is divided into three horizontally and vertically.

Three points of interest in the frame, arranged to draw the eye to them alternately.

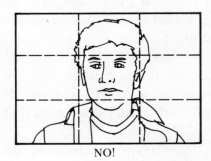

NO!   YES!

Keep your focus away from boring midpoints.

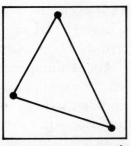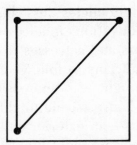

TRIANGLES OF FOCUS. Use ideas like these to "compose" your frames.

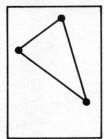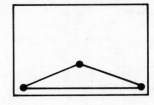

Continuity. In a video, the *continuity of action, direction, and detail must always be maintained* so the viewer does not become disoriented. For example, if a man is running from the left side of the screen to the right in a master shot, it would be confusing for viewers if, when we cut to a medium shot, he is running from right to left. His speed of motion in the second cut must be much the same as it is in the first, and if he carried a ball in his right hand in the first shot, he mustn't have accidentally transferred it to the left hand in the second shot. All these things sound simple, but when you are shooting scenes out of continuity—that is, one shot at a time, and possibly doing master scenes on Monday and no close-ups until Tuesday—the simple things can go awry. To avoid messing up on such details, a "shot list" is made. It records every scene shot for your video, and the action that takes place in it.

A shooting script contains both more and less information than a writer's earlier scripts. More, because it includes essential information about actions, locations, costumes, props, and camera angles; less, because it excludes details of character motivation, nuances of behavior, and suggestions for the actors and actresses to interpret. The shooting script is for technicians to follow. Each shot is numbered, however brief it might be. Whereas the writer's earlier scripts of "the Barclay house" scene might have been written in two "master" shots—an exterior and an interior—the shooting script is divided into eight different shots.

Sample Page of Shooting Script

47. EXT., NIGHT, FRONT OF BARCLAY HOUSE. LS, policemen GRAY, BROWN, and GREEN, in uniform. They MOVE AWAY FROM CAMERA TOWARD the lit windows and dark porch of the house.

Camera movements, angles and character names are in capital letters to make them stand out.

48. SAME. MCU, GRAY, who TURNS TO BROWN and GREEN, GESTURES for them to get down and spread out.

49. SAME. MCU, reaction shot of BROWN and GREEN as they LOWER TO GROUND. GREEN EXITS FRAME LEFT, BROWN remains.

Screen direction may be important for later continuity.

50. INT., NIGHT, LIVING ROOM OF BARCLAY HOUSE. MS, card table and people near window. We see only three men in white undershirts and shoulder holsters, PLAYING CARDS. Beer bottles empty, ashtrays full.

Only important details are mentioned.

> GEORGE
> I'll call.

With no indication to the contrary, it is understood that the editor will cut from shot to shot.

51. SAME. CU of GEORGE's hands as he PUSHES chips to center.

52. SAME. CONTINUE 50 and PAN RIGHT from GEORGE to REVEAL fourth player, JANE, in evening gown. She GRINS, then LAYS DOWN three jacks, two sevens.

> JANE
> (mock innocence)
> What d'you call this again—big house? full deck?

53. SAME. GEORGE, MCU, as he disgustedly THROWS IN his cards.

Calls for special effect—needs pre-planning!

Off: sounds of GROANS from other men. Cloud of cigar smoke OBSCURES THE SCREEN.

Important sounds also in capitals. Off-screen sounds may be added in later, rather than shot at same time as master scene.

54. SAME. MS, JANE FANS AWAY smoke, REACHES OUT for the pot. Then, off, sound of a PEBBLE HITTING THE WINDOW. Many hands UPSET THE TABLE and it obstructs camera's view of JANE.

This off-screen noise helps link inside and outside scenes that may be shot at different times.

Calls for the shot holding longer than usual at its end, to allow space for this technical manipulation during editing.

> JANE
> (OS)
> Ah, nuts. Just when I was gonna take the jackpot, the cops hafta show up!

> DISSOLVE TO:

SHOT LIST FOR SHOOTING SCRIPT PAGE

Exteriors, BARCLAY HOUSE lawn, night.
Personnel: GRAY, GREEN, BROWN.
Costumes: Police uniforms.

47. LS of all three men, backs to camera, moving toward lit windows of house.
48. MCU GRAY, who turns.
49. (a) Reaction shot: BROWN and GREEN lower to ground.
    (b) GREEN exits frame left.

Interiors, BARCLAY HOUSE living room, night.
Personnel: GEORGE, PLAYER A, PLAYER B, JANE.
Costumes: men in undershirts, shoulder holsters, JANE in evening gown.
Props: cigars; playing cards; poker chips; ashtrays; beer bottles.
General scene: card table and group near window.

50. MS, group of three men playing. GEORGE, one line.
52. (a) Same, pan to JANE.
    (b) JANE lays down cards, two lines.
53. MCU GEORGE, throws down cards. Hold for cigar smoke across screen.
54. (a) JANE fans smoke, reaches for pot. Two lines. Hold, for OS sound at window.
    (b) Many hands upset table toward camera. Extra hold at finish for dissolve.
51. CU GEORGE's hands, push chips forward to pot.

wild sound: (a) OS groans from male cardplayers.
            (b) Sound of pebbles hitting window outside.
            (c) OS JANE line, sc. 54.

As mentioned earlier, close-ups, the fourth C, are a particular type of camera angle—a view taken extremely close to a person or object, usually revealing small details rather than the whole person or object. Close-ups are important transitional images that are used for continuity, and in editing or cutting. Cutting is the fifth C, and what Mascelli means by including the idea of cutting in the arena of camera work is that directors and camera people must shoot their scenes with an eye toward the fact that they must eventually be edited before they are seen by an audience. Shooting with this in mind, directors and camera people make an extra effort to provide shots which maintain continuity, such as close-ups, reverse angles of people "reacting" to others, establishing shots, and so on.

Telling a Story Visually. Imagine that the following scene has been written into a script that you, as a cameraperson, are about to shoot:

> A dozen people are gathered in a large conference room to decide the fate of a small company. They include the company PRESIDENT, his "YES" MAN vice president, a UNION REPRESENTATIVE, and a female SECRETARY to take notes. During the scene, the "YES" MAN can't come up with any ideas, but the SECRETARY has a good one that will definitely aid the company's sinking fortunes. The PRESIDENT says he's going to make her a new vice president.

How would you visualize this essentially static scene? First, make sure that you understand the intent and context of the scene. This is obviously a pivotal scene that marks the transition of the woman from secretary to vice president. At the start of the scene, then, we'll probably want to see her only in passing, as a minor cog in the machinery of the company, almost passed over at the table. (Maybe a long, moving shot along the table.) Later on, as she comes to the fore in the meeting, we might choose to do many more close-ups. (Maybe a series of them; each time we cut back to her, she is larger in the frame.) Near the end of the scene, when she has triumphed, we might consider something to emphasize her newly elevated status. (Maybe a low-angle shot that makes her seem tall in the frame.) We may also want to use some "rack-focus" shots in which the camera holds still, but its focal point is shifted in the frame from an object or person near-by to one further away—let's say, from the "YES" MAN in front, to the SECRETARY in the back—to underline visually what the scene should be conveying to the audience.

Second, try to decide on your "in" and "out" shots. Perhaps the most important moments in a scene, visually, are its beginning and ending. In this one, we might want to start with a shot that gives us some hint as to the company's business or the traditions that go with it: maybe a zoom-out from a portrait of the company's founder on the conference room wall; or possibly we would want to cut into the scene as it is in progress, and would use part of that long trucking shot to open. Our closing would probably be used to point up the main aspect of the scene, the secretary's rise in position. This could be accomplished by a close-up of her looking pleased with herself, or by a shot of the disappointed "YES" MAN, or by the image of someone turning out the light that illuminates the founder picture.

Third, having decided on the general flow and on the in and out points of the scene, we can go on to choose angles, positions for the camera, certain people to highlight or obscure, etc. Many choices are available, even in a static scene; in fact, the scene will remain static and unmoving only if choices are *not* made. Choices that make the meaning of the scene clearer and more striking for the audience are at the heart of telling any story visually.

PRE-PRODUCTION
At CBS studios in New York City (*top*), script and floor plan (*center*) are readied for today's episode of the long-running soap opera "As the World Turns." At Strang Middle School in Yorktown Heights, New York, students go over the script for a daily news broadcast (*bottom*).

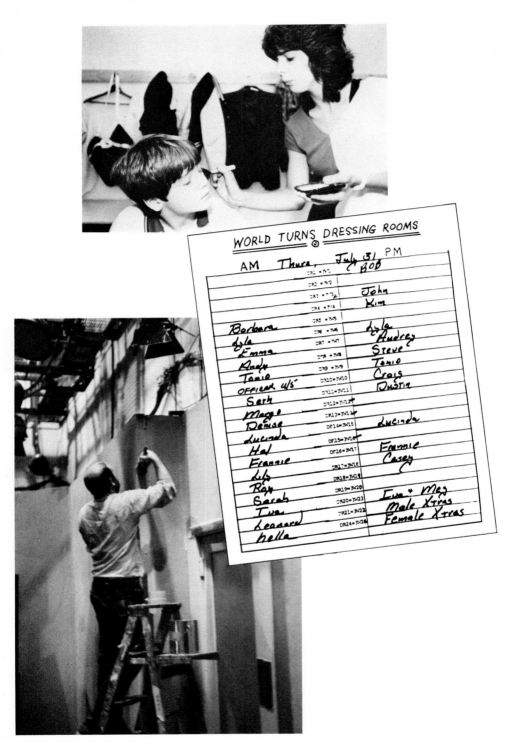

BEHIND THE SCENES

A thousand details must be attended to: set, wardrobe, properties, and makeup.

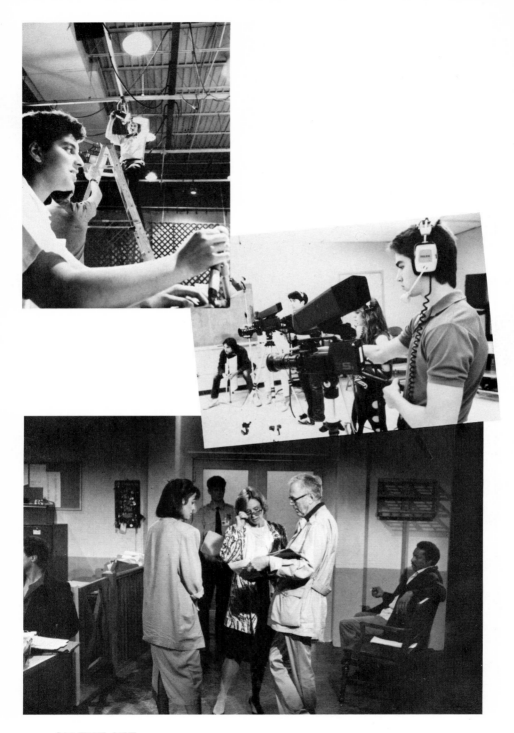

ON THE SET
There are last-minute adjustments of camera angles and focus, lights, sound levels, and placement of actors and actresses.

PRODUCTION
Action! On the set and in the control room, everyone has a specific job to do.

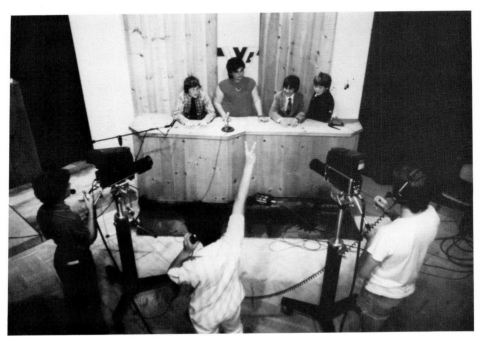

POST-PRODUCTION
Editing with small or large machines completes the product: a video to
be proud of.

/// **8** ///

Environment: Sound, Lights, Set, Props, Wardrobe

In an earlier chapter we talked about the concept of "milieu," or the setting in which the action of a video takes place. This chapter examines the ways that a videomaker controls and creates the milieu, through the use of various elements such as sound, lights, set, props, and wardrobe.

A television picture has two dimensions, but to enrich the sense of reality we must try to create in the minds of the audience a third dimension—depth. In this context, depth means not only the size of an object, but also how it "feels" to an audience. What we want is to make the audience believe in the "reality" of the video they are watching and hearing. Sound, lights, set, props, and wardrobe help us to enhance that reality.

Sound

Television is not a silent medium; sound has accompanied video pictures since their inception, and sound is a vital element in video's ability to communicate. In order to make good videos, a knowledge of how to produce "audio," or sound, is essential.

An audio system is generally made up of three component pieces of equipment: the microphone, which collects sound;

55

the audiotape recording device, which records the sounds; and the playback system, which allows the previously recorded sounds to be heard later. Just as the television camera provides video input to the video recorder, the microphone provides audio input to the recording system.

Microphones

There are several types of microphones, but most can be divided into two categories, the *omni-directional*, and the *uni-directional*. Omni-directional microphones are those which pick up sounds coming from all directions around the device. Omnis are ideal for situations in which you want to record several different types of sound at one time—say, in the midst of a band, or choral group—and you want those sounds to be blended *before* they reach the audiotape recorder. The "natural" sounds of a location are usually recorded with omni-directional microphones. A hanging microphone in a scene, or a small "lavalier" microphone clipped to someone's tie or hung around their necks, is a version of an omni microphone.

Uni-directional microphones are built so that they pick up sounds in a well-defined, small area which extends directly in front of the instrument. Most directors prefer uni-directional microphones because they are selective. When pointed in the direction of the sound source they are to pick up, the unis catch just the sound that is wanted, and eliminate unwanted "ambient" sounds (random location noise). Hand-held mikes used in reporters' interviews or in performances by individual singers are uni-directional, as are the "shotgun" microphones generally used when at a distance from the subject. Shotguns allow the recordist to pick up sounds selectively while staying outside the range of the camera's viewfinder.

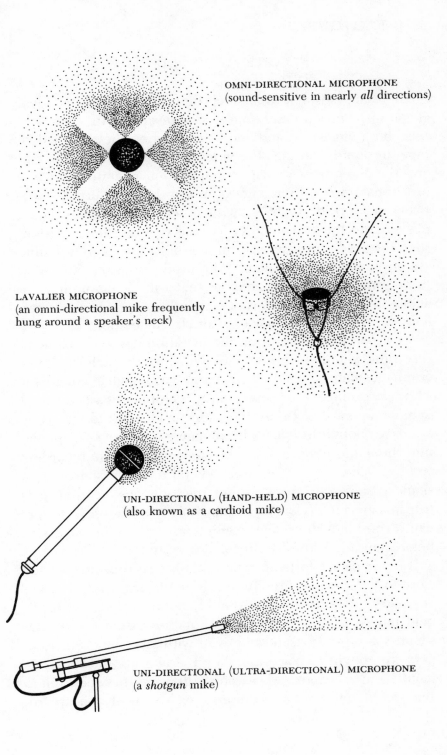

OMNI-DIRECTIONAL MICROPHONE
(sound-sensitive in nearly *all* directions)

LAVALIER MICROPHONE
(an omni-directional mike frequently
hung around a speaker's neck)

UNI-DIRECTIONAL (HAND-HELD) MICROPHONE
(also known as a cardioid mike)

UNI-DIRECTIONAL (ULTRA-DIRECTIONAL) MICROPHONE
(a *shotgun* mike)

Recording the Sound

There are two modes for recording the sound for a video, *single system* sound and *double system* sound. In single system, both video and audio are recorded on the same videotape; in double system, the video is recorded on videotape, and the audio is recorded at first onto a separate audiotape in a separate recorder, and later may be transferred selectively or "mixed" together with other sounds before being placed onto the videotape in its final version. Single system sound is used for most fairly simple productions, but double system sound is recommended for productions that are going to be somewhat complicated, or that will have a number of audio "tracks" (such as location sound, narration, music, effects) all brought together on a single videotape.

Most portable cameras on the market today are capable of recording sound along with video images, through small microphones housed inside the cameras. Although adequate for a few close-range interviews, these microphones are not good enough for most of the productions you'll want to try. They are easy enough to bypass by plugging a better microphone into the audio plug, or jack, of the camera or the recording system. When recording from several different sources in a single scene—say, from lavalier microphones on three participants in an interview—you may want to add a small "mixer" which combines the signals coming from all the microphones before sending it into the recording system.

It is important to hang or "set" mikes so they are not too close to the sound source they will be picking up; if they are very close, they distort the sound being recorded. For hand-held mikes, a minimum of 6 to 8 inches distance from the sound source is advised, and even with lapel mikes or lavaliers, you ought to place them a bit away from the speaker's mouth and voicebox. Always test distances between mikes and sound sources before taping, especially if you are recording inexperienced performers or interviewees. Similarly, all cable connections should be checked to ensure that they are in working order. When choosing volume levels, all controls should be set to record at upper levels of intensity as measured on the mixer or recording device: remember that before these sounds reach the ears of the audience, they will be sent through speakers that are, in general, fairly small and certainly not as sensitive as the earphones through which the person recording the sound at the location hears the audio. Recording at high levels will prevent the broadcast sound from being too low to be enjoyed.

Most people don't realize that it is the quality and quantity of the recorded audio that often shapes the content of most videos. It is therefore important to consider the needs of the editor when recording sound. It's helpful for the editor to have as much recorded audio as possible to work with; for this reason, audiotaping should begin at the very top, or opening, of a scene or interview, and then continue on through the time the event is completed and even afterward—without stops. The sound recorded with pictures at the time of taping is called "synchronous" or "sync" sound.

It is also a good idea to record audio that is supplemental to that heard in the actual scene or event as it is taped. Usually the sound recordist takes a minute or two of the natural sound of the studio or location site at a time when no one is talking or making unnecessary noise. This ambient sound, known as "room tone" if the recording is done indoors and as "natural sound" if outdoors, may be taped before or after a scene is shot. The editor uses this to help link together materials recorded at different times, to blend them so that no sound gaps are noticeable.

Another good source of supplemental audio is "wild sound." We record "wild" sounds such as applause, conversation, automobile honking, or birdsongs that take place at a location but may not be present during the exact moments when the main scene is recorded. The recording of sounds that are unattached to pictures is a good idea for all productions. For example, interviewees frequently talk more freely when off-camera. Separately recorded interviews often provide "voice-over" material or replacement audio for situations when the camera malfunctions or misses something important. While the rock band is rehearsing and you're still calibrating the camera and setting lights, take down the audio of their song, even if you have to use a blank videotape to do so. Then you'll have another "take" should you later need it in the editing process. Recording supplemental audio gives you flexibility in editing and insurance in case of problems during the regular taping.

Lighting

Everything reflects light; that is how—and what—and why—we see. In a video system the light reflected from an object is captured by the vidicon tube and recorded in the form of an image on the magnetic tape. But cameras see the reflected light of objects with far less sensitivity than the human eye does. Our eyes can see things that are too bright or too dark for a camera to properly record. Our eyes can discern contrasts in thousands of small increments of light and color, while video cameras can only capture hundreds of small steps.

This means that cameras need far greater amounts of reflected light in order to "see" what the human eye can view unaided. And video cameras need more added light than film cameras, because while the sensitivity of film in a movie camera can be varied, the videotape in a television camera cannot. Adequate lighting, then, increases the chances of capturing good video images.

For black-and-white videotaping, almost any added sources of light are acceptable, whether you're indoors or outdoors.

That's *not* true for color videotaping—and, in general, you will always have to take into account the large differences in illumination level between outdoor "natural" light and indoor "artificial" light.

Natural outdoor light is far stronger than artificial light. The sun's rays are diffused and reflected in many ways, so that no matter whether you have predawn haze, cloudy glare, dusky dimness of full midday brilliance, the intensity is usually high enough for the video camera. Also, outdoor light helps create a sense of visual depth (or three-dimensionality) by clarifying and emphasizing the spatial relationships among objects or people in a scene.

Indoor Light

Artificial light for television generally comes from quartz-halogen, tungsten or fluorescent lamps. Fluorescent lamps are hard to avoid in places such as schools, but because of their chemistry they tend to cast a greenish glow over a scene—a glow, incidentally, that is not visible to the human eye—and have to be "balanced" with other lamps to eliminate the green tint. To add intensity to a scene, tungsten or halogen lights are the best alternatives to natural sunlight. Both differ from ordinary lightbulbs that you have in your home, and are considerably brighter. Tungstens and halogens for video can be bought or rented from larger camera or video supply stores. Use tungsten or halogen lamps in an indoor setting to:

- raise the level of illumination,
- imitate the effect of natural sunlight, and
- enhance the sense of depth by accentuating the distance between objects or people.

Three-Point Lighting

To best achieve the proper illumination in a scene, and to enhance three-dimensionality, lighting designers recommend that videomakers use a minimum of three lights. In a three-point lighting plan:

1. Place your strongest light 6 to 8 feet above and 6 to 8 feet in front of your subject, but slightly to one side. This placement, known as the *key* light, imitates the direct light of the sun. Its beams should create sharp outlines, crisply defined features and well-modeled contours. It should also cast heavy shadows behind the subject.
2. Place your second strongest light above and behind the subject, directly opposite the key light. Its reflections should outline the subject from behind, and create a sense of separation and depth between the subject and the background. This is a *back* light.
3. Place any additional lights to the side of the subject, in between the key and back lights and on the same level to soften harsh contrasts in a manner similar to the way that diffused light in nature softens direct sunlight. *Fill* light fills in the contours outlined by the key and back lights.

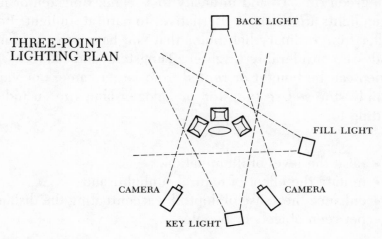

THREE-POINT
LIGHTING PLAN

BACK LIGHT

FILL LIGHT

CAMERA

CAMERA

KEY LIGHT

Lighting is a prime element in the creation of milieu and mood. For example shadow-filled lighting maximizes mystery and suspense, while bright lights convey gaiety. Sharp contrasts in lighting underline a director's point of view on the characters or situation. Variously colored spotlights can reinforce characterization. Red and yellow lights are often used to create a rosy glow and a feeling of warmth. Blue lights bring out coolness and a sense of foreboding. Green light, particularly when used in individual spotlights, creates an impression of ill health.

Experiment with different lighting set-ups until you get the ones you want for a particular scene or production. Here are some common pitfalls to guard against in lighting, indoors and out.

Insufficient light. Poor, gray pictures result from not enough light in a scene. Indoors, this inadequacy is usually quite apparent when you look through a camera or at a monitor—but outdoors, it's not so obvious. Avoid dusk and dawn shots unless you can add fill lights to the scene. Also, if possible, avoid shooting in the midday sun, because there may be too much light for the camera to handle. The best days on which to shoot outdoors are those with even cloudiness.

Uneven light levels. Light levels that are of comparable intensity are always preferable, even if they're not very dramatic. Strong, harsh light creates shadows which are very dark and which the camera may be unable to "read." To counteract this problem outdoors, take along sun reflectors—good, cheap ones are large pieces of white cardboard—and use them to reflect or "bounce" light into dark areas. They will act as a fill light and soften the harshness. Indoors, experiment with light bouncing by aiming some lights at reflective surfaces such as walls or ceilings, to create softer light on your subjects—but always make sure that the light level is high enough so that the camera will be able to record all aspects of the scene.

Severe Backlighting. This occurs when the subject to be photographed is positioned in front of a brightly lit background—outdoors, the sky or horizon; indoors, a window on a sunny day, or a brightly lit doorway into a darker room. Remember that the mechanisms of the camera are naturally drawn to the *area of greatest brightness* and when that area is the background rather than the subject in the foreground, you've got problems. In such a situation, the human eye can adjust to make out the details of the subject, but the camera's eye can't. Change your lighting balance by adding artificial light in front of the subject, or manually overriding the camera's internal automatic controls so that the lens will filter out some of the background light, or move the subject to be photographed to a less hostile place. Remember, also, that if the subject is dark-skinned, this problem may occur with more frequency in usual settings; to get more details, be sure to add light on the subject.

SOLVING A LIGHTING PROBLEM

SEVERE BACK LIGHT
(figure in doorway of brightly-lit room)

CORRECTED BACK LIGHT
(add key light in front of subject to balance back light from doorway of brightly-lit room)

Lighting for Movement. This requires special care both inside and outside. Lighting must be preset for all the twists and turns taken by a subject during a movement so that the subject doesn't go too deeply into or out of the light. This is mainly a problem for fill light, but it is also a problem for the director to solve by advising his actors and actresses to keep their movements within the pools of light that are set up for the scene. Block out and rehearse all movements as much as possible before shooting to make sure the camera is able to "see" the subjects being photographed. And remember, do *not* try to move lights while the subjects are actually moving in a scene. If the light source and the camera subject both move at the same time, unwanted light flares or light "trails" may be picked up by the camera and result in an unacceptable recording.

Set

The set is the physical location where the action of a scene is taped. It may be an anchorman's desk in front of a map of the world, a rock star's stage outlined in neon, a chemistry laboratory, or a tide-pool above a rocky beach. Whatever the content of your video, you'll have a set—either it will already exist, or you'll have to create it.

Dramatically speaking, the set is also the symbolic and physical re-creation of the world in which the story of your video unfolds. A set is, then, one of the most important components of milieu. Through the set and everything contained within it, the re-created world of your video becomes a tangible, three-dimensional illusion shared by the creative people behind the camera, performers, and audience alike. Creating that illusion means paying attention to detail, whether the set is a natural landscape or an intricately designed studio setting.

When designing the set for your video, there are some basic considerations you may want to keep in mind. The set should visually reflect the content and story line of your video, reinforcing rather than getting in the way of what you are trying to communicate. If you're conveying the news, make the set look professionally efficient with a no-nonsense quality. If you're taping a performance, emphasize the theatrical aspects of the scene. But, remember to keep it simple. You don't want to distract the audience. You want them to concentrate on what you have to say. Sets work best when they are suggestive of an environment, conveying only what you want your audience to know and feel. Everything doesn't have to be visible or solid. A corner of a library can convey the same feeling as shelves filled with thousands of books.

The set also may reflect or enhance characterization in a video. The type of rooms in which your main characters appear, the colors of the rooms, the age and condition of the furniture, all reveal the personalities and eccentricities of the characters your actors and actresses portray. The set defines the circumstances in which the story line of a video takes place, and as such, is a vehicle for the director and producer to communicate things that are otherwise unsaid. We can all imagine what a room in the home of someone who is rich in material goods, but poor in spirit, looks like. To create a set that reflects such a room, or one appropriate to any other story line, careful attention must be paid to the nuances and overall impact of chosen details. An effective set is a powerful theatrical device.

Properties and Wardrobe

Properties or props are objects of an incidental nature added to and used on the set by actors in the course of a performance.

Anything can be a prop—cigarettes, a book, a musical instrument, some knitting.

Props provide a means for the dramatic and visual portrayal of character. People are often defined in real life, as well as in dramas, by the idiosyncratic things they do. You can also convey mood and state of mind through props. Imagine a scene of a young man waiting for a phone call. In version A, he's calmly leafing through a book while waiting for the ring. His choice of a book indicates his relaxed mood. In version B, the young man is nervously chain-smoking, while waiting for the phone to ring. His tension and apprehension are helped along by the prop—the cigarettes. In such situations, props are devices which support the actor's interpretation of the role, helping him to define and establish his character.

A prop in an actor or actress's hand very often aids in conveying emotions by giving them something to do with their hands other than hold them at their sides. The same effect can be observed in an interview with a nervous subject. By giving him or her a cup of coffee or a soft drink to hold, or a dog to pet, the nervousness often is displaced or disappears, and the result is more "natural" behavior and a better interview. But try not to make props so complex that people can't communicate because they're worrying about how to work some gadget.

Wardrobe

This is the clothing or costumes worn by people on the set. In the broadcast media, this includes the use of makeup and hair styling which are appropriate to the physical presentation of the character being portrayed. These last elements are particularly important indoors, when there are high levels of illumination used for the cameras; such levels may not always accentuate what an actor or actress—or a guest on a talk show—wants to convey. Wardrobe, makeup, and props should be carefully chosen to illustrate the content of your story and the personality of your characters.

Because of the special requirements of the video camera, there are some specific things a videomaker should keep in mind in relation to wardrobe.

Avoid shiny fabrics and the use of colors which reflect a lot of light. Mylar or satin fabrics, and clothes in fire-engine red or bright white (or other very bright solid colors) will appear to "glow" when the camera records. This may be fine for science fiction and visually shocking music videos, but may be distracting for other types of productions.

Avoid closely lined or patterned fabrics. A video camera has difficulty in holding a steady image of pinstripes, herringbones, and paisleys; they create a shimmy or moiré pattern, and the fabrics appear to take on a life of their own. Again, this may be great for your outer space opera, but unacceptable for most videos.

/// 9 ///

Editing

Editing is the craft—and art—of putting together two or more images and sounds in a moving series in order to create an impression or tell a story. We edit in order to compress, rearrange, and change the emphasis of previously recorded material. With the exception of programs broadcast live or recorded tape-to-time, most videos are edited. The more complicated the production, the more likely it is that you'll have to edit.

Although the artistic principles of film editing and video-tape editing are much the same, the physical process of videotape editing differs markedly from that of film editing. In film, individual pieces of film—some as small as one single frame—are spliced together. In videotape editing, the tape is not actually cut; usually, the original tape is not altered, but images are copied from it, one after another, onto a second tape.

How you edit your tape depends on the equipment available. Single-machine editing is possible. Some machines have controls that allow you to erase and eliminate unwanted portions of tape; with this, you can close up gaps and string together useful shots, but you can edit material only in the order in which it was shot and you can't transpose a shot from late in the roll to an earlier position.

Most videotape editing is done with two machines. One

plays back the original material, which is called a "source tape." The second is used to re-record selected portions from the first, to make what we call an "edited master." The process of re-recording one tape onto another is called dubbing, and two-machine editing is really selective dubbing. Using two machines does not mean you are limited to using two tapes— you can change the source as often as you like, substituting one tape for another, or skipping backward or forward in a tape to find the shots you want to re-record onto the edited master.

Two home VCRs with special adaptors (available from some manufacturers) can be used for two-machine editing. Best results are usually achieved with two machines of the same make.

Major productions use more than one source machine at a time, but still place all the images onto an edited master. To use several source machines you also need to employ special switchers that can go quickly from one source to another; switchers are available from video equipment suppliers, and can be somewhat expensive. Although it's nice to have several source machines, it's not necessary, and two-machine editing can accomplish most of the tasks you'll want to try on your first productions.

Getting Up to Speed

In order to make a proper edit, both machines, source and edited master, must be rolling at full and correct speed. Getting both machines "up to speed" at once is a problem because it can take different machines different amounts of time. To do this you must:

- determine the precise spot where you want the edit to begin;

- roll the source tape back approximately five seconds before that "start-edit" point and also roll the master tape back in a similar manner;
- start to roll both machines forward; and push the "record" button on the master-tape machine at the exact point where you want the edit to start.

This is a clumsy and imprecise method, which often turns out to be a hit-or-miss proposition; you may need several tries to complete a successful edit. Practice helps, and so does a knowledge of the particular machines you're using.

The key to success is locating an action, a sound, or another "cue" point on the source tape that occurs at least five seconds before the start-edit point. You can do this with the tape counter on a VCR or, more precisely, with a stopwatch. With either, you time out the distance (in tape-feet or in seconds) between cue action and start-edit point, and use that to aid your button pushing. For example, you might determine that footsteps are heard precisely 12.6 seconds before you want to cut to the medium shot of the door opening.

Better Control

If your editing machines were bought in the 1980s, they probably come with a device which makes editing less imprecise. Control track pulses which are placed electronically onto the tape itself guide the system and make it easier for two machines to work together. With a control track system, you position both machines at the start-edit point; then, by pushing the "cue" button, you are able to make both machines move back simultaneously. They go back for about five seconds—just far enough—and then course forward and are thus able to reach full forward speed and mesh properly before they get to the edit point.

Going up the scale in "control" systems, some schools and larger facilities use electronic time codes. These give each moment of a source videotape an electronic address, usually stated in numbers. They allow for even more precise locating of frames in the tape. Such codes are electronically placed on the tapes after they are shot and before they are edited. Time codes are centered in the lower third of the frame and are visible for use during editing but are removed when the final tape is made for broadcast. In a more advanced version, computer-assisted editing, you are able to punch in the time code addresses of two segments that you want to view in contiguity, then hit a button, and the computer will line up the right segments and show them to you, connected.

Assemble Editing

There are two distinct modes of video editing. One is computerlike, and the other more closely resembles a typewriter. With insert editing—as with word processing computers— you are able to make a sequence of shots and then insert a new shot into that sequence without otherwise altering the sequence. You can put in a shot which you forgot to use the first time around, or you can change your mind about the order of the shots.

Unfortunately, insert editing requires more sophisticated equipment than is generally available in schools, and so we usually have to work in the mode known as assemble editing.

In an assemble edit, shots from the source tape (or tapes) are copied onto the master, one after another, from beginning to end of a sequence. If, after editing, you want to change the order of the shots or to insert an extra shot within the sequence, you must re-record them anew in the correct order.

In writing a composition with a typewriter rather than with a computer, you have to be more careful with your thoughts, because errors or changes are more difficult and time-consuming to make, but the writing process remains the same. So, too, with video editing—insert or assemble mode—the principles are still what counts.

Editing Concepts

The basic purpose of editing is to make the action believable to the audience. If, in Shot 1, a man throws a ball, and, in Shot 2, another man catches a ball—the edit which connects these two shots must help the audience believe that the ball is being thrown and caught by the two men, not that a video crew has taken two isolated shots and simply placed them in juxtaposition. This is a matter of rhythm, flow, continuity of action, and of making transitions and emphases.

We've touched upon the idea of *continuity* in the chapter on cameras. Action in a video must appear to be continuous; a motion in the master shot of a scene must be followed through in the medium-shot of the same scene. There is an *invisible line* through the physical set-up of a scene that separates the people on the left side of that line from those on the right. This idea derives from the live theater, where actors and actresses do not face one another directly in a dialogue, but, rather, stand at 45-degree angles so that the audience can see part of their full faces, not just their profiles. On the video screen, dialogue scenes are structured in the same way for continuity. Person A, on screen left, is taped at a 45-degree angle to the camera, facing right; then person B, on the right, is taped at an opposite 45-degree angle, facing left. When the shots are intercut, the people appear to be talking to one another, having a dialogue. If we do a two-shot, we'll see the people talking to one another naturally. But if, in the individual shots, the invisible line is crossed—say, by having both people appear to face in the same direction—the audience will not "read" the action in the same manner. The invisible line actually means that the camera may be placed anywhere along a 180-degree arc which goes around the front of the people in the scene.

What happens if you as an editor get shots that cross that 180-degree line, or that don't match easily? You can blame your cameraman and/or your director—and you will!—but it'll still be your job to "fix" the scene. How will you do that? Most probably by using a *cutaway*.

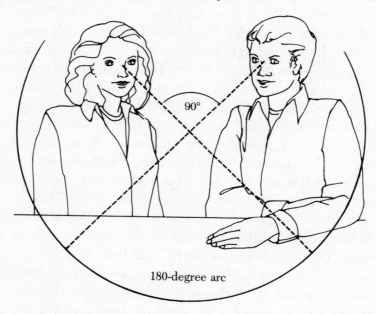

90°

180-degree arc

Cutaways, or inserts, are any shots which enable you to "cut away" from the action of the scene, and later to come back to the scene proper, without losing "believability." A cutaway can be a close-up, an isolated detail, a point-of-view shot of what the people in a scene are looking at, a reaction shot of one of the participants—almost anything can be used, if it will complete the flow of the scene. Using the example above, we'll insert a close-up of the woman's hand, drumming on the table, to make the cuts "work."

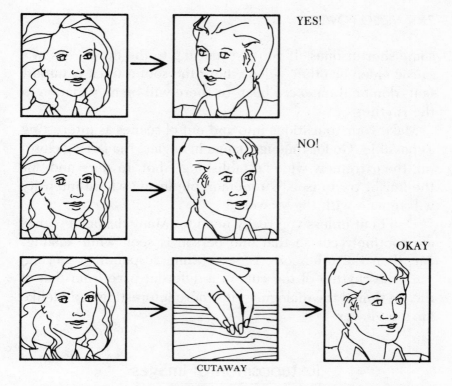

YES!

NO!

OKAY

CUTAWAY

There are no real rules for the art of editing—only a few suggestions about cuts that "work" (in the sense of maintaining believability) or don't work. Here are a few such suggestions:

It seldom feels right to cut from medium-shot to medium-shot. Much better are transitions which include a change of width, from wide to medium, medium to close, etc. But close-ups often cut well with other close-ups.

Cuts work best when they are in the middle of an action. It is better to move from a long shot of the car in motion to a close shot of it in motion, rather than waiting to see the car come to a stop in long shot, and then going to the close-up.

It's important to vary the rhythm or pacing of edited footage. If the screen seems to change every six seconds, the viewer will soon expect to see something new on that sixth second—this distracts the viewer's attention from the scene. Use some shots which last a fairly long time, mixed in with some shorter ones. If you are "cutting to the music," as in a music video or other video where the sound track is important, don't cut on *every* beat, or there will be no variation in the rhythm.

Make your transitions into and out of scenes as interesting as possible. Go for the big change in angles, the jarring close-up, the extremely wide "establishing" shot, to start; and, for the finish, try to isolate a memorable image whose intensity will remain with the viewer.

Don't cut unless you really need to. Many dialogue scenes are routinely cut so that one person is seen while talking, and then the other one is seen while responding. Boring! Vary the rhythm of the cuts in a different pace from that of the rhythm of the dialogue—it's more interesting and lifelike for the viewer.

Juxtaposition of Images

The main purpose of editing is to ensure that the audience will understand the director's sympathies and intentions, and will experience what the director of the video wants them to feel. This is accomplished primarily through juxtaposition of images—by simply putting one shot before or after another.

Here are some examples of sequences of images, drawn from scripts and ideas we've described in earlier chapters.

First, some nonfiction editing. You'll recall our discussion of the Middleburg High School championship football game, and various news reports and documentaries that we could make using that game as subject matter.

A. Shot 1. The winning touchdown.

Shot 2. The home crowd, cheering loudly.

Shot 3. Close-up of a cheerleader doing a cartwheel.

In this sequence of shots, the videomaker's statement of purpose is clear. The intent is to demonstrate delight in the team that has scored the winning touchdown, and to re-emphasize that excitement by the third shot of the cheerleader.

B. Shot 1. The winning touchdown.

Shot 2. The losing coach, chewing his hat.

Shot 3. A small boy in the stands, asleep.

Here the videomaker's sympathies are more blatant—rooting for the home team and relishing the disappointment of the losing coach. In conjunction with the first two, the third shot seems to express the philosophy that, win or lose, it's just a game.

C. Shot 1. The winning touchdown.

Shot 2. The groundskeeper, seemingly watching the game from underneath the stands, as many feet leap up in excitement.

Shot 3. Close-up of what the groundskeeper is actually watching—a small TV set which shows a baseball game.

Here the comment on the action is ironic. The first two shots underline a theme of behind-the-scenes people who don't get to see the game as the spectators do. But then the third shot adds a humorous postscript by showing that the groundskeeper really prefers to watch something else.

For fiction editing, let's take some examples from the proposed video script about the rise and fall of a rock band. Most often, in editing fictional pieces, the difficult choices must be made when interweaving scenes or images.

Suppose the videomaker wants to condense material to show a short sequence from the rise and fall of the band. Choosing from material already shot, we might put together shots for the female drummer:

Shot 1. Hands with sticks playing the drums.

Shot 2. Hands on man's back.

Shot 3. Hands signing autographs in a crowd.

Shot 4. Hands cutting meal with plastic knife and fork on an airplane.

Shot 5. Hands drumming idly on table.
The cumulative impact of these close-ups creates an impression that no single shot can convey.

We'll use another example from the same script to show how editing can be used to demonstrate a character's mental state. Suppose that in one scene, the female drummer has come back to a hotel at which the band is staying on the road, and by chance discovers her lover, the guitarist, kissing another woman. In another scene, the drummer is playing on stage during a concert. The editing problem: to intercut these two sequences in order to convey her emotional state after being betrayed by her lover.

We'll key the sequence to the rhythm of the song being performed as beaten out on her drums: one, two, three, *Four*, five, six, seven, *Eight*—with the emphasis on the last beat of each measure. On one, two, and three, medium or long shots give us an overall impression of the band in performance, but, as we come to *Four*, we use a close-up of her, crashing down hard on the drums. Then, for the next three beats, we use images from the hotel sequence: five, she approaches the hotel door; six, she puts the key in the lock; seven, her hand turns the doorknob; and *Eight*, she sees them. After this build-up, we immediately cut to her furious drum solo, and expect the audience of the video will understand that in her energized beating of the drums she is taking out her anger at being wronged by her lover.

Editing a video can often be a long procedure, filled with attempts that seem right at first but later don't work properly and have to be redone. Nevertheless, the extra care spent on the editing process can make the difference between a video that is just okay and one that is really terrific.

/// 10 ///

"Be Prepared"

Successful productions at all levels of expertise share the Boy Scout motto, "Be Prepared." Now that you are comfortable with the tools of production, here are a few guidelines for making sure you're ready for anything in the preproduction, shooting and postproduction phases.

Try to make a workable production schedule that includes all three phases. The key is back-timing. Start with the date on which you want to complete or deliver your project. Then work backward through the editing phase, the shooting, and, last, the research and scripting. In making the schedule, all sorts of questions will arise, such as:

How many shooting days (or hours) should you allow or budget for? How much screen time should you try to complete on a shooting day? It's important to estimate realistically what you can do on any given day in a studio or on location. Don't attempt too much at once, but, on the other hand, do try to move your production forward at every moment. Each tape day and hour must be planned so that important production decisions won't be made under pressure, and you won't have to do tiring retakes and retaping. Where do you plan to shoot? If on location, scout it beforehand to know how difficult it is to prepare it for taping. If in the studio, reserve the time and equipment.

How many days or hours will you need to edit? That de-

79

pends on the amount of taped material and its complexity. What's your shooting ratio—the amount of tape shot versus the amount that will actually be used in the edited master? Are you shooting ten hours of tape to make a half-hour production? If you have such a high ratio, you'll probably need more time to edit. For special effects such as split-screens, dissolves, or wipes, you may have to book time on an advanced editing system. That costs money (rather than just time on a less fancy school-editing system) and brings up the matter of balancing resources and requirements.

Your production may or may not have a budget that includes actual dollars, but you need to know what's available to you both in terms of real money and in equipment that you reserve from the school's facilities. Most productions do end up spending money even if equipment is not rented—for special editing, tape stock, meals, transportation, costumes, phone calls, etc. So, make a budget: two days of one-camera shooting, six hours of school editing, one hour of special effects, $25 for meals at the location. (That $25 could buy you ten times that amount's worth of production time: If you bring in a lunch, and keep your people on site, you'll be able to do more shooting than if everyone took a ninety-minute break to find the local pizza parlor.)

After your shooting script is prepared and "broken down" into scenes, make a list of what you have to shoot and what must go into the editing. Then you can ask yourself better questions. For example, are the dissolves really necessary, or could you go from scene 32 to scene 33 without that added postproduction expense? Do you have to shoot that exterior scene with all the actors in it, or could you get by with a less expensive close-up? In answering these questions, what you're actually doing is comparing your requirements for completing your production to the assets you have on hand.

Quite naturally, there will be some gaps between your resources and your requirements. The art of producing is to fill these gaps by learning how to budget production facilities, time, money, and people.

This will probably mean such time-tested economies as shooting your exteriors on one day, your interiors on another, or sending a soundperson out to do "wild" tracks without benefit of three other people along to direct and produce. If you're working with school equipment, your lists of resources and requirements may help you defend reserving, say, two cameras for a day when another group needs one—because you're doing several complicated crowd scenes at once and thus condensing two shooting days into one.

The balancing act is aided by ingenuity. Cut corners, beg, and borrow to get everything you'll need for your production. The budget may not have money for costumes, but you might be able to find what you need in family attics or thrift shops. If you've budgeted $25 for a meal on location, don't go above that—unless you're ready to scrimp on some other essential item.

In addition to script breakdowns and budgets, a good producer is always knee-deep in lists. Shot lists. Prop lists. Equipment check lists. A list of all the telephone numbers of everyone connected with the shoot. Can you imagine getting to a location (Did you give everyone a map and directions?) and finding it locked up, and then not having the number of the building's superintendent because you left it at the studio?

When making a video, you need to do as much homework as you can. Check out every detail before tape day. Do the actors know their lines? If you're using another person on camera, does he or she know what time to be loaded up and ready to leave the studio? If you're shooting early in the day, will anyone require a wake-up call? The telephone is a producer's best friend. A call in time saves nine retakes and three headaches.

Despite the best laid plans, disaster can always strike while you're in production. A camera can go on the blink. An actor or actress can become ill. The weather can turn a picnic into a mud party. Being prepared also means having fallback strategies, so that if something goes wrong during a production you can still accomplish part of what you set out to do or an alternate plan that may serve just as well.

If a camera breaks down on a two-camera scene, try shooting the scene twice, with a single camera positioned differently each time. If the action is continuous, such as at a football game, take two or three times the usual amount of cutaways so that editing can cover the loss of that extra camera. If an actor or actress is sick, see if there are other scenes in the script that you can shoot without him or her that day. (Accomplishing that is much easier if you have a full script and shot list with you on location.)

If the script calls for a sunrise shot to emphasize the idea of a just-breaking day, but a downpour has turned dawn into mist, think about what might convey the same mood. In a recent production, this was done by substituting an interior scene (alarm clock, breakfast being made and eaten) for the rising of the sun. Fallback saved the day (and the producer's shoot).

The cardinal rule on tape day is to work in advance of the scene being shot. Whether or not you pay out real money for it, every aspect of the production has a time value attached to it, and you can't afford unused time. For example, if the actors must rehearse their lines or put on new make-up in between scenes, the camera crew might use that time to adjust lighting or move equipment to a new location. Often, if there are enough people on a crew, an assistant is sent ahead to the next location to prepare it for shooting.

Punctuality is the hallmark of good productions. Arrive early at locations. Have a stopwatch on hand so that each segment of tape can be accurately logged. Time each sequence, and, if possible, each shot. Check the actual time elapsed in taping a sequence against what you previously estimated. This may seem an excessive practice, but you'll be glad to have such a log later, during editing, so you can skip over takes that weren't successful.

It's in the postproduction phase that the old adage "time is money" is most often heard. Even in schools, there's always a crunch on editing time, so you have to budget your own as carefully as you can. Plan what you're going to do before you sit down at the machines.

First, if it hasn't already been done in the field, log the footage that has been shot. Often, you can do this on your home VCR, or on a facility that isn't part of the regular editing equipment, and save a little of the expensive editing time.

Second, make some "paper edits." Write out on paper the order in which you think the shots ought to go, and discuss this with someone else involved in the production, say, the director or the editor, before using the machines. Paper edits help pinpoint places where the shooting ran into (or even created) problems which must be solved by editing.

Third, divide the editing process up into many small sections by placing each cut segment onto a separate tape which you can later transfer to the master. If you try to build the whole program on one master tape, you may find yourself endlessly dubbing and redubbing the same string of sequences in order to change one interior part.

Make an overall rough cut—or close approximation of the sequences of the program—before fine-cutting any individual sequence. By working in rough, you'll be able to see big mistakes and correct them early. Then, you can more easily fine tune your end product.

In short, plan your editing time as you plan every other aspect of your production, in order to make the most of it.

/// **11** ///

Finding an Audience

The video revolution has distributed large amounts of video equipment throughout the country—tens of millions of TV sets, dozens and dozens of cable channels, hundreds of thousands of VCRs and video cameras and machines capable of doing video editing. All this equipment provides many and varied opportunities for a person who is eager to make a video.

As we have seen in the earlier chapters of this book, making a video is well within your grasp. It is not a mystifying task that can be done only by those who have studied it extensively for many years. Of course, the best videos take a great deal of thought and a certain level of expertise, but the tools and the techniques for achieving your goals are available and relatively easy to master.

The key to making videos is not simply a knowledge of the workings of the tools of the trade, but also an understanding of the purposes to which these tools will be put. Knowing your objectives and goals, as well as the capabilities of your equipment, is an integral part of the process of making a video. As in the handling of most mechanical things, people get better at using video cameras, microphones, lights, recorders, and editing equipment when they use these tools repeatedly. As in athletics or in playing musical instruments, practice makes perfect.

Showing Your Video

Having conceived, shot and edited your video, you'll want your creation to be seen and enjoyed by as wide an audience as possible.

Many videos are made specifically for certain outlets such as regularly scheduled programs, video jukeboxes, or particular school classes. However, your production may not fit into these categories, and you may have to search for a place to show your video. To increase the potential of obtaining a good showing for your video, try to:

- Use program lengths and formats which fit into regular program "slots." A show which is thirty-seven minutes long might be rejected for broadcast because the only slot available is for a half hour.
- Study the potential opportunities for showing your video before you complete it. Tailor your product for specific programs on cable channels, or in school.
- Make several copies of your video. This is relatively inexpensive and will ensure that you can keep one copy for reference, and send out as many as you can afford to all the various potential outlets. Don't be shy. If you hide your work, it will never be seen.

Possible Markets: In School

Many classes would benefit from having a video shown in them. Try to convince a teacher to let you produce a video project that will be of use in his or her class. Often, a teacher will be excited at the idea of someone doing something extra for the class.

If you're making a video, chances are there are other people in your school or community who are making videos as well. Start a club, and show your work to one another; positive criticism can help you improve your work. You might even initiate a festival for videos; works can be judged and prizes given. Often, video equipment dealers and other local merchants can be induced to sponsor individual awards. Try narrow category delineations, such as Best Video for a School Class, or Best Video Featuring a Local Band. Deadlines and categories help producers shape and complete their works on time.

Possible Markets: Community TV

Most commercial cable channels need three-, five-, and ten-minute "filler" pieces to show in between regularly scheduled programs; others have specific weekly or monthly shows devoted to short works and to student productions. Many states require cable broadcasters to provide "community access" channels, and these can become vehicles for almost anyone who has anything to say or show. Community access will mean that a producer with a completed production can rather easily obtain air time. Also, with community access, you can create your own show—say, a monthly "magazine" which features short videos. In all cases, it's advisable to do some research on available cable and community television outlets before you start sending out your tapes.

Contests and Awards

At last count there were over 200 awards and prizes given out to television programs and videos in this country, and the number of awards is growing all the time. Many are specifically for programs that have been broadcast, others for videos that haven't been widely seen. Some are open to students, and although most of these are for college students, a number have categories for high school productions.

Surprisingly, not all the contests are for artistic quality. Many deal with specific subjects—Jewish affairs, or medicine, or mathematics—and are sponsored by organizations or foundations concerned with those subjects. Contests for specific formats, such as ½-inch Beta, are run by equipment makers. Cable producers run contests for videos of specific lengths—generally, very short ones, used as fillers.

Here are a few nationwide contests for student videos:

Community Video Festival
87 Lafayette Street
New York, New York 10013

JVC Tokyo Video Festival
41 Slater Drive
Elmwood Park, New Jersey 07407

San Francisco Video Festival
650 Missouri Street
San Francisco, California 94107

Slice of Life Video Showcase
740 Elmwood Street
State College, Pennsylvania 16801

NJ Video and Film Festival
Newark Media Works
P.O. Box 1716, Dept. F4
Newark, New Jersey 07101

To enter these or any other contests, first write for guidelines, including a self-addressed, stamped envelope to facilitate correspondence. One of the best guides to up-and-coming contests, including requirements, entry fees, and closing deadlines, is the newsletter of the Foundation for Independent Video and Film, available for a fee from FIVF headquarters at 625 Broadway, New York, New York 10003.

Unfortunately, no single organization has an accurate list of all the contests because more are cropping up all the time. To find out about them you need to do some research. Try the following sources:

- the communications or radio-TV-film department of a nearby university
- your state or county council on the arts, or broadcasting association
- local cable channels and broadcasters
- equipment manufacturers or facilities that service professionals, and that sometimes sponsor contests and/or scholarships
- reference books about organizations that encompass a subject of interest to you—scuba diving, dog handling, rock 'n' roll—and that may sponsor contests

Keep a list of when and where your applications were sent. And, if a contest is being held near you, make it your business to attend and view the winning entries. Even if you haven't won, you'll want to study the winners so that next time around you'll have a better understanding of what the judges look for.

Selling Your Video Services

There are dozens of ways to make money out of home video. For example, you could make a video portrait of an infant which the parents can buy as a keepsake. Or do the same with a wedding, or a birthday party. Videotape your school play or the annual graduation exercises—people will want copies. Make a videotaped introduction to a bicycling or walking tour of your city. Build video portfolios for friends who study art or music. How about video portraits of blind dates, so people can get acquainted with one another before the first meeting? Ask lawyers in your neighborhood if they could use videotaped depositions of witnesses for their court cases. For elaboration on these and other ideas, read "Home Shooting—Make Money with Your Camera" by Frank Lovece, in the March 1985 issue of *Video* magazine.

Further Education

Today, most colleges and universities offer courses in television and video production. Some have full departments which specialize in television and film. Among the best known of these are New York University (New York City), Syracuse University (Syracuse, New York), the Annenberg School of Communications at the University of Pennsylvania (Philadelphia), and, in Los Angeles, the University of California at Los Angeles (UCLA) and the University of Southern California (USC). If you are applying to a college or university and are interested in video, be sure to inquire if the institution has a television studio and video equipment, and what courses allow the students to do "hands on" production.

Video production courses are also offered in many cities by institutions other than colleges such as "universities-without-walls," or YMCAs. Often such courses are taught by full-time professionals in the video field, and can be quite valuable. These courses also have the advantage of being offered to anyone who can pay for them, rather than only to matriculated college students.

Also, some community facilities offer video production

workshops for young people, as an adjunct to other community services. Check with local youth-service bureaus for any of these available in your area; these have the added advantage of being inexpensive, or, sometimes, completely free.

Jobs in Video

Because of the video revolution, and the importance of communication in a vast, industrialized society, video will become increasingly important in the future—and, with that increased importance, more jobs will be available that use video. Today, almost all corporations in the medium-to-large size range have corporate communications departments and video facilities. The explosion of community access and cable channel possibilities means more job slots available, too. Similarly, our society's growing appetite for information, entertainment, and instruction has opened up new markets for videotapes to be sold directly to consumers, or rented to be played on their VCRs—and, as a consequence, is expanding the number of program producers. Colleges, exercise clubs, hobbyists, department stores, and other people and institutions with information to get out are taking to using videos, and need people to produce them.

In short, the only limit to video power is your own imagination.

GLOSSARY

Aperture: a circular opening in the front of the camera which controls the amount of light allowed to pass through to the film (in a still or motion picture camera) or to the vidicon tube (in a video camera).

Assemble Editing: the process of editing in which sequences are placed one after another onto the master tape. *See also Insert Editing.*

Broadcasting: the transmission of sounds and visual images through the air, usually by a television or radio station.

Closed-Circuit Television: a private television system in which images are transmitted by wires to limited numbers of receivers.

Close-up: a magnified, close view of a person, object, or scene detail.

Continuity: in a scene or between scenes, checking the physical action for correct sequence of events and checking the details, such as props, costumes, and lighting for consistency.

Contrast: the range in brightness (from light to dark) capable of being photographed.

Cut: in editing, the instantaneous transition between one scene and the next.

Cutaway: a shot inserted into the action of a scene that may interrupt the physical action but that usually adds visual detail.

Depth-of-Field: in a frame, the range of distances within which objects or persons will be in relatively sharp focus.

91

Dissolve: in editing, a transition between scenes in which the first image is faded out while another is faded in.

Documentary: a type of film or video essay which uses journalistic techniques to comment on the meaning or impact of events.

Double System: a camera system and sound system which are recording, respectively, images and sounds separately, but which will later have their products synchronized.

Dub: to duplicate a videotape; in editing, to re-record material onto a second tape.

Editing: the condensation and/or rearrangement of previously taped or filmed scenes.

Establishing Shot: a first, generally wide view of a scene; its purpose is to tell the audience where in time and place the events are occurring. Also called a "master shot."

Fill Light: light aimed at the side of an object or person being photographed to soften harsh contrasts from other light sources.

Focus: in a camera shot, the clarity of the image; in a scene or script, the center of attention.

Format: type of program. Examples: quiz show, documentary, tape-to-time.

Gray Scale: a bar chart of gradations from white to black used to determine how well a camera can distinguish between objects of varying brightness.

Horizontal Hold: a control device on a camera or monitor used to stabilize the resolution of video images and prevent rollover. *See also Rollover.*

Insert Editing: editing in which scenes can be inserted in any order between previously recorded images.

Key Light: the strongest light in a lighting plan, usually placed in front of the object or person being photographed.

Lavalier: small, omni-directional microphone, often worn on a loop around the neck, or as a lapel or tie clip.

Lens: series of curved glass structures which control the focus and depth-of-field on images for a camera. Examples: zoom lens, telephoto lens.

Master: an edited tape used as an original, and from which duplicates can be made.

Master Shot: see Establishing Shot.

Microphone: an instrument for recording sounds and translating them into electrical impulses, which are then sent to recording devices.

Milieu: the setting or environment in which the action of a story takes place.

Minimum Illumination Level: the lowest level of light intensity required in order for a video camera to record images.

Monitor: a television set whose primary use is to display video signals in a studio or control room or on location, rather than to receive broadcast signals.

Narrowcasting: types of programs produced to appeal to specialized audiences; these are generally transmitted by cable or direct broadcast, rather than over the public airwaves.

Omni-directional: a microphone that responds equally well to sounds coming from all directions. See Uni-directional.

Pan: physical movement of the focal point of a camera from one object or person to another. Such a movement along a horizontal axis is called a pan. Along a vertical axis, *see Tilt.*

Playback: on a videotape machine, the regeneration of previously recorded images, so they can be seen and heard on a monitor or television set.

Point of View: in camera work, a position that mimics what a character might see; in a production, the slant with which the maker of the program presents material to the audience.

Postproduction: the editing phase of making a video, which begins generally after shooting or field production work is done.

Preproduction: the planning and organization phase of making a video, which takes place before the shooting and editing phases.

Production: the actual recording of a live or staged event.

Props: objects of an incidental nature, used by people in a scene.

Recorder: that part of a video or audio system in which images or sounds are electronically stored.

Rollover: an image on a television screen in which top and bottom portions appear to have exchanged places; the result of an error in the control of the horizontal hold on a camera or monitor.

Scan: in a playback system, a device which allows images to be viewed at six times normal speed; in a monitor or television set, the process by which horizontal and vertical lines (which make up the image) are placed onto the screen.

Scene: an event which is either self-contained, takes place in a single location, or which accomplishes a single dramatic or informational purpose.

Set: the physical location in which the action of a scene is recorded; a set is sometimes an artificial replica of a real or imagined location.

Shooting: the process of photographing and recording events and images; the production phase of a film or video.

Single System: a camera system which records video and audio images on a single tape.

Synchronization: the simultaneous, linked running of sound and visual images so that they appear to be lifelike and connected. Often abbreviated as "sync."

Tape-to-Time: the recording of an event in the same time period as it actually occurs; a format in which no editing is anticipated.

Telephoto Lens: a camera lens that greatly magnifies an image or that brings a distant image closer.

Three-Point Lighting Plan: a plan which uses light generated from three different points, usually front, back, and side, to create the sense of depth and perspective.

Tilt: a camera shot in which there is physical movement of the camera up and down the vertical axis.

Truck: in camera work, the physical movement of the camera, usually on wheels, toward or away from the action of a scene.

Uni-directional: a microphone which responds to sounds coming from one specific direction.

Vidicon Tube: a device in a video camera which collects light energy and then separates and transforms it into electrical impulses to be transmitted through the camera system.

Video Cassette Recorder (VCR): a device for recording and playing back video cassettes.

Videotape: the recording material used in video systems; comes in several widths.

Voice-Over: a voice heard without a narrator being seen on screen; often, the voice of a scene participant or narrator, recorded separately from that of the visual scene.

Wardrobe: clothing or costumes (including makeup and hairstyle) worn by people appearing in a film or video.

Zoom Lens: a type of camera lens which is capable of varying the image from close-up to long shot while maintaining correct focus.

BIBLIOGRAPHY

Anderson, Chuck. *The Electric Journalist*. New York: Praeger, 1972.

Bensinger, Charles. *The Home Video Handbook*. Third edition. Indianapolis, Ind.: Howard W. Sams & Co., 4300 West 62nd Street, 1982.

Bretz, Rudy. *Handbook for Producing Educational and Public Access Programs for Cable Television*. Englewood Cliffs, N.J.: Educational Technology Publications, 1976.

Canape, Charlene. *How to Capitalize on the Video Revolution*. New York: Holt, Rinehart & Winston, 1984.

Eargle, John. *Sound Recording*. New York: Van Nostrand Reinhold, 1976.

Marsh, Ken. *Independent Video*. New York: Simon & Schuster, 1974.

Mascelli, Joseph. *The Five C's of Cinematography*. Hollywood, Calif.: Cine/Graphic Publications, 1965.

Mattingly, Grayson, and Smith, Welby A. *Introducing the Single Camera VTR System*. New York: Scribner's, 1973.

McQuillin, Lon. *The Video Production Guide*. Indianapolis, Ind.: Sams & Co., 1983.

Murray, Michael. *The Videotape Book*. New York: Bantam Books, 1975.

Quick, John, and Wolff, Herbert. *Small Studio Video Tape Production*. New York: Addison-Wesley, 1972.

Ritsko, Alan J. *Lighting for Location Motion Pictures*. New York: Van Nostrand Reinhold, 1979.

Sambul, Nathan, ed. *The Handbook of Private Television.* New York: McGraw-Hill, 1982.

Smith, Welby A. *Video Basics.* Alexandria, Va.: Development Communications Associates, Inc., 815 North Royal Street, 1982.

Wurtzel, Alan. *Television Production.* New York: McGraw-Hill, 1979.

INDEX